Two Trees

BOOK ONE OF THE MELKIZEDEK SAGA

Christopher Beck

The Rural Publishing Company

First published by The Rural Publishing Company 2023

Print (Paperback): 978-1-923008-07-6
eBook: 978-1-923008-08-3

Cover Design: The Rural Publishing Company
Layout and Typesetting: The Rural Publishing Company

Email: hello@theruralpublishingcompany.com.au
Website: https://theruralpublishingcompany.com.au/

Contents

PROLOGUE

Dear readers, before this story begins I would like to make some things very clear.

First of all, although this story is a work of fiction, there are elements that are drawn from history, from myth and legend and also from the Bible. Some of the ideas I speculate on might be seen as controversial or at least as not "orthodox" in the minds of some, particularly as I use material from the Bible.

I would make this disclaimer though, that I make no claims of theology nor doctrine and that this story is fictional and meant to be enjoyed as such.

Chapter One

Introduction - 1917

The fact remains that the world is not the way most people think that it is. It wasn't that long ago that I too had been blissfully unaware of the reality of the Vansadagaadians and other Eldar races. Before the Great War I was a career soldier, but my real passion was archaeology and history. I was also good with languages and so I ended up in intelligence when the war began. I was under the command of General Edmund Allenby, who recruited me because of my historical background. He was the one who told me the truth about the Vansadagaadians, the Faerie, the Anunnaki, the Nephilim and the other alien races who live among us.

In a strange way it all made sense. I knew all the old mythologies about the ancient gods. To find out that these so-called gods were actually real beings and that they had been living among us without our awareness was a bit of a shock. Most of them were content to just live out their lives, but some had formed powerful groups or factions. General Allenby was a member of the Order of Melkizedek, an ancient Christian order of knights that served an alien faction called the Seerlie Court. There were twelve A'sidhe Noble families in the Seerlie and they led a surprisingly large community of Faerie tribes based in Britain. In fact, the largest Faerie community in the world was living in Britain and doing very well. Many of them were members of the aristocracy or gentry and together they wielded considerable power not only in Britain, but all over the world. The Seerlie, thankfully, were friendly to mankind and were determined to help us in any way they could. But one thing for certain, while it could be said that the Seerlie were friendly towards Christian civilisation, they were nothing like angels from heaven as I imagined them to be as a child. There were no feathered wings nor glowing halos or white robes - nor were they the proverbial fairies at the end of the garden either. Oh no, they were real people, but they were also very, very special.

When I entered the old Order and took my vows I realised that I had entered a much bigger world. I also realised that mankind had some formidable enemies as well. While the Seerlie Court did have allies, such as the Malakim who were based in Jerusalem, and friends among the Huldre, the Djinni and many of the Solitaries, some of the factions were notoriously self-serving and a few were completely evil and even "Satanic". The main faction in Germany were called the Ouroboros, ruled by the shadowy Elvish Circle of Ring Lords, who were self-serving tyrants, interested in power. While not really evil, the Circle did have a bad reputation for being ruthless. Nevertheless, while the Circle was the real power behind the German war machine, and were as such, for now, our enemies, the Pandemonium and the Atalanti factions were much, much worse. That was why I was sent to see General Erik Ludendorff, the German chief of staff, in my last mission and make the deal with the Germans that I did. The Atalanti and Pandemonium had formed an alliance, and their agents had infiltrated the German government. I'd just spent a whole year hunting them down. Giving the Ring Lords the list of

Pandemonium and Atalanti agents would probably prolong the war, but it most certainly guaranteed the defeat of Germany and Ludendorff knew it.

The Pandemonium in particular were very dangerous. They had been poised to strike the Ouroboros down and take over the Central Powers by the end of the year. They planned a secret treaty with the Americans to end the War, but with Germany and her allies still holding all their occupied territories. That was unacceptable. Ludendorff on the other hand was a warmonger and his tactics of unrestricted submarine warfare was provoking the Americans. That was something that the Seerlie wanted. If America entered the War, Germany and her allies would most certainly be defeated, on our terms.

All of that though was politics. What really concerned me though was the escape of a particularly nasty Pandemonium agent named Graud. I was determined that I would hunt him down and take him out. I had a very bad feeling about him.

I'd just come back from my mission. Disposing of the motorcycle and the German uniform I returned across no mans' land back to the British lines. I went to report immediately to General Allenby. After our recent victory, I expected to find the General at the 3rd Army Headquarters, located temporarily at Messines. Instead, when I arrived I was sent in to see General Douglas Haig.

The General didn't say much to me. I knew that he didn't like Allenby and he liked me even less. I entered the office and saluted.

"I suppose an explanation is in order, Major Ryan." The General said, "General Allenby has been recalled home for new orders. You are to also go immediately to London and join him there. You have both been asked to see the Prime Minister as soon as possible. I have your orders here."

Haig passed an envelope to me.

"There is an escort waiting for you outside." he looked down at the work on his desk, "You are dismissed."

I saluted again, although as far as Haig was concerned, I no longer existed, so I left. Outside the office a young looking orderly was waiting for me. He was tall, very handsome, with almost white hair and piercing blue eyes. He saluted me and I stopped and looked at him.

"Major," he said, "I'm private Goodfellow. I'm to escort you back to London, Sir."

"You're my driver?" I asked after a short pause. There was something distinctly odd about this

man, like I should be saluting him rather than the other way around.

"Yes Sir."

"Well I suppose that we better get my gear packed …"

"Already done Sir!" he saluted again.

"Please don't do that." I shook my head, "Good job and all, but I'm not one for too much enthusiasm. I'll pack my own bags in future."

"Yes Sir." he began to lead the way towards a car parked across the street, "Sorry Sir."

Private Goodfellow walked to the car and opened the roadside door for me, but I frowned and ignored the offer.

"Look," I waved at him, "I'll drive. You just need to keep me company and be an extra gun in case of trouble."

I got into the drivers' seat, while he went around and got in the passenger side. I started the car and we drove out of Messines along the road to Paris. At first we were quiet. I was thinking about my mission and wondering about what was waiting for us in London, but my eyes kept looking over at my strange companion. There was something about him…

Then it was obvious. Once out in the countryside I pulled over and turned to face him. I had to be careful how I did this, I might still be wrong.

"Alright." I said it then sighed, "What exactly are your orders regarding me?"

"My orders," he said, "are to guard your life and get you to London."

"Who gave you those orders?"

"It was Lord Fisher." he replied.

"The First Sea Lord?" I was staring at Goodfellow now. Fisher was Melkizedek.

"Yes Sir," Goodfellow nodded, "he told me to pack some bread and wine for the journey, Sir."

"How much did the wine cost?" I asked.

"About a tenth of my salary." Goodfellow smiled.

With that I smiled as well and reaching across, I shook his hand. As I did I felt a tingling sensation, a bit like static. I looked at his hand and saw three fingers instead of four. Private Goodfellow wasn't just a Melkizedek agent as I was. He was one of the Faerie who served the Seerlie Court and he had just revealed himself to me. This was something new.

"It is an honour to work with you." I gave a nod of my head, "I have never had the opportunity to actually work in partnership with one of the Folk before."

"Actually," Goodfellow looked at his hand and watched as the glamour flowed over his skin, as the fourth human finger reappeared, then he smiled again "the honour is all mine. You are very highly regarded Walter. We are about to embark upon a very important mission and you have been chosen by the Seerlie to lead it. You have formidable skills. I actually requested that I be your partner and companion."

"What exactly is our mission?" I was feeling excited.

"I have not been given the details." he said, "Lord Fisher knows."

"Then we had better not keep him!" I started the car again and we continued on our way.

Chapter Two
Angels

We drove through Paris, stopping for lunch, then onto Calais where we caught a boat across the channel that night. The drive was pleasant and uneventful. I took the opportunity to get to know my new partner. I had worked with partners before, but they had all been short lived - usually only as long as the mission we were on and they had all been human. In some cases they were literally short lived – survival in a war zone wasn't easy. As I said, I had never worked alongside one of the Faerie folk before. His full name was Robin Alaquandi Goodfellow and he was an English Faerie of some renown and a member of one of the A'sidhe ruling families of the Seelie Court. In Paris we had gotten rid of our military uniforms and become civilians again. Robin, or Al, as he preferred, had hated wearing the army uniform, which he had called "atrociously unfashionable!" Instead he preferred a rose coloured suit made from the finest silk, along with a similarly coloured trilby hat, with a feather in the band and willow wood walking cane. Next to him, in my rather more practical black suit and bowler, I looked quite ordinary. Despite Al's appearance, he wasn't in the least bit arrogant, but he did take pride in his appearance as well as his work. He considered himself to be a good actor, a skill always useful for those doing spy work. One thing that certainly impressed me was that when it came to the crunch, Al was no fop. Like the infamous Scarlet Pimpernel, he led his double life well. In Paris, as we changed in the safe back room of the café where we had lunch, we also checked our various tools of the trade. We both carried firearms under our jackets. While I preferred a regular Webley Mk5, Al carried two sleek custom made silver plated handguns. We also had fighting knives, mine a Bowie and his, a slender stiletto. I liked to carry extra bits like grenades, spare loaded gun barrels and a wicked looking set of knuckle dusters in webbing which I wore under my coat. I was what one might call a meat and vegetables man. Al on the other hand liked fine dining. His walking cane turned out to be a weapon as well - a concealed sword, which he was proud to show me. His spare ten bullet clips he kept well-hidden about his person. He carried no other weapons, except a garrotte, but he also had various poisons and other chemical substances, including gelignite and fuses which he kept, along with a gold flask filled with "medicine" all inside a well-crafted leather shoulder bag which he always kept with him at all times. As a Faerie, Al also had other abilities at his disposal. We were both experts in unarmed combat, but watching him doing exercises on the boat trip that evening convinced me that I wouldn't want to challenge him, even for fun. Also, like all of his species, Al had the abilities of mental empathy and glamour. While he couldn't read minds as such, Al could tell what other people were feeling and he had the ability to influence the minds of others. This was useful when it came to women in particular, he had told me with a wink! Glamour was the ability to make things appear differently than they actually did. This was a vital skill for the Faerie because in their true forms they appeared quite different to us. To live and work among the human population, all of their species had learned to have a constant shield of glamour on themselves. The glamour was also useful in other ways as it could be used to make people see things that were not there and also make things that were there, invisible. I had a feeling that I would enjoy working with this man.

Our boat took us right up the Thames into London and we were dropped off at the docks, where another car had been left for us. It was early morning and for June it was unusually foggy. Al drove this time and took us to a particular gentlemen's club called "Angels" in the city. We went into the courtyard and were met there by doormen who were agents like us. The seneschal was waiting for us at the door and he, being a Faerie, stopped to empathise before letting us in. Once he was sure who we were we were let in and taken to one of the private rooms in the club. General Allenby and Lord Fisher were already there waiting for us.

The two men were sitting beside a small table upon which breakfast was set. There was of course, tea, toast and conserves, but also a selection of fruit and cereal. Lord Fisher was eating some porridge covered with milk and honey, while the General, a more humble man, was cutting up an apple for himself.

"Welcome gentlemen, welcome!" Lord Fisher cried enthusiastically, "Come on in and have some breakfast with us before we talk business!"

Lord Fisher, despite being quite elderly and having resigned in 1915 in protest over the Dardanelles debacle, was still very much active and involved in things. His role in the Melkizedek Order was still a vital one of leadership and counsel.

As we moved into the room he began beckoning us over to some chairs, muttering cheerfully to himself. We shook hands all around the table in greetings. There was no saluting, nor any formal recognition of rank in the Order, except for the recognition of wisdom. Lord Fisher, or Jackie as he preferred to be called, even poured us tea.

"I'm very pleased to see you two working together." Jackie addressed us, "Some of us have been talking about working partnerships between the two peoples for some time now as a matter of course. It is good to see you again Al. Have you and Walter gotten to know each other over the last few days? And you Walter, I want to know all about our little meeting with Erich."

We enjoyed breakfast together, especially as the old admiral began to tell old war stories and about one of his loves, the dreadnaughts. Nothing at first we talked about was terribly serious, except mentioning things in passing. It seemed that Jackie was waiting for a signal before getting down to business. Then some servants came in and cleared away the breakfast things. At the same time a distinguished looking man entered the room as the servants left. There was no doubt that he was Malakim, one of the angels of Israel, and in particular, a guardian prince. By this time, of course, Al had relaxed enough so that he had been able to shrug off the lingering protection of glamour. He was, like all the Folk friendly to the Seerlie Court, absolutely safe within the walls of the Angels club. Our new visitor entered the room in the form of an elderly Jewish gentleman, but he quickly flicked off the glamour like a wet dog shaking off water. The difference between the Folk under the cloak of glamour and their appearance once free of it always fascinated me. Both Al and the other now appeared smaller in stature and more slender of limb. Their hands now had three rather than four fingers. They had long faces with prominent noses and large wide eyes, with oval shaped pupils that reminded me of cats, and like cats all Faerie Folk had extraordinary night vision. Unlike modern humans, they did not have our high skull, but rather a low skull, with a larger brain capacity, that sloped back from their foreheads. Most, because of this, liked to decorate their foreheads in particular - the women often wearing jewellery, and the men wearing hats or crowns. Al still wore his pink trilby, even though he was indoors, and I noticed that a golden torc now encircled his neck as well. Our other visitor wore a white yarmulke. Both men had a glow around their foreheads that made me think of halos. They also had the distinctive pointed ears of their species.

But there were also significant differences between the two men that marked them as members of their different tribes. Al was a member of the infamous warrior tribe, the Tuatha De Danann. He had fair skin and pale straight hair, but no body hair nor beard. The Malak on the other hand was bearded and his dark hair was curly and streaked with red. As a resident of the Middle East, his skin was olive and his eyes were dark.

We all stood for our new guest as he came to the table to join us.

Of course we all knew who he was, Michael himself, the Oberon of all those loyal to the Light, and the High Melkizedek of our order.

"Shalom brothers!" he said as he sat down, "Be seated! Be seated with me, please."

"It's a shame that you missed breakfast with us Michael." Al said.

"That's alright." Michael replied, "I've ordered another pot of tea. In the meantime there are a lot of important things to discuss. Jackie, you have no doubt already spoken with Edmund here about his new mission, would you care to explain to the others please?"

"Of course Michael." Jackie cleared his throat, "But I think that it would be good if Edmund tells us about it all."

"Well then," Edmund began, "once back in London I was to go and see the Prime Minister first. He told me that poor General Murray had been suffering setbacks in Palestine and that in fact he was being recalled and invalided due to illness, and that I was to replace him."

"But that wasn't all, was it!" Jackie chortled.

"No it wasn't!" Edmund grinned, "He told me that I was being sent to take Jerusalem before the end of the year, to make it a Christmas present to the nation!! I wasn't very confident about it and so Lloyd George sent me to see Jackie. Of course Jackie set me straight."

"The bottom line is that it is prophesied to happen this year!" the old Sea Lord declared.

"Yes." Edmond nodded, "Isaiah 31 clearly speaks of the deliverance of Jerusalem from alien occupation. Jackie spent a long time convincing me that it was our responsibility to make it happen. But the clincher for me was the timing of this.

Haggai chapter 2 gives us the date of the liberation as 24 Kislev. Daniel chapter 12 verse 12 gives the years as days, thirteen hundred and thirty five years under foreign control. The Jewish calendar shows that this year that 24 Kislev is December 10th, or Hanukkah, the celebration of the dedication of the Temple, the festival of lights."

"Yes," Michael nodded, "You're right about that."

"And," Edmond continued, "this year is, according to the Moslem calendar, the 1335th Year of Hijra. In other words, Turkish control of Jerusalem is finally going to end, according to Bible prophecy. As a servant of the true God, I know that I am called to make this happen and it will happen as God has destined it to. Later today I will be returning to 10 Downing Street to draw up my plans for the liberation of Jerusalem. Already I am hearing favourable reports from Palestine that Colonel Lawrence is doing very well against the Turks and that the Turks are not prepared for a new offensive. I plan to give every soldier in my army a Bible, and go into every battle covered by prayer."

"That's the spirit!" Jackie patted Edmund on the back, "But what is the mission for our two agents here, I wonder?"

That's exactly what I wanted to know, I thought!

"I can reveal that." Michael answered, paused, then said, "The liberation of Jerusalem from the Turks is the first step towards the return of the people of Israel to the Holy Land, beginning with Judah. But the battle is more than just a matter of soldiers, aircraft and cannon; it is also a spiritual issue. In order to defeat the Turks we must also defeat the Djinni who support them. The Djinni presently occupies the Splinter Mountain of Utnapishtim, which is Mount Ararat, called Agri Dagh by the Turks. On July 2nd 1840 the Djinni elementals engineered a huge earthquake on the mountain causing an avalanche which destroyed the Arminian monastery of St. Jacob and the town of Arghuri. Many of our people lived there and most of them were killed. This enabled the Djinni to possess the Rath of the mountain, including the Gate Ring there and of course, the ark of Noah in its protected resting place. Since that time the Djinni have strengthened the Ottoman armies. What we need to do is take the Rath back into our possession. That is why I have asked Alaquandi here to go with Walter on this mission, because from ancient times, Utnapishtim was guarded by the A'sidhe kindred tribe of the Tuatha De Danann. By repossessing this mountain, we can use its Gate Ring to send our people into Jerusalem. Along with the Avalon Gate Ring here in Britain we can launch a far more effective attack and so reclaim the Zion Rath as well."

"How are we going to fight the Djinni?" I asked, "They won't just let us walk up the mountain and then let us in."

"In fact," Michael grinned wolfishly, "that is exactly what they will do!"

"What do you mean, Michael?" Al asked.

"Well," Michael continued his explanation, "right now there is a Russian Army expedition exploring the mountain. The summer in Anatolia this year and last year has been particularly warm. We had an agent upon the mountain that was able to disable the field of glamour just long enough, twice actually, to enable some Russian fliers to spot the Ark on the mountain where it is exposed. They of course reported their sighting to the Tsar. As you know, the Tsar is a member of the Order and so he commanded the expedition to scale the mountain. For the last month they have been cutting a path up above the snow line and they are getting very close to the Ark as well as the hidden entrance of the Holy Way into the Rath. The Djinni have been doing everything they can to prevent this, but the Russians have been equipped with bayonets made of Elf blessed meteoritic iron, and this confuses the Djinni and prevents them from attacking. Also, our agent is there to help and she is carrying a Gate key Staff."

Al and I grinned at each other. So we were going to Mt. Ararat.

"What will we be up against once we are inside?" Al wondered.

"We suspect the possible presence of a Pandemonium agent in the area." Michael turned to me, "He's someone you have met before, just recently in France."

"You mean Graud?" I asked.

Michael nodded.

"There is also the Guardian of the Rath to deal with as well. Her name is Surreya and she is a powerful Djinn. At the moment we have isolated her and she is alone. And there are ways to defeat a Djinni and even make them obey your commands. The Djinni, like the Ouroboros are our enemies, but they also hate the Pandemonium. She will respond to the challenge to fight against Graud - use her pride to make her an ally. The Djinni are known to switch sides if offered something they want - use her greed to capture her."

"How are we to get there?" was my next question.

"I'll answer that!" Jackie exclaimed, "You'll be travelling by submarine E11 under the command of Captain Martin Nasmith! They are known for their daring raid at Constantinople back in 1915. Since then we've been using them for various Secret Service missions in the Black Sea region. They will get you to your Russian contacts who will then take you to Ararat. To make this mission a little easier, and to keep the Turks off your backs, General Maude is going to make a strike north from Baghdad at the same time. We are sure that he will draw some attention; he's not called 'Systematic Joe' for no reason!"

We all grinned at each other and nodded. This was going to be a very interesting mission indeed!

Outside, Michael took Al and I aside on our own. "You need to be aware that Jackie and Edmund are men of deep faith. They believe the prophecies they spoke of literally."

"And it's not as simple as that...." I could feel Michael's empathic sense touching my mind "is that what you are telling me?"

"Yes," Michael nodded, "I know that you have faith too Walter, actually a greater faith because you see more, know more and you understand that there are no certain victories here."

"We can still lose." Al nodded.

"We will fight anyway." I grinned.

"This is why the Seerlie trust you Walter." Michael led the way to the docks and the waiting submarine.

Chapter Three

Agri Dagh

A bit over a week later we were brought ashore somewhere along the Turkish Black Sea coast north of Mt. Ararat. It was one of those dark cloudy nights with no sign of either stars or sky. Still it was warm enough that our short swim to shore wasn't uncomfortable. I looked out towards where I knew that the submarine was and I thought that I could see the outline of the coning tower. There was a brief flash from a torch to which I replied so that they knew we were on the beach. Al and I turned quickly towards the cover of the trees and we dragged our gear inshore. While I fumbled a bit in the darkness to get all my equipment unpacked, Al had no problem seeing what he was doing. Still, we both sorted ourselves out quickly, quietly getting changed into the clothes of Turkish farmers. For the last week I'd been growing my beard to make myself look a little more realistic. Al couldn't grow a beard, but he had the benefit of glamour if required. Both of us wore fur caps on our heads, which were supposed to help make it easier for the Russians to identify us as their contacts. In our packs we carried our usual assortment of weapons and survival gear; we also both carried modified Lee-Enfields, camouflaged to not look like English made weapons. Without hesitation, I followed Al as he confidently moved inland in the near total darkness; we wouldn't stop to rest until daybreak.

The next morning as the sun rose, we climbed a hill so we could get a better look around. It was still partly cloudy, but getting hot very quickly.

"I can see them." Al said suddenly, his very keen eyes scanning towards the south.

We decided to stay on top of our hill, light a fire and have something to eat while we waited for the Russians to get closer. After finishing breakfast, Al sat down and went into a meditative state, closing his eyes and breathing deeply. I watched him as he used his empathic ability to probe towards the minds of the Russians, to see if he could draw them to us. Suddenly he jolted awake and stood, looking a bit shaken.

"What is it?" I asked, also standing and automatically grabbing my rifle and knife.

"I managed to, ah, there's no English word for it, well, touch the minds of them out there." he seemed a bit drained, "I'm pretty sure that they will head this way and find us in the next few hours. It's just that I also sensed another presence, a powerful spirit. It took all my strength to pull away before being detected. I don't think that they sensed me. We don't need psychic warfare just yet."

On the submarine Al had been very cheery and talkative, but now he was quiet. He just sat there and stared towards the south as though searching for something. He raised his hand as though trying to touch something there that I couldn't see. He looked frightened, and that was scary to me. After some time he turned towards me and spoke.

"Hey, I'm sorry Walter." he patted my arm, "Thanks for your concern, I was a bit rattled that's all. It won't be easy fighting this Surreya at the mountain. I've always had a bit of a problem with overconfidence, but now I've had a reality check. Still, I'm confident that we can do this. Remember that there is another of the Folk with the Russians. She's been working at the mountain for some time and together, along with some support from our Russian friends, we should be able to do this."

"Do you know who she is?" I asked.

"I have a pretty good idea who!" Al grinned, "But I'll leave that as a surprise for you. Anyway the Russians are nearly here. We better go to meet them."

So we packed up our little camp and put the fire out, then began to walk down the hill. About half way down a group of Russian Imperial Cavalry rode up to the hill. There were about twenty of them. They stopped at the bottom of the hill and we waited for them.

"Welcome friends!" I called out to them in Russian, "Do you have any spare vodka?"

"Certainly!" came the reply, "Have you brought the caviar?"

With that we climbed the rest of the way down the hill and were greeted by friendly hugs and kisses!

The journey south to Mt. Ararat was a long one, especially riding on horseback, but at least we were relatively safe, remaining for most of the time in Russian held territory. The first destination was the town of Dogubayazit, where the Russian 19th Petropavlovsky Regiment was stationed. As we rode into the town, it was largely deserted. When the Russians had arrived to occupy the area, the Turkish population had fled, leaving only the small Armenian minority, who seemed to be staying indoors and out of the way. The town was dry and dusty and falling down. We were introduced to Colonel Koor, the commanding officer, who had set up his headquarters in an Armenian church in the town.

The Colonel invited us into a small back room where he opened a huge door facing west. Framed before us was the great mountain, looming close and huge. It was very impressive. I finally felt that I had arrived. We sat down and food and vodka was brought. Seated around the table were some other officers and the Colonel introduced us to them.

Firstly, there was first Lieutenant Vassilli Zabolotsky, the pilot who had first flown over the mountain last summer and spotted the ark. With him was his wing commander Captain Kurbatov, who had sent the report to the Tsar. Standing behind them was Sergeant Boris Rujansky who was the chief engineer of the railroad battalion, made up of one hundred and fifty men who had been charged with climbing the mountain and actually conducting the expedition.

All the officers were young men, in their twenties, and I realised that this was probably because the casualty rate had been high and that they had all been field promoted. The fighting had been fierce. Not only had these men had to face the Turks, but there were problems with Communists as well, often working against them within their own ranks.

Kurbatov was the nominated leader of the mission, despite being an aviator, because the Tsar had so ordered it. He was young, blonde and enthusiastic.

"It is so good that you are finally here brothers!" he grinned at us; "We have just completed the final survey of the mountain and have carved out paths for easy access. We have already located the ark of Noah! This is very exciting for all of us. Sergeant Rujansky has done an excellent job!"

"Thank you sir," Rujansky took the Captains' praise to be permission to speak, "but we did have some initial difficulty on our first attempt. We sent two teams up the mountain. One team, the largest, made up of one hundred men, attempted to climb the mountain directly up the northern slopes to about the fifteen thousand foot mark to the foot of the Parrot Glacier. There is a large flat area there which at the moment is going through a melt. Because of the warm weather, we have been able to see the ark quite clearly and even take photos. Sadly though, the melt water has made the whole area very dangerous. There is a swampy area and lots of water infested with mosquitos and venomous snakes, as well as other dangers. We were not actually able to get to the ark itself that way. But, our second group, led by Lady Niamah, our local guide and advisor on the mountain, attempted another path from the east. Although dangerous, and subject to avalanches, they climbed up the Ahora gorge along an ancient path. Not only did they carve a path to the exterior of the ark, but Lady Niamah also located the entrance of a cave that leads into the mountain itself. We have decided to wait for your arrival before proceeding."

Al and I looked excitedly at each other.

"Your report is very good news." Al nodded, "Your advisor, Lady Niamah is well known to me as she is kindred. What has been her involvement in this mission so far?"

"I have been working with her." Zabolotsky replied, "She is at this moment still upon the mountain. Not only is she an expert on the mountain, but the Lady has been a great encouragement to the men. In particular she has been encouraging the men to pray and pray they have been doing! We are very aware that there are spiritual forces upon the mountain that do not want us there! I suppose that is why you two are here, to help us in regard to the next stage of this mission?"

"There is a lot to discuss, including specific things with the men." I said to everyone, "It is true, there is an enemy that we have to face within the mountain. Noah's ark is certainly a prize, but we may have to fight for it... and I'm not talking about Turks."

"The Lady Niamah has told us as much." Colonel Koor said seriously, "We have also received the shipment of special bayonets and they have been distributed to the men. What exactly do we have to do?"

It was Al's turn to speak.

"Alright," he began with an involuntary sigh, "the Tsar has ordered this expedition, as part of a much bigger combined operation, which includes the capture of Jerusalem before the end of this year. We have secretly been planning this for some time. Mt. Ararat is an important part of the plan because the Turkish commander Enver Pasha has formed a secret alliance with a dangerous enemy who call themselves the Djinni. The Djinni are very powerful and have been helping the Turks. This mountain is a holy place, to Christian, Jew and Moslem alike, but the Djinni have occupied it for some time and used it as a base for their attacks. This summer, we have caught them off guard and most of their forces are elsewhere, so we can take the mountain back from them. Right now the British forces in Baghdad under General Maude are preparing for a major assault, but it is actually a diversion. Enver Pasha has called many reinforcements away from Jerusalem to face what he thinks is the real battle, but Allenby is about to invade Palestine and take Jerusalem. Most of the Djinni have joined the Turkish reinforcements and are heading for Mesopotamia."

Al paused at this moment for effect, then continued, "You have already been informed by the orders you received from the Tsar that our enemies have spiritual power. I should tell you bluntly that the Djinni are not even human." another pause, "The Djinni and others like them are allied to the Pandemonium, literally devils in human form. The Germans also have an alliance with another group, the Ouroboros, but recently we have been able to gain an advantage over them, thanks to Major Ryan here."

Al patted my arm. While the Ouroboros was far from defeated, they owed us one for helping them against the Satanic Pandemonium and that was almost as good.

"At the moment there is only one of the Djinni Guardians on the mountain." Al continued, "She is a very powerful enemy in her own right, and she has command of many lesser Djinni who do her bidding on the mountain. Our job is to capture her and occupy the mountain stronghold. That is why Lady Niamah has been encouraging the men to pray, for prayer is a powerful weapon against the Djinni as their primary weapons are spiritual and mental ones. Men with faith are hard to defeat. Lady Niamah and I are here to conduct spiritual warfare against this Djinn while the men take out her servants who guard the mountain."

The Russians became very thoughtful and looked at each other a bit uncertainly.

"A few questions please." Colonel Koor frowned, "Firstly, who on earth are you?! And, how the hell are we supposed to fight against spirits when we are but men?"

At this Al laughed, quite loudly, which unsettled them even more!

"If I ask you this question, you should know the answer for yourself." Al looked at them with eyes ablaze, "You are men of faith, and so, if our enemies are demons, then who or what do you think Lady Niamah and I are?"

"There is only one answer to that!" Rujansky cried, "You must be angels!"

"Right you are!" Al grinned and nodded, "We're not what you expect are we?!"

Everyone, strangely, seemed to relax at that. Then I realised that Al was probably using his empathy to calm them.

"And who are you?" Zabolotsky looked at me.

"I am," I said proudly, "an Englishman!"

The following morning we boarded the only truck in the village along with members of the engineering battalion, leaving the colonel and his regiment in Dogubayazit. From there we drove out to the village of Ahora located at the base of the mountain, where the rest of the battalion and the Lady Niamah waited for us.

Upon arrival Rujansky began growling orders at the troops and they lined up with their equipment in the main street of the village. The villagers who were mostly Armenians were used to having the Russians around now for over a year. They just continued about their business. Still, they recognised that there were some new comers and that caught some interest. Al, who seemed to know his way around, headed for the house of the village headman and returned with someone

I assumed to be Lady Niamah. She wore men's clothes, but her head was covered by an Armenian scarf. She was also carrying a long staff.

I was with Kurbatov and Zabolotsky when Al brought Niamah over to introduce her. While much of her face was covered by the scarf, her long golden blonde hair peeked out. She had blue eyes and a fair complexion. My first impression was that she was very strong and confident. I was fascinated and curious.

She shook our hands pleasantly, "Today is the day gentlemen!" she said.

"Walter Ryan," Niamah stopped a bit longer with me, "it is so good to meet you. I have heard a lot about you. When we go up the mountain and Al and I engage the Djinn, we will really need you to lead the physical battle. We are heading into very dangerous territory. I'm sure we will do well with your exceptional talents."

She smiled at me then, but it wasn't just politeness. In that moment, as she turned towards the others, I was utterly disarmed by that incredible, wonderful smile, and also fortified. I felt ready to fight.

Just then Sergeant Rujansky approached me. "The men are ready for your inspection Sir."

I looked them over. There were one hundred and fifty in the battalion, all lined up in neat rows, their field packs resting in the ground beside each man. They were looking at me with some suspicion since I was this strange Englishman. I cleared my throat and stepped toward them confidently, and then in perfect Russian, I addressed them.

"Brave men of the 19th Petropavlovsky Regiment engineering battalion, I am Major Walter Ryan, the ranking officer of this expedition. You may have noticed that I am British and some of you may have some reservations about that. But I want you right now to put those reservations aside. For the last year you have been living in this region and climbing this great mountain, building pathways for climbing and guarding against the attacks of the Turks. You have been told that I am an expert, but you are the true experts here. I salute you!" and I saluted.

The men saluted back, "Mutual respect and trust is going to be needed here if we are going to survive this mission. I trust your knowledge of the mountain, your toughness and your obedience, so trust my experience that I know how to kill the demons that live up there on that mountain!"

I could see some of the men smiling at that. The fact that I spoke Russian like a native would have helped immensely as well. I nodded to Sergeant Rujansky.

"Bayonets!!" he bellowed.

The soldiers pulled their bayonets from their belts in a smooth fluid movement then attached them to their rifles, which they then presented with a snap of their feet. Rujansky passed me a bayoneted rifle. I pulled the breach and opened the magazine of my weapon and let the bullets drop to the ground.

"An excellent weapon!" I said, "The most advanced semi automatic rifle on the planet I am told. But you are used to shooting it. But up there against the Djinni which occupies that mountain, your bullets would be utterly useless. But the bayonets are a different matter! They are made of a special metal that not only confuses the Djinni but which can deflect their attacks and which is lethal to them. They will attack you in a number of ways. They will attack your spirit and mind. You have a defence from that though. Lady Niamah has been encouraging you to pray. Your prayer, your faith will defend your mind and your spirit. You will need all your faith and courage to stand before their swords with these bayonets. But remember - they are disabled by the metal, it can kill them, so they will be afraid of you!"

I removed the bayonet from my rifle and held it before them.

"The bayonets have also been lengthened and sharpened." I slashed the bayonet sword like,

"The hilt has a good hand grip and a knuckle guard. It is also double edged. While not a sword, I have discovered that a weapon like this can be even more deadly. It is light, easy to use and once you get in close to your opponent, it will cut them." I smiled wolfishly.

"You must realise this," I continued, "that as men of faith, you have spiritual power. These weapons amplify that power. Your faith is quite literally your shield. Whatever weapon they come at you with, pray against it. Your faith will deflect arrows, spears and swords. Just keep your courage and don't believe what you see, see by your belief."

I waved at Al and he came over grinning like the Cheshire cat. He had his cane with him. With a flick he slipped the scabbard off and without a warning he came at me. He moved with uncanny speed around me, looking for a way in. I followed his moves, praying silently under my breath. I wasn't going to wait for him, I moved in first. I could feel the power of the faith in my arm. I had entered the battle trance.

The Russians watched us with horrified fascination as we danced. Al was still fast, but I could see the strain in his eyes, that the Elf blessed metal was rattling him. Metal flashed but met metal each time. We dodged and wove around each other, but the trance vision enabled me to anticipate him and suddenly I had him on the ground, with the bayonet at his throat.

"Got to draw blood old chap to end the trance." Al grinned at me, panting with exertion.

I was panting too, exhausted. I made a tiny cut on Al's neck which bled then healed immediately. We got up. I turned to the Russians.

"With this weapon, you too can fight like this," I said, "Let God guide you and you'll win."

After the demonstration, Rujansky dismissed the men. I would have liked more time to train them a bit more, but we had to start the climb quickly. But one thing I knew, it wasn't training which made the real difference. I was told that each of these men had been trained in knife fighting and edged weapon combat. The reality was though that either they had faith, or they did not. The battle trance was a spiritual gift, a work of grace that fell upon the warrior. The Spirit used the warrior as a channel. These men were mostly Christians, as well as a couple of devout Muslims and one Jew. They had been brought from many places to be part of the battalion because of their spirituality as much as for their skill as soldiers and engineers.

The men did one last check of their equipment, filled their canteens and report-ed back to the centre of town. We all met there with the equipment. Everyone, including the officers, was to carry their own pack and weapons. Niamah and Al led the way, heading up the mountain from the eastern side, along the Ahora gorge. Despite the height, it was hot and buzzing insects soon began to pester us. The path that the engineers had cut out up the gorge made the going easier, but we could hear rock slides in the distance, sounding like cloudless thunder. Looking back down to the valley below, the view was absolutely astounding. Armenia was in the distant east and looking south I could see the smaller peak of Little Mount Ararat. It was easy to forget that we were heading into a dangerous battle zone.

As we headed up the gorge a cool breeze blew down from the glacier above, cooling us down, but it also brought with it the smell of decaying plant matter from the swampy pools of melt water created by the hot summer. Above us we could see the ice of the Abich glaciers and under the dripping overhang some caves further along the carved out track. That was where we were heading. Carefully, because the track was wet and slippery, I moved up the column in order to catch up to Al and Niamah. They had stopped and were doing something. As I passed Rujansky I patted him on the shoulder and gave a serious look.

"Keep alert!" I said, "Looks like trouble!"

The men began to crouch with their backs against the mountain as the column came to a halt. They were uneasy and there was a feeling of static in the air.

"Courage!" I said quietly to them in Russian as I passed.

Finally I caught up with Kurbatov and Zabolotsky. The path had come out to a large flat area. To our right were a number of smaller gorges and caves slicing into the mountainside. They were mostly filled with slush and ice. But that wasn't what I noticed first. I let out an involuntary gasp because up ahead was a large rock ledge protruding out from the glacier above. Sitting on the ledge was a very big black rectangular object which was obviously man made. While the back end was still encased in the ice above it, I was clearly looking at the end portion of a large barge-like vessel, the Ark of Noah! All around me the men were breathing hard. That and the noise of dripping water was the only sound. Some were crossing themselves. The two officers stood before me, stunned. Kurbatov turned and faced me, his eyes filled with wonder.

"There is even less ice covering it this time." he said, "It is truly incredible!"

Kurbatov, always thoughtful, called one of the engineers over. He pulled a camera out of his pack and began to take some photographs of the ledge above. Up ahead I could see Al and Niamah holding up a long staff together, pointed towards the Ark. They were praying out loud in a language that I had never heard before. I could see an aura of green blue light forming around them and occasional sparks of light. I felt tingling sensations all over my body. I wanted to step closer but Zabolotsky stopped me, shaking his head. I began to also feel a distinct feeling of menace, as though we were being watched. Of course, we probably were.

Then, Al and Niamah's chanting became more intense and they swung the staff around towards the mountain. I could see light shining from it like a beacon, striking deep into the ice of one of the nearby gorges. Suddenly I could see it for what it was, an illusion of glamour dissolving before our eyes. The ice and much of the rock wall vanished, to be replaced by a large open cave, which was really a carved doorway. The rock curved forming an arch and was carved with images of Mesopotamian style cherubim standing guard with swords drawn. Their eyes stared at us, daring us to enter their realm.

Al and Niamah came over to us to speak. The photographer took more pictures behind us.

"This is the entrance to the Holy Way that has been blocked since 1840, when the Djinni first came here and troubled the mountain." Niamah explained, "We will need to go in here. The Djinni know we are here, but we won't be attacked because we have closed their eyes to us."

"Now is the time to draw our blades." Al grinned, "Be alert, the tunnels are narrow and the enemy are cunning."

Al and Niamah entered first and we followed with swords drawn. The staff lit up the way ahead and covered us with an unearthly glow so we could see in the darkness. I noticed that the bayonets we carried glowed as well. We moved down a narrow path carved directly into the rock of the mountain, but then came out into a circular room. Other tunnels led in various directions and there were stone seats carved in the middle of the room. Also in the middle of the room were some stone benches. The benches were covered with ancient and old fashioned weapons. There were all kinds of swords and spears, shields and even armour – from every age, ancient Urartian, Hittite, Assyrian, Babylonian, Greek, Roman and Byzantium and Ottoman. There were even some old rifles, probably from a pre 1840 visitor. The weapons were all in excellent condition, non-rusted and without the expected layer of dust. It was so unusual. It was then I noticed something very strange. Al noticed it as well. Sitting in a corner was a modern weapon, a German pistol.

"Someone has been here before us." Al said, picking the weapon up. He passed the pistol to me and I looked more closely at it.

"Why would someone leave their pistol here?" Zabolotsky asked me, "Why are all these weapons here?"

"Because of the glamour that covers the Rath." Niamah explained, "The Djinni which occupy the mountain have placed a cloak of glamour over this place. No normal metal weapon, no man forged steel or iron can enter the Rath. Only blessed steel, like our bayonets, can pass through the field. Try it and see."

Zabolotsky looked a bit unsure, but he picked up a sword, a Roman gladius, from the floor and walked with it towards one of the tunnels. As he approached, the metal began to glow with red heat. Zabolotsky yelped and dropped the sword.

"This is why I was so concerned about the equipment that we brought with us. There must be no steel nor iron." Niamah pointed at all the littered weapons in the room, "But we are well armed and the enemy are afraid of us. Still we will need to be cautious. We are entering their lair and they will be waiting for us. Keep alert and faithful."

Many of the men crossed themselves at this or pulled crosses (wooden ones on leather thong) out from around their necks and kissed them. Quickly we did our final checks. We removed our heavy jackets and left our rifles behind. Our packs were put back on. Both Al and Niamah also stripped off their coats, revealing that they wore nothing but chainmail hauberks over their bare skin and torcs around their necks. Both of them slung their swords over their shoulders. I nodded, and our guides, leading the way, took us down one of the dark tunnels.

Moving into the tunnels felt a lot like trench warfare. It was tight, hot, and death was probably just waiting for us around the corner.

We moved carefully along the tunnel, but also quickly as our two guides led a physically punishing pace. They seemed to know where they were going. Along the way we passed bodies, dry and mummified or bones scattered in the tunnels, evidence of battles and blunt and violent ends. This might have caused lesser men to become afraid, but we had our weapons and we were already praying earnestly. There was no time to stop and think about things.

Then suddenly we did stop! The men took defensive positions.

"Keep praying!" Niamah hissed back at us.

"They're coming!" Al added, "Prepare yourselves!!"

I gritted my teeth and prayed ... "deliver us from evil..."

Suddenly they were upon us. Out of the dark tunnels around us the Djinni attacked. Male warriors, naked except for their sword belts and helms clambered along the walls and even upon the ceilings of the tunnels, moving like slithering quicksilver. They were incredibly beautiful, but I could see through the glamour that they were actually quite small and waifish. They literally dropped upon us, but we kept our discipline and fought back fearlessly, despite their almost animal-like ferocity. They not only slashed with their weapons, but also bit and clawed like wild creatures. This made their beauty to me something almost obscene and I dispatched them as I would wolves or tigers.

Then, again suddenly, they withdrew back into the tunnels, leaving their dead behind.

"Keep praying!" Niamah warned again.

"Dear Jesus," I whispered, "give us victory over your foes..."

A great howling began. I could feel the force of spiritual fear hit me like a wave. I held up my weapon and focused my prayer.

"Though I walk through the valley of the shadow of death I will fear no evil..."

The Djinni attacked this time by flying into our tunnel. They were females this time, larger and equipped with wings. Like the males they too were naked, but they were just as well armed and their long dark hair flowed behind them like a mane. They flew at us but at the last moment they hovered before us, just out of reach. Then they began to pose and posture for us, leering at us and calling to us with lustful looks. They were beautiful and naked and it was impossible to tear our eyes off them. I was still praying under my breath, but I was unconscious of the words and my breathing became shallow and I felt light headed, clammy and sweaty. I was responding sexually and gritted my teeth in deep frustration. I wanted them yet I feared them. I was hardly aware of what was happening when they began to attack us. Almost casually they alighted upon the ground and approached us. Our guard was down and our eyes utterly preoccupied - I could see her standing before me, the vision of her naked body caused me to shudder with desire. Waves of empathic glamour flowed over my senses and .... then I heard a clanging noise. Some of the men had dropped their bayonets to the stone floor. I could see them enraptured, their eyes full of desire. I could also hear another sound. It was Niamah yelling at me! At first it was just a muffled voice, but suddenly it was as though the spell was broken. It was as though the world had started again, and I was aware of another feeling, one of shame and violation. The Djinni female knew that her hold on me was broken - with a bloodcurdling scream she attacked!

"Jesus!!" I screamed, and lunged in counter attack. With all my strength and all my spirit I had but one word in my mouth, "Jesus! Jesus! Jesus!"

The battle was on! It was like the dream was over and we had all been awoken by a very loud sound. Some of us had fallen and were dead, but most of us had come to our senses and we realised just in time what danger we were in. But we had let them in among us!! They were upon us and pressing in hard. In desperation we drew upon all our faith. I could hear the men invoking the Name, or crying "the Lord rebuke you!!" and even "Allah yarham!"

The physical fight was hard and we all fought with all our strength. With grim determination I knew that I was not fighting mortal human women, that they were diabolic creatures that only had humanoid forms. They were beautiful, yes, but as we fought I realised just how alien these creatures were. It gave me the stomach to kill them. Some of them begged for mercy as we drove in for the attack, trying to evoke pity in us, but they had already made the fatal mistake of revealing their true selves and we saw through the lie. The one who had attacked me had drawn blood. She was taller than the others and formidable. I could feel myself tiring – the spirit is willing but the flesh is weak – I felt my muscles burning with exhaustion! Suddenly, Niamah barged in sideways, knocking the Djinni off her feet into the wall of the tunnel. She collapsed unconscious, and I too dropped in exhaustion to the floor. This Djinni, whoever she was, must have been important because as soon as she fell, all the others wailed in distress and fled or dropped to the floor cowering in terror! It was a remarkable sight to see these previously powerful beings suddenly stripped of their strength and will to fight – they surrendered and were utterly defeated. The men, panting with exhaustion, gathered up the enemy weapons and herded the ones we captured together. It had all ended so quickly, too quickly, I thought.

Chapter Four

The Rath of Utnapishtim

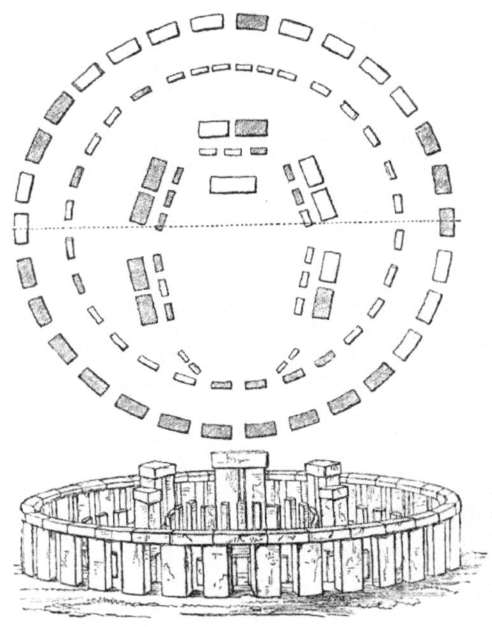

I looked at the whimpering Djinni curled up on the floor. Her chest was heaving with an exhaustion of her own, and a look of terror was in her eyes. She looked up at me with pleading eyes.

"Kill us." she begged.

"What?" I was astounded, but turned to Niamah who was standing beside me, "She's terrified of something," I said, "but it isn't us."

"What do you want?!" Niamah squatted down next to her and grabbed her long hair, "What are you so frightened of?"

"He's here in the mountain!" the Djinn whined, "He will punish us! But if you kill us first, we may escape. Please kill us!!"

Niamah and Al sat down next to the Djinn. She was shuddering with terror, and so were all the others curled up all around the tunnels. A strange groaning was coming from them all. They had failed and they knew it. As I watched, Niamah and Al let their glamour down. I was astounded to see that they didn't look too dissimilar to this Djinn, but with a strange beauty that came from an inner goodness. They reached out to the Djinn and drew her into an embrace, stroking her hair and body as though she was a cat. The Djinn seemed to visibly relax, and so did the others in the caves.

I knew why this was so. With the Faerie Folk, death was not a one way trip as it is for us mortals. The whole basis of their life cycle was that they had spiritually evolved into interdimensional beings, who could perceive the non-corporeal world. But they also liked to inhabit corporeal forms, and so they would incarnate and reincarnate as they needed to. But between incarnations, they entered an invisible world, a world few humans could perceive, but which was dangerous and full of peril. We live in a fallen world, occupied by fell creatures – the Pandemonium were there waiting in the spirit realm, just waiting for any opportunity to incarnate themselves or to drain the life force of an enemy.

I could feel the malevolent forces that were invisible around us. The Djinni were not the real enemy. They were being controlled by an enemy far more sinister.

I turned around when I felt a hand on my shoulder. It was Niamah.

"The Djinni were enslaved by the Pandemonium." she said, "Surreya has told us everything. She wants us to help her free her people from the enemy's control. She's told us that a Nephal has come into the Rath and he is the one controlling the Pandemonium. We need to get the Djinni to the centre of the Rath and then we can help them."

I called the Russian officers over.

"We need to get the Djinni to the centre of the mountain." I said.

"For the moment we have pacified them." Niamah said, "But they were controlled by evil spirits that could return if we do not get them to the centre of the Rath quickly."

"We will have to carry them." Al added.

So that is what we did. Rujansky ordered the men and because the Djinni were so small and light, we were able to carry a couple each but there were still some that we had to leave behind, those we hadn't captured, as we ran deeper into the mountain.

We ran down a long tunnel with the Djinni, who appeared to be in utter agony. Al and Niamah were trying to pray as they ran, because Surreya was not the problem. We carried the Djinni, and for now they relied upon our strength.

"KEEP PRAYING!!!" Niamah yelled at the men as she ran past them.

In the moment of our victory against our physical adversaries we needed to not become complacent as our non-corporeal enemy was even more deadly. There were shadows following us, looking for spiritual niches in our armour through which to strike at us. There was also among us a well-hidden Nephalim agent. He could be anywhere. I had never been more terrified in my life, yet in my terror I sought courage from Divine help. My determination to beat this enemy was stronger.

So we ran. Suddenly we came out of the tunnels and to the edge of a wide chasm. Before us we could see the continuing tunnel... on the other side of the gulf. Al stepped forward quickly. He was the one carrying Surreya as well as two males of the Djinn. He put the two males down and lifted Sureyya up and spoke to her. She nodded and although exhausted and diminished, Surreya flexed her shoulders. For the first time I noticed the two large protrusions running along the edge of her shoulder blades. There was a sudden flash of light and a pair of wings, like light shimmering upon water, shot from her shoulders. Surreya leapt into the air over the chasm and hovered there briefly, looking back at Al and Niamah who had just joined him. We watched as Al put the staff he was carrying into a slot in the rock ledge and turned it like a key. Lightning flashed from the top of the staff and Surreya seemed to catch it in her hand. She flew over the chasm, drawing the lightning after her. She landed at the other side and with a smack of her hands upon the stone, attached the lightning to the other side.

"She has made a bridge for us to cross!" Al cried, "We must cross quickly!"

Indeed she had. The light played and formed into what looked like a fine bridge made of luminescent spider silk. Al grabbed his staff and after scooping up his two Djinn, ran without hesitation across the bridge. We followed him. Just then we heard horrifying screams echoing along the chasm! We looked up searching for the source of the sound but I couldn't see anything. Then, yes! There were shadows flashing in the dark cave above us. I had just crossed the bridge and put my burdens down. By the light of my blessed blade I looked again. I could see them coming. They were Pandemons, like black smoke shadows, hideous bat-like and vicious. Others were still crossing the bridge, and the Pandemons were almost upon them! Niamah was just then at my side. Quickly she passed her two female Djinn to me and in one swift motion she pulled at the clasps at her shoulders and disrobed. Now naked and glowing with glamour fire, Niamah screamed at the Pandemons with a scream like the cry of an eagle. She had those same shoulder protrusions which she flexed and with a leap was flying up into the air! Hurtling with incredible speed and aggression, and covered in blue-white light, Niamah met the Pandemons with a violent crushing collision! The shadows were scattered and she tore some of them apart with light flashing from her fingertips and her eyes. But some had flown around her and attacked those still crossing the bridge. In horror, I saw the Pandemons tear through the bodies of several men and the Djinni they carried, dragging their life forces from their bodies! Dead, without a mark upon them, the bodies were hurled by the force of the impact over the edge and into the chasm! These beings were incredibly powerful!!

I gritted my teeth and ran back out onto the bridge, yelling at those still crossing to move faster! Those of us who had crossed and placed our Djinn upon the safe side returned to the bridge. Holding up our blades and crying in rage and faith, we attacked the Pandemons flying around us. The noise of battle was even louder than before and we kept our focus this time as we drove the enemy back to where Niamah waited for them in awful and deadly beauty. Our blades and Niamah's light seemed to tear them apart and burn them. They retreated into the darkness of the tunnels in panic, screaming in their frustrated rage.

My heart was pounding and chest heaving. We were all astounded by the attack. The last of the Russians made it across the bridge to safety with their Djinni.

Captain Kurbatov was doing a head count and the men were forming a defensive position in an open space, just in case of another attack. As for Niamah, she had flown after some of the fleeing Pandemons, but I could see her flying back already. Meanwhile, Al turned his staff in the key lock on our side of the chasm and the bridge vanished.

"Aren't there more of us over there?" I called to him, "And what about the other Djinni?"

"They're dead." Al's expression was grim, "They are all dead."

Niamah landed next to me and picked up her clothes. She looked exhausted and a bit unnerved, yet the light in her eyes still shone with victory. I could see a burn across her collar bone.

"You're injured!" I exclaimed.

"We Tuatha De Danann are fast healers." Niamah said, pulling her clothes back on over her head.

"We must continue into the city itself and strengthen the wards that protect us from the Pandemonium, before they work out a way to break them down." Al warned, "There is more work to be done yet."

We gathered ourselves together in the mouth of the tunnel and redistributed the Djinni who were still unable to walk. But Surreya and several others seemed revived enough to stand by themselves. They were a proud species, but they had been humbled. It had all seemed so surreal, but invisible forces had been the main enemy in this fight.

So we continued down the tunnels, with Al, Niamah and Surreya leading the way, the light of the key staff shining before them. Finally we came out into a large gallery. We could hear the sound of running water nearby, there was another bridge ahead, this one made of stone.

The bridge itself was ornately carved and in the middle was a stone structure that looked something like a bee hive. There were lights flickering within. As we passed over the rushing torrent below, a few of us stopped to look at this strange thing. I looked closely and discovered that the hive was some kind of habitation. There were little windows and inside the rooms within, tiny sprite-like faeries, looking back out at us. One of them, wearing what looked like a skirt made of flower petals, got such a shock at seeing me peering into her room that she fell over! My laughter seemed to offend her and she flew out of her hive, along with dozens of others of her kind and they chattered and flew around us.

The Russians were fascinated but wary. Some of them were concerned that we were in danger again. Surreya took to flight again and she hovered over the bridge, surrounded by her little companions. Some of the other Djinni soon joined her.

"These are the Renim." she explained, "They are chariots of God and gate keepers. We will need their assistance to enter the Rath of Utnapishtim."

The bridge ended at a wall of rock, but there was a wooden door there. The wood looked old and black. Ancient carvings covered it. Two carved Mesopotamian sphinxes stood guard on either side. We watched with the Djinni as the Renim flew up to a hole in the rock just above the door. There was loud clunking noise and the door opened. The Renim were waiting for us on the other side. Surreya led us into the Rath beyond. At first, everything was dark, but the Renim flew forward to find lamp posts which they lit up. The lamp posts were stone columns with flames above a bowl at the top. The light of the flames appeared as the Renim flew outwards, revealing the city. They were now inside an enormous cavern that seemed to fill the whole interior of the mountain. Far above there was a sphere of what looked like iron hovering in the hollow space over the city. Before us was a wide boulevard which crossed the city. Stone buildings were all around us. I stood there with the others transfixed with wonder. All the buildings and structures were magnificent and palatial. There were wide streets and gardens and fountains. Everything had been carved from the virgin rock long ago. Surreya and the Djinni, most of whom were walking now anyway, led us down towards the centre of the Rath. In the centre was a large open plaza, with large columned buildings, which looked like temples on either side. Al and Niamah took Surreya and physically pulled her to the centre of the plaza. In the floor of the space there were large rectangular stones, crystalline quartz forming a series of rings. At the middle of the rings was a single square stone, slightly raised above the surface of the plaza floor. Like at the bridge, Al placed his staff into the keyhole in the stone, but he pushed Surreya towards it and she actually turned the key. As she turned the key she said a word in Angelic or Enochian, the language of the A'sidhe, the word was "phoosh-ee", which means "activate".

Another loud clunk noise, much louder this time, could be heard deep in the bowels of the mountain. The floor of the plaza began to vibrate and the stone pattern in the floor began to rise. Al, Niamah and Surreya stepped off the stone upon which they were standing, Al bringing the staff key with him. The rest of us, even the Djinni, watched the stones rising with fascination and interest. The Renim were swarming above us, lighting up the plaza like fireflies. As the stones rose up around us I suddenly realised what I was seeing. The rectangular stones formed lintels on top of other megaliths, standing in a large ring around us.

"It's Stonehenge!" I exclaimed.

Yes, all the trilithons were there in place and unbroken, as were the other marker stones and the various other sarsens. The stone in the middle was the so-called altar stone, which only rose up to about hip height, while the rest rose to their full height. All the stones seemed to be humming and vibrating with a strange inner light.

"We need you to finish the activation process." Niamah beckoned me over to where she was standing with Al and Surreya near the altar stone. The stone was low and wide, facing towards the open end of the horseshoe of giant trilithons in the middle of the larger ring of sarsen stones. Al stood at one end and Niamah at the other, and Surreya stood at the back facing toward the opening of the horseshoe of trilithons.

"Stand there opposite me." Surreya said in Russian.

She beckoned me over to the altar stone. I was a bit wary still of this Djinn because not long before she had been my deadly enemy. She was also stark naked and beautiful. That was unnerving enough. But as I approached the stone I could see lights flickering within and right in front of me a pair of hand print shaped lights. Similar hand shapes were in front of the three others and it was obvious that they were intended for them because the hand shapes had only three fingers and thumb, just like the Faerie hand and the hand shapes lit before me had the four fingers and thumb of the human hand.

"We need a mortal to make it work." Surreya added, "The gate is off."

"It's alright." Niamah added, "Place your hands on the stone."

We did it together at the same time. I suddenly became aware of the empathic connections between my companions, including the strong feelings of remorse and sorrow coming from Surreya and the compassion and forgiveness coming from the other two. But then their thoughts and feelings shifted to focus upon me. There was also the sense of a fifth mind with us. The Rath and the stone ring had suddenly vanished. Instead there were five people standing together. The two A'sidhe, the Djinn and myself of course stood facing each other, but another man had stepped into the circle to my right. We all looked at him. He was middle aged in appearance, with dark hair tinged with grey. His hair and beard were carefully curled and styled in the Mesopotamian way and he wore a colourful patched kilt and reed sandals.

"Hello." he spoke in ancient Sumerian, a language which I'd never learned, but apparently could now understand.

"Hello." I answered in Sumerian, "Are you Noah?"

"No!" the man laughed, "If you mean am I the actual man named Ziusudra born in the ancient city of Shuruppak before the time of the Deluge, the man who built the Torbor which floated upon the waters, the man whom your Bible calls Noah, then I have to disappoint you. I am not Noah, but I am an artificial intelligence which is based upon him. You can call me Atra. By the way, all the systems are now activated. Is there anything else in particular that you want or need?"

"You better ask them." I said pointing to Al and Niamah.

"Oh," he said, "the Seelie agents. By the way, the psychic barriers protecting the city have been breached and Pandemonium forces are trying to enter the Rath."

"That is what we needed to know." Al said, "Can you restore the barriers?"

"Yes. I've already done that." said not-Noah, "But, while the Pandemons themselves can be repulsed, some of them have recorporealized and are gathering in the lower levels of the Rath."

"How many are there and where are they?" Niamah asked.

"I can give you a holographic representation."

He waved his hand and a picture of the mountain appeared in the air. He waved his hands again and the side of the mountain was erased and the interior revealed. Looking carefully I could see the city and other chambers as well as the ark itself. The Rath was glowing with light, but there were some dark patches, which soon closed over. I could nevertheless see small red points near the breaches, moving together in groups. They were inside the Rath. I counted them. There were only a few of them.

"I know where those places are." Surreya said, "We can stop them."

"It won't be easy." not-Noah said, "They're ghouls. But yes, it is possible to stop them."

"Ghouls?" I asked, "Where did they come from?"

"The Pandemonium stole the bodies of those of us who died!" Surreya growled, "They commit

an abomination! It is not respectful!"

"We will track them down and exorcise them." Al said, "And when we have full control of the gate, we will purge the entire mountain."

"Yes," Niamah agreed, "we must get the gate opened as soon as possible and get reinforcements here into the city. Then we can start moving troops from Zion and help Allenby take Jerusalem."

"We were ordered to shut the gate down," Surreya said, "and sabotage it. It will take some time to undo the damage, but we should be able to get it fixed by tonight."

The picture of the city grew and Atra seemed to be looking intently at the iron sphere that hovered over the plaza.

"Hmm," he mused, "I will get the Renim to undo the damages that you made them do in the first place, Djinn, but you are a bit optimistic, it probably won't be fixed until tomorrow. In the meantime there are a few ghouls to deal with and you need to get your Russian guests settled in. A tour of the Rath might be a good idea, and show them the boat as well. Oh, and feed them too!"

With that, we were back standing around the altar stone.

"How long were we away?" I asked Zabolotsky who was standing nearby.

"You didn't go anywhere! You all put your hands on the stone and then asked me how long you were away? What is this?"

It had all happened in a split second!

"Don't worry about it." I shrugged, "It is too complicated."

I could see Niamah and Surreya talking, and some other Djinni were coming out of a building nearby. Those whom we had rescued and brought back with us were quietly taken away and so were those Russians who were wounded. Some of the men got a bit indignant about that, seeing their comrades placed into the care of the Djinni, but Al quickly stepped forward to address those who remained. Behind him I could see Surreya and Niamah now talking to some Djinni warriors, presumably those who were being sent to deal with the ghouls.

"My fellow warriors," Al said, "do not be alarmed that your friends are being cared for by the Djinni. They have been defeated by us, but also liberated. They were slaves to the Pandemonium and now they are released and willing to be our allies. Even now, our true enemies are trying to gather their forces, and Surreya has sent some of her remaining warriors to fight the intruders."

"Then we should go and help them!" one of the Russians cried. There were general calls of agreement. Some of the men stood up and drew their bayonets. Surreya stepped forward.

"There is no need." she said. "Some of the Pandemons have taken possession of five of our Djinn dead and turned them into ghouls. It would not be right for you to fight them. It is the responsibility of the Djinni to take care of our own. Let our warriors exorcise the evil spirits and bring the bodies of our people home to us. You have already saved the lives of many Djinni today."

That kind of honour was something that the Russians could understand. They nodded in agreement.

"Besides," Niamah had appeared beside Al, "there is a lot to explain to you all. We have brought you here for a special reason."

"This is new to me." I said.

"It is meant to be a secret." Niamah responded, "But now I will tell you, men of Russia and Britain."

Niamah winked at me. Djinni individuals and the Ren were active all around us in their city, but we were led by Niamah and Al to sit down in the middle of the Ring.

"You are among a number of specially selected individuals who come from many nations, members of the Melkizedek Order." Niamah continued, "who have all proven themselves in battle on behalf of the alliance between our two peoples. You are all spiritual men, good soldiers committed to fighting against evil. You have seen the enemy up close and personal, so you know what we are up against. Few mortals are invited into our world, but we feel that we can trust you. Now I am going to tell you the truth of our story so you may be better equipped."

Niamah paused and sat down among us. We were all tired and stressed, but also keenly interested. Revelations were coming.

"Major Ryan," Niamah pointed at me, "has been an agent of the Melkizedek Order for some time, as you all are. You might think of us in terms of angels fighting, but we are not of your world, although many of us were born and raised here. Our species, both the good and evil, are descended from an ancient Eldar race called the Vansad. We physically evolved over twelve cycles, each a different universe. We developed the Ring Portal technology you see here in this ring of standing stones. We use these stones to travel to other worlds, to replicate and heal bodies, and even transcend our physical forms. This technology has made us effectively immortal as we can create a new body, if our old one dies. The Vansad now come in many forms and tribes. Some of us are very ancient, such as the Seelie Court of the A'sidhe. While most of us have chosen to remain in the path of life, some have fallen away and love the darkness. Great evil Satans and the Nephalim Baal Lords lead the Pandemonium. Our race, and many of our tribes have fought against the Pandemonium for millions of years. Some tribes, like the Djinni, have in the past, kept to themselves or remained neutral. But as the battle rages, we are all forced to take sides whether we like it or not."

Niamah looked at Surreya, not with condemnation, but squeezed her hand in encouragement.

"You humans, and other races, have at various times and places met us and taken sides as well." Niamah continued, "Your religions attest to this. Your world is located in a pivotal and strategic place in the universe, and your human race, although mortal and subject to decay, is beloved of the Seelie Court. In fact, your race has been given powers that you do not yet know how to use. You are special, and although only very young as a people, your role in the battle against the darkness is vital."

Niamah stopped for a bit and let that sink in.

"There have always been special chosen ones among you that have stood with us," Niamah said, "the Children of Adam and the chosen families, and those who joined them. But the enemy was always powerful and violent and manipulative, controlling men from behind the scenes with cunning. It is the nature of your history. The enemy has infiltrated and corrupted the world, your nations, your religions and economies. They have persecuted or killed anyone who got in their way. It is why we have so often had to work in secret ourselves with small groups of humans, such as the Order of Melkizedek and some spiritual individuals. But now the enemy has taken a more aggressive strategy, and we must respond to it - which is why we need you."

"Retaking this Rath within the mountain," Al continued, "will certainly mean that it will be a lot easier for us to take Palestine and defeat Turkey, so moving closer to winning this conflict. But there is more. The Djinni have been guardians of this mountain for a long time, along with other Faerie tribes. In the past this mountain was a great place of learning and a gathering place for wisdom. When the Djinni entered the service of the Pandemonium and were enslaved, it was a great loss. In the battle, many Faerie and humans died."

Al paused and sighed inwardly. He and Niamah seemed to be communicating empathically with each other.

"There is much that you will need to know." Niamah finally said, "Not only you, but your families as well are invited to come here and live not only in this Rath, but in a network of such hidden cities around the world. Each of the Raths has a circle of rings just like this one. In reality there is actually only one circle, but it exists in many places at the same time. The staff that Alaquandi carries with him is, it should be obvious to you, a key which unlocks the circle and enables us to use the circle to open portals between the different Raths, including those

Raths existing upon our other worlds, and even in other times. We have also placed "traveller stones" in different places around this world and we can open portals between the circle and those stones enabling us to move quickly around the planet. We angel-types have been getting around like that for a long time!"

"The problem is," Al continued, "that the Pandemonium control some of the Raths and so they sometimes intercept travellers. So, the more Rath circles we control, the safer it is to travel. Taking this Rath means a lot to us Faerie because this Rath was the first to be established after the Deluge. Utnapishtim is also important because within the Torbor, what you would call the ark, is a great historical library containing all the knowledge of the antediluvian world and also many secrets of the Vansad species. We want to give you access to this library so you can learn those secrets."

The three Faerie stood up together. Surreya stepped forward and bowed to us all. She had tears flowing down her cheeks and she seemed very humbled.

"I wish to apologise deeply for the evil that I have committed against you all. In fact, I have always secretly served the Light, although I have been a slave of the Darkness." Surreya declared, "The Djinni have kept this mountain hidden from the Light for centuries, and now you have access to that Light. My people are preparing for you a meal and places to sleep, but before we eat, I think that you should see the Torbor first. It is important for you to understand just what a resource you now have in the battle against our common enemy, those who used to enslave the Djinni, the Pandemonium."

We all stood up. Despite our tiredness, there was an expectation, an excitement among us.

"Should we bring our cameras and other research equipment?" one of the soldiers asked.

"No need yet." Niamah shook her head, "We know that you will need to make a report of what you see here to the Tsar and to the King, but there will be time for that tomorrow."

Leaving our packs behind, we were led by Surreya out of the plaza and towards the other side of the city and through another doorway. We crossed another bridge and were joined by a host of happy Djinni and Renim, who followed us. They constantly smiled at us, the Renim flew about our heads, cavorting and laughing. Sometimes a Djinn would reach out and touch one of us. On the other side of the bridge, there was one of the Portal Stones, a pillar made of the same stone as the Ring at the centre of the Rath. A Djinn placed his hand on the Stone and spoke some words. A portal opened nearby. Some of the small Renim, who were tiny and sprite-like in size, flew in one side of the portal and stepped out the other side, now full sized. I recognised one of them as the tiny creature I had frightened in the bee-hive home outside the Rath. She looked at me with a look of reproach, but then just poked out her tongue and laughed! I laughed as well!

"They are thankful for the way that you have rescued them." Al told me, "The Djinni have been slaves of the Nephalim for a long time and now they are free."

Surreya looked back just then and smiled. Her eyes glistened with tears of happiness. Other Djinn walked close to us, some holding the hands of the soldiers who had carried them to freedom. These people had once been deadly enemies, and while there was a part of me which still had a healthy fear of the Djinni potential for violence, I knew that we were in safe hands with friends now.

The Djinni led us down some stairs to the waters' edge near the bridge we had just crossed. There was a stone platform, like a jetty projecting out into the water and tied to the jetty was a barge-like boat. At one end of the boat was a mast with what looked like a seat on top, which in fact, that was what it was. Surreya called to one of the full sized Renim, a buxom female with short hair and a cheeky face, to sit in the chair. We all got on board, along with a considerable number of the Djinni and the Renim flew around nearby. Then the Ren in her chair began to glow as she opened her wings and we pulled away from the platform. Despite the fast flowing water, our pilot kept the boat balanced and gave us a smooth journey. The water flowed into a tunnel, lit up with the light of flying Renim. Their sparkling bee-hive shaped houses were built into the tunnel rock face, and reminded me of the so-called "Peri houses" of Cappadocia.

Finally, the boat was slowed and came to a stop in front of another platform. Light was filtering down from above via a spiral staircase. We disembarked and were led up the stairs, then along a long tunnel. As we went it began to feel colder and there was a lot more moisture and even a bit of ice here or there. The sound of the running water below and dripping from melting ice echoed around us and there was a slight breeze blowing down the tunnel. We came out onto a ledge, and there before us was one end of the huge boat we knew to be Noah's ark! It was bigger than I first thought and the pitch, which covered the bundles of reeds which were tied together to make the "gopher wood", was black and shiny. The ark was a massive barge made from reeds covered in tar, rectangular in shape, with a flat bottom, but with a wide prow that curved up at the end. Above this prow, which was quite thick, was a structure, the long cabin of the vessel, also made of bundled reeds, packed together and covered in tar. The rock ledge upon which the ark rested was protected by an overhang of rock above and on the other side of the ark we could see what looked like a wall of cut stone, where the blocks were even bigger than those used in the pyramids. This end of the ark was therefore quite sheltered. Surreya led us down a path which ran along beside the ark. We looked up at it with wonder. We came to another wall of cut stones, this wall was built across the middle of the ark, over and above it, forming an arch. There was a passage running along-side the ark through the wall and we went into it. As we walked along the passage, it was easy to just reach over and touch the ark itself which formed the wall of the passage to our left. While the surface of the wood looked rough, it was actually very smooth to the touch. The tar which covered the reeds was petrified long ago and felt like glass or hard resin. I was expecting us to exit somewhere on the side of the mountain, but instead we came out into a large stone chamber, made of monolithic white marble stone blocks. Looking around I could see clearly the end of the ark behind us, actually broken open. It was as though someone had taken the ark and cut it into two pieces then tried to re-join the two parts with this massive chamber of white stone, forming an open space in the middle. We could see both ends of the broken ark where the wood had been cut and made square on both sides of the chamber. The chamber we were now standing in seemed to glow with light from the stones themselves. Before us in the middle of the huge room was a wooden platform. We climbed up some steps and there were what looked like gold sarcophagi in the middle of the chamber, rising up from the floor, through the wooden deck. These gold sarcophagi had round dome shaped caps on top with cuneiform carved around the peaks of each. Surreya went over to the nearest and sat down upon a small couch that rested against it.

"Please be seated," she invited, "Let me tell you the true story of the Torbor."

As Surreya reclined back on her couch she waved her hand and called out. "Atra!"

Immediately, the being who was not Noah, but some kind of image of Noah - who had called himself an "artificial intelligence" (whatever that meant), he materialised before us.

"Mistress." he bowed.

"I am about to tell our guests the story of the Torbor, would you like to illustrate for us?"

"A pleasure! I have archival images in my memory including the neurological scans of Atra-hasis himself, that is Ziusudra, the members of his family and crew, as well as library recordings going back to the time of the First Nephalim War. There is also a comprehensive visual and sound library as well as generated projections and holographic simulations."

"Very well Atra." Surreya nodded, "I will need appropriate illustrations as I tell the story. Will you be able to do that?"

"Certainly!"

Although a bit stunned by all the strangeness of the situation, the advanced technology of the Djinni and Faerie people, I was surprised at the fortitude of my Russian companions. They had sat down and were eager to listen to Surreya's story. I suspected that Niamah, Al and the Djinni were using their empathic powers to calm us, and it must have been working because I was feeling quite content.

"Most of you would be familiar with the Bible stories of Adam and Eve and the story of Noah and the Ark." Surreya began, "But there is a lot more to be said about your ancient times. For example, how old would you say the Earth is?"

"About six thousand years?" Zabolotsky suggested.

"Oh, no!" Surreya smiled, "Much older! This universe is nearly fourteen billion years old and is part of a much larger continuum we call the Multiverse, which is infinitely old. The Multiverse grows and is alive. Your universe is like a single cell of an infinitely huge Being, the Source of All Being. From the Source of All Life is created all conscious beings throughout an infinite continuum of universes that are born and die and are reborn. Great ancient civilisations have arisen and have evolved to travel across the Multiverse, seeding their kind wherever they went. An ancient alliance of Elder races entered the Universe when it was young. They were called the Elohim or the Powerful Ones. The Elohim established colonies or seed worlds in the Universe. This Earth, your world, was one of those planets, among many others that the Elohim terraformed and settled long ago. They supervised the colonisation of this universe billions of years ago and have been visiting periodically ever since then to continue the creation process by seeding this world with organic life, then genetically engineering and modifying those life forms at different times. What Atra will show you is an illustration of what took place in ancient times."

An image of a lifeless planet appeared in the air above us, but with different shaped continents and the Moon orbiting much much closer, looking huge in the sky. Floating in space over the Earth in space was a huge asteroid with what looked like a city built into a crater at the top end. Above the city towers was a glowing sphere of light emanating a field of energy. The asteroid descended to the Earth and as it landed it partly submerged itself in the Earth, becoming a mountain. The process was spectacular as the huge Splinter stabbed itself like a blade into the Earth. On the plain near the new Mount, a portal opened, like a door in space, and three people, who looked remarkably human, stepped out, followed by a group of other beings. The world was barren and lifeless, although there was a thick fog of carbon dioxide cloud swirling around them. The Three were led by a tall beautiful woman, with skin blue black like deep space and clothed in robes made of energy. Her male companions were like her, but one was older looking than the other. The Three all had pure white hair, and the mature looking one was bearded. Then five Elementals stepped forward from the portal out into the world. In their pure spiritual forms they were shimmering light, forces and energy in a simple humanoid pattern. Although only vaguely human looking, we could see that they had different character and personality, shifting colours in their energy fields that pulsed. I knew what these alien beings were. They were ancient members of an

Eldar race, even older than the Vansad. The Three were the Logoi, Avatars of the Source, known as the Progenitors, the Founders of the Elohim Council.

The Aesir air Elemental hovered above, and he gathered the gases around himself, clothing himself, looking like cloud in humanoid form. Standing below him was a Triton water Elemental who seemed to call water droplets from the air, forming a shimmering robe of flowing liquid. Together they began to sing and clouds formed in the sky. It began to rain. The raindrops fizzled and evaporated where they fell upon the Astari Fire Elemental who stood nearby, her (she was definitely feminine) spirit form clothed in burning flame. The Terrestrial Earth Elemental was huge and masculine, like a strong man in a circus. His form was clad in rock and dirt, drawn up from the earth around him. He clapped his hands once and the ground opened up, and huge rock formations rose up. The Astari found a cave among the rocks and flaming lava could be seen rising in the depths of the Earth. The last Elemental, a green Gaean with branches and leaves for hair, growing alive over her spirit body, joined in the song. All sang together. The barren land shook and became darker in colour. Plant life sprang from the Earth, ferns and cycads and tall trees. It appeared to us to happen quickly, but there was a sense that what we were seeing was taking a long time. The Elementals and the members of the Elohim collective, were actively working and working hard.

Other images appeared one after the other, of Zoel who were also other members of the ancient Eldar Races. The Zoel were different to the Elementals. Unlike the Elementals, whose physical bodies were formed from matter around them, the Zoel were actual living beings, with biological bodies, alive and in a true sense, members of distinct races. There was a Mer, swimming with the fish in the sea. An amphibious Tor-Ahn in his pond, watching as reptilian Tor-Gar rode past through the swamp on the backs of dinosaurian mounts. Standing on a grassy hill was an antlered Behemah beast lord with a sabre toothed cat at his side and a tiny flower Sprite sitting on his shoulder. Nearby were a male and female Faerie, their sleek bodies tattooed with wode.

The Zoel races were the original races of the world and they lived here long before human beings even existed. There were other races, such as the bird-like Ziv and the insectoid Deborah. Unlike the Russians I was already aware of some of these races or had heard rumours about them. Most of the Older Elementals and Zoel races had left the earth long ago, although some visited sometimes. These were all allies of our world. For reasons that I could understand, Atra didn't show us examples of the fallen races of the Pandemonium. They were part of the earth's past as well.

"The Elohim also brought us children of the Vansad to this world and placed the world under our protection."

Surreya paused as images of our planet appeared before us. We saw the rise of the dinosaurs and the rise of an ancient Saurian civilisation. This was particularly surprising for us and something I wasn't aware of.

"These beings are the original indigenous species of this world." Surreya answered our unspoken question, "They were the seeded offspring of the Tor-gar, an Eldar race, and were called the Gorenge. They built a great civilisation and were a noble people. But the end of that age had to come."

What came next was even more surprising. Starships landed on the Earth and made contact with the Gorenge. The inhabitants were very clearly human-like. They reminded me of the Australian Aborigines, dark, handsome and slender.

"These are the Lahmu, who are another seed race, this time from the world you know as Mars." Surreya explained, "The Lahmu and Gorenge formed an alliance and set out to explore all the galaxy together. But they met disaster. They met the Pandemonium."

Indeed, the whole galaxy did. We saw images of Pandemonium star fleets conquering system after system. Many species banded together to fight them, but eventually they reached our solar system. The civilisations on both Mars and Earth were utterly destroyed. On both worlds, the survivors fled underground into arcologies or they fled into space. Earth descended into a series of glacial ages, while Mars fared much worse, their atmosphere stripped away and all surface life exterminated. This is what ended the Age of Dinosaurs, and what turned Mars into a dead world.

"What became of the Gorenge?" one of the Russians asked.

"Watch and see." Surreya responded.

Images of life returning to the Earth began, including the rise of new mammal species.

Survivors from the long war return to Earth. New civilisations are built.

"Mu and Lemuria." Surreya said as we watched, "The Lahmu people and Gorenge who had been fighting the Pandemonium returned to the Sol system. Contact with survivors on Mars and Earth is made and new civilisations soon develop. The Gorenge by this time have become two distinct species. There are the Subterranean Gorenge who continue to live in the inner Earth arcologies, and the Spacer Gorenge who have developed the ability to shape-change their bodies. The Shape-Changers chose to live among the Lahmu people in the Martian arcologies and in the new cities of Mu and Lemuria they built on the Earth."

"Where does Adam and Eve fit into all of this?" one of the Russian soldiers asked.

"Good question." Surreya replied, "We are getting there. The first humanoids to live here on Earth were from Mars originally, the Lahmu. They were quite a distinct species and they are still around. There are other humanoid species in our galaxy too. One of these species is the Nebiruim, a distant relative species to the Vansad. They arrived in the Solar system nearly three hundred thousand years ago. By this time, Earth had its own seed humanoid species developing. The Elohim Progenitors supervised this themselves. Homo Erectus lived in Africa and Australia and Homo Neandertalensis and others were in Eurasia. There were also other minor branch species. This is what the Bible talks about when it says, 'God created Mankind, male and female they were created.' Then the Nebiruim arrived in a ship the size of a planet. They were a giant race, and very powerful."

I knew about the arrival of the world-ship Nubiru and how they resisted the Elohim and the Eldar for a time. Under the Leadership of Anu, the Nubiruim did join the Elohim Council, but Anu's sons, Enki and Enlil plotted conquest.

"The Nebiruim warrior caste, the Anunnaki, attacked both Mars and Earth and occupy both worlds. The Lahmu and Gorenge were enslaved and joined to the worker caste of the Igigi. The Anunnaki had Saurian troops called Rahab-Devar who they used to enforce their will. The Anunnaki ruler, Anu, also known as Elyon, sent his son Enlil to supervise the occupation. Later on, Enlil's brother

Enki and sister Ninhursag began the process of mining monoatomic gold from the oceans, an element needed in Nebiruim technology. The Igigi and the enslaved peoples were put to work. After some time though, the Igigi led a revolt against the Anunnaki and demanded better working conditions. Enlil wanted to exterminate the workers, but Enki had a better idea. Enki and Ninhursag collected genetic samples from the indigenous hominids in Africa and mixed in their own DNA to genetically engineer a new species that was called the Adapu. The Adapu were still not very intelligent and they were infertile, but they made excellent workers for physical labour, and so the revolt ended and work began again. Enki wanted to improve the new worker species, but Enlil flat out forbade it as he was determined to keep the Adapu as a slave species to a race of angry gods."

There was some disquiet among my Russian friends. This wasn't the story they were expecting at all.

"There's more." Sureyya continued, "Enki was a great scientist and he loved his Adapu, but Enlil insisted on keeping them as dumb slaves. So Enki secretly came to the Edin, Enlil's garden and he modified the Adapu genetically so that they became aware of good and evil and were able to reproduce. They became a new species, called the Adamu. Enlil found out and was utterly enraged! He expelled the Adamu from his Edin and confronted Enki, whom he called a Serpent and a rebel. There was war as Enki took the Adamu away to protect them. The two brothers have remained in perpetual war ever since.

"This isn't the story you know," Surreya stated the obvious, "The Serpent isn't the Devil, but is Enki, raising Humankind to true self awareness. Enlil used the name of Serpent as an insult, but Enki bore it proudly and took on the snake as his personal heraldry. Today, the same symbol is used by doctors as the caduceus or the rod of Asclepius. It is Enlil, calling himself Yehowah, the God of this world, the Great Dragon, who is the real Adversary of Humankind. These days he goes by the name of Graud."

"You are saying that Enlil and Graud are the same person?! Enlil is, ah, Jehovah, ah Yehowah!!" I exclaimed, "I was hunting Graud just a few months ago in Germany! How is it that Satan became God??"

"Yes," Surreya nodded, "they are one and the same - just different incarnations. We Eldar races live long lives, but we can be killed or we can choose to let ourselves die. When that happens, we return to the non-corporeal state of spirit. The Spirit Realm is the energy field that sustains all life and to which all life must return. The Elohim and Elder races, both they and we have the power to take on corporeal form, to become reincarnated beings. It is how we walk among you. Both the Spirit Realm and the Physical Realm coexist alongside each other and are dependent upon each other. Never let anyone tell you that your physical body is evil or unspiritual. Even the Elohim seek to take on physical form many times - it is what we are all meant to do. Spirit must give birth to life. And the Baal Lords know this, but they use their spiritual powers to dominate and control life. They are predators and Graud is one of the most vicious of them. He is also a masterful liar, the Devil, masquerading as God."

"Was Graud the one who had enslaved you?" Vassilli Zabolotsky asked, "Was he the one who made you attack us?"

"Yes," Surreya clenched her fists in rage, "he has come here and is nearby. We can sense his presence in this very mountain. He is angry that we have changed sides and he will no doubt have plans to take this Rath back. We must repair the damage done to the circle and use the portals to bring Faerie and Melkizedek forces here if we are to maintain a strong occupation. Graud is very intelligent so we shouldn't underestimate him. He was underestimated back in the time before the Deluge and he was able to establish a Nephalim Empire of genetically engineered monsters that conquered most of the world. The Nephalim Empire used advanced technology to conquer anyone who tried to fight against them. They hunted down and killed all the heirs of the Sethani royal house, descended from Adamu and Titi, but Atra-hasis, the one which you know as Noah, escaped and found sanctuary among the Shile. The Shile were the only ones on Earth at that time who had sufficiently advanced technology to fight and prevail against the Nephalim. Both the Shile and the Nephalim had already established colonies on other planets in other star systems and they also had colonies and military outposts in this star system. In fact, they controlled almost everything between them in this arm of the galaxy. The Shile asked the Seerlie Council of the Eldar nations to intervene. There was an alliance formed and the Eldar and the Shile went to war with the Nephalim Empire. In the end, the Shile evacuated the Earth and Ziusudra and his supporters went into hiding. The Elohim used Enki, who warned him of a final attack and Ziusudra built the Torbor. As you can see, while the Torbor was a wooden boat, it was also very advanced technologically. Let's show you what that war looked like."

A scene of desolation appears. The Earth is burning and stripped of plant life. Bomb craters and even trenches can be seen.

"That looks familiar!" says one of the Russian soldiers.

Suddenly the ground begins to shake and moving towards the trenches are huge war machines walking on mechanical legs. Turrets are mounted along the sides and there are two large guns, one at the front, and another at the back. In the background other war machines can be seen being dropped down by even larger aircraft - huge barrel shaped dreadnaughts that look similar to dirigibles covered in guns begin firing particle beams at the trenches ahead.

"Those are the Nephalim attackers landing a raiding party near a Shilean evacuation area. Watch what happens next."

Out of the trenches poured forth soldiers in dirt coloured armour. They swarmed towards the enemy war machines fearlessly. Behind them the ground began to heave upwards and break open. From the ground crawled what could only be described as giant spiders. These were not machines which looked like spiders, but actual living creatures. But it was also obvious that they had been "modified" in various ways. On the sides of their heads were cannons which fired superheated plasma. From their mouths squirted acidic poison. Their spinnerets fired web the strength of steel cable, tangling up the enemy battle wagons, knocking them down so the war spiders could tear their hulls open, allowing the soldiers to swarm inside.

"Those soldiers don't seem to be human." Kurbatov said.

"You are right." Surreya nodded, "They are genetically engineered soldiers, bred by the Shile, called Pigrians - the infamous Boars Tusk Brigade. They are the best soldiers this planet has ever produced and that is saying something!"

"They're pigs!" someone shouted.

"Yes." Surreya answered. "The Shile bred all kinds of servant species which they called Humanimals. That is what the Shile are known for - their mastery of genetics."

In the background, large manta ray shaped aircraft were approaching. They landed and the Shilean forces began to retreat towards them.

"Those are Shilean space whales," Surreya said, "living creatures bred by the Shile capable of flying into space."

The Boars Tusk Brigade began their tactical retreat but the Nephalim war machines kept up their assault. It wasn't looking good for the Shilean forces, which were taking a pounding. One of the space whales took a direct hit from a plasma cannon and exploded spectacularly. Then, in the sky of the distant background, a large airborne object could be seen approaching. Bigger than a mountain, it was soon obvious what the object was.

"You can see the large craft approaching." Surreya said, "It is what we call a "splinter". You can see the Rath located at the top with the weapons and propulsion sphere above. In fact, this mountain, Agri Dagh or Mount Ararat, is a buried splinter, left here on the Earth, one of twelve actually which are still here."

The implications of all this had to sink in, and so we watched the battle continue. From the Rath fortress at the top of the splinter swarmed thousands of lights. It was soon obvious that they were Renim, but they looked different.

The angle of view changed from the battle on the ground to a battle in the skies. The glowing balls of light were the individual Renim, but spinning around each of them was a metallic looking wheel with lights around the rim. The wheels that spun around the Renim gave off bolts of lightning as they attacked the Nephalim ground forces. Incredible firepower lanced down at the Nephalim war wagons, and even targeted specific troops on the ground, which we were seeing for the first time. It kind of reminded me of that Bible passage in Ezekiel of the flying wheels within wheels, with eyes all around their rims. While the Renim wheels took out smaller targets, the big sphere over the splinter fired huge bolts of energy at the Nephalim battle wagons, utterly disintegrating them. The field of view kept changing, from the sky to the ground, but our hearts were beating because this kind of warfare was unlike anything we had seen before. The noise and energy of the attacks were unnerving and deadly.

But the objective of the Elder attack was successful as the Shile space whales laden with passengers retreated. The wreckage of Nephalim war machines and thousands of bodies remained behind. The Renim did one final sweep of the battle ground then returned to the splinter. Then we watched them land along a wide flat area of rock running around the edge of the Rath of the splinter, hovering high in the atmosphere. The Renim transformed as they landed, the light of their bodies diminishing and then somehow vanishing. All the weaponry and other mechanical equipment harnessed onto the glowing hulls of the Renim was gone as well. The Renim themselves and their crews stood there on the landing ledge and I realised something as they headed for passages into the Rath. The Renim were not pilots that flew in some kind of aircraft, but they were the air crafts themselves, living flying beings, able to carry others within themselves and weapons upon their glowing bodies. How utterly fantastic!

The splinter itself then withdrew from the earth and headed out into space. There in close orbit it joined others.

"Once the Shile had been fully evacuated," Surreya said, "as well as many others, one thing was necessary, the Nephalim had to be utterly destroyed."

Silently hovering in space, the splinters watched as a huge meteor, followed by other smaller rocks dropped towards the Earth. There was no sound as the meteors struck the targets that they had been aimed at. But the explosions were unimaginably horrifically huge, sending colossal plumes of fire and ash out of the atmosphere and shock waves across the entire planet. We watched in shocked fascination as the death of an age unfolded.

"And what of the Torbor and its passengers?" Surreya asked.

Our viewpoint moved from orbit, down through the clouds. Already it was raining hard. Below we could see the ancient Sumerian city of Shuruppak, already being flooded by the waters of the swollen river. People were trying to flee, some even climbing up the ziggurat in the middle of the city. Near the ziggurat and floating in the Euphrates river, which was now greatly enlarged, was the Torbor. It was a huge black structure. On the other side of the river from the Sumerian city was what at first looked like a garden. There were lots of large trees, now swaying in the howling wind, and open areas now inundated by water. In the middle of the garden was a huge plant of some kind. It was part tree, part fern, and covered with pod shaped growths and leafy branches. Strangely it looked like some kind of house. This strangeness was compounded further by a bridge of living trees running from the centre of the garden to the main hatch of the Torbor.

"What you are seeing here is the Shile compound at Shuruppak. Ziusudra and his family were under their protection. But the area was also a border zone and the Nephalim were constantly preventing us from getting in there. Just getting this vision was difficult. There was no way to evacuate people. But, with the help of the Shile, Atra-hasis and his sons built the Torbor. The animals were genetically engineered and placed in suspended animation in the Shile facility before being loaded aboard the Torbor."

The view switched to down on the bridge, as though we were looking through someone's eyes.

"This is a memory recording of one of the Torbor's crew members, a Chipperwaal named Took. He was one of seven Chipperwaals, or ape Humanimals, as well as seven Bardel bears and a seven member squad of Pigrians."

A sudden shadow moved over everything and through Took's eyes we looked up. The rain was flashing down in torrents, and lightning that looked unnatural arched between the sky and Earth continuously. The thunder was horrifically deafening. Even though I was safely removed from these events by many thousands of years, a part of me was terrified. I wondered how Took felt in that moment. But that was not all - worse was yet to come. Everyone had gone into the Torbor except for Took who stood by the open hatch and tried desperately to get it closed. For some reason the mechanism just wasn't working. The poor Chipperwaal was horrified. Someone was yelling from further inside and he yelled back. A man came and side by side they pulled on the lever that would close the hatch, but it refused to work. They looked up again because just then the rain stopped. The clouds were moving around and forming into a huge funnel. If anything, the lightning was only getting worse! But for that moment, they could look up through the eye in the storm as it was forming above them. We could see stars, but also something else, something unthinkable, something I just couldn't believe!

"What you are seeing now is one of our most closely kept secrets." Surreya cried out over the noise of the holographic scene above us, "You must not tell anyone of what you are seeing here!"

Briefly I looked at Surreya and she looked at me. The look in her eyes told me that she meant business. I was at a loss of what to think about this thing I could see unfolding above the skies.

Strange light, bright red and orange flashed over the scene and then there was an earthquake! Took and his human companion both fell over and a wave of water came washing in through the hatch upon them as the whole Torbor was suddenly lifted up by a swell of the river. The Torbor was torn from its moorings and the bridge had broken away as well as the great boat began moving upriver before the ocean swell that was pushing it. Took looked out the hatch and down the length of the Torbor, down river and he yelped in shock and fear. The man looked as well and both he and Took got busy on the lever for the door which stubbornly refused to move. What we had seen looking down the river was certainly horrifying, in fact it was one of those things so terrifying that one would wet one's pants! Because relentlessly moving towards them was a wall of water, a giant wave, bigger than any wave I had ever seen or ever heard of! The sound of it coming was like that of a locomotive getting louder and louder. Took looked outside again and groaned in despair. Above was one horror and to the south another, fire from above and water from below! He and the man both fell to their knees and cried out with their arms outstretched, imploringly! They were praying, I realised, but their voices were drowned out by the noise. Soon they would be literally drowned if that hatch didn't close! And then it did! The lever, by itself, moved, and the hatch, like an iris of a camera, slid shut! We all cheered in relief and thankfulness for their sake at what was certainly a miracle. The Bible passage came to mind in Genesis 7:16 "And when they were all in the boat, God closed the door."

The view switched to orbit again and we could see the splinters hovering there as the Earth was torn apart far below. The cause of this destruction was right there too, horrifyingly close and menacing. We were silenced by what we were seeing, this secret that we were not allowed to repeat.

Up from the clouds below came some craft, ships flying in space. There was no sound, but the splinters actually withdrew. Then a great blast of fire and energy descended upon them, and like insects, the space ships were evaporated! There was to be no escape for the Nephalim.

"What followed was a systematic search of the solar system." Surreya continued, "The Eldar forces hunted down and exterminated the Nephalim where ever they hid in their bases, on Mars, out in the asteroid belt. They were utterly destroyed. Only then did the Eldar draw back to see what would happen next. Down below of course the Torbor survived. The splinters descended down to the Earth, where they built mountain sanctuaries, well-hidden cities, whose purpose was to protect the Earth in case the Nephalim ever returned."

The splinters did indeed descend below the clouds, which were, after many days, beginning to disperse. One of the splinters came down in the midst of the flood waters that were receding from Mesopotamia and gently lowered itself. The soft wet Earth opened up beneath it and it settled there, drawing the mud up around itself, so that it towered over the flood below. As I see this, it sounds such a simple thing, but it was actually very violent and volcanic, with great clouds of steam and lava blasting up over the splinter, changing its form and shape. All the time the great sphere of power that hovered above, radiating belts of force and rainbow light mixed with lightning, seemed to be shrinking. With great clouds of steam, the splinter stopped its descent and with boiling waters around it, took on the appearance of an island. Portals opened all around and Renim glowing and wearing their rings flew out, flicking around like spinning tops, glowing like sprites. Nine Renim flew in formation, three triangles forming a larger triangle, the Renim headed out over the flood waters, which were beginning to flow away already.

The Renim sped southwards. Below the waves were choppy not only due to the fact that the water was receding, but also because of a strong wind. They found the Torbor and did a fly over. The roof of the Torbor was a flat deck, but with a long narrow raised section running down its spine, which appeared to be rows of window shutters. The shutters were open for ventilation, and there were also a number of hatches spaced along the raised section. One of these hatches rose open and Ziusudra himself stepped out and began to wave.

One of the Renim broke away from the formation and descended right down to the deck of the Torbor, not far from where Ziusudra, the real Noah, stood. By this time, others were coming out from the hatch, including Ziusudra's family, and some of the Humanimals. The Ren dissolved their body of light, but kept the spinning ringed harness above them. The Ren, in humanoid form, stood beside a single Vansad warrior. The warrior bowed and saluted before Ziusudra.

"My lord." he said, "We have come to safely transport you and your vessel to the Rath of Utnapishtim. The Elohim await you. They are pleased to know that you have all survived this terrible conflict and they apologise for not rescuing you with the earlier evacuations."

"The Elohim are gracious." Ziusudra nodded, "But it was they who gave us the design for this Torbor through their Messenger Enki, and the vital mission to preserve the animal and plant life of our world, as well as the cultural records of our civilization. It had to be done this way, secretly, in order to avoid the eyes of the Nephalim, who can rot in their graves. But I praise the Light, for we are rescued."

"Lord Ziusudra," the warrior bowed again, "I am your servant Melkiel. We will use tractor fields to lift you to safety."

The Eldar warrior bowed again and then turned and went back to his Ren. As he turned, it was obvious to me, I recognized him. He was younger looking, but his face was unmistakable. This was Michael, the same Michael with whom I'd had breakfast back in London. I shook my head in wonder.

As the Ren pulled away, the others broke their formation and gathered around the Torbor where it floated in the water. Ziusudra and his people quickly returned inside and closed the top hatch along with the shutters. Waves of energy flowed from the Renim and formed a kind of shroud over the Torbor, which was gently lifted up out of the water! In this fashion, the Renim carried the Torbor towards the splinter. We could see it ahead, and the familiar outline of the mountain, even now was obvious, the larger and smaller peaks, which were in reality the tip of the splinter rising up through the earth, which now held it fast.

Approaching the larger peak of the "mountain", we saw an amazing thing. Above the peak, the glowing sphere was shrinking and cooling down. It was slowly lowering itself and as it did so, the top of the mountain seemed to peel away, becoming a large circular opening. Around the rim of this opening there was also forming a series of ledges, with other openings into the interior of the mountain. The Rath itself, including the ring of standing stones at its centre could clearly be seen through the large opening because a column of light flowed between those stones and the sphere above.

As for the Torbor, it was lowered upon one of the ledges, the very ledge where we were right now. The lack of snow meant that all was revealed, but it was obvious that the ark of Noah was placed right where it was meant to remain.

The final images were of the sphere dropping, now completely cooled, down into the opening above the Rath, and that opening closing over. Clouds were pierced with light above, and snow was falling, but a great rainbow also arched above the mountain. It was a beautiful and fitting end to the images that ended then.

"Ziusudra and his sons supervised the re-seeding of the world." Surreya said, "With the help of the Elohim and Eldar, he re-established animal and plant species in their right habitats and also searched out and helped the survivors of the cataclysms which had devastated the planet. The Torbor became a place of pilgrimage for those seeking knowledge and aid, especially knowledge about the ancient world which had been destroyed. Eventually the Nephalim did return, but only in very small numbers and much weakened. The Eldar garrison at Utnapishtim and also of the other splinter Raths around the world continue to remain on guard to this day against them. Having been a slave of the Nephalim, I can personally attest to their determination to restore their lost empire."

Chapter Five

Torbor

After Surreya's demonstration, I think that we were all a bit stunned. All my Sunday school preconceptions of the creation and flood stories had been "washed away" quite dramatically. And here we were actually sitting in the middle of the thing itself!

No one spoke. We just sat where we were and looked around at the two sides of the ark, or Torbor, that at some point in the past had been broken then mended.

"Would you like to have a closer look at the Torbor?" Niamah asked us suddenly.

There were general nods of ascent and "da" was said enthusiastically. We all got up and were led into the section of the Torbor behind us. Walking into the lower deck area, which was well lit by what I had to assume was electrical lighting, there were large metal tanks and piping as well

as storage areas, now mostly empty.

"The lower deck of the Torbor was mainly used for storage and these tanks here held fresh water, while other tanks processed waste or bilge." Niamah pointed, "Machinery for pumping water and air for ventilation is further forward, and between here and there are general store rooms for food and other stores. There are also some large refrigerators on the other side of this wall."

Niamah led us to a very large service lift and we went up to the next level in two groups. Everything about this ship seemed to be technologically advanced. My conception of Noah and his times was certainly being shaken. We came up to the middle deck. There was a wide open space running right down the middle forming a kind of gallery, with open balconies through the decking above. There were lifts at each end of these open areas leading up to the top deck above, as well as strong columns holding everything up. At our end of the space, there were pens and cages and spaces large enough to hold dinosaurs. Feeding bays were located in convenient places and slots for waste removal were in the floor. Further forward on either side of the open space was something which was obviously Shile in origin. They looked like huge pods, all clumped together. I could see clear windows in their sides. Curiously we moved closer.

"These are gestation pods installed by the Shile." Niamah touched one of them and pushing on a pad caused the clear window to open up, irising with a slurping noise.

"Their purpose was to grow various animal species from embryos which were stored in suspended animation. These animals were designed to reach juvenile adulthood very quickly while growing in their pod. They could then be released. The large pods are here at this end and smaller pods are further down, for smaller animals. Most of this middle deck - called the bio-deck, was used for storing the animals and plant seed. Some animals were actually kept alive as well, for use during the voyage time."

To one side of the open area was a passage. There was a noise as the hatch at the end of the passage opened with a hiss and light streamed in from the space outside.

"This is the hatch that wouldn't close!" cried the soldier who had just opened it.

"Yes indeed!" we all laughed, "That is the main access. The door still sometimes fails to close even to this day!"

The soldier tried pulling on the lever. It wouldn't budge!! We laughed some more.

We moved on, looking at other pods, work areas and a laboratory. Later on, we would come back and photograph everything and look more closely. But this was just a basic tour for now. This half of the broken ship ended with some bannisters and a set of stairs climbing up and down. We could see the central room one deck below us. There was also another set of smaller lifts. We moved up to the next level. Upstairs was the habitation deck. Niamah and Surreya showed us the apartments of the passengers, which were still finely furnished and comfortable looking. There were other living areas, a kitchen, which was still obviously being used by the Djinni who had been living here, and a communal bath, which was filled with warm water. But most impressive was what Surreya called the "library". Actually, this was only one part of the library complex, which also continued on the other side of the Torbor as well, and was connected by a walkway between both sides, running high along the side of the room connecting them. The place was more like a museum. There were viewing rooms for looking at "movies", and whole wings filled with "books". These books included some scrolls, but not many. There were also some historical objects, like Sumerian clay tablets covered in cuneiform, or ring seals. But most of the data was kept on pages of clear material. Each book was a single page. I picked one up and to my astonishment the cuneiform writing moved. Touching the corners of the page seemed to move the page, like a scroll. There were even colour pictures.

We were then led across the walkway that connected the two sides of the Torbor. The other end included more library space, but the most interesting thing we saw there were what Niamah referred to as "artificial reality couches." She explained that it was possible to actually record peoples' memories, or even create false memories and then replay them again. Being connected to the couches would enable us to experience those memories as though we were actually there! I was utterly astounded and wanted to try it out for myself.

"Perhaps another time." Niamah just smiled and shook her head, "The couches also do other things as well. They actually create a whole artificial world and also act as suspended animation pods and auto doctors. They have many functions that we can't look at now. But we will do so later. There is lots of time."

"Besides I won't let you touch them!" said Atra, whose image suddenly just walked out of one of the walls, "I have been keeping the Djinni away from these machines and out of the Torbor systems themselves for the last few years, and I won't let just anyone play with my systems. Not even these Seelie who have their key!"

"You are supposed to be helping us!" Al complained, "We have returned the Rath to Seerlie control. The ring will soon be repaired..."

"Yes!" Atra interrupted, "The operative word here is "soon", which is not yet, and who said anything about the Rath being under your control? The Nephalim are still about and not until the ring is fully functional and reconnected to the transit network will I let you even near A.M.I. systems."

"What is he talking about?" Kurbatov asked.

"A.M.I." Niamah explained, "It stands for Artificial Machine Intelligence..."

"No." Kurbatov shook his head, "That's not what I mean. Just how safe are we?"

"He means that he is detecting enemy movements which might threaten our security here." Al said, "Also, I don't think Atra quite trusts us to be up to defending ourselves, do you Atra?"

"Quite right boy-oh," Atra poked Al, but his holographic finger just passed through him, "You need to be on your best guard tonight. I think that old Enlil is planning something."

"Thank you Atra." Niamah said, "We will respect your system integrity and be alert for danger, but in what ways can you help us?"

"I'll certainly give warning if anything goes amiss," Atra now poked Niamah, "and keep a guard during the night, and make sure your men sleep with their blades."

"Do you have an armoury?" Rujansky asked, "Are there any better weapons we can use?"

"Yes, there is an armoury," Atra answered, "but I'm not giving particle blasters to primitives! Besides, I'm not so concerned with who is outside the Raths protective wards, but rather who is inside. Beware of traitors in your midst!"

"We've already suspected as much." I said, remembering the gun we found at the Rath entrance.

"And we are still in the lair of the Djinni!" Atra pointed out, then turning to Surreya, "No offence to you lady."

"No offence taken." Surreya answered, "I may have capitulated to the Seerlie, but there are some among us that would welcome the return of the Nephalim. I can feel the empathic vibrations. It may come down to a fight eventually, but I know who is loyal to me. The Renim are loyal and so are my clan. There is only one way for us to stop rebellion."

"Kill the rebels?!" Atra laughed.

"No!" Surreya scolded, "Have a party!"

"Have a party?" Captain Kurbatov exclaimed, "Parties do not stop rebels!"

"Oh yes they do." Al was grinning, "You need to understand the way we Faerie folk think."

"Of course," I nodded, "it'll work. It is almost built into you lot like a biological instinct. We humans host the party, we give away our food, and they will owe us. Whatever we do, don't eat the food of the Djinni, at least not until they have eaten our food first."

"But our food is...ah, not gourmet, it is basic soldiers rations!" Rujansky was astonished.

"That does not matter to us." Surreya assured, "If my clan and the Renim eat your rations, and the other clans are not invited to eat as well, it will be considered an act of war. Most of the Djinni will not want that. It will force the disloyal to either submit or fight. Djinni honour demands that such a fight be done openly and without deception."

"So there will be a fight." Kurbatov said, "Where and when we want it."

"Yes." said Surreya, "But they will demand a single combat. It is the only way that they will be able to save face."

"What if they win the fight?" I asked.

"Then they will set conditions for our surrender." Surreya answered.

"That depends upon whom they have to fight." Niamah added.

"Their champion will fight me." Surreya insisted.

"No." Niamah shook her head, "Their champion will have to fight a human because it is the humans who are hosting the party."

"Who is able to fight such a battle?" Zabolotsky cried, "Who will be our champion?"

"I will." I said, "And I will win."

"But what if you lose?" Zabolotsky asked.

"Then I do."

"But we will defend you if it comes to that." Surreya said, "Even if it means a full scale war. The Nephalim will not retake this mountain!"

"Let's hope it does not come to that." I said gratefully, "But let's pray that lives can be saved and it is they who have to surrender to us, not the other way around."

Chapter Six

Celebration and Confrontation

So we returned to Surreya's boat and the Ren steered us out into the fast flowing waters.

"These waters flow in an extensive system of channels and underground rivers that are part of the splinter's internal habitation zone." Surreya told us, "Over the millennia the various inhabitants of the Rath have extended the underground caverns and cave systems beyond the rock of the splinter itself. This is so we can get rid of excess water and also have access to tunnels that connect to other Raths in this region. There is a significant Rath near Yerevan in Armenia and also another ancient Rath near Tabriz in Iran, the location of the old Garden of Eden. The largest Rath in the region is under Judi Dagh, which the Muslims believe is the real mountain of Noah, the resting place of the ark. They are right, in a sense, because the Torbor did briefly run aground there before being picked up by the Ren. It was upon Judi Dagh that Ziusudra released the dove and the raven. Anchors from the Torbor are still on Judi Dagh and so is the remains of one of the Torbor's explorer boats. We could follow these underground streams to any of those places, but we are going to somewhere very special."

We must have been deep under the mountain, right in the centre of the splinter. The underground river was flowing very fast and descending steeply. There was also a lot of fog or steam rising from the water and we realised that the water was actually getting hotter.

I wondered about that. Mt Ararat was an extinct volcano, but the Rath and the Splinter that had impaled itself into the mountain most certainly was not. The last big 'eruption' in 1840, was not actually an eruption, it was when the Djinni took the mountain from the Tuatha who were guarding it. It must have been quite a battle. A whole side of the mountain slid down into Ahora gorge and destroyed the monastery. There were Melkizedek Order people there. None of them survived. I should hate Surreya and her people, because they had done that killing. But strangely I didn't. They had been slaves. It didn't make the deaths alright, but it did give me focus for my anger, at the real enemy, the Nephalim.

That some of the Djinni would still choose to serve the Nephalim after we had set them free, well, that made me angry as well. We weren't safe yet. I had a fight ahead of me.

Finally the boat came out of the channel and into a patch of dark and still water. It was much colder here and we could actually feel a faint breeze. I looked around at where we were. Some of the Russians were talking loudly because only moments before we were in rapids and they had to shout to be heard over the noise of the wild water. They had been arguing over food, in particular over the food we were going to give to our Djinni 'guests' at this feast. It wasn't much. I shushed them.

The cavern we were in was enormous! Our boat moved out from the passage behind us into open water. Looking around we could see the walls of the huge cavern rising up around us into the darkness. The only light was that given off by our Ren pilot. Still, she seemed to know where she was going and steered us out into the darkness confidently.

It didn't remain completely dark for long. Up ahead we could see a light, or rather a series of lights. There were poles rising up out of the water, with lanterns upon them. They were quite large and lit up the subterranean sea we were on, forming a path leading us forward. As we moved onward, some of the poles were more like pillars. Some of them were covered in lanterns or had Djinni dwellings built into them. The Djinni who dwelt there came out onto their balconies to see us and Surreya called out to them in her ancient tongue. Some flew after us, but many took to boats of their own and followed.

Sometimes we 'sailed' past small islands, also inhabited by the Renim and Djinni. Once we saw, not too far away, a massive stalactite hanging down from the ceiling of the cave which had a point that didn't quite touch the surface of the water. Not only had the Djinni carved a small township out of the stalactite, but they had also constructed a ship port of sorts, floating on the surface of the water. Large numbers of boats shipped out from there as well and joined us.

Finally, we could see our destination ahead. It wasn't an island. Rather it was a boat, a very big boat. Our small boat approached the bigger ship and the Ren guided us up to the ship and we floated along-side the main deck and settled into a cradle projecting from the side. We were welcomed aboard the larger ship by a group of Djinni warriors. They were big men, and they carried very big scimitars. One of them in particular, was looking daggers, not just at us, but also especially at Surreya.

"Hello brother." Surreya greeted him.

The big Djinn ignored his sister and walked boldly right up to me. He looked over at the rations which were being piled up on the deck nearby by some of the Russian soldiers and snorted rudely. He then looked me right in the eyes.

"You are the champion? Hmff." he punched me on the chest, "I will kill you."

With that he stalked off and his men followed him below deck.

"Well," Al said, "That went well."

I felt quite numb.

"Who the hell was he?" I asked.

"My brother Enmesharra." Surreya said, "He is the chosen champion of the pro-Nephalim faction. It is now time to meet the leaders of that faction."

Coming down from the bow of the ship towards us was a group of Djinni, led by an impressive looking man in a Sumerian style kilt. He also wore a black hood and cloak and held a long staff in his right hand. Standing on either side of the leader were two giants with bright red skin and purple hair.

"Welcome aboard my ship!" the Djinn's voice was deep and frightening, "I am Humut-tabal boatman of the Netherworld. When you fail we will sail upon the Hubur river to Irkalla, city of the dead. If you succeed, only then will we return to the Rath of Utnapishtim. You have brought food here to share with us. Your challenge is acceptable to us. We will eat and rest and then your champion will fight Enmesharra. But now my master Namtar wishes to meet you."

We were led forward towards the bow of the ship, climbing up some stairs to a large open area of the foredeck. Tables had been set up and also seats and cushions and other soft furnishings. There was a large round table in the middle of the deck with platters upon it. Surreya spoke to Captain Kurbatov who told Sergeant Rujansky to have the men put their rations up on the table. There was another odd looking fellow watching us from where he was sitting on the other side of the deck from us. He wore a long black woollen hooded cloak. He was thin and very tall, clean shaven with a sharp, beak-like nose. His hair was long, black and greasy looking. His face was gaunt, like a skull. Humut-tabal and his followers went over and sat down on the deck next to him.

The packs were opened and the food set out on the platters provided. Rujansky organised it all very efficiently. There were a number of loaves of dark bread, some hard biscuits, dried fruit, jerky and of course, numerous bottles of vodka. It was pretty poor fare, which was only to be expected from a White Russian unit at this point of the war, but it was enough to make a meal for our 'guests'. In the end there were about twenty Djinni who arrived at the 'feast', including Surreya's brother Enmesharra and his entourage of warriors. I looked over to the strange looking man in the black robe. He was rather creepy looking. His name was Namtar. I tried to remember my Sumerian mythology. Namtar was the son and sukal, like a prime minister, for Ereshkigal, the Queen of the Netherworld. He was called the 'Harbinger of Death'. I smiled at him.

Namtar got up from his place on the floor and approached.

"I sense in you feelings of mirth," Namtar said, grinning back at me, "I also sense something else about you that I haven't sensed in a long time. You are confident yet it is a confidence based upon a realistic self-appraisal. Who are you to be so confident? Does not Enmesharra frighten you?"

"Not now that I have looked the grim reaper in the eye and lived." I grinned again, "The ancient Sumerians believed you to be the personification of Death, did they not?"

"Ha!" Namtar laughed out loud, "The grim reaper! Are you disappointed?"

"No! Not at all!" I extended my hand to shake and he shook hands with me, "You are not Djinni are you?"

"Not Djinni, you are right. I am of the Anunnaki."

"I think I understand now." I nodded, "Death is neither good nor evil, but rather is a transition. I have nothing to fear from you. I can trust that you will act appropriately in the transitional state after this is all over."

"You know our ways well."

"I've known a few in my time."

"Then let's get this transition done," he said.

We all gathered around the table. Surreya whispered in my ear what to do. It wasn't very complicated. Captain Kurbatov and I broke up some of the bread and other foods and handed it out to the Djinni warriors. I had to give some to

Enmesharra. The Djinni ate, but we did not. We then handed vodka to them and they drank the strong alcohol as though it was water. Enmesharra sculled half a bottle without flinching. I was impressed.

We spoke no more, but rather moved down to the open space of the mid deck, Enmesharra at one end and I at the other. Everyone else sat around the sides in order to watch. Surreya, Niamah and Al helped me get ready. I stripped off my shirt, trousers and shoes and sat to meditate for a few minutes, holding my bayonet in my lap. Enmesharra also sat preparing himself, and he too had selected a medium sized blade as his weapon of choice. But I needed to get calm, to get into the zone of concentration. This was no exercise. We were fighting to the death here, and I would have to kill him or be killed. I breathed in and then exhaled. Something in my spirit stirred and came alive. I knew that it was more than just the blessed weapon. My consciousness was heightened and my senses too. Neither Enmesharra nor I wasted time with talk nor ceremony, we leapt at each other with deadly coolness.

There is nothing romantic about fighting with an edged weapon. It isn't like it is in the books and plays. There is certainly no time for long speeches nor fanciful and dramatic death scenes. No, it is usually over quickly and there is blood and pain and struggle to survive. Both Enmesharra and I fell into the fighting trance and to observers we became deadly blurs of movement. Knives flashed and sometimes clashed, but mostly we dodged each other, sometimes we cut each other. One part of me felt the pain of my wounds, but another part remained in the trance and just kept going. Moving in and out we attacked again and again, leaping over each other or diving past, drawing blood almost every time. That was the idea. It was a contest of stamina and strength. Being a human fighting against a Djinn, I had a disadvantage in agility and skill, but I was physically bigger and stronger and I had been trained to fight the Faerie way, something I don't think he expected. I could see Enmesharra tiring. He pulled back to rest for a moment, which I also welcomed. His concentration dropped, just for a moment. It was all I needed. I leapt over him and as I passed I drove my bayonet down into the back of his head as he tried to twist away. I landed upon the deck slick with my own sweat and blood, but firm on my feet. Enmesharra dropped to the deck dead, with my bayonet still in him.

There was no cheering, no noise at all, just my heavy breathing. I went over to the dead Djinn and retrieved my blade. I kneeled beside Enmesharra for a moment in respect, then turned to face Namtar. There was no anger, no sense of loss, just acceptance in his eyes.

I looked over at Surreya. After all, I had just killed her brother. But Surreya, Niamah and Al all came over to me with eyes of compassion and comfort. I looked Surreya in the eyes and she knew what I was thinking.

"He ceased to be my brother many years ago," she said, "let's get you cleaned up. Now we can have a real peace between us all."

I was taken below in the ship and Niamah took charge of me once Surreya showed us to a cabin and had a servant bring in some water, ointment and bandages, as well as my clothes and shoes. Niamah did a good job. A couple of the wounds required stitching, but most were superficial. Niamah seemed to be personally distressed by my injuries, something unusual for Faerie, who are often reluctant to reveal their inner feelings to others. I got a surprise when she held me for a moment and kissed me softly. For a few minutes she held onto me. She said nothing, but I appreciated her closeness, and so I caressed her hair. She was one of the fair folk, whom many considered to literally be an angel. She was also incredibly beautiful and I could feel my heart beating. I felt privileged and honoured and loved. I also knew that it would be easy to fall in love with her, but I dared not hope. We were literally from different worlds, but Niamah didn't seem to care about that.

There was a knock at the cabin door which startled us both and Niamah answered it. It was Al who came in and sat down next to me.

"Alright," he said with a grin, "It seems that Namtar and his people have decided that they are on our side. They have set up a feast for us on deck. Surreya is playing hostess and all the girls have come out! The men are tired and hungry. They deserve to have a big break and have some fun! Come on, hero of the hour! It is your celebration."

As I climbed the stairs up to the deck, I realised that the ship was moving, quickly enough for there to be a breeze. The whole deck from bow to stern was lit up with faerie light and there were at least four Ren propelling the ship through the netherworld sea. But it was the deck itself that was now covered with tables laden with food and drink that caught my attention. I suddenly realised that I was incredibly hungry. My stomach growled loudly in anticipation. Everyone on deck turned when I came up and the Russians all cheered loudly and slapped my back.

Captain Kurbatov raised a glass of vodka and with a flourish smashed it onto the deck in typical Russian enthusiasm.

"God bless our good English Major and his victory!"

All the Russians cheered, "Huzzah!"

"God bless this good food!!"

"Amen!!" they all shouted and swigged mouthfuls of vodka.

And the party was on!

"Was that grace?" Al asked, a bit awed.

"Yes it was!" I grinned. A Russian handed me a glass, and without hesitation I downed it and thrust the glass out for it to be refilled. Al tried the same thing and the Russians all roared with laughter as he spluttered and coughed, nearly dropping his glass!

As for me I was ravenously hungry. Niamah seemed to understand this and so she led me to one of the tables and sat me down. She then proceeded to load up my plate with all sorts of nice things and I ate.

The Djinn put on an excellent feast, and I wondered where the food actually came from. A lot of it looked like local Turkish food, but there was fish and other sea creatures, including some large crayfish with pale shells. Pretty soon we were all eating our fill. The Djinn, like all Faerie folk, liked to party. They made a point of eating all our food first, passing the hard bread and dried meat around and washing it down with vodka or wine or using the meat and bread to dip into pesto or spicy sauces. I was even interested enough to give that a try. The wine that the Djinn produced was mulled but almost icy cold, and incredibly refreshing.

Many of the Djinn had taken their clothes off and they reclined on thick colourful mats on the deck or on the raised cargo hatches and stairwells. Uninhibited and unselfconscious nakedness was another Faerie custom which the Russians had to deal with. Even Niamah and Al stripped off their mail and got comfortable. But the good Orthodox boys couldn't quite go that far. I wondered what I should do. I didn't have a problem with nakedness as such, but was of two minds as to how I should act in the presence of my Russian friends. Niamah could sense the Russians discomfort and so she whispered in my ear.

"It is not a good thing that these men have been brought up by their parents to believe that their bodies are shameful things." She said, "If they are to live here and be part of the alliance between our peoples, they will have to be re-educated."

"No need to get dressed on my account." I flashed a cheeky grin.

"You mortals always only have one thing on your minds!" she wagged a finger at me, "You are only joking, and you know our ways well enough to get away with it, but these men will need time to adjust."

Again I could feel the Faerie glamour doing its work upon the Russians, and me as well. Nothing had changed, but I was beginning to feel very relaxed and we all began to settle down to our food and incredibly, talking with our angelic hosts. Surreya sat on the edge of one of the tables, and looking beautiful, she began to sing, like an angel. It must have been an old song, because many of the others began to join in and some of the Djinni started to dance. As the song ended we all sat there in awe. I was literally tingling with a feeling of ecstasy. After a while, it was Boris Rujansky who began a song of his own, an old Russian folk song. He started out slow and his deep voice was wonderful in a way that only a Russian can sing. His comrades soon sang with him and the song took on a quicker beat and the soldiers began to clap and then they got up to dance as well! A different type of joy came upon us as we celebrated as men. Rough as we were, Russians not being faeries, even the good people couldn't help smiling and clapping to the Russian song. Pretty soon, the Russians drew the beautiful Djinni women into the dance. Djinn musicians improvised and soon got the tune, and the party took off! We danced and laughed into the night.

Chapter Seven

Love and War

While the rest continued to celebrate, Niamah took me aside and we found a quiet balcony out of the way. "I have something very important to discuss with you, but we must be alone."

The balcony was located off a stateroom, one of the grand cabins of the ship. The ship itself was called 'Netherworld' and it was absolutely luxurious, a finely built work of art in its own right. Everything was made to be beautiful. Walking out from the stateroom onto the balcony, we could see the magnificent under-ground world of the Anunnaki and the Djinni. This had become their home, huge caverns, some filled with literal oceans. Massive columns of stone, stalagmites and stalactites could be seen, because the folk had placed glowing lamps everywhere. There were also a lot of natural phosphorescent fungi growing everywhere and so it wasn't difficult to see this strange, dim world that few knew existed. Strangely, there was a light cool breeze which was very refreshing.

I looked around and could see that Niamah was behind me. She was still naked and looked absolutely gorgeous. I had to admit, I was unsettled, butterflies filling my chest. Niamah smiled and tilted her head slightly, she could sense my embarrassment and she was enjoying it.

She came near and hugged me close to herself. We were like that for some time and then we just stood together and looked out at the dark world beyond the ship. Then she turned to me. There was a bit of a wild look in her eyes.

"Walter." she put a hand on my forearm, "We are about to awaken a city that has been desolate for centuries. Even before the Djinni came here, there were only a few of us and the Anunnaki were reluctant to let men into their world. But now you have defeated Enmesharra, both Humut-tabal and Namtar agree, with Alaquandi and I that you should be the new Oberon of this city."

"You...agree..." I stammered, not knowing what to think about this.

"Yes," Niamah continued, "the Oberon must be a human, and the city did accept you when you put your hands onto the altar stone..."

"...the altar stone, yes, I, what exactly did I do again?"

"You woke Atra up." Niamah smiled at me, "He's been asleep since 1840, and he slept for thousands of years before that. He doesn't just wake up for anybody you know."

"So what does all this mean for me?" I asked.

"It means that you will rule Utnapishtim and also all the ancient Raths of Eden." Niamah paused and took a deep breath, "It also means that you will need a Queen, one of the Seelie matriarchs, to rule with you. It is vital that a new alliance is forged between our two peoples, a covenant relationship."

"Do you mean that I have to get married?" I was beginning to feel even stranger, then a thought came to me. "Are you talking about Surreya?"

At that Niamah laughed out loud, then very delicately she touched my cheek.

"No, my dear friend!" her smile was so disarming, "Surreya has declined. Besides, she has other duties to Utnapishtim. No Walter, I am to be the new Morrigan of the city."

"You and I, get married?" I was quite astounded at that, but I would be even more astounded by her response.

"No!" Niamah was actually laughing, "You know that none of the Eldar races get married! There is a lot that I need to tell you. There has got to be a paradigm shift with you humans!"

"Alright! Now wait a minute!" I exclaimed, taking Niamah by the shoulders, "You are here alone with me, you are stark naked and you are not going to marry me, but you are going to be my Queen, and I am going to be King of this city and you are talking about paradigms?"

"Yes!" Niamah grinned at me, and I could feel her empathy power washing over me and making not one ounce of difference. "Gee, you humans have got to get over this whole sex problem you have. Just calm down and tell me what you know about us Walter."

I stopped for a moment and thought deeply and quieted myself.

Finally, "I'm sorry." I sighed, "I'm a cad, and I'm human. I'm also quite intoxicated and I think that I love you and despite having been part of the Melkizedek Order for the last four years, I still don't understand enough about you and your people. Please let me just sit down and you can explain everything. I'll listen."

So I actually sat down, right there on the deck of the ship, and Niamah sat down next to me.

"Walter," Niamah began, "you are not as ignorant as you think. But I'll tell you what you need to know." She paused, then, "We Eldar peoples do not marry, that is we do not engage in the kinds of contracts where women are given as property from one man to another. The very idea is repugnant to us. Also, we do not marry because in one sense we already are joined to one another, both spiritually and as a community of people. For us, we do not need the permission of the state, nor religion in order to love each other. Sex is not a sin, it is an expression of love that for my people, who are already so connected by our love for each other, is just a natural reality that binds us all together. Love is the Divine nature, it is what we were made for. It is you humans that have made it a filthy thing, a dangerous thing, a tool of power and control. You will be Oberon and I will be Morrigan. We will be equals, our love is a sacred symbol of the unity of our two peoples, together to build a new kind of community that will change the world. It must be done that way. We are examples for others to follow. We are not building an empire, but a growing family. We want everyone to be a part of it."

"I understand." I said, "But that is not the way that the world sees things. It isn't even the way that Christianity sees things."

"That is the whole point!!" Niamah suddenly turned and sat astride my legs, looking right into my eyes, "This is the one thing, the one thing that after thousands of years of Divine Revelation, that you stupid humans just don't hear! The Divine Being is a family bound together by love. But instead of building a loving family community, men have dominated others, build systems to control people, enslave people. And religion is the worst system of tyranny of them all. We must be different. Our love is meant to show the way. And we will begin in the Splinter cities, and gather together spiritual people of faith who will learn how to love, to really love. We will go out into the world and find others who share this spirit of love and restore God's people so they can be again, who they are supposed to be. Even those of the East need to know that karma is not about punishment, but about a willingness to learn, be teachable, and that the consequences of bad karma are only undone with love which is passed on into the future."

"And what about the Nephalim?" I asked.

"We will fight them as we always have." Niamah nodded, "But the greatest weapon of all, is a community of spiritual people who love each other and who are willing to love others. We will not defeat them by killing them, but they will lose because they do not know how to love at all."

"Niamah." I touched her face with my hands, "We will do it together."

We kissed, passionately.

Something began to happen. Niamah was already naked and her body seemed to be glowing. Quickly and assertively, she stripped my trousers off and lay down very close, running her hands over my body and guiding my hands to touch her as well. At first I thought it was the empathy sense, but I could feel her emotions flowing in and through me and I could tell that she was responding to my feelings as well. Then it got very strange and wonderful. It wasn't just the physical pleasure as we touched each other's bodies, it was so much more. We began to hear each other's thoughts! The empathy sense deepened and I felt like I was falling. Breathing deeply. Her eyes framed by her blonde hair cascading down over me. Her fingers burning my spirit with her touch. Niamah shuddered in spiritual ecstasy and I felt it like a shock wave passing through me.

Walter... she thought... *Niamah* ....I thought ...it went beyond words. For a moment we just lay there looking into each other's eyes as the psychic connection deepened and opened into full blown telepathic union. We were still aware of our physical bodies, in fact more so. I could actually feel the pleasure she was feeling and visa versa, so it was with a great sense of joy and anticipation that we knew exactly what felt the nicest, what gave the most pleasure. Our breathing and heart beats became one, our telepathic laughter filled our minds as we plunged into the feelings. We explored each other's bodies, touching, kissing, and caressing. We discovered every pleasure, but not just the physical pleasure. At the same time we entered each other's minds, and our spirits joined.

In that moment I had to make a decision, a momentous and terrifying thing, but something that I would never regret, to go to that place of utter trust, to let another person, this woman, have the right to enter my mind and I into hers, to see all memories, all feelings, the deepest darkest secrets, the sins and hidden thoughts, but also the dreams and desires and the love. In a moment that lasted an eternity, I learned all there was to know about Niamah, all her lifetimes, her past and what it was like to be a member of her tribe, the Tuatha De Danann, in their strange and wonderful ways. I could feel her exploring my humanity as well, looking into rooms in my consciousness that I hardly knew existed, opening me up to me as well. She was better at it than I was, but I was a fast learner. Our bodies continued to make love, and it was that sexual magic that opened us to each other. It was a distinctive gift that the Seelie tribes all had, that with physical sexual union, their spirits would also find complete union as well, the only time they could transcend the empathic sense and reach true telepathy with one another. I wondered how it worked for me, being a human, but I was to discover something I didn't know until then, I had the gene. Sometime in the distant past, I had a Seelie ancestor. That also meant something else, it meant that I knew the exact moment, when the conception took place in Niamah's womb. I could see the new life spark into being.

He won't be Seelie.... Niamah thought, *he is a Halfling, a hybrid, and he will be a leader of both our peoples.*

A feeling of great joy and contentment washed over us in that orgasmic moment. It was a perfect instant in time, as though God had brought all the good things together into one place. We had a future, made between us and a goal. I also felt deeply certain, absolutely focused and clear headed. Having found union with Niamah, body, mind and spirit, meant that I knew everything she knew and she knew everything I knew. So many questions and gaps in knowledge were answered. I knew that I would never be the same again. I was no longer human, I now belonged to another world. Niamah looked into my eyes and we could feel the blissful connection beginning to untie. We both yawned and smiled and fell into sleep, entering each other's dreams, where we danced and enjoyed and found rest together.

At first the dream was sunshine and flowers in her hair and sweetness, but sometime in the night, clouds began to gather. Quickly, the dream turned into a nightmare and we found ourselves standing in a dark wet mist.

Something must be wrong. Niamah thought, *We need to wake up!*

I certainly want to, I replied, *but we are still here.*

All around us the mist was becoming thicker, colder and more ominous. Shadows seemed to be moving, just beyond my peripheral vision. I knew that we were dreaming together, but this seemed so real. I also knew that we were under some kind of spiritual attack. It was subtle but I could feel a creeping sense of depression and hopelessness. Niamah seemed particularly affected by it. She was terrified and so I held her close to me.

Walter..... Niamah's thought could hardly be detected, *....you can summon Atra.*

I looked around and I soon found what I was looking for. A patch of mist flowed away and there was the altar stone. I had to pick Niamah up and carry her to the stone. As I crouched down, I could see the hand print, the human five fingered one in the middle, light up. I placed my hand and instantly I was standing in that place where I'd been before, and Atra was standing before me.

Atra immediately stepped towards me and placed his virtual hands on my virtual head.

"You have been psychically sedated." Atra looked very concerned, then he looked upwards, as though searching for something, "God help us! You are all sedated! There is a powerful mind ...

... hmm, outside of the wards of the Rath.. it's a very subtle influence. It should be possible to wake everyone up. But I will need to wake you up first."

"But why have we been put to sleep?" I asked, "What is going on?"

Atra looked around. I could see what he was looking at. The image of the mountain Rath appeared before us. Deep under the mountain, there was the huge bubble which was the Netherworld and its subterranean sea.

"You are....there." Atra pointed at a red dot which appeared, "Humut-tabal's ship is presently drifting rudderless. Everyone, everyone is asleep."

Atra sighed, "We need to find the enemy. They've gotten into the Rath somehow. I can't see the Pandemonium ghouls that were there before, it's like they've just vanished."

For a moment I just thought about it.

"Alright," I concentrated, "Graud is the enemy here. I know you, you bastard! What would you do? What is your objective?"

I looked intently at the image of the mountain before me.

"This just doesn't make sense." I shook my head, "It makes no military sense. It's like he wants to be noticed. Atra, can you give me an update? Have the repairs to the Gate and the Sphere been completed yet?"

"Yes!" Atra exclaimed, "Within the last half hour! We have a fully functioning Splinter Sphere and the Gate Stones are recalibrated. But no-one can use the Gate without the Gate Key, which master Alaquandi has in his possession."

"I think that I need to make sure of that!" I looked at Atra in alarm, "Can you wake me up?"

"Yes." Atra nodded, "But you will have to wake up anyone else."

"How?"

"A medical stimulant should do it." Atra produced a schematic plan of the ship, "You and Lady Niamah are here in this cabin, the ship's medical clinic is located on the same deck, here."

"I can find it." I nodded, "What do I do then?"

"I keep forgetting that you're a primitive!" Atra cursed under his breath, "You can't possibly know how to administer or even identify the stimulant!"

"Don't be so certain!" I wagged a finger at him, "I think that I do. Niamah and I have... ah...we have..."

"You had sex." Atra rolled his eyes at me, "You are the new Oberon and she the new Morrigan. So, you've conjugated the covenant! Great! So you do know what a hypo-spray is then? Load it with, ah, torashaan, one shot should wake anyone up. Not more than one shot, two would stop their heart, you don't want that."

"Alright!" I cried, "Get me awake now!"

I was suddenly awake! Gasping and more alert than I'd ever felt ever before. I was still on the floor of our cabin aboard ship and Niamah lay curled up close by me. I tried to shake her awake but there was no response. So I leapt to my feet, grabbed my blade and pulled my trousers back on, thinking momentarily how stupid and time wasting that small modesty was, but what the hell, I'm human! I ran into the hall and right to the medical clinic. Having just shared such a close telepathic union with Niamah, a lot of her memories were now just there in my mind as well. It made me kind of dizzy, or was that Atra's wake up still hitting me? I worked feverishly and yet competently. I found a hypo-spray in a drawer and the torashaan in a cupboard along with a lot of other drugs and healing agents. Niamah's medical memories and experiences were there in my mind. Not as strong as my own natural memories, but enough for me to have some understanding of what I was doing. I ran straight back to the cabin and pushing the torashaan cartridge into the hypo-spray, I placed its nozzle to the back of her neck and squeezed the trigger. Niamah gasped loudly and sat bolt upright, nearly knocking me over in the process!

"I think that Graud is after the Gate Key!" I cried, "Where's Al?"

Niamah jumped up and moving quickly, grabbed her mail surcoat and her sword, "This way!"

Running out the other direction down the hallway, we nearly tripped over a sleeping Djinn guard passed out on the deck.

"Al first!" I stepped over him. Niamah led on.

We ran up onto the deck, all along the way passing sleeping individuals, until we came to the main wheel house. We found Al unconscious inside with some of the ship's crew. There were playing cards scattered everywhere, where they had been dropped when sleep had overcome the players. I quickly injected Al and pulled him to his feet. He was quite responsive, nearly stabbing me with his stiletto, before realising it was Niamah and I.

"Where's the Gate Key Al?" Niamah almost yelled at him.

Al looked around, puzzled at first, then became very, very concerned.

"It was right here with me!" he looked around in near panic, "I was sitting on it!"

"It's Graud!" I cried, "He put the whole ship to sleep and has stolen the Gate Key. I think he's going to try opening the gate! We have to stop him!"

Al suddenly raised his hands.

"I can sense something strange!" Al headed out of the wheel house onto the deck, "We are not alone, I think that he's still here. But it feels really weird."

Al and Niamah both drew their weapons simultaneously and became fully alert. We moved out along the deck. I drew out my blade as well and headed for some steps leading down to a lower deck. Just then I noticed something. There was a strange light coming from the water.

"Hey!" I called out, "What is that?"

Al ran over to the railing and looked over into the water, which was now bubbling so much that the ship was rocking. "Oh, shit." Al said under his breath.

There was a shocking explosion of water and we were knocked off our feet. The whirring noise was deafening and there was a flash of blinding light. I looked up in shock to see a glowing disk of light hovering over the ship. There was a blade of metal, looking like a scythe, its handle following the curve of the hull and the blade itself curving around the edge of the disk, which was spinning and looking very dangerous!

"It's a Shrike!" Niamah cried, "A Pandemonium Renim!"

"Run!!" Al grabbed my arm and we leapt for our lives.

The hum of the disk grew louder and the Shrike spat great wads of energy at us, blowing holes in the deck! In that moment I thought that we were dead. This enemy had us in his sights and we had nothing to stop him. He'd destroy the ship, open the Gate and that would be it. It just didn't seem right. But it was worse than that! He didn't seem content to just blow us away, the Shrike extended its blade, flicking it around the disk and heading for me! Niamah screamed and the three of us scrambled across the deck to try and escape the whirring blade as the Shrike flew relentlessly closer.

Another explosion! Then another! The Shrike was knocked sideways, its blade smashed off! I was momentarily confused, but the pilot of the Shrike wasn't interested in hanging around anymore. He fled, flicking off into the higher cavern. A second later, three other Renim, flew over the ship. Two flew in pursuit of the enemy, while the third hovered over us. We stood up under its light and the breeze of its spin buffeted us. This Ren was different from the other, it was Djinni. Its disk was more elliptical and a metal band studded with lights spun around its rim. A silver weapons pod could be seen on the upper side of the disk with a cannon. As the Ren lowered to the deck, there was a flash of light and Surreya appeared with her Ren companion standing behind her, the ship vanishing as the Renim wings folded and retracted into her back. It was a spectacular transformation. I felt very relieved.

"Are you alright?" Surreya cried, rushing forward to meet us.

"Yes." I told her, "But everyone here is asleep, and I think that the ship is sinking! We need to stop the enemy. I think that it's Graud and he's heading for the Gate."

I looked around for the hypo-spray, but I had dropped it sometime in the confusion, but Al found it.

"We better get busy." Al nodded.

"I can do it faster." Surreya's Ren companion stepped forward. On her left upper-arm she was wearing a bulky looking utility armband. She took the hypo-spray from Al and put the torashaan cartridge into a slot in her armband.

"I can fire doses of stimulant using my glove." she said, "One touch and they're awake."

"We'll need to get it done quickly." Surreya nodded, "Some of us can fly to escape the ship, but most of us can't. We'll need the ship's away boats and other Renim to get people off before the ship sinks."

Surreya looked down through one of the holes that had been blasted through the ship. The ship was already listing and we could hear water bubbling up from underneath. Any thought of pursuing our enemy had to be put off for now. Lives had to be saved. Surreya's Ren took off, moving quickly, while we four got the away boats ready. It wasn't long and others soon joined us in the work. We soon had the boats ready and even began to carry unconscious people and put them aboard. Some other Renim turned up and lifted people away to safety, flying to a nearby Djinni settlement on the shores of the lake.

The ship was breaking apart and we had gotten all the away boats filled and shoved off. We were still on the deck, watching the water splashing over the edge when Surreya's Ren returned.

She had some of the Russians with her, including Zabolotsky, Kurbatov, Sergeant Rujansky and four others.

"We are coming with you!" Captain Kurbatov exclaimed, "We have an enemy to stop!"

"Good on you gentlemen!" I then turned to Surreya and her Ren, "Can we all fit?"

"Absolutely!" the Ren spread her wings and floated above us. There was a flash of light and we found ourselves standing in a circle of light. Surreya was seated in what had to be the pilot's couch. She appeared to be asleep. All around us there were what appeared to be windows, looking out at the outside. We were already moving, and moving very quickly, manoeuvring along the corridors within the mountain. It was incredible, we had absolutely no feeling of inertia at all, and yet we must have been moving incredibly fast.

"We will be there very shortly." Surreya's voice told us, then, "Hilli, we need to get to the Gate without being seen if possible."

"I can't cloak in here," Hilli replied, "but I can fly us right to the rear entrance of the forum building, that's as close as I can get."

"Sounds good." Surreya said, "We will need to be ready to fight."

Our movement came to a sudden and sickening stop, followed by a flash of light, and then we were standing on a balcony next to water on one side, rushing down a cascade and a set of steps on the other side. Drawing our weapons, and whispering a prayer, we ran up the stairs and along a corridor lined with columns. On our right, the columns opened up to a broad sloping pavement and we could see the standing stones of the Ring beyond. We stopped and hid for a moment. There was movement down among the stones. I could see some light, like a reflection of water.

"They've opened a portal already!" Niamah whispered, "We must attack before he resonates it with the Key."

We moved quickly and without much time for strategy. We got to the Ring of stones without being seen, but without hesitation, we ran into the interior of the Ring. With deadly silence we sized up our enemy and then attacked. I could see Graud himself at the Altar Stone. He had the Key staff and was turning it in its lock. The staff itself was glowing and the interior surfaces of the great stones seemed to glow as well. Graud was a young looking blonde man, very proud and strong, although he was much older than he looked. His Shrike was nearby, one of her arms was burned. Standing with her were about a dozen others, a couple of Djinni and the others were Ghouls. The Ghouls wore Russian uniforms, but they were certainly Ghouls, with their dead looking eyes and pale skin, drained of life. Without much sound, the fight was on. While the Ghouls fought with hellish viciousness, they were ungainly and not difficult to fight. The two Djinni warriors were a different matter. They were big men, strong and skilful. But I left them all for the others and ran straight for Graud. Without hesitation, Graud pulled the Key staff out of the Altar Stone and ran to the largest trilithon, the one right in the middle of the Ring and he touched the left sarsen stone. A portal opened immediately and Graud and his Shrike leapt through. The portal began to shrink and with a loud cry I leapt after them.

I rolled and blinked in the light of bright daylight. I could see Graud and his companion running ahead of me towards a small building. Behind me was another Ring just like the one I'd left behind inside Mt. Ararat, but the portal had opened on the outside of the Ring. It now closed behind me, blocking off my return. I didn't have much time to appreciate my surroundings, but what I could see was fascinating. This Ring was located in a large open space all by itself on what appeared to be the edge of a cliff. On the other side of the Ring I could see a huge city and mountains beyond, but Graud had fled to the small building located right by the cliff edge. I ran after them.

I got to the small building and carefully looked through the door that was before me. The building was empty, but I could see another door on the other side. Beyond the open door I could see, strangely, a telescope and then clouds, nothing but an endless rolling carpet of clouds. It was as though these clouds were a carpet that flowed without break from the edge of the cliff edge on into infinity. But then I noticed that the telescope was pointed out towards something. Out beyond the horizon of the clouds there was a light, three glowing threads of light, woven around each other rising up out of the clouds and up into the sky above. These threads glowed like a sun, and they were unlike anything that I had ever seen before.

Suddenly there was pain, incredible, excruciating pain! I fell to the ground and it felt as though my whole world was spinning. I could see Graud and his Shrike standing over me, mocking me, but I couldn't hear their voices. I knew instinctively that I was fatally wounded, I was going into shock and I was dying. The last thing I saw was Graud leaping over the edge of the cliff and his Shrike drawing him into her wings and her disk flying away towards that strange thread of lights beyond. There was a sensation of a man standing over me, a look of concern on his face, and warriors nearby, but then everything became dark and I fell into oblivion. I thought that I'd be afraid of dying, but at the time it was living that was just too inconvenient. I felt happy, content and looked forward to seeing what happened next.

Chapter Eight

Avalon

Now, about dying. Some people I know talk about seeing their life flash before their eyes. Others talk about a tunnel of light and visions of angels in heaven. Well, for me there was none of that. There was nothing, absolutely nothing. No heaven, no hell, not anything. There was this odd feeling though of floating and the presence of eyes watching me, of hands carrying me. It felt like a dream. But there it is. The only reason why I can even have anything to say on this matter at all, the fact that I was dead, is because I got to be not dead. It was quite strange, all of this. The thoughts all came into my head all at once and I actually felt very annoyed. My annoyance was unexpected because now it was quite obvious that I was alive again. My annoyance turned to surprise. I wasn't in any pain, I felt no different. In fact I felt really good. I opened my eyes.

I was in a large, very comfortable bed in a rather nice looking wood panelled room. There was a large balcony to one side, with a curtain drawn across and a small table beside the bed. Strangely there was no door that I could detect. I sat up. My clothes were missing. I also noticed a few other strange things as well. All the cuts and bruises from the fight with Enmesharra were gone. I was completely clean, even my finger nails looked perfectly manicured. How strange. How long had I been unconscious? Long enough for my wounds to heal certainly. That was a frightening thought! I was feeling annoyed again.

"Mustn't be in heaven then. Nor reincarnated as a cockroach!!!" I said to myself, chuckling a bit.

I got up and wrapped the sheet that had been covering me around myself. The obvious first step was to look at the room a bit more closely. I still couldn't find a door, so I pulled the curtain aside and went out onto the balcony. My room was quite high up and I whistled at the impressive view. The balcony I was standing on looked out over a wide moat which was far below. Beyond the mote was a wall and beyond that were the cliffs where I could see the other Ring of standing stones. Beyond that were the endless fields of clouds and the strange threads of light on the horizon.

I looked down at the ring of stones far below and realised that was where Graud had hit me. I also looked up, and to the sides. The building I was in was absolutely huge, bigger than any other structure I had ever seen. Its wall was even higher above me than below, and I could see clouds moving past in the wind. To the left and to the right, the building just seemed to go on forever. I had seen this city from below when I had first arrived. It was bigger than I first thought. No hope of tying a bed sheet rope together to climb down on to escape!!!

I went back into the room and got a surprise. There were three people there, two female Vansad and a human man. One of the women was an armed guard, tall and watching me like a lioness, the other was sitting on my bed, a rather cute looking redhead. The man was quite large, bearded and with long hair. He wore a gold torc around his neck and was very well armed. Despite this, he smiled at me and looked very friendly.

"I see that you are awake." he said, "Are you feeling well?"

"Ah, yes thank you." I responded, realising that I could understand the language he was speaking, and also that I replied in his language as well. "Where am I and how long was I out?"

"Out?" the man said, "Oh, you mean unconscious." He laughed,

"No, you were dead my friend and we ring cycled you."

"What?"

"Put you through the ring portal, but instead of sending you off to somewhere else, we brought you right back." he explained, "It is one of the characteristics of the ring system that it dematerialises you and genetically scans you before rematerialising you. That means that things like wounds, scars and even illness and death can be undone. We can even program the ring to bring you back at whatever age you like. You are in peak physical condition. Now we have your scan record, you are pretty much unkillable. We can even make copies of you, complete with your memories."

For a moment I just looked at him incredulously, but he was talking about Vansad technology and so I wasn't too surprised.

"Alright, so I'm back from the dead. I don't remember a thing. So, who are you and where am I? I need to go back to where I came from. It is important."

"You came from Utnapishtim." he said, "But we can't open a portal out to there yet. The system is down. But you are now in the city of Avalon. You are not on Earth but in the Vansadagaadian Corridor, the world of Tur-Nan-Ogg. My name is Arthun ap Meurig, but people usually call me Arthur."

"As in King Arthur?!" I grinned stupidly.

"Yes." Arthur sighed loudly, "But I wasn't really a king. We can talk more about history later, we have more important things to discuss. The man who killed you was a Baal Lord. He had a gate key and stone. That is what he hit you with. Nearly caved your skull right in! Very nasty."

"His name was Graud." I growled, full of fury, "He was a Nephalim, Atalanti faction. He was also once known as Enlil the Anunnaki. I'm Melkizedek Order and we have just occupied the Mt Ararat Rath, but Graud went through the ring portal and I followed. Then you know what happened."

"He's known to me." Arthur frowned, "He's got a gate key and stone. Riding the corridor he can go almost anywhere or even any when."

Arthur led me back out onto the balcony and he pointed at the threads of light glowing up in the sky.

"That is the Vansadagaadian Corridor. Three cosmic strings are there, forming a helix. The physics is hard to explain, but those strings cause all kinds of interesting gravitational phenomena as well as temporal displacement all along the corridor. Our world is one of many that orbit the corridor like petals of a cosmic flower. The Corridor links all our worlds together and the helix gives us light and warmth. This is the Vansad home system. They came from here a long time ago. Because of the helix the Vansad and other Eldar were able to establish the ring system and so travel around the Multiverse. Their Splinter ships have travelled to many worlds. But if this Atalanti has flown along the helix itself, he can use the stolen gate key and stone to open up time portals. Fortunately we can track him."

"So where did he go?" I asked.

"Back to Earth, but he used an unusual frequency." Arthur frowned, "We think that he travelled back in time, back a very long time."

"What?" I was puzzled, "Why would he do that?"

"He's a Neph and Anunnaki to boot, so he has a plan, no doubt something unpleasant." Arthur growled, "The problem is that he has gone so far back that we can't get a precise trace. He wanted to disappear. We could try following him, but we could miss the window by hundreds of years."

"So how do we find him?" I asked.

"We have to wait until he uses the gate key and stone to open another portal into the present. Once he does that we can read the frequency and follow the portal back to its point of origin. But we will need to be close to the portal when that happens."

"Which won't be easy," I shook my head, "even for the Vansadagaadians."

"We've got to be prepared." Arthur placed a hand on my shoulder, "There are a lot of things I

need to tell you about and there is a lot you need to tell me. Tell me what the Melkizedek and their allies are up to in Utnapishtim."

So I told him about the war that was presently being waged across the globe and how the different A'sidhe tribes had taken sides. The Seerlie plan to take Jerusalem and Ararat meant that we would recover two Splinters and in effect push the Turks out of the war. I also told Arthur about the deal we made with the Ouroboros Ring, that we gave that enemy faction the information they needed to crush the Pandemonium and Atalanti agents that had infiltrated Germany. Strangely I felt that I could completely trust this man with the Intel I was giving him. Being in this strange world seemed to give me an almost Faerie empathic sense, and I felt I was in a safe place.

"That means that they would owe you." Arthur grinned wolfishly, "What are they offering you in return for saving them from the Satanists?"

"Unconditional surrender when we win the war." I said, "They recognize that allied victory is now inevitable, especially since the United States is now involved. Naturally, the Nephalim Baal lords are upset with us and with the Ouroboros."

"And so the battle lines are being drawn up. While one war, the visible one, is coming to a close, another one between the hidden powers is just beginning." Arthur nodded, "Graud is their first countermeasure. He got through the gate and knew exactly what to do when he got here. He used a Shrike to run along the corridor and escaped into the ancient past."

"Got any idea of when?" I asked.

Arthur turned to one of his female companions, a red haired Sprite wearing a pair of shorts and chain-mail top. She pulled what looked like a small slate out of her pocket and after pressing some buttons, she passed the slate to Arthur.

"Thank you Danu." he looked at the slate, "Hmm, we are talking antediluvian times, around 9000 to 12000 BC or earlier even. In other words, during the time of the early Adamic patriarchs and the rise of the Sethani Kingdom in what is, eastern Turkey. Doesn't that seem interesting?"

"Not likely to be a co-incidence." I remarked, "So, do you have any knowledge of the history of the times that can help us?"

"Good thinking!" Arthur exclaimed, "We do have records on those times, very good records. It was a very interesting time, for obvious reasons."

"We're talking about the time of Adam and Eve aren't we?" I asked.

"Yes." Arthur began to push buttons on the slate, "Let's look at some details."

He took some time reading the slate, but then seemed to find what he was looking for.

"You need to understand that this was one of the most formative times in human history. The agricultural revolution had just begun and people were building cities and the Old Stone Age cultures just couldn't compete with the Adamite peoples as they began to spread out over the world. The Nephalim and Pandemonium were particularly active at that time and they often openly sought to conquer new lands. Sometimes they succeeded. Perhaps Graud was posing as one of these early Pandemon warlords. Here's something interesting...."

Arthur read some more and then looked at me with concern in his eyes.

"Just before the rise of the Sethani Kingdom, founded by Seth, son of Adam, there was an invasion of the Adamite lands by a powerful warlord, leading an army of ....."

"Rah-hab?" I offered.

"Correct!!" Arthur nodded, "A subgroup of the Rah-hab, a very nasty race of reptilians, notorious for their speed and their deadly attacks. It says that this army attacked using boats that flew in the air, and that the warriors had weapons that could kill from a distance, weapons that sounded like thunder."

"Sounds like modern weapons to me." I said, "Perhaps they were armed by someone from our time."

"From your time." Arthur corrected me, "We living along the Vansadagaadian Corridor are affected by relativistic time distortions, who knows exactly *when* we are, but yes, I think that this record is talking about weapons, circa early twentieth century. There are other details here that seem to confirm that, but of course we can't be sure unless someone goes back and looks."

"Is that possible?" I wondered.

"Time travel itself isn't difficult." Arthur answered, "It is getting exactly to where and when you want to that is difficult. That is why we need a frequency to follow. I can send teams back in time into the antediluvian period, and we can get pretty close to the right time, but each time we do that the fluid of the space time continuum is stressed and so multiple time jumps soon causes serious problems and things get dangerous. Very dangerous. People can get lost. It is better to wait and be sure. We need to know exactly where and when we are going."

"So what do we do now?"

"We need to get the gate system working again and reopen a portal to Utnapish-tim Rath so that you can go home." Arthur said.

"Then what?"

"Then we all talk about the future." he said, then paused for a bit, thoughtful, "I have lived for a long time, at least in human terms, Walter Ryan, and I have been watching the struggle being played out on Earth. In particular, I have supported the work of the Melkizedek Order and the fight against Satanist factions like the Atalanti and Pandemonium. Such monsters deserve to be made extinct. For too long we have been complacent and have let things run as they may. But there are some of us here in the Corridor who want to have a more direct role in things on Earth. Up until now, the Eldar of Vansadagaad have pushed a policy of strict non-intervention."

"There are A'sidhe on Earth who think the same thing." I frowned, then laughed, "The only thing that stops eighty percent of the gentry from leaving the Earth is that they make too much money from us!"

"The truth is that inter- world travel is greatly restricted." Arthur said, "Infil-tration events by the enemy, who we are trying to keep blockaded on Earth, would be a lot more common if there was too much regular traffic. The Nephalim Baal lords have been trying to escape out of the blockade for centuries and reconnect with their allies in the Milky Way Galaxy. If that happens, the Earth will fall to the enemy. That is something we obviously cannot allow. The Eldar have been protecting the Earth from invaders for thousands of years."

"Then why don't the Eldar or Seerlie send more people to the Earth and put an end to the Nephalim once and for all?" I asked the question I had been wanting to ask for a long time, "If they are such a threat to the Earth, why can't we just exterminate them?"

"It isn't as simple as that!" Arthur growled, "I wish it was, but think what we would have to do. How do we find them? They have been living on the Earth for many thousands of years and they have made themselves very much at home. They are powerful, and have human allies who fight for them. We would have to do again what was done last time, and the price which was paid was too great."

"You mean the Deluge?" I asked, "I get your point. Atra showed us what happened. Scary."

"So you understand why we must do what we do secretly." Arthur nodded, "Knowledge is power and the enemy wants more power. But I get your frustration."

Arthur paused for a moment, thinking about what to say next, how much to tell me I supposed.

"Look," he put a hand on my shoulder, "we would have brought you here eventually. You are the new Oberon of Eden, so we would be letting you in on a lot of things. Your coming here just now, however unfortunate the circumstances, was good timing. I think that you need to meet some people soon, but for now, I'll take you on a tour of the city and explain some of our history."

Chapter Nine

The Tour

Arthur and his two companions led me out of my room. There was of course a door concealed in the wood panels and Arthur simply pushed it open. On the other side there was a hallway and a number of other rooms of what was obviously a comfortable private residence.

"Welcome to my humble abode!" Arthur grinned.

We walked across the hall, which had a large table in the middle with comfortable furnishings, soft rugs on the floor, carved wood panels and large tapestries all around. The hall was also filled with many people, presumably members of Arthur's household. A human woman stepped forward and stood next to Arthur.

"This lady was my wife, Gweneffar, when we were mortal, and she remains the matriarch of our clan." Arthur introduced her.

She was an attractive brunette, but there was something puzzling about her. I had to look twice when Arthur's other armed companion stood on the other side of Arthur. In many ways, this Vansad female and Arthur's Lady were like twins, although Gweneffar was certainly human. Still, the look on my face must have been obvious. Arthur laughed and put his arms around both women.

"Welcome to the interesting worlds of the Corridor, Walter!" Arthur wiggled his eyebrows at me, "Yes Gweneffar is human, and like me she was born in post-Roman Britain, and like me, she also died there. But the Faerie brought our bodies here to Avalon through the hidden Rath Gate located in Britain and like you, we were ring-cycled and restored to our youth! HA! What a day that was! I know what it is like to die violently too. I also know what it is to reawaken in this alien place. I have played host to many others like you, to make the transition easier. But you have need of a more immediate explanation. Gweneffar is the original, and Charis is a copy of Gwen, created at the same time when Gwen and I were cycled. She's Vansad because Charis was what the Eldar call a familiar, or a 'guardian angel'. Many of us humans have familiars, especially those who are spiritually sensitive. I don't have a familiar because Merlin took an interest in me. You also have the support of very important people."

Suddenly I began to feel very disoriented. I searched my own mind. I could still feel Niamah's memories there in the back of my mind and a whole lot of things began to make more sense. I also realised that I had new powers of my own. I began to feel dizzy, then I fell over. Strong arms caught me. I slipped into unconsciousness.

My sleep was full of dreams...

Knowledge of many things exploded in my mind...

It was as though a whole new universe had been opened up to me. In one sense that was literally so.

The Vansadagaadian corridor was a kind of pocket universe that ran through the Multiverse, connecting it all together. The corridor was where the Vansad species first left their original native universe twelve cycles ago. They had watched as worlds were formed, as the spiritual creative energies of the Divine Being gave birth to worlds teeming with corporeal life.

The Vansad and other Eldar had then been given the task of guardians. The very first guardians with the Elohim, engineered our world. They also did the work of engineering bodies for new sentient species from the DNA of living things.

The Zoel races were born, and they built ancient civilizations. But with life, also comes the inevitable end of life in death. So the Zoel, with the help of their cosmic parents, engineered the first circles of stone and the way was opened to explore the wider Multiverse. The stone circles were more than just gateways to other worlds across the Multiverse, but were to become the foundation of all of the formidable technology of the Vansadagaadian civilization. With the stone circles, they could open portals to other places and even times, they could also design and then create things, all kinds of things, drawing upon the energy of the cosmic strings running through the corridor. But the circles also meant that they had found a way to solve the problem of death. The dead could be brought back, bodies could be healed, and almost anything was possible.

It was a power though which could be abused. Dreadful wars were fought to control that power..... I gasped inwardly as I saw the horror of it. I understood at last why the Eldar races were so determined to protect us from the dark enemies who wouldn't hesitate to enslave us or destroy us just because they could.

As sentient races developed upon many worlds, the cost of failure for the Eldar rose, as new peoples everywhere needed protection. The humanoid races of planet Earth were especially vulnerable because the Pandemonium had managed to infiltrate the world. Our planet has been a battle ground from almost the beginning.

Meeting Arthur and in particular Gwen's familiar Charis had opened knowledge to me, knowledge I'd always known, or rather she had known it and given it to me somehow. The role of familiars in the Corridor were as direct links to the Ring A.I.s and nanotechnology was used to transmit data. I must have just got a huge download and I was able to know the truth for myself. It was all too much for me, but dreaming now, my mind could process it all, albeit slowly. I had been resurrected. That much was evident. Most people wouldn't have that privilege, not for a long time. Most people would die and stay dead for a long time. I remembered the way that I'd had no consciousness of anything before I'd awakened in the fine bed in Arthur's house. But as I looked more deeply, I could feel that I'd really been sleeping. Ghosts were the dead who woke up before they were supposed to. That was generally a quite traumatic thing. So there is something left after death, a trace of energy which can be awakened. The Elohim and their Eldar races could wake up the dead with their formidable technology and give us new bodies so we could live again. No matter what people say about dying and going to Heaven, or being reincarnated, it's all more complicated than that, and living is still a whole lot better than dying. We need help to come back. I could see that the Elohim hoped to do that for everyone eventually. It was this realisation, that death was able to be conquered this way that gave me a renewed hope...hope...

My eyes opened. I was on the floor of Arthur's hall and there were lots of faces looking at me. They were smiling.

"Your awakening has begun Walter." Arthur helped me up off the floor, "Coming back from death is a learning experience. The recycling process usually does it. Your mind and body are perfect. You will remember things, including race-memory, the memories of the Ring A.I.'s and because you are life mated with a Vansad woman, you have her memories too, and that means you know everything she knows, and that includes the collective knowledge of her ancestors. No wonder you fainted! But it will take time for the memories to arise into your consciousness."

"My head hurts!" I did indeed have the mother of all headaches!

"Some food and drink will help." Gweneffar said, "Come on, we need to get our guest looked after everyone!"

Gweneffar and many of the others moved away to the other end of the hall. I could smell the wonderful smells of good food. Arthur and Charis led me over to the great table.

"It isn't round!" I giggled to myself as they sat me down in a big chair. My head continued to hurt horribly. I was feeling very unsettled. All kinds of strange thoughts, memories which were not my own, and feelings were still confusing me.

Charis returned to the table carrying a large jug. Arthur held a cup and Charis filled it with a sweet smelling wine. It was thrust at me and I took it and drank deeply.

For some time I just sat there and drank wine as Arthur refilled my cup. The headache slowly subsided and I began to feel more human again. I also felt incredibly hungry.

Somehow I was given food. A spicy broth, meat, lots of sweet bread, fruit and more drink. I ate like I'd never eaten before.

"Walter," Arthur was saying something a long way off, "You are remembering a lot of things. Most of it will be new memories that you've inherited from others. You don't have to hold onto those memories consciously, you have to sublimate them or else you won't be able to function. Breathe deeply and let it go...that's right. Focus upon eating and what you are doing, don't explore the memories or you will be overwhelmed. There's time for that later....eat man! You have to metabolise some energy or else you'll collapse again."

The next few hours were a blur. I knew that I was eating and enjoying it. I was like a small child, just enjoying the tastes of the food and drink I was being given. Slowly I began to feel much, much better.

At some point I was given over to some of the women, who bathed me and dressed me in some new clothes. I wasn't in any state to complain. I remember, almost like a vision of something happening to someone else, of leaving Arthur's house and stepping out onto the streets of the city. There was a strange feeling then of a sudden catch-up, like I was travelling very, very fast. Then, just like that, I was myself.

"Whoa!" I shook my head, which no longer hurt, "That was a rush!"

"Welcome back to life Walter." Arthur said, "How do you feel now?"

I had to think about it for a bit. I searched my mind - yes... all my new memories were there and I could see it clearly, and I felt very comfortable.

"Hmm." I smiled at Arthur, "I actually feel 'right' for the first time in my life. What's next?"

"You tell me." Arthur said, "You know whatever there is to know."

"I'd like to see Avalon." I looked around. We were standing not far from the entrance to Arthur's town house. Gweneffar and Charis were standing there just on the threshold, watching. Nearby was a great balcony looking across into the interior of the city. I looked with wonder. There was a part of me which had never been here before, which saw this as new and strange. I could see the ring road, which strange memories told me ran around the interior of the cathedral of the city. Avalon was a great cube, but the cathedral within it was a hollow dome. Below us was the harbour with sailing ships entering and leaving the port. I could see the grand plaza and the arcades that ran in all directions of the compass through the city. Row upon row of other town houses could be seen, their lobbies, like the lobby we were standing in, all facing the ring roads that circled the levels of the cathedral. This was wonder, to see it with new eyes, but yet I still remember this place as though I had grown up here.

I pointed suddenly across the cathedral at one of the upper levels and a great balcony.

"There!" I cried, "That is the ancestral home of the Tuatha de Danann, Niamah's people. She grew up there!"

Arthur nodded.

"Down there!" I pointed down towards the grand plaza, to the deck that jutted out into the harbour. I could see the crowds of people. "That is the annex. That is where the Oberons meet and judge the people. We will have to go down there. I need to see the Oberon of this city."

"Then that is what we will do." Arthur replied, "Lead the way."

I looked out towards the interior of Avalon, but I knew that we wouldn't actually reach the annex by going along the ring road on our level of the city. We would have to take one of the great carriage ways that spiralled up and down the city, or we could just portal down.

"We'll take a carriage." I said, "I want to see the city."

Arthur nodded and laughed. He clapped me on the shoulder and we walked away from his lobby and the balcony that led to the ring road. Instead we walked down the arcade towards the market place of the Pendragons.

I had the memories of people who had lived here. But to actually be here for myself, well, that was wonderful. The city was huge. The cathedral in the centre of the city, the huge dome was ringed by hundreds of mansions all around the interior wall, they were magnificent. The balconies were beautiful, like the proverbial hanging gardens of Babylon. And although hundreds of different races from many different worlds shared this city, it was no Babylon, but a unified community of people who shared their lives together.

As we walked down the arcade, the foot traffic heading towards the market got thicker. Many of them were obviously humans, Romanised Celts, Arthur's people. They were speaking a dialect of ancient Welsh, but I could understand them. They seemed a proud and strong people. But there were also others. I recognized the Peeleens, the indigenous people of this world of Tur Nan Ogg. They were a large grey skinned people, with flat faces and small piggy eyes and wide lipless mouths. They were a quiet and peaceful people, hard workers and good crafts workers. I also saw humanimals, ape-like Chipperwaals, bear-like Bardel and a few Pigrian sires.

"How did these humanimals come to live here with your people?" I asked.

"They are self-governing peoples." Arthur told me, "They have been free since the time of the Deluge, and were brought here as refugees. The Shile, their ancient masters, are not welcome here in the corridor."

"That's good." I nodded.

We finally came into the market itself and we stopped and had a good look around. There were dozens of stalls selling-no, not selling but giving all kinds of wares, food, and there was a stage nearby with a dancer performing there. She was a Rogan, an anthropoid rat-like being, not native to Tur Nan Ogg, but to one of the other nearby corridor worlds. They had been here almost as long as the Peeleens. They were notoriously sensual beings, who also liked to drive fast vehicles, the faster and more dangerous the better. Some of the male Rogans watching the female dancer, who was quite attractive and very skilled (for a Rogan) were wearing racing gear.

"Do you have races here?" I grinned, "I wouldn't mind seeing the Rogans race."

"They race out in the high desert." Arthur laughed, "But they come down here to the city to spend their time relaxing. Do you like to race?"

Now it was my turn to laugh, "The internal combustion engine is being used for racing on the Earth, but we are too preoccupied by war at the moment!"

"The war will be over soon." Arthur reassured me, "Then there will be peace."

"I hope so." I said, but not quite believing it, "But there will not be any real peace until the Nephalim are removed from our, mine and your world."

"Then we need to get on with it." Arthur slapped me on my back, then led the way through the marketplace to the carriageway at the other end.

So we walked, Arthur and I, along with Charis and Danu. But as we walked through the marketplace, I could see lots of people talking and watching us as we went past. Some of them even began to follow us.

"Hey! Earthman!!" someone called from nearby.

I turned to see and was confronted by a very large Pigrian, a Boars Tusk Brigadier wearing his full battle harness.

"You that cycled sapiens come through from Utnapishtim?" he demanded.

"Yes." I replied, a little uncertainly.

"I wanted you to know," he said, "that I am descended from one of the seven of my species that were saved on the Torbor. My clan came here after we fought the Nephalim. I hear that you are fighting them again. My name is Grrr-tuk-moor. The Tusk Brigade will fight the Nephalim for you."

I didn't know what to say, but I just looked at this remarkable creature. His eyes blazed with determined zeal, not hatred for the Nephalim, but perhaps a certain intention to rid the multiverse of a pest.

"I will remember your name, Grrr-tuk-moor." I said, then turning to Arthur, "I mean it. I know that your people are the best soldiers anywhere. There will come a time when we will need you."

The big Pigrian struck his chest in salute. "I await your orders, Oberon of Utnapishtim."

As we continued our walk, many others either saluted or bowed as we passed. Everyone stopped to watch us. I realised that they were not looking at Arthur, although they were his people, but they were looking at me.

"What is it that just happened?" I whispered to Arthur, "Why are so many people looking at me?"

"They know who you are Walter Ryan." Arthur replied, "You faced up to Enlil himself and you have been made an Oberon by the Bene Elohim. It isn't every day that happens to a man. The last time that happened, it was me!"

"But I was killed!!" I protested.

"And so was I!!" Arthur rolled his eyes and laughed at me, "But that won't stop us will it?!"

I laughed with him, "Definitely not!"

We soon came to the end of the market. There was a large open space there with several carriages waiting, parked in a circle. The vehicles looked like old fashioned horse drawn carriages, but without the horses. Instead, up front was a chair with a Ren driver. We climbed into a carriage and quickly, the carriage pulled out onto the road.

I was soon to discover that even such a pedestrian thing as a road in Avalon was made to be beautiful. The road itself was wide and carriages moved freely alongside walkers and those using smaller personal vehicles. Roadside verges and islands were all beautifully landscaped with gardens or artistic monuments. There were tall pillars holding up crystal ceilings like stained glass windows in a cathedral. The ceilings and vaults above were big enough to allow some flying traffic as well, Renim and winged individuals. Here and there we passed other marketplaces and parklands or clan households with their huge gates. There was enough parkland under the bright glass ceilings that there was room for animals and birds and small pools of water. Then we took a spiralling ramp that descended down the levels of the city, with walls lined with glistening mother of pearl.

Finally we drove out into what was the 'political level' of the city. While the arcades and galleries of this level were still beautiful, this was the home of the various embassies and trade guild houses. We got onto one of the main artery roads that headed into the centre of the city. The place was absolutely huge. I could see literally millions of people coming and going. This was also 'ground level'. The main roads also led to the outside of the city, where I knew some of the leading households had their great estates, located out in the tropical forests or up in the nearby mountains, or even along the edge of the world facing towards the cosmic strings of the corridor. But we sped up and our driver took us up onto the highway. Despite the size of the city, the traffic wasn't as heavy as I thought it would be. Literally a billion people lived in Avalon, but the highways were only there for a more relaxed aesthetically pleasing kind of travel. Most people preferred to use portal technology to transport themselves and things directly. But I had wanted to see the city. Many people in Avalon walked. When one was immortal, there was no need to rush anywhere.

But I was very aware of time. Back on Earth, there was a war being waged. I needed to get back. There were things to do, but first of all, there were some important people to talk to.

Finally we came to a stop at a large circular parking area. We were quite a distance from the actual arcade that led into the central gallery of the city, but there were literally thousands of carriages and other vehicles coming to rest on the parking decks. Beyond there was a garden. We disembarked and Arthur led me into the park.

"We'll have to take a portal from here." Arthur told me, "It is just too far to walk. They are waiting for us."

Up ahead there was a plaza, basically a circular paved area. But there in the middle of the circle was a portal key. Danu walked up to the key and turned it. Immediately the air nearby began to shimmer and the portal 'popped' open. We all stepped through and the portal closed behind us. Just like that we were right beside the water of the harbour at the centre of the city. We were standing in the middle of another paved circle, but now the circle was surrounded by hundreds of people all talking in small groups. I could see various delegations of people, each with their own cases to bring, talking with tall Tuatha De Danann officers. But nearby we could see the actual court up against the main wall. Already a troop of ceremonial Danann warriors were coming towards us. Like they used to in ancient Britain, these ghost warriors, six men and six women, were naked and painted with blue wode. Their hair had been bleached and spiked up. They carried spears and had swords slung over their shoulders. The captain of the guard stepped forward, drew her sword and handed it to Arthur, who took it, kissed the pummel and handed it back.

"The Oberon of Avalon, Lord Enoch welcomes you and wishes to speak with you." the captain said, "Also, seer Merlyn is here with another Oberon who also wishes to speak with Walter Ryan. Come with us please."

The guard turned and the two rows parted to let us pass through, then they followed us. The whole crowd of people filling the courts of the harbour suddenly stopped their talking and turned to look at us. A chill went up my spine as the crowd silently began to follow us on the walk towards the court platform of the Oberon. I looked around and I could see that the crowd was actually huge. It was as though all of Avalon was there to watch us. It took us a good ten minutes to walk across the width of the harbour. I turned to look at Arthur and he was grinning like the Cheshire Cat. Up ahead I could see the judgement seat. It was actually a raised platform covered with pillows and rugs. Waiting there for us was a man sitting on the pillows and standing nearby was a woman. Both of them, like the Danann guard, were naked, and yet they were incredibly noble in their bearing and completely unselfconscious. There were some others watching nearby, in an archway, another man, well armed and a woman robed in transparent silk. We approached and I went to bow, but Arthur held me back.

"No bowing here," Arthur shook his head, "we are equals."

"Greetings Walter Ryan, Oberon of Utnapishtim and Eden," the man nodded to me, "I am Enoch son of Jared, Oberon of this city and my companion is Morrigan D'Anu. Welcome to this presbytery." Out of the archway behind the judgement seat stepped the other couple, now accompanied by another man.

"Greetings Enoch," Arthur said, "I attend as elder, and Charis comes with me to speak on behalf of Gweneffar my co-elder."

"Good." Enoch nodded.

"I am Merlyn, seer and elder," the armed man stepped forward, "with my co-elder Nimue."

"There are seven of us." Enoch said, "Who is the eighth?"

"I am the eighth." the other man approached, "I come to represent Zion."

The eighth member of our group was a man appearing in his thirties, Semitic by the look of him with short curly hair and a tuft of a beard on his chin. At first appearance he seemed to me to be unremarkable, but his eyes were kind and he smiled at me. Everyone else seemed familiar with this man and he sat up next to Enoch on his left on the judgement seat. Enoch didn't introduce the man, so I was left to wonder who he was.

"We can now proceed." Enoch announced. There was a silence around us from the watching crowd. I felt very honoured and a little strange.

"The issue at hand and the purpose for which you have been brought to meet with us here today Walter is of great importance." Enoch began, "According to the covenant between the Seelie Court of Earth and the Melkizedek Order, you have been made Oberon of the Rath of Utnapishtim and the Netherworld realm beneath Eden. As such you are effectively Prime of the Order and we recognize you as such here, that you have authority to speak for Earth concerning the war with the Nephalim. Are you willing to represent your people and your world?"

"Yes." I replied, although I didn't feel very competent.

"It seems that a great disaster has fallen upon us," Enoch continued, "a Baal by the name of Graud, also known from ancient times as Enlil, the Lord of the Air, of the Anunnaki, styling himself as Yahweh, the God of Earth, has stolen the key of Utnapishtim and a ring stone. He has then opened a portal along the corridor into the past and has escaped, free now to commit evil as we do not know where he has gone."

"But the Order has occupied the Rath of Utnapishtim and the Djinni are now our allies." Arthur added, "The Rath intelligence is awakened and we will soon have the portal to Earth open again once we have a new key and stone to replace those which were taken."

"I have brought the new key and stone with me." said the man sitting next to Enoch, "The purpose of taking Utnapishtim was so we could unlock the portals to Jerusalem and Sinai. The Holy Land will be occupied by the Allies."

"But the carnage of the Great War will continue." Enoch's companion D'Anu said, "New forces for evil are rising in the East, the Bolsheviks."

"Tell us Walter," Enoch turned to me, "give us a report on the progress of the War and what the Order are doing now."

I could sense even then that things were divided here. Arthur and Charis were obviously on my side, as was this anonymous man on the judgement seat, but the other four, Enoch, D'Anu, Merlyn and Nimue seemed to be cautious. I saw where the conversation could head. It didn't look good. I also knew that I was dealing with spiritually powerful people here. There would be no smart talking here. I would have to be utterly transparent.

"We have dealt a heavy blow against the Atalanti and Pandemonium factions." I said, "Just recently I personally gathered intelligence within Germany revealing that the enemy were planning to attack the Ouroboros and take over Germany from within. Many Melkizedek agents were killed attaining the identities of the Atalanti and Pandemonium agents working in Germany, but we were able to not only warn the Ouroboros, but also help them track down and remove those enemy agents. While we effectively strengthened the power of the Ouroboros Ring Lords, we broke the power of the Atalanti and Pandemonium forces in Europe and weakened them greatly in America. Their evil alliance has effectively fallen apart, and the Americans are now free to enter the war, which will end the war quickly. The Ouroboros have promised to remain neutral from now on, and they are no longer at war with us. The Djinni too are now our allies. General Allenby will have occupied Jerusalem by now and Turkey will be removed from the war. The Central Powers cannot maintain the war for much longer. We will soon be at peace."

"What about Russia?" Merlyn asked, "D'Anu's point needs to be answered. Also, what is Graud planning to do? What will he do?"

"I have fought against Communists in Russia and we have a strong network in Russia, including most of the White Russian leaders, and of course, the royal family." I replied, "It was with Russian help that we were able to occupy Mount Ararat, that is, Utnapishtim."

"But be honest with us Walter," D'Anu pressed on, "what is our real strength in Russia?"

"The Communists are stronger than we can presently deal with," I replied, "and we even have an evacuation plan in place for the Tsar's family. There was a particularly powerful Pandemonium agent named Rasputin within the royal household who has done a lot of damage. The Russians are likely to withdraw from the war and the Communists are in control of much of the countryside."

"We will need to realistically consider the loss of Russia then." D'Anu concluded, "You will need to act quickly upon your return to Earth. Even if we were to put our full support behind the White Russian resistance, do you think that we could push the Communists out?"

"I think that we should try." I said, but then admitted, "But I think also that we would lose. Tsar Nicholas is a member of the Melkizedek. But Nicholas has been foolish in some of his decisions. He isn't popular with his people because he has failed to hear their concerns. Despite working hard with the Mensheviks for constitutional government, the Communists still dominate Russian republican politics. There have been several assassination attempts. It is just too late. Russia is effectively an old style feudal state and the serfs have had enough. Nicholas knows this. He seems resigned to die for his people."

"He needs to be resigned to live for his people!" Enoch said loudly, "We need to evacuate the royal family immediately, make them disappear and consolidate our strength. Our people in Russia can find refuge in Utnapishtim, we will need them there anyway."

"If we withdraw them from Russia," Arthur said, "then it is inevitable that Russia will fall to the Communists. We will pay for that later."

"We need to be strong enough to fight Graud when he eventually returns." Merlyn countered,

"And he will return, you can be sure of that. That must be our primary concern."

Right then, the unnamed man stepped down off the judgement seat. All conversation stopped as he walked over and stood right in front of me. I knew what it was like to be 'read' by an empath, but this felt different, deeper and warmer. He looked me right in the eyes and then he smiled at me, patted me on the shoulder and went back up to his seat. No one spoke. The man looked thoughtful. Then he looked at me again.

"Tell me about Graud." he asked.

I thought for some time myself.

"He's a ruthless murderer." I said quietly, but I wasn't thinking of my own death, "He is personally responsible for the deaths of thousands, our people, soldiers on both sides of this conflict, and many civilians too. In fact, I think he is insane. He seems to gain pleasure from the suffering of others, and he likes large demonstrations of his ability to kill large numbers."

I paused, paying my respects for the dead. No-one said anything.

"But he is also incredibly efficient, very German in that respect... of course he's not German."

"This incarnation is." the man said, "It is the nature of the A'sidhe, and the Anunnaki, both those in the light and those in the darkness, to find affinity with the cultures of their incarnated forms."

"He likes having power," I continued, "and he has been close to General Erik Ludendorff and influential in the German High Command for a long time. Despite having power and the potential to gain promotion, he has never gone above the equivalent rank of Major. Still, he is known as the 'Little Kaiser' by the general staff. He remains at the low rank he has so that he can participate in actual raids and military missions. He lets others give his orders for him, then he goes out and makes it happen himself. He is, as I said, utterly ruthless and his soldiering ability is excellent. I have fought against him in hand to hand combat a few times. He just kills without hesitation, as quickly and as efficiently as possible. He is personally good at killing. He is also a good battlefield officer. The men he gathers around himself are handpicked natural born killers, cold and ruthless like himself, and loyal to him personally."

"That is Enlil's way for certain." Oberon Enoch nodded grimly.

"Yes." the man agreed, "Quiet and deadly. You don't see him there until he strikes and then he strikes hard."

The man then looked right back at me again, "Alright Walter, what do you think Graud will do? Don't try to reason it out with your head, listen to your spirit."

I closed my eyes. There was a part of me that knew that now I was different, that I had new spiritual skills since my resurrection, what they called cycling here. I also knew that of all the people here, I was *the* Earthman. I was there and they were looking to me for the answers.

In my minds' eye I could see Graud as he was the last time we had met each other. It was in France, after my mission to meet General Ludendorff, and was returning across no-man's-land. I had come across an abandoned farm house, or rather what was left of it. He had been waiting for me there. The whole place was flooded with mustard gas and we were both wearing full kit including gas masks. I had been riding a stolen motorcycle when he began shooting at me from the farm house. I was forced to take cover behind a stone wall, and followed it along towards the ruins of the house. I had managed to cross behind the house from the wall, dodging fire from an upstairs window. Then he did something which was humanly impossible, he jumped out of the upstairs window, twisting in the air and firing as he fell, and landing squarely on his feet, not two metres from where I was crouching!! I should have died in that moment, but by some miracle his gun had jammed, and so he flung it away from himself and pulled out his combat knife. I shot him with my rifle and lunged with my bayonet, but he rolled aside. He was bleeding, unbalanced, and yet he spun around and thrusting with his knife, he stabbed viciously. I deflected his knife with the butt of my rifle.

The wood of the butt splintered with the force and I was thrown back into the wall of the house, smashing through the wooden walls and into the building itself. There was a popping sound and the entire side of the building literally fell apart, with boards splintering and falling all around us! A whole section of wall fell down and drove down onto Graud where he stood. As the dust was clearing, I realised that I was in pain, yet incredibly nothing was broken. I staggered as I stood, and went over to check the pile of wood that had fallen upon Graud, to see if he was dead. Incredibly, he shoved the planks aside as though they were straw, and I was faced with a decision. I turned and ran. There was no way I could win against that strength. I don't know why he didn't follow me immediately, perhaps he was more disoriented than I thought, or more likely, he had lost a seal on his gas mask (and that would have been unpleasant). But I'm sure he would have gotten me if I hadn't fallen arse over elbow, down into an abandoned trench. On the way back, I had to evade a squad of stormtroopers, and then a bombardment of mortars. Somehow I survived. He seemed determined to kill me, but I lived. I stole another motorcycle and returned behind allied lines.

It seemed strange that I would remember this episode so vividly, but I had learned a lot about Graud the man in those violent and desperate moments. He was relentless. I only survived because of a set of fortunate circumstances. In the year before that meeting in Angels in London, I'd lost four partners to violence. I only survived because I had been trained by Seelie fight trainers, and as they put it, I had the instinct. I'd overheard one teacher say that I had the gene. I knew how to enter the fighting trance, which made all A'sidhe warriors so formidable. But what did I *see* while in the trance that day?

...Graud had a plan, even then. He had been watching me, provoking me, NOT killing me, following me. I'd met him in Germany, in the Caucasus and in France, and each time I escaped by the skin of my teeth and others died in my place. It was like he knew. Perhaps he did. His escape through the stone ring in Utnapishtim was not opportunistic, it was planned. He planned everything.

"Graud has gone back in time to create an army." I finally said, "He will return when the time is right and will strike with overwhelming force. The present political situation is exactly how he wants it. He wants a destroyed Germany, Communists ruling in Russia, and he wants a strong America. I don't think he will rush his plans though, but will gradually sneak up on us, when we least expect it. He has his people, here in our time, working to his agenda as well. We think we have won, but in reality, he has gotten what he wants."

"And what does he want?" Enoch asked.

"He wants the Seelie Court to continue their policy of non-interference, and do nothing." I said.

That stung. Murmurs could be heard in the crowd who were watching silently until now. I could feel the empathy moving in my favour.

"Up until now," Merlyn said, "it is true that we have been merely maintaining a holding action, just containing the enemy. The Blockade of Earth has been successful because we have not provoked the enemy. But now it is possible that Graud plans to break that Blockade. He provokes us, perhaps to act prematurely."

"What are you suggesting we do Walter?" the man asked me.

"I have a plan, I think." I replied.

Chapter Ten

Petra

For the rest of the day, the man from Zion and I talked in a private office not far from the judgement seat. I poured my heart out. Later we continued our discussion over food and drink and it was then that I began to get some thoughts about who he actually was. But like all wonderful things in the Vansadagaadian Corridor, I wasn't so surprised. What I was surprised by was his 'normalness', so I felt very comfortable with him as we discussed ways to save the world from the Nephalim. It was such a big thing really. I was just a soldier, a common man and I felt very small, yet the man insisted that I had something he wanted to hear from me.

Sometime later in the day, the man told me that the new gate key for the Avalon ring had arrived and that we needed to go to the ring for the new portal opening. I expected that we would use one of the Renim or a carriage, but instead he waved a hand and opened a portal in the room with us and he led me through. At the ring, Arthur, Oberon Enoch and Merlyn were there waiting for us, as well as a sizable force of Tuatha De Danann warriors and technicians. They were properly suited up in metal battle armour, mail and armed with advanced weapons. The key was placed in the altar stone in the middle by Arthur and turned. The captain of the warriors touched the gate stone on one of the big trilithons and the portal opened. The squad of warriors went through to Utnapishtim. We waited for a few minutes and the portal reopened, Niamah, followed by Al and the Russian officers, accompanied by one of the warriors appeared. Niamah and I fell into each other's arms and just held each other. Waves of empathic relief washed over me. Niamah held on and we wept with joy.

Quite a big expedition returned to Utnapishtim. After I'd leapt through the portal to Avalon, only to be met with violence on the other side, the portal had closed behind me. Without the gate key and the Avalon gate stone stolen as well, there was no way for those in Utnapishtim to follow me. But as it was, they were busy for some time anyway. Graud had secretly gathered a small army of ghouls. He had collected the bodies of the dead left behind in the tunnels, killed during those first battles with the Djinni and using fell knowledge he'd reanimated them with Pandemonium spirits. Somehow they had evaded the powerful wards of the Rath and when the battle started that night, it didn't stop for three days, fought all around the city. But eventually our side had prevailed when Atra, after pleas from Niamah and Surreya, finally gave Vansadagaadian energy weapons to the Russian soldiers. It was then a matter of hunting the ghouls down and burning them out. The Russians were still proudly carrying their 'blasters' when they arrived in Avalon. The expedition brought almost all the bodies back with them, and I got to watch the 'cycling process' this time from the other side. The portal from earth opened and the Russian and A'sidhe soldiers carried the bodies of those who had died, but who were now alive again, through the portal on stretchers. I checked one of the bodies, a young Russian who had died in the tunnels during the first fighting, and then who was killed a second time as a ghoul. He lay on the stretcher, unconscious, yet breathing. The transition from death to life, as they say, is traumatic. Few cycle back in a conscious state, which is what had happened to me. I hadn't woken up immediately either, but had slept while my spirit reintegrated with my living body. I also noticed that there were some A'sidhe going back through the portal, unarmed. Arthur told me that there were some of the dead whose bodies weren't recoverable. Those A'sidhe were going to Utnapishtim 'astrally' to recover the spiritual traces of the remaining dead. I was learning a lot about the way the Vansadagaadians do things. The process of resurrection or 'cycling' was complex and risky. As a child I'd believed that 'going to heaven' was something that just happened automatically. Apparently not. Death was and is a terrible thing. When mortal beings die, their lives end. But the Elohim and Eldar had found a way to bring us back to life. I watched this process of 'cycling' carefully, travelling myself to Utnapishtim and back a number of times. I stood with Atra and watched the A'sidhe 'trace hunters' seek out the bodies of the fallen. All that was left of them was their quickly extinguishing life trace. This 'trace' was what was left of the soul or life force of the living person. Seeing with the A'sidhe empathic vision, the traces or ghost balls were like little lights lost in the dark. The trace hunters would dematerialise when they crossed the threshold of the portal and in their disembodied state they would bring back the spiritual remains of the dead, held carefully lest they extinguish altogether. As the trace hunter and their charge returned through the portal to Avalon, the Artificial Intelligence residing in the ring would read the trace and rematerialise a new body for both the trace hunter and the trace of the dead person they carried. For humans, this process was very traumatic. For the Eldar races, the transition from corporeal to non-corporeal and back again, happened all the time. I understood now what had happened to me, and why my memories had been so messed up as I recovered. Watching the invisible spirit world around us I could see familiars as well, coming and going hovering protectively next to those they protected. I also understood just how dangerous this process was – I could see the Pandemons hovering nearby as well, hoping to slip through the portal when we weren't looking. Both guardians and trace hunters sometimes had to fight to keep them away. The Christian hope of 'Resurrection Day' is a vital one to the faithful, but I could see that cycling an entire world, billions of traces, would be a huge undertaking fraught with terrible danger and battle. So, while Avalonian troops occupied and guarded the Rath, we were all asked back to Avalon, to gather again and so I could reveal the new plan for defeating Graud and the Nephalim.

After a short time alone with Niamah, the first thing I wanted to do was talk to the Russians. I met them in Avalon, in the same room near the judgement seat where I had spoken with the man earlier. They came in, all quite overawed by the things they were seeing in the Vansadagaadian Corridor. The officers, along with Al, Niamah and Surreya sat down with me around a large round table, which seemed very appropriate since Arthur soon joined us. The man from Zion remained outside, talking with the other Oberons, leaving us to talk.

"All the men who were killed have been brought back to life." Captain Kurbatov said, looking stunned, "All our injuries were also healed when we passed through the portal from earth to this strange new world."

"Is this Heaven?" Zabolotsky asked, "A lot of the men are astounded."

"It is more complicated than that," I replied, with a smile, "but essentially, yes, this city of Avalon, the whole Vansadagaadian Corridor is Heaven."

"It better be." Sergeant Rujansky pointed out the door, "Do you know who is standing just out there? And this man sitting with us is King Arthur? I am much more than astounded!"

I looked out the door and saw the man. He looked back at me and he seemed exhausted, tired, as though he'd poured his life out for all those who lived – in one real sense, he had done exactly that, paying for the bad karma of others.

"But it is you men of Russia who astound me." Arthur's voice cried as he bowed to Rujansky and the others, "You have shown yourselves to be courageous and faithful men, true warriors. Even as we speak, Tuatha De Danann warriors are destroying Nephalim enemies all over the world, using the portal networks now available since we have recovered the Rath of Utnapishtim and the recovery of Noah's ark, the Torbor, is a great victory in its own right. General Allenby has occupied Jerusalem."

"But our homeland, the Russias, is falling into the hands of evil men." Captain Kurbatov looked crestfallen, "It is hell in Russia, while we sit here in comfort. It is victory for your people, you Britons, but not for my people."

"Friend, Captain Leonov Kurbatov," I said in careful Russian, "it was your own Tsar who ordered you and your men to Ararat, to find the Ark which you yourself saw from the air. His Majesty knows what is happening to his country. He is prepared to lay down his life if need be for his people. There is a bigger picture here, not just our countries are at risk, but our entire world, in fact, many worlds could fall if we fail in this moment."

"How many Russians will have to be sacrificed?" Kurbatov continued, "Will any of them be brought back to life through the power of those portals down there in the ring? Will the Tsar

and his murdered family be given new lives as we have? Why can't we go back to my country and fight and die with them?"

There was silence for some time as we sat together. There were also tears. We wept for Russia.

"There will come a time," I continued, "where you will return to Russia and will get your chance to fight. But it is not to fight Communists, or Germans. The Nephalim Baals are in retreat, but they are not defeated and they are still plotting their next attack. What they will do next has something to do with what Graud has just done. He has escaped, but we think that he is gathering a great army somewhere in the ancient past and that he plans to return. We need to be ready for him. If he is intending to gather an army, then we need to do the same. It is easy to die, my friends, but much harder to live. You need to live because one day your people will be free. In the meantime, we have the help of the angels, and believe me, they intend to fight alongside us as they never have before. I need you to trust me, to trust the plans of God, and stand with us in this time of trial, but also great opportunity."

The three Russians looked at each other.

"Brothers, Boris, Vassilli," Leonov Kurbatov said to them, "Not as the commanding officer, but as a man to other men, do we stand together?"

"HA!!" Boris Rujansky slapped his fellow Russians on their backs, "Of course 'we will!"

Vassilli Zabolotsky was grinning too, and nodding.

"Good." I smiled, "Tomorrow I want us to gather here again. Arthur has offered us the hospitality of his household. He is also going to equip us with the best armour and weapons they have. What we will be doing with our new weapons and strategies is going to change the world. You are about to become the first of a new Order. The old Melkizedek Order has had its purpose and we have done well, but it is time for a new approach to the Nephalim threat."

"Friends," Arthur stood up, "gather your men and come with me. Tonight we will celebrate our victory and prepare for tomorrow. Be encouraged, we will see wondrous things."

I could see the fire in their eyes. There were no more tears, only hope and a new sense of joy. Arthur led them out of the room. Al joined them, winking at me as he went. Niamah sat with me for a bit longer, then she kissed me and we followed them out. A large portal had opened and I could see the gate of Arthur's house beyond. There were a lot of people, of many species, passing back and forth. I could hear music coming through the portal, and smells of food. Niamah took hold of my hand and squeezed. I swam in the joy of her love. My vision was before my eyes. We were about to cross through the portal, but then the man met us.

"Can I join you?" he asked.

"My Lord!" we shook hands, "Of course!"

I still didn't dare actually say his name.

"You are doing very well. I'm proud of you." he put an arm around my shoulders, and looked right into my eyes, "But now it is time for a bit of fun! I need to rest and recuperate too!! Arthur knows how to host a party!"

The next day it seemed as though all of Avalon had come out to the Great Plaza to see us. There were ships crowding the harbour, every balcony and walkway was full of people. Air cars hovered above us. But the plaza in front of the Judgement Seat was empty. Niamah and I were waiting there at the Seat, with the man and the Oberons sitting behind me. A portal opened down by the water and out marched Arthur, leading a battalion of British horsemen, the Cymbrogi, his own royal guard. The horses they rode were not animals, but were machines called constructs. Like the knights, the horses were clad in bright silver armour, their bodies shining like mercury, and moving with liquid fluidity. The Cymbrogi were wearing Roman legionary style helmets and plate, but instead of mail, they wore skin tight silver uniforms. Around their shoulders they wore tartan cloaks with gold brooches and golden torcs around their necks. They carried power lances and their mounts were equipped with cannon, particle beamers and missiles, mounted on their heads. They looked powerful, formidable and deadly.

Through the same portal next came the Russians, wearing white skin tight uniforms, wide bowl shaped helms, chest armour, gauntlets, grieves and long white sleeveless overcoats. Like the Britons, they were equipped with power lances, but they also wore bandoleers of grenades and proudly carried the blasters they won during the fighting in Utnapishtim, strapped to their left thighs, while the bayonets were strapped on the right.

Al was nearby with a detachment of Tuatha de Danann warriors, wearing a uniform similar to that worn by the Russians, but with Greek Corinthian style helms and capes. Along with their power lances, they also carried swords and round shields (strapped to their left arms). Their uniforms, I knew, were normally coloured the blue-grey of wode, and often decorated with runes and magical symbols, but this time I had to actually look carefully for them because their camouflage was turned on, which made them almost invisible. It was one of the reasons why they were known as ghost warriors.

Then, everyone looked up when a cloud of Renim swarmed into the city harbour, flying along the water entrance of the city. They hovered over the plaza and a few of them descended to the causeway in the middle of the harbour. Surreya, Humut-tabal and Namtar disembarked with their Djinni. They wore black battle skins, pointed helms and black turbans and were lightly armed with scimitars or long knives and gauntlet blasters.

Now that all the main players had arrived, the Oberons of the cities stood and their guards, now wearing their gold dress armour, saluted, drumming their power lances against their elliptical shields. A great hush came over the crowds, and the man stepped out into the middle of the plaza. High up in the tiers of the city above, someone blew on a shofar, the haunting noise echoing across the heart of Avalon. Then everyone cheered, millions of voices all at once! I stood transfixed, shivers up and down my spine. In that moment, I almost fell over. I looked at him. The man from Zion was smiling, but he looked almost embarrassed. He looked around at me and wiggled his eyebrows, then he laughed, joyfully. Others laughed with him. It wasn't some flattering thing, but pure and uninhibited. I couldn't help grinning. It was a moment of true happiness. I put my arm around Niamah and gave her a squeeze.

Then the man walked over and took me by the hand and led me out into the middle of the plaza. I was a bit perplexed, but then he bowed to me! I looked around and I could see all these balls of light hovering above. The memories I gained from Niamah told me what they were. They were called 'witnesses' and were the astral projections of those who couldn't be here physically, but who still wanted to be here to see what was happening. Normally they would be invisible, and usually were, on earth, but now I had the empathic sense, I could perceive them. I realised that they were there, incredibly, to see me!

"They want to hear what you are about to say," the man nodded at me, "to hear your vision for the future of earth. Maybe no-one knows your name now, Melkizedek agent, but most of these are witnesses from the future, and I think that you are famous!"

I could feel their eyes upon me, and the emotion of approval, but also expectation.

"Time to begin." The man said, and he led the way into the meeting room. Quite a lot of people followed us in, including all the Russians, the Oberons and Arthur and his Cymbrogi. The room was quite large, with high stone walls and hovering glow globes above. The witnesses floated among the globes. In the middle of the room was the table that I'd asked to be placed there. There were rows of chairs, in circles all around the table, with plenty of space for people to sit. The soldiers who entered the room formed ranks along the walls, but the officers sat at the table. Arthur came up behind me and passed his sword over.

"This looks familiar!" he smiled, then sat down.

I placed Arthur's sword on the table and also sat down. Arthur was next to me on one side, and Niamah on the other. Others at the table included the man, who sat across on the other side, Kurbatov, Zabolotsky and Rujansky, Al was sitting next to Niamah, who I suddenly realised was actually her son, and by extension my step-son!!! He looked over at me with one of his cheeky grins. Everyone seemed happy and chatted with each other. Surreya and the Djinni leaders Namtar and Humut-Tabal were over near the man, and talking animatedly with him. The Oberon Enoch and Merlyn, sat together as well as the Morrigans, D'Anu, Nimue and Gweneffar. Charis was there as well, sitting next to Gweneffar, looking like her twin sister.

I waited a bit, until everyone settled down. I looked over at the man and he nodded at me. I picked up Arthur's sword, Excalibur, and knocked on the table with the pummel.

"Ladies and gentlemen, it is time to discuss some serious matters." I said, "I call this presbytery in order to propose a new plan for the defeat of the Nephalim enemy on earth. Until this time, the Eldar and Seelie Court have worked hard to protect mankind from the Nephalim threat. At times, there has been open warfare and this has usually led to incredible destruction and death, which is unacceptable. This Great War that still rages in its last stages is a testimony of this violence. Since the time of the Deluge, the Seelie Court has been cautious in their actions. So, the plan to defeat the Nephalim has involved humanity. A people were raised up, descended from Adam and Eve, and then a new Logoi was born from the Source of All, Yeshua."

We all stopped at that moment and I looked across the table at Yeshua himself, sitting there among us. He smiled, but held up his hand. He was notoriously humble, and wouldn't want any adulation. I was very aware that while religion loved to worship the Son, but not serve Life, we were here to serve Life together, and that is what pleased Yeshua the most. Still looking at him, my heart swelled with respect and loyalty and love.

"Yeshua established the community of people who love Life and did so by sacrificing his own. Since that time, that community has worked to bring goodness to the earth and make our world free. But this process of life giving transformation hasn't been easy. The enemy has been at work and has corrupted and infiltrated the people of the Light has established religious systems and empires to destroy Life. Still, we have quietly prevailed, with the power of the Spirit, our Mother, guiding us."

I paused again, letting the story sink in. We all knew it, but we still needed to be reminded of the cost.

"Behind the scenes the Eldar races have continued to aid us. Most humans though are completely unaware of this angelic help, which has remained very much done in secret. There are only a few humans who know the truth, such as the soldiers of the Melkizedek Order, of which I am one. Since the time of Abraham, the Order has worked alongside of the A'sidhe tribes, and we have fought against the Pandemonium, and those humans who serve Graud and the Nephalim Baal Lords. But the Melkizedek are few, and the power of the enemy has often been overwhelming, while the religious have remained apathetic, comfortable and ignorant. Now, what we are seeing is a new Nephalim strategy. Until now they have operated in obscurity and their power has been limited, but more recently they have gathered their forces and powerful leaders, like Graud, and some of the old gods have returned. Alliances have been formed between the factions. The Atalanti of America and the European Pandemonium, along with some of the other smaller Satanic factions have formed an alliance they are calling Medusa. Despite our recent victory in bringing the War to End All Wars to an end, the redemption of the Djinni and the reoccupation of the Raths of Utnapishtim and Zion, Graud was able to use the Ring-Portal system to escape into the past, where we have a suspicion that he is raising up an army. We also suspect that they have other plans, to break the blockade of earth and unleash their cosmic allies upon us!!"

At that there was some murmuring among those at the table. Was I really talking about an invasion? Yes, I suppose I was.

"We need a new plan." I said, once the talking died down.

Yeshua stood up, "The Enemy is making plans." he said, "The Enemy is on the move. It is time for us to be revealed to the world."

"Do you mean that the A'sidhe will reveal their true nature, their non-human nature to the world?" Enoch asked, "That would be very provocative, it might bring Armageddon down upon us!"

Yeshua sat down and looked at me, "Yes and no." I said, "What I'm proposing is the forming of a new Order and a new strategy of action, which will see the A'sidhe and other Eldar becoming a lot more publically active alongside of faithful humans. Please let me explain. The new Order is the Petra Order, which will replace the Melkizedek. Petra will include both humans and fair-folk working together, and covertly using advanced Vansadagaadian technology to continue the fight against the Nephalim. What will make Petra different is that they will operate openly as a security and aid agency on earth. I envision seeing Petra's membership being much greater than the Melkizedek Order ever was, with whole garrisons of well-trained operatives in every nation. There is also something new and this is the key difference. The Petra Order is also to be a civilian alliance of communities loyal to Life. These 'Petra Communities' will be self-governing spiritual communities, an alliance, a spiritual movement, not to form a new denomination nor a church, but rather to bring communities together in co-operation. The communities will be intentional and bring together all kinds of leadership together. Petrad, will be a local and global research and development organisation. Petrad will also be our mission arm, and will work to develop new Petra communities all over the world. Naturally, Petrad people will work very closely with the agents of the Order to ensure that people are protected from the Nephalim threat."

"Will the people of these Petra communities be aware of the existence of 'angels' living and working among them?" D'Anu asked, "Won't that knowledge put our people at risk?"

"As with the Melkizedek," I replied, "the agents of the Order will be aware of the folk living and working with them. The leadership within Petrad will also, as will certain key trusted people."

"But won't there be leaks in security?" D'Anu protested, "It will get out and become public eventually that 'angels' walk among men! This has been the most closely guarded secret we have!"

"I actually hope that these leaks happen!!" I laughed, "While there will certainly be no way for strangers to prove anything, for the grassroots people in the movement it will be very encouraging to know that heavenly forces are here working with them. Are there any other questions?"

I looked around the room. Arthur and my Russian friends were grinning quite happily, and Al, Surreya were too. Lots of others were thinking through what I'd said and projecting the implications and consequences in their minds. Yeshua was silent, I knew because he was determined to make this our common decision and not something he imposed upon us. To know that I had his approval was enough for me, but the members of the isolationist faction, led by Enoch, didn't know that. While Enoch was human, he was also an antediluvian patriarch and he'd been living in the Corridor for many thousands of years, removed from life on earth. But he was also very, very wise.

"You have done very well." Niamah whispered in my ear.

"We need to adjourn for now." Yeshua said finally, "And think very carefully through everything. We also need for the people of the Corridor some time to consider as well. Pray also and Wisdom will know. She will tell me the verdict of the people. I will call another presbytery when that happens. For now, goodbye."

I could already see the witnesses floating above beginning to move away and all the leaders began to walk out onto the plaza, where portals opened to whatever destination they were going to. Arthur, the Djinni, Al and my Russian friends followed, leading their troops out of the room in ranks. Niamah and I followed as well. Yeshua met us at the Judgement Seat.

"Do you know what they will decide?" I asked him.

He grinned at me, "I am a Logoi member of the Elohim." he rolled his eyes, "But I am also a man, and that is why I am fit to be High Oberon. No, I don't know, and in this matter, I do not want to know. Be patient my friend, it is not for the Son of Man to know either the time or the hour. Abba knows more, but even he is keeping his own council this time. The River of the Spirit flows all around us and is in us. The right decision will be made."

He gave me a hug, and smiled warmly and turning onto the plaza, opened a portal with the wave of a hand and stepped through.

Chapter Eleven

Transition

The War to End All Wars was nearly over and there would soon be peace, at least between Germany and her enemies. There was still fighting going on in Russia, as the White Russians resisted the Communists. Kurbatov, Zabolotsky and Rujansky, along with the 19th Petropavlovsky Regiment, equipped with the new Excalibur equipment and weapons returned to Russia for a very special mission.

On 22nd March 1917, Tsar Nicholas had abdicated. It was in August, while the Romanov's were in exile in Tobolsk, in the Urals, that the message of the discovery of the ark was smuggled in, and Colonel Koor of the 19th Petropavlovsky Regiment hatched the plan to climb the mountain in the hope that if the ark was discovered, that the Communists would be discredited and The Tsar vindicated and returned to the throne. Nicholas himself supported the plan, but being a member of the Melkizedek, he had other reasons, and could see the big picture. That was why Al and I were sent to Turkey the following summer. The Bolsheviks came to power in October 1917, and we climbed the mountain in June 1918, three months after the royal family had begun to be moved to the Ipatiev House in

Yekaterinburg. Early on the morning of 17th July, Petra agents, including members of the White 19th Petropavlovsky Regiment performed their first mission. Lenin had ordered the secret police in Yekaterinburg to execute the Romanov's, so we ported in and snatched the Romanov's out. We also grabbed Yurovsky, the chief executioner and his fellows, and gave them false memories, and left behind copies of the family's bodies. It had been a tricky mission, but we succeeded, bringing the Romanov family back to Utnapishtim. The War itself ended in November, but the fighting in Russia continued well into 1919, including several more secret missions, which I took part in, that is until March 28th, when Niamah gave birth to our son Kit.

In the years following the War, Kit spent his childhood either in Utnapishtim or back in England at the Albion Rath, home of the Avalon A'sidhe, the Tuatha De Danann, Niamah's tribe. Kit got a good Seelie education and training. As a Halfling, Kit had a number of advantages. As he grew up he discovered that he had the spiritual powers of the Folk and he was particularly good at glamour, the ability to change the appearance of things and himself. Kit also grew tall and very strong. In fact, his physical strength was considerable, a common characteristic of Halfling children. In many ways, Kit had the best characteristics of both races. Al personally trained Kit in Tuatha De Danann fighting techniques and by the time Kit was fifteen, he was a better warrior than his teacher! That was saying something.

Kit went on his first mission as a Petra agent the following year. 1935 was a bad year for Jews in Germany and Kit went to Germany to set up the first cells for resistance in Germany, and begin the process of getting people out, especially persecuted Jews and other political dissidents. After that, Kit became involved with the Petrad people and the Petra communities that were being formed all over Europe.

Something needs to be said about the Petra communities. While the Order certainly continued to operate as a paramilitary and intelligence organisation (i.e. They were spies! Like the Melkizedek before them), the real work of the new Petra Order was in the development of intentional communities. It wasn't religious proselytization but rather building strong communities, united by a common spirituality, and a desire for justice, mercy and compassion to be lived out in practice. In the twenties, and especially in the thirties during the Great Depression, the Petra Movement took off because people were looking for a place and a people to belong to, a way to share the burdens of the times and give hope to whole communities struggling together just to survive. Practical social welfare was a big part of what Petra did. Kit would, even as a child, often be out on the streets doing his bit to help. New communities were formed firstly in England, and then in Australia, New Zealand, Canada and then, in Germany. Other nations were to follow, Scandinavia and America and South Africa, and we were looking at wider Africa, Asia and South America too, but that was when Hitler rose to power in Germany, and we became preoccupied. The way Petra built community was to establish 'hamlets' or 'villages'. Hamlets were groups of houses or whole street blocks in major cities, which were collectively owned by the Petra community. The communities often grew as people of good will entered the community and quite literally added their homes and businesses and lands to the community. While we didn't collectivise our properties, we did often work together to help people buy collective properties for the communities, to set up syndicalist businesses, schools, hospitals and other community projects. In some parts of Germany, as Nazism rose to power, the Petra movement became a 'third power' in the local politics, hated by both the Nazis and the Communists. Our villages were intentional communities, often in the country, and again, in some places Petra farm cooperatives owned a lot of land. But in Germany, in 1935, Hitler not only attacked the Jews, he was also determined to exterminate Petra as a movement in the Reich. It was in that year that we learned something very important, we learned that Hitler had the full support of the Nephalim Medusa Alliance and that the Nazi's were being supplied with advanced technology by the Nephalim. As Kit led the teams to pull our people out of Greater Germany, leaving everything behind, Order agents were involved in some very nasty fighting with very well armed Medusa agents, including members of the Pandemonium. Hitler and his Medusa allies believed that they had driven us out, but our withdrawal was really a ruse. The Order remained in Germany.

There is of course, a lot to be said about all of this, and I could write whole volumes of books about what my son Kit and I did during the Second World War.

But this is not the place for those stories. We were all involved in that struggle because unlike the German leaders during the first War, Hitler was a true occultist, and he served his Nephalim masters well. But it is probably worth saying here that Hitler escaped and didn't die in 1945 in that Berlin bunker. But he, and a very large number of Nazi supporters were taken into hiding in the last weeks of the war to secret Medusa bases. These Nazi forces and their descendants after them would continue to be a threat for a long time.

After the War, another war began, the cold war between the new nuclear powers of the United States of America and the Union of Soviet Socialist Republics. But this was only the surface of things. At various times during and just after the War, advanced Nephalim, Seelie or other non-human technology inevitably fell into the hands of various nations. In the late forties and early fifties there were a number of times when our hidden war almost slipped out. But both sides knew that if the wider public were to know the truth about the war between the Seelie and the Nephalim that it would inevitably escalate into another global conflict, this time with very advanced weapons that made even the nuclear threat look tame in comparison. So, sometimes we actually 'leaked' technology to the Americans or to other friendly nations. In July 1947 we actually held a conference at the Albion Rath and invited President Truman, along with other western heads of state to discuss the Roswell incident. The electro-dynamic vehicle that crashed near Roswell New Mexico on July 7th was actually a Humdrid raider, in the service of a Shile breakaway faction, who were interested in breaking the blockade into the solar system so they could acquire new genetic material for their biological technology. In fact, there were many off world powers getting very interested in developments on the earth, and the Seelie and Eldar allies were almost constantly chasing blockade runners from that time on. This led to an alliance, firstly with the Americans, but also other nations. In September, Truman set up the CIA and the National Security Agency in order to directly work with the Order in combating Medusa, who had Atalanti allies working in the Americas.

The Russians had captured Nazi Haunebu E.D.V.s at the end of the war, including some of their cigar shaped Andromeda class big ships. The Chinese stole the technology from the Russians and the Japanese, sometime in the seventies, stole the technology from the Chinese, although some people believed (and I suspected it) that a rogue faction of Vansad, called the Immortals may have set up their own political connections with certain Japanese companies and Yakuza elements.

All this might sound incredible, but everything changed after 1947. It was the year that the UFO phenomenon began. A lot of it was either our people or else it was Medusa, but a new element also entered the mix. Blockade runners from outside the solar system increased one hundred-fold. Some of them got through. The two main players were a Shile faction called the Archons, who became notorious as the 'grey aliens', but who also used Humdrid mercenaries and their ships. The other group were the Valorians of Cootac. Like the Humdrid, they were very good mercenaries, but this time they were working for a rather powerful Satanic Baal named Falshon. Falshon had his eyes on the earth, and was working with Medusa to break the blockade once and for all. The Valorians that made it through the blockade were infamous for wearing black, and people would often refer to them as the men in black. The Seelie tribe called the Pladan had a settlement on Pluto, from where they held the blockade. Pluto was a super-splinter, with a huge power sphere over its gate stones that not only provided artificial sunlight to their colony, but also acted as a primary weapon, used effectively to destroy any raiders that dared to enter the solar system without permission. Enemy E.D.V.s would have to drop below lightspeed way out past the ort cloud, and then run the gauntlet of deadly fire to get in system. Even heavily cloaked vehicles would have their fields disrupted by the wards that protected the solar system, and even if they were able to sneak in, the powerful empaths on Pluto could sense the minds of the passengers, and the Pladan primary weapon would disintegrate them. The Valorians tried robotic ships too, but the remote signals were easily jammed. But after 1947, both the Archons and the Valorians opted for the strategy of mass numbers running the blockade. The Pladan would destroy huge numbers, and sometimes it came down to full blown space conflicts between fleets of ships, but some got through. It was a very serious situation. Then, in 1969, the same year that man officially landed on the moon, (I just have to laugh at that one!!!!), Kit led an expedition to Pladan where he met with a defector from the Medusa side, who we now know as John James. The defector was switching sides for a number of reasons, but the main issue was that Medusa were massing a space fleet on Mars, the so-called Plazash base, and they were going to execute a coordinated strike, with the Valorians against the Pladan. This in itself was bad enough, but the purpose of the attack was even more frightening, apparently they knew where the Daedalus was.

The Daedalus was a very old legend. At the time of the Deluge, the Nephalim Baals had three super-dreadnaughts, huge spacecraft that enabled them to dominate the solar system. One was the Icarus and its twin was the Daedalus. The third was the Minos, even bigger than the other two. At that time though, the Minos was not in the solar system, but was on its way to Cootac, a world used by the Nephalim as a prison planet, notorious for its harsh environment. The story of the Minos is itself important, because it was a group of slaves aboard that ship who rebelled against their slave masters and then settled on their own world of Zioron. The Zioronians were to become very important allies, and they were vital in the battle with the forces of Falshon in 1969. Back in Sol, the Seelie launched their war with the Nephalim and the Deluge happened as a result. In the fighting, the splinters attacked the Icarus and Daedalus and during the battle the Icarus was broken and it fell into the sun. But the Daedalus, also damaged in the fighting, spun out of control, out of the solar system into deep space, where it was lost. It was always assumed that the Daedalus was dead, never to be a threat again.

But John James had found the Daedalus, had actually boarded it, and he didn't like what he found there. He realised that if the Daedalus was to fall into the hands of Medusa it would be a very, very bad thing indeed. Without John James, we would never have known about the Daedalus, and the blockade would have been broken. As it was, there was a battle. Order and Medusa E.D.V.s did battle out past Pluto, and we nearly lost, but then the Zioronian fleet turned up and saved the day. Kit led the boarding party that boarded Daedalus. On board, deep in suspended animation, were millions of Pandemonium warriors. If Medusa had awakened them, it would have been a disaster.

So, we had the Daedalus. The Pandemonium captives were transferred to Pluto and kept safely locked away by the Pladan. We refitted the Daedalus and then went to war with the Valorians. The blockade running was stopped. It was our greatest victory in centuries. What followed was decades of peace and relative quiet, although the Nephalim were still there, plotting what to do next.

Chapter Twelve

2018

It was one of those perfect sunny days, with barely a cloud in the sky over the South Pacific. The nearest land was New Zealand's North Island, over a thousand kilometres to the south west. There was nothing but ocean as far as the eye could see. At least that was how it seemed. There was an odd noise, kind of like someone breathing out and a sliver of light, growing wider, appeared in the blue sky, like a doorway. The doorway grew, sliding open. Inside, walls could be seen and lights around the rim. Then lowering itself through the gap at one side there appeared a tube, with a sphere on the end. The sphere swivelled around and it was obvious that it was a mounted weapon of some kind. A moment later a single aircraft emerged, very similar to the VTOL design of the osprey, but with a single rear rudder. As the aircraft descended its rotors swivelled up into the hovering position, unfolded and began to rotate. Falling almost to sea level, the scorpion B-VTOL hovered for a moment over the water and then the rotors, turning forward, propelled them ahead.

The scorpion flew over the water and soon was approaching a ship. The ship was a Petrad research vessel, the Deep Water Explorer. But the ship wasn't alone. Not far away there were other ships too. Most of them were large research ships like the D.W.E but there was also a United States Navy aircraft carrier watching on the horizon, and not far from the carrier, what looked like an old oil tanker, one of the big heavy carriers, converted into a general sea platform. On board the scorpion, there was a pilot and her co-pilot, and a single passenger.

"Check out that tanker platform." the pilot told her co-pilot, "Looks suspicious to me."

The co-pilot activated his virtual reality visual display in his helmet and began scanning ahead.

"They have a cloak on that ship." the co-pilot said, "I'm picking up energy signature leakage."

"In other words," the passenger added in, "they have advanced tech. We'll have to watch them carefully."

The pilot turned around and grinned at her passenger, she was none other than Surreya herself, and her passenger was Kit Ryan, son of Walter Ryan and Niamah Golden-hair. Even sitting in his seat, Kit looked tall and physically powerful. He had his dark hair worn in long dreadlocks and he had a short stubbled beard. His brown eyes were smiling.

"Something big is happening here." Surreya grinned back, "This is going to be fun."

The VTOL scorpion turned a circle around the Petrad ship and the co-pilot radioed for permission to land on the helipad deck. The rotors turned upwards and the scorpion made a smooth landing. The rear ramp was lowered and the wings folded back. Crew members locked the wheels to the deck. The three stepped out and were met on the deck by a woman. She was a very attractive indigenous Australian, and hugged each of the visitors warmly and then led them up some steps away from the helipad and inside the ship.

Once inside, away from the noises outside, she introduced herself.

"Welcome aboard the Deep Water Explorer, or as we affectionately call her, the Dwee." she led them into a large cabin and to a table with an urn and a hot drink machine. The great ritual of making tea or coffee, prelude to every meeting there ever was, was done quickly and cheerfully.

"I'm Kit Ryan," Kit began introductions, "This is Surreya Kara-Su, and Newton James."

"My name is Clarrissa Maris, but my friends call me Rainbow." she handed the cups around, "I've been asked to brief you about something we discovered that is quite mind blowing."

"What exactly have you discovered?" Kit asked.

"Let me give you some background first," Rainbow led them over to what looked like a large table in the middle of the cabin, "and then I'll use the holo-projector to show you."

Filling the middle of the cabin was a large circular thing. It was lower than a table ought to be and was a solid elliptical shape. It had a white glass top. Rainbow pressed a button on a panel on the side of the projector and a remote control 'gizmo' popped up into her hand. She switched the machine on. The room went dark and a column of light was projected up to the roof.

"The Dwee is a research vessel and Petrad has been using this vessel to explore the Pacific Ocean. We have a number of things we are looking for in particular. We are doing a detailed survey of the sea floor looking for sites for future sea colonies. We have already been instrumental in setting up five colonies already. We are also very interested in looking for thermal energy sites and exploring the deep trenches of the world. But on the quiet, we are also doing some stuff for the Order, looking for Nephalim underwater activity. It was on one of our security sweeps that we discovered this..."

There was a bleep noise and the light over the holo-projector went digital, with lots of pixels flicking on, and finally forming into an incredibly clear image. It was a three dimensional picture of the ocean. The surface of the sea had the ships floating there, and below was the sea floor itself.

"What you are looking at here is the Kermadec trench, one of the deepest sea trenches in the world. It is over ten thousand metres deep in places. We were mapping the trench in this area looking for thermal and volcanic activity because lately there has been an increase in sea quakes. We picked up some unusual electromagnetic signatures, here.."

Using the gizmo, Rainbow pointed at a section of the trench, which enlarged. The wall of the trench could be seen clearly, and there was something unusual there in the side, sticking out of the mud. It was a section of a sphere. Although the sphere was covered in a layer of mud, it still glowed faintly, shimmering like quicksilver.

"Although this is a simulation," Rainbow explained, "the sphere does glow like that because it is actually a stasis field, a very large and powerful one. It reflects all forms of energy, but now, for at least a few days, it is also giving off energy. In other words the stasis field is beginning to resonate again."

"What exactly do we have here?" Kit asked.

"What we have is a disaster of horrific dimensions." Rainbow was almost shaking with obvious fear, "Everything that exists has a vibration or resonation frequency. Atoms, the very structure of space-time itself is pulsing with energy. A stasis field acts to freeze time and space within a specific sphere, and that is what we are seeing here. But this field is destabilising and beginning to rise to a higher frequency. As it begins to re-resonate, huge amounts of energy is being released into the environment. Usually, things decay and are subject to the normal process of entropy. Inside the sphere, entropy is greatly slowed, but now is beginning again. While kinetic energy is being released, which is destabilising the tectonic integrity of the region, it is the cascading entropy which is actually affecting the physical structure of space-time around the sphere that is doing the most damage. Time-space is breaking apart. There are all kinds of strange time anomalies taking place. But worst of all, actual atomic and subatomic integrity is being damaged. Eventually the stasis field will equalise and 'pop', releasing all its energy. We are not sure what will happen, but it will be catastrophically violent."

"Which is why we are here," said Surreya, "with the particular equipment we have brought with us. What can we do to stop this?"

"There may be a way to greatly reduce the damage, or even safely shut this stasis field down." Rainbow said, "But it will be difficult. We have to actually go down to the sphere and find a way to get inside. The field generator is inside. If we can switch it off or better still, restore its power, the Daedalus can then tractor the sphere out of there and it can be shut down safely."

"How do we get inside?" Newton asked.

"We brought an adapted battle suit with us." Kit nodded to himself, "And I can see how we can use it. The flight platform uses a resonating field, and we can use an E.D.V.s ship field to give the whole suit a higher resonation frequency."

"You will be able to literally walk into the sphere." Rainbow smiled, "That's the plan!"

"Yes," Surreya warned, "but we are not alone here. It looks like there is a cloaked ship nearby."

"We're already aware of them." Rainbow said, "In fact they were here before us and have been mining the whole trench."

"Have they tried to approach the stasis field?" Newton wondered, "Why would the Nephalim be putting mines down? It's as though they are protecting it."

"Should we bring the Daedalus in?" Kit suggested.

"That might be a bit of overkill." Rainbow shook her head, "It might be best to run the mines using the scorpion under a cloak. We don't want to start a full blown sea battle in front of all the ships in the area and have the world's media see it!"

"Even so," Kit said, "the Daedalus isn't far away. They could get here in minutes in an emergency. Just what kind of emergency, I have no idea."

"I can give you a few scenarios." Rainbow answered, "That disaster of horrific proportions I talked about could happen. In about twelve hours the clock starts again for whatever is inside that stasis field. This whole region will convulse with huge earthquakes and super storms, tsunamis and the ocean will literally boil. That's a conservative prediction. Then there is the Nephalim ship - what they actually want here is unknown. If they try to capture the stasis sphere we will have to try and stop them. Even if we keep the battle submarine, it is going to be noticed. The Nephalim might want this disaster to unfold. In one sense, we will have to come to terms with this fact that something is going to happen here, something big. Our job will be to retrieve that sphere and I think that the Nephalim will try to stop us."

"I think that the answer is to bring the 'Arrow' in." Newton said, "They can launch their pylon fighters and they have the tractor field to pull the stasis sphere into their hold. They can effectively cover our ass when we go in to check it out. Sometimes we just have to go for it."

"And keep Daedalus nearby in case it goes to hell." Kit added

"Alright." Rainbow nodded, "That's what we do."

Chapter Thirteen

Into the abyss

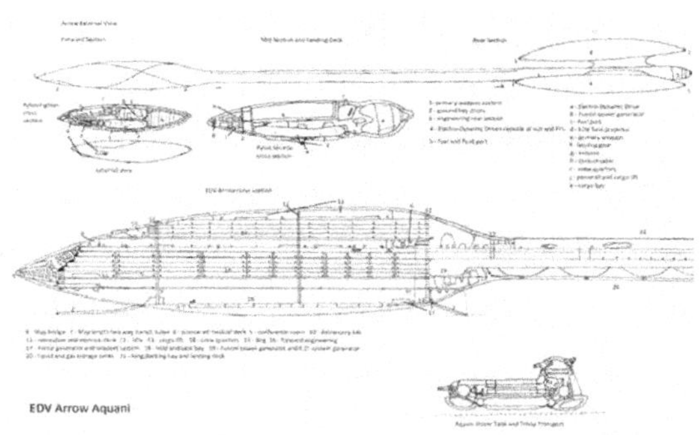

EDV Arrow Aquani

Surreya and Newton prepared the scorpion for flight, while Rainbow and Kit collected all the right gear on the deck. Ship crew were also busy. Other scorpions from Daedalus were flying in and landing on the deck. The captain of the Dwee came down with the radio handset and handed it to Kit.

"Captain John James for agent Kit Ryan." the com officer's voice said.

"Yes Sir." Kit responded.

"Give your report," the captain said.

Kit said, "We need to station Daedalus nearby, because we anticipate Nephalim activity. They have mined the Kermadec trench and we think that they want to prevent us recovering the object we discovered. I recommend that we take a single scorpion down into the trench and I go exterior and enter the object using the modified suit. We will need the Arrow to guard our backs and then tractor the object out if we need to. Rainbow says that we definitely need to do so, and prevent the object from resonating. If the stasis field collapses..."

"I get it." the captain understood, "Go for it. Report back if you find anything unusual."

From now on, Kit knew it was a matter of trust. He would do what he had to do, and the crews on board the Daedalus and the Arrow would do their jobs.

"Alright," Kit turned to Rainbow, "nothing for it, but get moving and do it."

Rainbow nodded, picked up some sensor gear and led Kit down to the Scorpion. The back ramp was down and Surreya and Newton were waiting.

"It's a go." Kit said. There were no words. Everyone strapped in and Surreya began the start-up procedures.

"Dwee tower." Newton spoke into the radio, "Scorpion flight Dad twelve, we're ready for take-off."

"Scorpion flight Dad twelve," the ship radio officer replied, "you have clearance, the other birds are all roosting. Good hunting."

The rotors were already turned upwards and Surreya gunned the engines, and the Scorpion seemed to leap of the deck of the ship and swing away. Turning and flying to the south west, away from the flotilla of ships, Surreya kept the Scorpion just above the water.

"We've got to fly out of visual range over the horizon." Newton told everyone. "Not long."

"I'm preparing the radar drone." Newton continued a few minutes later. The drone was a small rocket pod and Newton fired it from the nose of the Scorpion, "It's away."

Surreya brought the Scorpion into a sudden hover as the radar drone flew onwards. The idea was that anyone, including the Nephalim in their ship, would see the Scorpion flying on their radar and scanner screens.

"We're cloaked." Newton grinned, "No need for all this pretending anymore."

"Ok," Surreya patted Newton on the shoulder, "time to convert the drives."

Newton flipped a series of switch covers and pressed the lighted switches. Still hovering over the water, the rotors slowed and came to a stop. The rotor hubs were glowing with electro-dynamic magnetic fields, which were holding the craft up. The rotor blades folded up and then were withdrawn into the engine housing.

Surreya turned the engines around, so the electro-dynamic hubs were now facing down. The Scorpion made a little hopping motion.

"I'm powering the E.D. fields up for submarine propulsion." Newton said, "Time to submerge."

"Submerging." Surreya sang, and the Scorpion gently descended under the water. The electro-dynamic field around the Scorpion acted like a protective buffer around the hull, enabling the Scorpion to swim through the water almost as though the water wasn't even there. Surreya accelerated their speed and soon the darkness swallowed them.

Newton pressed another switch and a holographic display lit up the cockpit windows. There was a flight window showing Surreya where they were going. It was so dark now, they were completely dependent upon instruments alone. Newton had pulled out a keyboard and was giving instructions to the Scorpion's on board computer.

"We're doing well." he said.

"Scorpion flight D2." the radio squawked, "Arrow bridge control here, Tarmal for Kit Ryan."

"G'day Tarmal!" Kit used the Aussie greeting, a personal thing between the two friends because they had both lived in Australia together for some time, "How's it hangin' mate?!"

"Everything's bonza mate!" the Zioronian prince laughed, "We are following you into the trench and have our Pylons deployed in a protective formation. We are detecting some bandits – it's only cloak shadows, but we are pretty sure that ship you told us about was their origin point. No ordinary ship that."

"Thought so." Kit replied then looked over Newton's shoulder at his screen, "Ah, we'll be at the target in about nine minutes. It is tight down here. I'll be going exterior in about ten."

"K'ma-shah brother," Tarmal used his Zioronian blessing, "we will be watching you."

"Alright then," Kit got up out of his seat, "Rainbow, could you help me with the suit please?"

"Sure." Rainbow was already in the back of the Scorpion and had opened the boxes containing the suit components. She began the process of hooking up the power leads and assembling the helmet and backpack unit. Kit stripped down to his underwear, a pair of grey tight boxers and black t-shirt. He grabbed the boots off Rainbow and slipped his feet into the padded centre. The boots made a beep noise and with a smooth movement, the front and sides closed and snapped in place. The boots, like all the suit components, were all chrome metallic, and they fitted snugly around his lower leg, looking like rather fashionable ski boots.

The technology for the suit was Vansadagaadian, but had been used and developed by the Zioronians for over eight thousand years and they had perfected its use. The suit was a helmet with a full suite of scanners and projectors, a backpack which included a power unit, small missile launcher and the camouflage technology. The gloved gauntlets had force projectors, particle weapons and a retractable mono-molecular blade which could cut through almost anything. The boots had repulsors which enabled one to leap long distances. But, most importantly, the boots fitted into a flying scooter, which meant that it was actually possible to fly or in this case get great propulsion underwater. What made the suit practically invulnerable though was the force-skin that, once activated, covered the exposed limbs and body. The whole body was covered by the skin, which gave full protection, and enabled the camouflage to work. The Zioronians first were given the suits by an Eldar Oberon named Hexagon and they used them to fight against the Dar Mae Kae who were invading the galaxy about eight thousand years ago. The Zioronians had been fighting the Pandemonium, and other enemies as well, like the Humdrid, the vampire-like Bursar and their allies the Ragdelon Matriarchy. In more recent years they had come to Sol and became members of the protective blockade. But how that happened is another story, for another time. For now, the Zioronians were Earth's greatest human ally, and their power suits were incredibly useful.

As Kit had the final connections plugged in and he slid the helmet on and had the neck sealed, he was thinking about his Tuatha De Danann mother and his friends the Zioronians and how so many people of the Earth depended on so few to keep them safe from a very numerous and powerful enemy. Now there was this stasis field, a present left behind by some Nephalim or Pandemonium warlord from before the Flood, capable of causing so much destruction. What omen was this? What future would this bring? Kit was determined to find out.

While Rainbow helped Kit suit up, Surreya had lowered the back ramp. Normally this would be a stupid thing to do, being underwater, but there was a force curtain keeping the water out. Floodlights were switched on and looking out into the water, Kit and Rainbow could see the muddy wall of the Kermadec trench. Newton left his seat in the front and stepped up to the force curtain and 'bounced' his finger on the surface tension. Kit stepped forward to meet him. Newton tapped on the helmet, then pointed to the ear mike he wore.

"Better power up." he said, "Ready to go? Look-ee down there."

Kit spoke sub-vocally, "Suit computer, power up."

A feminine voice spoke in his ears, "Suit powering up."

Suddenly, silver mercury flowed over Kit's body, the force-skin enclosing him. Kit could hear the breather in his helmet working. The visual display on his helmet visor switched on and data began to scroll down.

"Display off for now." Kit said, and he stepped close to the force curtain to see where a grinning Newton was pointing. Moving in the powered up suit felt really good, natural. There was no sensation of weight at all. Looking down where the spotlights were pointing behind the scorpion, there in the mud, it looked impossible, but there were girders down there, really big human made structures, deep on the bottom of the ocean!

"Tarmal here Kit." said a voice in the helmet, "Time to go."

"Time to go." Kit exhaled, "Alright, then. Tarmal, have you got the feed to my viewer?"

"Coming through well." Kit was looking at Newton who was grinning like an idiot and waving at Tarmal who was watching on his ship, the Arrow.

"Stop wasting time you two!" Kit began laughing, "The water looks good, time for a swim!"

"God bless then." Newton shook Kit's hand. Kit turned and Rainbow looked into his faceplate and she nodded. Surreya grinned at him too.

"We will be watching," Tarmal said.

"And us too." Newton held up his lap top. The helmet camera was already sending the data.

"I promise," Kit said, "there will be quite a show!"

Kit turned and stepped onto the flying scooter. The boot clamps automatically sealed.

"Just give it a little test." Rainbow said.

Kit subvocalised and the visual display in his helmet lit up again. Kit could 'feel' the suit. His nervous system 'asked' the scooter to rise a few centimetres and it did. He bumped his head, and then, without hesitation, Kit launched himself out the back hatch through the force curtain and into the water beyond. Helmet lamps automatically illuminated the dark and also used other visual spectrums as well, including temperature and ultra-violet. His helmet told him that the temperature was below freezing outside. The water pressure was terrifying, but the suit protected Kit. The scooter propelled Kit easily through the water and he was soon down alongside the structure he'd seen before under the mud. Kit was scanning as he reached out to touch. Metal. Metal clad with stone. He reached out and pushed through a layer of clay and could feel the hard structure underneath. It was real. But Kit's scanners told him something else – the stasis field – was there, still further under the mud.

"Ok." Kit said, "You guys getting this? I'm about to do some excavating. What we have is a superstructure, what looks like the remains of a building. There's not much left, but the stasis bubble is there and I guess that what's inside is fully preserved. Here goes."

Kit fired up the force beams on his gauntlets, creating cones of force, sucking and expelling mud from in front and sending it down the trench. Kit moved into the cave he made, closer to the sphere of energy his scanner told him was ahead.

"Hate to say this." Tarmal's voice said, "We have bandits moving down the trench. Pylons have been sent to intercept. Gotta hurry my friend."

"Hurrying." Kit replied.

A few minutes later, a huge lump of mud fell away and Kit could see the stasis field. Like his suit, it had the appearance of mercury, like a mirror.

"I'm reading the resonation frequency." Kit said, "I'll match frequencies, and just like stepping through a force curtain, I should be able to just walk in. It's likely that we'll lose com so I'm recording everything now."

Kit subvocalised more instructions to his suit computer and watched as the frequencies changed. Suddenly the sphere became transparent, then opaque, then transparent again.

"Whoa!" Kit could see what looked like a room inside the now clear sphere. There was a door further in, "You see anything?"

There was no reply, "Com is down", the suit computer informed.

Kit stepped through the field into the sphere. He could see a faint glowing around him.

"I've got leakage." Kit recorded, "I'm still resonating and energy is leaching into the stasis field around me. Damn it! I'm accelerating the decay! I can't stay long ah – no more than a few minutes. Got to investigate though."

Kit moved forward. It looked just like a regular room. There were painted designs on the walls and a woven rug on the floor. The door was hinged on both sides and opened in two parts as Kit stepped through. There was light coming from somewhere. To the left Kit could see a window and surprisingly there was a view to a lost world outside. There was sunlight and even some clouds. Kit shook his head in amazement. He tried to look more closely, but the wall stopped him. In the second room, Kit looked across and found some steps descending deeper into the sphere. Going down, Kit found his first person, a dead body. Killed violently with a projectile weapon of some kind. It was a man, wearing a uniform that looked strangely familiar along with weapons and webbing belts. He was a large man, with long almost blue-black hair. Kit couldn't decide the people group. The closest he looked was native American, but there were some major differences. Kit recorded everything and moved on. More bodies. Then Kit found some 'live ones'. There were some people, four men behind a barrier and another entering the room right in the middle of a gun battle! There were some women nearby trying not to get shot. Kit quickly divided the group into defenders and attackers. There were other attackers in another corridor. The defenders wore simple woven cloths, covering their chests and genitals. Their weapons were simpler and not as complex as those of the attackers. If things went well, they would have to be knocked out. It could be done. Deeper into the sphere. There was a large room with lots of corridors and other rooms branching off it. Kit found the other side of the sphere. But in this large room was a machine of quite advanced technology. People were standing around it working with power cables on one side and internal mechanisms on the other. A woman was operating some controls using an unusual looking keypad. Almost all the people in the room were human. The 'defenders' were red haired and fair and smaller in stature than the 'attackers'. But there were also a couple of non-humans, a Chimp-like Chipperwaal Humanimal and another Humanimal, a Pigrian. They were Shile, a race that specialised in manipulating life, but what they were doing here, Kit had no idea.

Kit had a look at the device. It was certainly the field generator. But something was wrong. The people looked like they were trying to stop something, at least that was Kit's impression. He sighed. There was no time left. The stasis bubble had to be removed. Kit moved quickly going back the way he'd come using his scooter. He went out into the trench again and immediately sent a distress alert!

"Arrow - got to tractor this thing out of here right now! The field is decaying quickly! There are living people in here! What is the status?"

"Daedalus is engaging enemy forces and so are our fighters." Tarmal replied, "Your lift has had to get out already. Get back inside the sphere, it's safer there. We will get you out."

Kit did as ordered. He went back inside and went back to the gun battle room. There was a sudden physical vibration and it was obvious that the stasis field had collapsed. Kit had no time to think, he just acted. The Arrow had put a tractor field around the sphere before it collapsed, but the collapse was inevitable. Everything around Kit resonated and people were moving, faster and faster. This gave Kit around five seconds where he was faster than them. So Kit, very quickly began to stun anyone with a weapon, both sides of the battle, and he released a sleep gas as well. It was quick and relatively painless. In seconds, Kit had nearly everyone unconscious. Stunning surprised stragglers and those hiding down rooms or in corridors took a bit longer, but thankfully there were no fatalities. Then Kit got to sit and wait until it was all over.

Chapter Fourteen

Catastrophe

Inside the new tractor field with the sleeping antediluvians, Kit really had no idea what was going on. But he did scan through com traffic, which was now available to him. There were all kinds of messages being sent, but almost all the voices were tinged with panic!

What is going on? Kit wondered. It wasn't just a battle. A battle would come over a lot more easily. A battle was something normal, something expected. There was battle com chatter from Daedalus. Battle chatter from fighters and tactical code sounded normal. There was an air battle going on over where the Dwee and the other ships were anchored. The battle had begun when one of the ships, the one that was obviously a cloaked Nephalim vehicle, dropped its ship hull and propelled itself up into the air. Two bandit e.d.v (that is Electro-Dynamic Vehicle) snub fighters broke away as well. Kit imagined what that moment would have been like for those on the other ships. While the crew and other Petrad or Order personnel on the Dwee were not surprised by the advanced technology of their adversary, the people on the other research ships and the U.S. carrier nearby were not so casual about it. At the same time the Dwee launched all her scorpions to intercept. But the most shocking sight was the decloaking Daedalus. Of course the Daedalus was absolutely huge, a massive rectangular prism with a slot underneath which was actually the docking bay for thousands of smaller vehicles, including destroyers, carriers, troop drop ships and fighters. The Daedalus was perhaps ten kilometres wide and over fifty kilometres long. The top deck was domed over with a clear canopy and enclosed an artificial environment and lower decks included space for a whole city. The top of the Daedalus couldn't even be seen because clouds obscured it, but hundreds of fighter vehicles were dropping out the bottom and they swarmed out to fill the sky. The Nephalim ship and its snub fighters ceased to exist about a second later. But that ship wasn't the problem, it was the battle fleet dropping out of orbit that was.

It was about then that the Arrow put its tractor field around the stasis bubble deep in the Kermadec trench, and then a few seconds later, the stasis field disintegrated. It was as though the whole ocean just jumped. A powerful gravitational shock wave pulsed out and then the ocean dropped, suddenly and violently. The electro-dynamic fields of all the e.d.v's flying in the area were briefly disrupted and for about two seconds everything lurched in the sickening drop. Static electricity, like bolts of lightning, flashed across Daedalus and all ships, both those in the air and those floating on the ocean were struck by an electro-magnetic pulse.

It only took seconds, but the impact of that moment was huge. While the e.d.v 's, including the Daedalus, all had automated back-up systems that stopped them from dropping into the ocean, a lot of their other systems, including weapons and tactical computers were fried by the e.m.p. The Daedalus' main battle shields were down when missiles, fired by the approaching unknown enemy, before they were hit by the e.m.p, struck the Daedalus, causing terrible damage! The big ship staggered like a man king hit upon his head and the missiles tore gaping holes in the side of the hull. It seemed impossible but the dreadnaught was crippled, fire ripped into the interior of the ship, people died, and nothing worked – none of the ships or rescue systems functioned due to the e.m.p.

Inside the sphere, Kit could hear the panic as s.o.s. was transmitted from hundreds of sources. It was chaos. Switching to the Zioronian com band wasn't much better. There was a lot of static, probably because they were so close to the epicentre of the pulse, but Arrow was transmitting a rescue code. So, they were still functioning.

"Kit, if you can hear me," it was the voice of Clarrissa Maris, "We are aboard Arrow and safe. The sphere is also aboard in the hanger bay and has been encased in impact foam. It's not pretty but it works. We'll get you out soon, but right now we are incredibly busy. The Arrow and her pylons are the only e.d.v's actually operational in a thousand k radius thanks to the more advanced Zioronian tech. The Dwee's scorpions are still flying too, using conventional rotors, but they are currently evacuating the Dwee and the other ships in the area. Kit, we are in big trouble. When the stasis sphere went off, Arrow's scanners detected dozens of other spheres, small ones, but with high energy readings. I think that the big sphere was meant to trigger the smaller ones. Anyway, we have only a few minutes before they re-resonate and there will be more gravitational and electro-magnetic pulses. We can't stay here. Already we are picking up bad seismic readings. There's about to be a big quake, very big, very soon... oh my God!"

The transmission was interrupted with static. No doubt this time, Kit actually felt the shock waves, one, two, three, four and five! He ran to the wall of the sphere and could see the electrical shine of the tractor field and through the field, he could see the light grey of the impact foam forming a support containing the structure. Kit desperately wanted someone to turn that tractor field off, but if that happened the impact foam would collapse under the weight of the enclosed building remains. There was no coming out yet.

Arrow surfaced and lifted up into the sky. Dark and ominous clouds were gathering and the wind was like a gale. The Daedalus was still flying, but was listing badly to one side. Smoke was pouring out of one side where the missiles had struck. But it wasn't the burning dreadnaught making the clouds so black, it was a huge storm cell forming over the area. Then there was lightning, huge bolts beginning to strike Daedalus. The thunder exploded. It began to rain.

Down on the sea, the dozen or so ships were floating without power, their electrical systems burned out by the e.m.p's. The Petrad team on Dwee stood on the ship's mid-deck watching the storm brewing and also watched as Arrow moved closer. The ship itself did indeed resemble a huge arrow. The front was shaped like an arrow head, with a long shaft behind to the pylon docking bays along the shaft of the ship and the three main drive pods at the back. Arrow skimmed close to the water, which was now churning, not just from the wind, but it was literally boiling! The sea suddenly jumped again, tossing everyone on deck of the Dwee over. The sound was like a loud 'WUMP!!!' Catastrophic subterranean and submarine quakes and eruptions followed, with more loud noises. The nose of the Arrow hovered over the Dwee, casting a huge shadow. The Arrow was not as big as the Daedalus, but it was still a massive ship. In the forward section there were twenty decks, a large docking bay for the bigger shuttles and battle platforms carried by the Zioronian warship. The Arrow was too large to land on the Dwee, but from under the nose of the ship, there was lowered the big cargo lift, down onto the Dwee's deck. Zioronian troopers leaped down onto the Dwee and began to herd the ship's crew and Petrad team aboard the cargo lift, pushing them into the passenger tube and up into Arrow itself.. It took a few minutes, and thankfully there were no loud WUMPs of the sea to knock people over. Dwee was left abandoned in the boiling ocean. Nearby the scorpion VTOLs were picking up people, as many as they could carry, from the decks of other research ships. Arrow then headed towards the U.S. aircraft carrier.

Since the devastating e.m.p's, the carrier, like the other ships, was also dead in the water. Also, none of the aircraft or other craft were working. There was no getting off, and the ocean was boiling. Arrow flew over the main deck. Watching on the monitors from Arrow's bridge, Tarmal could see sailors and marines on the flight deck, some of them with small arms. Over the noise of the storm, which was too loud for loud-hailer, the Zioronians standing on the cargo lift deck resorted to flashing code at the ships bridge, hoping they got the message. As before, Arrow got as close to the tossing deck as possible, lowered and then opened the cargo lift ramp. Power suited Zioronian troopers jumped down led by the Arrow's second, Fay, who was also Tarmal's wife. On the flight deck there were confused sailors everywhere.

"GET ME SOMEONE IN CHARGE!" Fay's enhanced voice boomed at them. Some were pointing weapons but seemed frightened and didn't know what to do. "WE ARE FRIENDS!!"

A group of men pushed their way forward, led by a man who had obvious authority.

"Chief engineer Barker here!" the warrant officer yelled, "Who the hell are you and are you here to help us?"

"Yes! We are here to help evacuate your ship!" Fay had switched off her speakers and was resorting to yelling too, "We are friends of the PETRA organisation, no time to elaborate, get your people aboard Arrow! This whole area is about to literally erupt!!!"

Barker only thought about it briefly then grabbed a nearby crewman.

"Tell the Captain we have to abandon ship, it's ok, GO!"

Sailors were only told once, they jumped up onto the ramp and into the lift tube as quickly as possible. There were over three thousand of them that somehow had to be crammed aboard! The ship's captain was the last to enter the lift up into the Arrow after all his crew were aboard, then the Arrow drew away, calling all her smaller craft home to their docking bays. All those who had been rescued from the ships were taken up to the spacious recreation deck in the Arrow and they sat down on the playing fields and recreation malls in the heart of the ship, served by the Zioronian crew members.

On the bridge, Tarmal and his command crew were joined by Fay, who was still wearing her battle suit. Tarmal stood under the huge tactical 'tank' in the middle of the bridge, a holographic sphere of the area.

"Helm," he ordered, "take us up close to the Daedalus. Communications, we need to reopen the com channels with Daedalus. Try some low band frequencies. Scanner team, we need resolution in the tank. I want to see what is happening."

"The temperature is rising outside." The scanner officer reported, "We are picking up significant volcanic activity."

Clarrissa Rainbow, who was also standing under the tactical tank looked up at it with keen interest, then she gasped with shock. A Zioronian bridge officer stood next to Rainbow, and compared notes using a digital notepad.

"We really need to get away from here." Clarrissa said.

"Daedalus reports." a communications officer announced.

"James here." a scratchy voice could just be heard over the com.

"We must get out of here John!" Tarmal said anxiously.

"We know." the Daedalus captain replied, "This whole area is about to literally explode, it's a cataclysm! We're inertialess but have no engines, you are going to have to tow us Arrow."

"Where to!" Tarmal replied.

"Closest equipped port is Petra 18, Tasmania."

"Ok....." Tarmal hesitated, "You know we won't be cloaked. All of Tasmania will see us!"

"We don't have a choice! The ocean is boiling!!!"

"Good point."

"Also," captain John James added, "can your drop ships collect the bogies which hit us? We can't leave them floating around and I don't think we should just take them out."

"We are already tractoring you and I'll send my people out. We'll take the bad guys into you and your security team can have them. What's the damage?"

"Thanks Tarmal," Captain James said, "we have the fires under control. Casualties have been high, just over three hundred dead and around two thousand wounded. A lot of friends are gone, but we are surprisingly unscathed. We had no shields. If they had used nukes we wouldn't exist! I wonder why the enemy didn't."

"I think I know." Clarrissa interrupted, "We're towing the bogies in right now. Radiation levels reveal they have nukes, and these guys are Humdrid."

"There's an Aquani saying," Tarmal grimaced, "The Humdrid aren't bad people, they just have a bad profession."

"They're a race of pirates, cut-throats and mercenaries," Fay added, "born into their life."

"Fanatics." Tarmal nodded, "If they could have used their nukes, they would have. When your security lock them up, be careful John. Tell your people to take no chances. The Humdrid are fearless killers."

"Another headache we don't need." Captain James replied, "But we need the intelligence. For now we will lock them down and get the Daedalus repaired and see what has just happened."

And what had happened? Clarrissa Rainbow was watching the holo-tank aboard Arrow and her face became more and more concerned. Arrow towed the Daedalus west over New Zealand and then across the Tasman Sea. By that time, the ships which had been left behind had literally melted and sunk into the ocean, but now the ocean itself was spewing gouts of lava high into the sky. Sea quakes kept causing the ocean to jump, but most horrifying of all, the sea floor had opened its mouth and was rising up to meet the sky!

Clarrissa got the communications deck crew busy sending out disaster warnings to all the earthquake warning centres around the Pacific rim and especially to her contacts in New Zealand. She was almost frantic, and became even more horrified as the replies came back.

"Tarmal," she addressed the Zioronian captain, "we are going to have to call a full council of Petra and the Order - the world is falling apart!"

"What?!"

"I'm getting reports of quakes all around the ring of fire," she was breathless, "not just the Kermadec Trench, but also New Zealand, Antarctica, Indonesia, China, Japan, California, Hawaii and the Yellowstone Caldera. It is very bad, all the quakes are above magnitude eight. The Kermadec and Yellowstone quakes are immeasurably huge. We are picking up more stasis bubbles, not just in the ground or under the sea, but high in the atmosphere as well! We are talking about a global transformation event."

Tarmal strode under the tank and did some typing on the holographic work pad underneath. A tectonic map appeared showing the Pacific region.

"You can see the secondary stasis bubble locations at the epicentres of the quake regions." Clarrissa pointed, "That is where we just came from, with our stasis bubble, there and that plume of smoke is coming from Wyoming. The ocean floor is rising east of New Zealand, forming a series of islands running south to Antarctica that will be bigger than New Zealand itself. As for the United States, the nation probably won't survive this event."

"These events are NOT natural though." Tarmal growled to himself, "The stasis bubbles seem timed to all collapse together. Whoever created these bubbles wanted this disaster to happen now. Knowing that we are fighting the Nephalim is no advantage if we don't know what they are going to do next."

Tarmal went back over to the communications centre, "Get me Utnapishtim."

The face of Robin Alaquandi Goodfellow of the Tuatha De Danann appeared on the com holo.

"Tarmal." Al frowned, "we've been watching. But there is no general Nephalim attack. If they were going to do it, now would be the best time. All the Petra bases are on alert and we are doing evac and emergency in the danger zones. Our splinters are porting personnel and resources and our whole E.D.V fleet are up. There's nothing going on in the Solar system, it's all quiet. The only exception is that Humdrid attack. I've traced them off world. It looks like they just got lucky, a coincidence. There was only one Nephalim craft, the cloaked one that got vaporised almost immediately, and we now think they were there for the same reason we were, to investigate the sphere."

"So what do we do?"

"Get Daedalus to Petra 18 and we will get the ship repairs done. Then we have to get out and help people - a lot of people need us now."

"Rainbow is asking for a full council."

"It's probably a good idea." Al nodded, "We will be revealing ourselves to the world at last and the Nephalim will try to take advantage of this situation."

"Kit has also found survivors inside the stasis bubble," Tarmal continued, "We have him and the contents in Arrow's hold."

"It all gets funner and funner!" Al grinned, "Mum and I will try to come down to Tasmania. Looks like you will need our help."

Tarmal nodded, "Definitely."

The Daedalus flew over the eastern shore of Tasmania, then over Ben Lomond and the Northern Midlands, towed towards the heart of Tasmania, the Central Highlands of the island. There on a foothill of the Tiers was a town. Designated Petra 18, the village of Hopetown, was an intentional community, the headquarters of a number of Christian community organisations, including a Petrad science team, but it was also more. On its journey across Tasmania, a lot of people got to see the huge ship Daedalus as it headed for the interior of the island, one end of the stricken vessel hovering over Hopetown. The people of the village were already waiting expectantly as the sky over head grew dark under Daedalus' shadow. But just to the south of Hopetown, in the Tiers themselves were two mountain peaks, Batman's Peak and the Tor, both of which looked remarkably like pyramids. Arrow tractored Daedalus to park its forward end right over the Peak. At the top of the peak was a very large square stone which began to rise, revealing a tower, like a massive mechanical arm which reached up and connected to the bottom of Daedalus, forming a docking station. The Arrow hovered nearby, making sure that the procedure went successfully. Further south, from the Great Lake, a freshwater glacial lake above the tiers, there came a number of e.d.v's which were service vehicles. They quickly arrived and flew along the length of the Daedalus, examining the damage from the missile strikes. At the same time, medical and emergency crews came up the docking tower at Batman's Peak. Now that Arrow had finished its job of towing the Daedalus, Tarmal had the pilot fly over Hopetown and then up into the maw of the docking bay, which ran nearly the entire underside length of the dreadnaught. As the Arrow ascended, they could see the starboard blast damage had destroyed a whole section of the docking bays. The fires had been brought under control, but the damage looked horrific nevertheless. Thankfully it was largely docking bay rather than living areas or the more sensitive port side of the big ship that had been struck. Still a lot of people had died, and a lot of special purpose vehicles and equipment lost. Arrow parked at one of the docking bays along the port side of the ship located not far from the engineering and industrial deck and the university and science complex. Between the two important parts of the Daedalus main deck was an open deck space where the Arrow fitted.

Few of Daedalus' service vehicles were working, so Arrow quickly dispatched all her shuttles and drop ships to assist in the repairs, but also to lower the still impact foam encased sphere to the deck below. Some of the science and engineering people had come out onto the deck space but most of the work had to be done by Arrow's crew. The sphere was tractored down to the surface of the deck and engineers from the Arrow, with the help of Daedalus' crew, quickly constructed a supporting frame around it. More impact foam was added and with radio contact restored with Kit Ryan inside, a hatch into the interior attached and opened at last. It didn't look pretty, but this object was the cause of all the trouble in the first place. As Kit looked out through the hatch out at the interior of Daedalus, he was hoping that all the pain was worth it.

The engineers had set it up so that the large forward cargo lift of the Arrow was directly attached to the makeshift gantries bolted up around the encased sphere. It meant that people could come and go easily and that the sphere itself was well protected. Tarmal, Fay, Newton and Rainbow came down the lift as soon as possible and stepped out onto the gantry where Kit was waiting. Security and medical troopers had already gone in to see to the people inside.

"Busy day?" he grinned grimly at them.

"Still not over yet!" Newton commented.

"What's inside?" Rainbow added, "What have you discovered?"

Kit led his fellow 'earthlings' into the sphere, leaving the two Zioronians to follow as quickly as they could. Inside the security people had set up some lights and in the big room where the main fighting had taken place, they had set up a morgue and near the stasis field generator that Kit had discovered earlier the medics were setting up triage for the other survivors. The Zioronian head medic approached the group and he bowed to Tarmal, his captain.

"Tarmal, there are five dead bodies and we have twenty one other survivors all still unconscious from the sedative Captain Ryan gave them. They all seem healthy. There are two humanimals, a Chipperwaal and a Pigrian. What do we do with them now that we have them?"

"Treat it like you would a crime scene, Toran." Tarmal said, "Put the survivors in isolation wards. Full autopsies on the dead and record everything inside the sphere. I'll be sending in some engineering people, probably Fass, once you are finished with the scanning. In particular we want anything that can give us information. Fass will help with any unknown tech you find, especially any e-records or logs. We've done this kind of thing before. You're good at it Toran."

In the meantime, Tarmal was showing the others around. While careful not to disturb the Arrow crew members, Kit was showing Rainbow and Newton the main stasis device in the central room.

"There was a battle going on here when the stasis field was activated." Kit said, "But the question is, who activated the field and why. The woman who was standing here had her finger literally on the switch, here.."

Kit pointed to a button on the generator console, then pointed down the hall through the door.

"Though there was where the shooting was happening. The people in this room would have heard it clearly. In fact, there were some of them preparing to make a last stand. There were some non-combatants hiding in the other room. I had plenty of time to look carefully at this moment frozen in time. The attackers were coming into this building through an entrance that no longer exists further down that way. Only one of their number were killed in the fighting. The other four were defenders. I don't think that the defenders were soldiers. They weren't well equipped nor did they seem well positioned to defend themselves. There was a lot of panic. The attackers on the other hand look to me to be more like real warriors. What really happened here?"

Fay and Tarmal came into the room, followed by a couple of engineers, including Fass, the Arrow's head engineer.

"The stasis generator wasn't on." Fass announced, looking at her personal scanner, "It never was."

"So the female standing by the generator didn't turn on a stasis field," Kit shook his head in puzzlement, "what was she trying to do?"

"Someone else put them into a stasis bubble." Rainbow answered, "My theory is that she was trying to stop them."

"We probably should ask her ourselves when she wakes up." Newton added, "Things are always more complex than our simple theories."

"The stasis field still saved their lives." Rainbow retorted, "They were under attack. Actually, we saved their lives! They were on the bottom of the ocean!!!" Rainbow giggled.

Kit and Newton were grinning, but the Zioronians looked a little puzzled.

"Sorry guys," Rainbow got herself serious again, "been under a lot of stress."

"There will be more stress to come." Tarmal agreed, "Something significant is happening here. We have a lot of work to do. Daedalus needs repairs desperately, and the world's biggest natural disaster in ten thousand years is happening right now."

"And the Nephalim will certainly be on the move as well." Newton added, "They are behind all this somehow, we need to find out how and why."

"For now we will leave Fass here to investigate the ancient technology and Toran and our medical team to take care of our new guests. They will be kept isolated and when they wake up we'll see if we can talk to them. We have good data on ancient languages in the Utnapishtim library." Tarmal explained, "Also, Captain James wants to talk to us, sort out what to do next. His command bridge isn't flying and we need to go and pick him up. We also need new intelligence on the disaster. We will meet in the Arrow's tactical room in ten minutes."

Chapter Fifteen

Aftermath

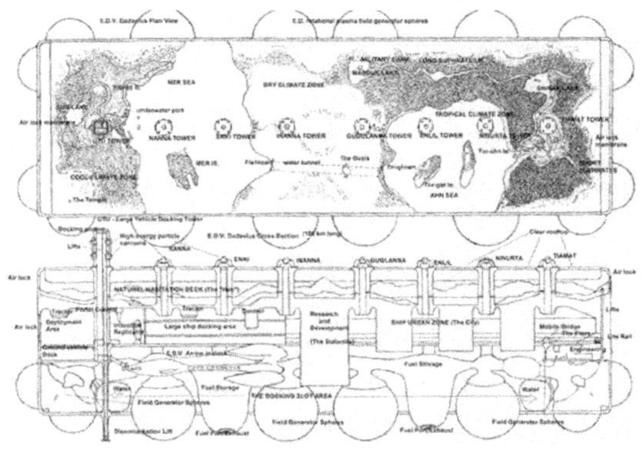

All around the Pacific Rim, the so-called Ring of Fire was burning. Rainbow's warnings sent out via her Petrad networks reached the right people, but there was still almost no time to prepare for what happened next. The whole South Pacific east of New Zealand was in upheaval as the Kermadec trench convulsed in a massive volcanic eruption. The Australian and Pacific plates were being driven together and pushed upwards. Whole sections of the western Pacific plate of New Zealandia were rising to the surface, spilling lava eastwards and forming a new landmass three times the size of New Zealand! The hot, displaced water either evaporated as steam or was propelled as huge walls of water in all directions. The biggest and most destructive tsunamis in recorded history first hit the eastern coast of New Zealand, and then smashed the Pacific island states into non-existence. New Zealand, at the same time, experienced an unparalleled quake and incredibly began to rise as well. Later survivors would describe it as a miracle that anyone could possibly survive at all, but most of New Zealand was above the water level when the tsunami's hit! Smoke and steam rose out of the ocean and blocked out the sun. People at Hopetown, underneath the Daedalus, could see the black clouds spreading across the horizon and the storms approaching. Soon the entire southern hemisphere would be covered in a belt of rain that wouldn't stop for two months.

The Yellowstone Caldera had literally exploded like a nuclear bomb. There had been another large stasis bubble buried deep within the magma hotspot and its resonation set off a chain reaction of movements within the caldera that opened fissures to the surface, releasing pressure, including explosive eruptions of lava and super-hot steam along with ash and a massive pyroclastic cloud. Within moments, everything within sixty miles of the explosion was destroyed and a huge cloud of ash was rising to fill the sky over the north western United States. It was the biggest explosion in sixty-five million years. Millions of Americans were about to die and the United States as a nation would cease to exist.

It seemed as though the world was shaking in its death throws, but emergency teams all over the world were rushing to those danger spots and huge armies of citizen volunteers were to be mobilised. On board the Daedalus, captain John James, was watching the events on holographic windows around this navigation deck. Standing in front of him though was a holographic projection of the Vice-President of the United States, as well as the Governor Generals of Canada and Australia and also the European President and His Royal Highness King William of Great Britain.

"The President is dead." the Vice-President said sadly, "She was flying from the Western United States back to Washington when Air-Force One was hit by the ash cloud and went down in the no-go zone. We attempted to send in a rescue team, but they didn't survive. In fact, nothing much survives in the north-west, and the ash cloud is growing. There are ash falls as far east as the Atlantic sea-board and the Gulf of Mexico. We can't fly anything, all our resources are stretched to their limits or no longer exist. FEMA can't cope. We have millions of people and nowhere to go."

"MR. PRESIDENT." Captain James said firmly, "You do have options. The Petra Alliance does have resources and we have our rescue units ready to be activated. You have, all of you, seen our technology and know what we can do. We can evacuate North America if we have to."

"Where to?" the new President asked.

"We have three main bases, the oldest and biggest is in Britain, Petra One, the Avalon Community. Petra Eighteen is in Australia, the Mu-Lemuria Community. Petra Nine is in the Armenian Republic, the Utnapishtim Community. Using the Daedalus we can open a portal. Most of the refugees can go to Australia and England, but we have a world portal at Utnapishtim. There are other places we can take people, safe places. Then we can work at rebuilding and figuring out what went wrong."

"But isn't the Daedalus damaged from a missile attack?" King William pointed out.

"Yes," James nodded, "but we have only to replace some components damaged by a powerful electro-magnetic pulse that took place in the South Pacific, north east of New Zealand. The missile strike did a lot of damage, but our main systems are able to be restored, and will be operational shortly. All that remains is that I brief our people and we will be able to get to work, with the full cooperation of our respective governments. Petra and our Security Order represent the government of the Seerlie Court and the Eldar nations who have been living here on Earth for a long time. Until now, we have remained a covert presence, helping wherever we can. As you all know, there are some very unfriendly enemies. The Nephalim factions might be behind this present crisis, so you will need us if a conflict escalates. We will also need your respective covert fleets, if it comes to war."

"You are talking about fully revealing our most secret technologies?!" the European President asked, "There has always been a balance of power. Russia, China, the Latin Federation, Japan and even the Islamic League all have been developing electro-dynamic technology."

"We have already been contacted by the Russians and Japanese. They are already being impacted by the disaster in Yellowstone. Japan is suffering from quakes of their own and are already using their own E.D.Vs, so the secret is already out."

At that point, the European President was interrupted by someone outside of the holo-field and he looked very concerned.

"Something is happening!" he apologised, "I have an emergency and will return shortly."

The man's image disappeared and the others looked at each other, bewildered.

At the same time, one of the Daedalus officers entered, "The shuttle from the Arrow is here to take you to the briefing, Sir." she announced.

"Could you ask them to wait," Captain James asked, "This is very important."

The holo-field flicked back on and the European President stepped back into view.

"I cannot stay long." he said, "Right now, over central Europe there have been a series of electro-magnetic pulses. We are using your shielded equipment, and that is all we have left. We have no communications. My advisers think that we may be under attack."

Suddenly, both the holo-images of the European President and the British King winked out.

"What's going on?" the President asked.

"We will find out." Captain James replied, "I'll send some of our people. If there is an attack of some kind in Europe, we will need to act immediately. We still need to concern ourselves with evacuations and rescue operations. Both U.S. and Canadian citizens need to be evacuated to pick up points. The Daedalus will fly into the danger zone and our E.D.Vs will search for survivors. We will need to work together, but we will be able to shift a lot of people to safety."

Both North American leaders agreed. Their images vanished, leaving the Australian Governor-General.

"You are in Australia right now?" she asked, "Tasmania? How long before the repairs are done? What are we to do here?"

"For now we need to prepare for refugees." James replied, "We will teleport them in manageable groups once you have set up camps in appropriate locations. We may also need to mobilise the special units. We can transfer the technology."

"How are we going to feed and house millions of people?"

"We will also take care of that. Our portal generators can also be used to replicate material, food, whatever we need. Your job will be to organise an army of volunteers to welcome the people when they arrive."

"New Zealand is also needing our help."

"We will have to do our best to help them as well." James nodded, "I need to coordinate my people."

"Alright," the Governor-General looked weary, "God's speed John."

"You too Robyn."

The holo-field shut down and Captain James was led out to the waiting shuttle.

High over Europe the storm clouds were building. Literally. Directly below were the fields that one hundred years earlier had been the scene of trench warfare, in the War To End All Wars. The trenches were long gone, replaced by quiet French farms. It was night, but the skies had been clear and there was no report predicting rain. Still, it was like a tornado, the clouds swirling around in a circular movement, lightning and thunder splitting the sky. People living beneath the storm could see strange lights high in the sky, almost as if the air itself was being torn asunder. Survivors of the event would be few, but they all reported the same thing. It was the worst storm they had ever seen, the wind demolished everything and then it rained, sheets of water. But then it got even more horrific. The sky began to vibrate and pulse until the ground too jumped, like an earthquake. Then there was a flickering of light, like a giant camera flash went off. There was no sound nor an explosion as such, but something that felt like an electric shock. Any lights or electric equipment still operating, any car still driving, they all died. The electro-magnetic pulses, over France, Belgium, over the cities of Paris and London killed all communications, all electrical devices, all computer systems. Cities and towns went dark as the powerful storms forming over them suddenly intensified. From Switzerland in the south, cutting right up through the heart of central Europe and up to England, the belts of storms tore the land beneath apart, with wind and torrential rain, sheet lightning and more and more pulses, shaking the ground! The super cells dropped twisters that ripped up everything in their paths. It became a hellish night, but it was to be only the beginning.

Even higher up in the sky, above the layer of dark clouds churning below, a line of hovering aircraft had appeared. They looked like old fashioned zeppelins but much larger and sturdier than those made in the early twentieth century. They were joined together, forming a cluster of ten. To the north and also to the south there were other clustered groups of zeppelins, each within visual distance of one another. The line of airships formed like this all along above the line of storms devastating Europe below. The storms were far more effective, along with the electro-magnetic pulses, than any bombardment could ever be. Now that the stasis bubbles which had contained these new arrivals had evaporated their kinetic and electrical energy, the storms below would soon evaporate as well. Still, the damage they caused was huge. That was all part of the plan. Each airship had four gondolas, below and above and at each side. One airship was larger than the others. It began to signal using a laser light up and down the line. The side gondolas on each airship opened up with roller doors retracting. Perched on the decks were creatures with wings. Armoured crew climbed into saddles on their backs and mounted weapons. Like the reptilian creatures they rode, these warriors were obviously not human. With a cry they launched themselves into the air and then dove through the clouds to the unsuspecting world below.

The tactical room was located in the forward nose of the Arrow, and was in fact two rooms. The main room was basically a large table with a tactical tank projector in the middle. A second room contained the ship's main computer and virtual reality couches for the ships systems operators. The command crews of the Arrow and Daedalus were gathered in the main room and holo-projections of the main Petra community leaders were seated along the big window of the room. Outside could be seen the Daedalus engineering deck and the sphere encased in its frame.

Captain James arrived and was greeted by Tarmal, Fay, Kit, Rainbow and his son Newton. A holo-projection of Alaquandi and Niamah, Kit's mother and Danann half- brother waved from the other side of the table. They were joined by other projections, A'sidhe tribal elders, and a representative from the Vansadagaadian Corridor, a Torgar named Grim. There were greetings all around, but then every-one sat down quickly.

"I call to order a formal sitting of a full assembly of the Petra Alliance." John James began, "It's twenty-eighth of July, twenty eighteen, ah, Saturday. It's Satur-day?"

There were some laughs from around the table, it had been a long day for most.

"We better open with prayer," John continued, "Grim of the Torgar, could you do us the honour?"

"Certainly," the Torgar stood, raising his reptilian arms. He pulled back his hood, revealing that he was a dinosaurian, one of the Kaloni anthropoids. He closed his golden green eyes.

"Great Creator stand with us today, your Spirit in our hearts empowering us to face this threat and bring victory. Reveal to us the truth and enable us to restore peace to this world. Until your Kingdom is restored and all our foes vanquished, we fight for Yeshua, Amen."

Grim sat down and raised his hood again.

"Grim is correct in saying that we need the truth to be revealed." John nodded, "Less than twenty-four hours ago, a powerful stasis field resonated in the south Pacific and now we are seeing other stasis fields in other parts of the world. As these fields resonate they emit extremely intense electro-gravitational waves and electro-magnetic pulses. These pulses have been the cause of volcanic and atmospheric disasters on an unprecedented scale, including the eruption of the Yellowstone caldera. While the south Pacific eruptions are spectacular and have had a major impact upon New Zealand and other Pacific Rim island states and Australia, casualties have been remarkably low. But right now we face a major loss of life in the north western United States, which will require immediate rescue operations. I have already committed the Daedalus and our e.d.v. fleets to help in this rescue. So, we are going to have to have the full cooperation of the Petra Alliance and the Order and be prepared to reveal ourselves, finally. But there is more to this. The stasis bubbles are not a natural phenomenon. We were able to recover the contents of the bubble that resonated in the Kermadec trench. You can see what we have recovered out our forward window. The bubble also contained twenty-one living survivors, who are in a secure military medical ward here in the Arrow. They are, our best guess, from the antediluvian era. We are yet to question our 'guests', but there are some individuals wearing uniforms which are almost identical to German army, circa 1918, yet these individuals are most certainly not Germans. We haven't been able to find out much more, but our best analysis is that these stasis bubbles are part of a planned attack from the ancient past. We are concerned that this might be coordinated with a Nephalim faction or factions in the present. We have in the last ten minutes also lost contact with Europe and Great Britain! A complete loss of communications, more stasis bubbles, this time resonating in the atmosphere. We have no satellite com either. We ARE facing a major threat."

Alaquandi's projection stood up, "I can speak for the cause of this crisis," he said, "We know the source of this threat and have been anticipating some kind of attack for some time. One hundred years ago the Melkizedek Order was dissolved and replaced by the new Order. You are all aware of the events that happened at that time at Utnapishtim. This attack has been anticipated. We just weren't aware of what form that attack would take nor when it would happen. Our enemy is a Nephalim Baal lord named Graud who escaped into the ancient past one hundred years ago. We have been trying to track him down but have been unsuccessful, all our agents sent back in time have not returned. He is using stolen portal technology to create the stasis time bubbles. We must mobilise all our security units, including the reserves immediately as there is an imminent threat of attack. We need to talk with these antediluvians because they may actually be able to give us a better time frame and location for us to counter attack."

"So these *unnatural* disasters are actually a form of attack." Rainbow continued, "This is a planned series of events. We have only been able to intercept one stasis bubble, one timed to resonate before the others, to keep us busy so the others could, ah, do the damage they were meant to. Those stasis bubbles located underground or in the ocean were, I theorise, meant to trigger volcanic or tectonic events as they released all their energy. Of course, a stasis bubble can contain living beings, time travellers, frozen in time until release when the bubble is timed to resonate. Subterranean or submarine bubbles would kill these people, our present guests included, if we had not rescued them."

"They were not meant to survive?" one of the Petra elders asked, "A form of execution perhaps? Prisoners sacrificed to the creation of a weapon?"

"Possibly." Rainbow nodded, "The building itself was made out of metal reinforcing and stone or concrete cladding. The remaining bits we have out there are very heavy, their mass would add to the energy release when the bubble resonated.

Whoever froze those people may have just considered them to be a useful mass to add to the package. But there was also a stasis generator inside the bubble and a battle was taking place when they were frozen, or rather, locked away within the stasis singularity. They were a threat to whoever froze them."

"But the real threat is yet to be seen." Alaquandi interrupted, "Stasis bubbles are essentially devices for time travel, to deliver, not just weapons, but personnel and possibly even armies to our present. What we need to know is, just how much stuff can be delivered? What is our biggest possible threat?"

"All the stasis bubbles we have detected so far have been similar in size to the one we captured. They were all essentially delivering weapons of mass destruction. Some of the other bubbles, especially those triggering the big American eruption, actually contained nuclear devices. But we have just, in the last hour, detected high atmosphere e.m.p's over Europe. The obvious loss of com is a direct result of this. The storms which are now raging over Europe and England are atmospheric phenomena also caused by these stasis bubbles. Our readings are alarming. These bubbles were much larger, and would have delivered a large package."

"What else do we know?" Niamah asked.

"Not much." Tarmal replied, "But I have dispatched a squadron of Pylons to investigate. The Arrow battle group is pretty much the only flight ready fleet we have as e.m.p's have disabled most of our e.d.v's all over the world. We do have a number of Renim based at the various Splinters, but a lot of them are heavily engaged in rescue ops or are having problems with the e.m.p's as well, which screws up their ability to use their chariot harnesses effectively. We will have our pylons at their targets within the next ten minutes. They will report to us directly."

"We have got to get all our e.d.v. fleets flight ready." Captain James added, "The Daedalus is still not ready for full restoration. Nothing works. Only the Arrow's Zioronian technology was able to survive the e.m.p's. So much depends upon our advanced tech getting back on line. We only just got our industrial and engineering replicators working and we are manufacturing replacement components as quickly as we can. One of our clever engineers has reverse engineered Zioronian tech for all our replacements so we are hardened against further electro-magnetic pulse."

"Our enemy," a Petra elder sighed, "seems to have caught us completely off guard."

Chapter Sixteen

War

Sixteen snub fighters and four pylon shuttles crossed the Mediterranean, flew over northern Italy, crossed the Alps and entered southern France. Scanning ahead the shuttle crews could see the storms that had been raging only minutes before were already breaking up. There was still a lot of wind, and some rain, but the worst of it was over. Or so it seemed. There was a lot of interference and all the radio and media channels were down, but the flight leader, aboard one of the shuttles was in clear contact with the tactical room aboard Arrow. Everything was quiet.

"Our initial area scans reveal extensive storm damage." the flight leader reported, "We have no radio traffic at all. We are picking up life signs, but some areas look utterly devastated. There will be a lot of people here needing help. We still have a lot of residual interference from the e.m.p's and it is hard to see what is here in the skies with us, but, yes, we have contacts. A long line of contacts, hundreds of aircraft of some kind. We are heading north to investigate."

In the Arrow tactical room, the scanner details were being displayed in the holo-tank.

It was a pitch black night, but the pylon shuttles and fighters were getting some good scans that made the night appear as day. Despite a blanket of interference, they rapidly approached their targets ahead, the line of airships. Suddenly, without any warning, a number of the airships that were previously forming two clusters, twenty airships, including the much larger one, vanished.

"Numerous contacts have just vanished..." it was all he had time to say.

Then the airships were right upon them. The air group broke up in evasive manoeuvres, but smaller dark forms hit against the shuttles and several of the fighters. There were explosions and the winged forms flashed away. Inside the lead shuttle, the flight leader was dead, along with other members of the crew and the shuttle was falling like a rock. Eight fighters and one shuttle survived the attack and withdrew as quickly as possible.

"We have just been attacked!" The pilot of the surviving shuttle cried in panic, "Enemy contacts rematerialized and smaller winged contacts attached explosives to a large number of our group, heavy losses! They are also firing upon us with large projectile rounds. We are evading."

The scanners would later record both the large airships and hundreds of smaller winged

'biologicals', dematerialising and rematerializing, with the winged creatures constantly trying to close on the remaining e.d.v's.

"Arrow flight group," Tarmal replied, "continue to scan and return fire!"

"They keep popping all over the place!"

"Use quick jump manoeuvres, shake them off!" one of the snub fighter pilots called, "Got one down in flames! They're biologicals with jockeys riding them!"

"Two more snubs down!"

"Flight group!" Tarmal ordered, "Withdraw! Break off! Head to Avalon!"

"Disengaging!"

The Zioronian electro-dynamic vehicles fled as fast as possible. The nearest Petra base was in England, the Avalon splinter. Thankfully the strange enemy didn't follow or continue the attack. At least, that is what the Zioronians thought. Attached to the back of the surviving shuttle was a cable and something alive was pulling itself along. The navigator in the shuttle could see something or a trace of something on his scanner screen, but he did nothing about it because it disappeared almost as soon as he saw it. What he didn't know was that there was something clinging to the hull of his shuttle.

Chapter Seventeen

Counter Attack!

Finally, the repairs to the Daedalus were completed and the big ship pulled away from its dock at Petra 18. The people at Hopetown watched from the ground as Daedalus ascended up into the high atmosphere, then disappear as the ship rose into orbit.

Now flying beside the Daedalus, having left the main dock of the engineering sector of the big ship, the Arrow remained as the main tactical centre for the Petra leadership and the main platform for the Excalibur fleet. The plan was for the Daedalus to begin the rescue operation in America immediately, but the threat of a military invasion of Europe by an unknown enemy couldn't be ignored. While the cargo-ships and many of the shuttles would remain with the rescue operation, the fighters and battle platforms would accompany Arrow. Arrow would also act as the platform for seven of the ten Order space marine units.

In the Arrow's tactical room, the main team leaders were continuing their meeting. As captain of the Arrow, Tarmal would lead the mission. Kit, who was a good pilot, would fly lead wing. Newton and Rainbow would remain in tactical, while Fay, Arrow's second officer, would lead any ground or air to air assault with the marines. Other wing leaders and the war leaders of the Order units were all at the briefing.

"Alright," Tarmal began, "we have a very difficult mission ahead of us. As you already know, our first attempt at investigating the objects that resonated in Europe left us with casualties from a very aggressive attack by a formidable, and we believe, numerous enemy, that although using dirigibles, has teleportation technology. They used teleportation to evade our ships as well as attack at close quarters. Their main tactic was to use biological fliers, which we are designating 'dragons' to close upon our shuttles and pylon fighters and plant high explosives directly on the hulls. They were almost impossible to evade and we had to bug out. Much of Europe has been shut down by the e.m.p's and the destructive storms caused by the resonating stasis bubbles which appeared over central Europe directly above the old Maginot Line. What intelligence we have coming from Europe is that our enemy has already landed troops in Paris, Berlin, and London. Some European military units have tried to resist them, but without armoured vehicles or air support, they are not able to stop them. We have reports of heavy casualties on the ground. Two things are most disturbing. One, our new enemy are apparently being supported by troops and equipment provided by some of the Pandemonium factions, especially in Germany. Two, beginning a short time ago, our Avalon complex in England is presently under attack. Somehow they tracked our ships to the splinter and enemy troops are on the ground."

Tarmal activated the tactical holographic tank. A 3D map of Europe appeared showing the main occupied areas shaded in red, with bright lights showing the locations of the enemy dirigibles and main troop movements were marked with arrows. Standing out was a bright red spot in Shropshire in England.

Tarmal sighed involuntarily, "You can see that we are going to have a big fight ahead of us. Our forces are divided between the rescue effort in America and what is effectively a Nephalim takeover of Europe. But the primary target must be for now to recover our Avalon Splinter Petra complex."

Tarmal used his hands to reach into the map and drew out a 3D view of the English Midlands.

"Here's the area we are heading for." he said, "This time it is occupied territory. The enemy have troops in Shrewsbury and Wroxeter and in the old Roman ruins at Viriconium."

The map showed the region around the English town of Shrewsbury, the Severn flowing south east past the small town of Wroxeter, which was the location of the ancient Roman fortress of Viriconium. Further east there rose a large mountain on the Shropshire plains, the Wrekin.

"As most of you know, the Wrekin is the location of the Avalon Splinter, the old Camelot fortress and the entrance into the underground Avalon complex. We have portal gates in safe houses in Shrewsbury and in the Viriconium ruins. Our fleet ships usually enter the complex via high atmosphere portals where no one can observe. In ancient times there were portal transit zones on the Severn River and around the Wrekin itself, which was often surrounded by water. But these days the fleet enters the complex via an underwater entrance in the Irish Sea."

"How did the enemy get into the complex?" Kit asked.

"We are not sure." Tarmal responded honestly, "It seems that they teleported right inside."

Twelve Splinters had descended to the Earth at the end of the Deluge and became the great mountain strongholds from where the Seelie would protect the world. There were Twelve Splinters - Zion, Sinai, Ararat, Olympus, Asgard, Shangri-La, Kilimanjaro, Mu, Lemuria, Atlantis, Atlas and Avalon. Each Splinter was the location of a portal circle and a large underground complex where many of the Seelie tribes still lived. Kit himself had been born and raised in the Utnapishtim Rath under Mt. Ararat, but he had also spent many years living in Avalon as well. For that reason especially, Kit had a personal reason for liberating the Splinter in England from the enemy.

There were other reasons of course. This enemy had now occupied a Splinter, along with its portal ring. If they could control the portals, they could attack other Raths and even return to the Corridor. But occupying a Rath and keeping it were two different things. The Avalon Rath was the most heavily populated complex and included sections running under Wales and the English Midlands, and a branch beneath Ireland as well. The Seerlie and the Tuatha De Danann ruled this underground realm, collectively called Albion and they would fight to keep it.

The mountain known as the Wrekin, located in Shropshire, England, was only the tip of a very large Splinter of rock that existed deep underground. As the Seelie and Eldar always did with their Splinters, they excavated a large underground complex and built a city around the portal stones. They almost always tapped into the vast reserves of subterranean water, and in this case had carved out a complex of lakes and islands connected by underground rivers. Some of the galleries and cathedrals were enormous. There were two submarine entrances to the Albion Avalon complex, one not far from the mouth of the Severn River and another out in the middle of Cardigan Bay. This second entrance was well hidden, but also large enough for the Daedalus to enter the complex. Only the Mu complex, underneath Tasmania, had a similar entrance, and so, the Daedalus was usually 'parked' either at the Avalon or Mu Raths. These hidden entrances could fit the Daedalus, which was huge, about fifty kilometres long! Huge portals were used to enter. While the enemy were most likely aware that the complex had such entrances, their numbers were too small to effectively guard them. At least that was the hope.

The attack began in the air. The Arrow and her pylon fighter wings began with a direct approach, flying in a close formation. The idea was to crowd out the enemy if they tried to teleport into the formation. The pylons were packed so close that there was no room for the large dirigibles to materialise. If they appeared too close to the formation, combined firepower, it was hoped, would drive them away. Both the pylons and the shuttles had been fitted with particle weapon cannons, and it was hoped that these would give them more fire power against the dragons, when they did materialise and try to engage at close contact, as they did before.

They dropped out of orbit right over Cardigan Bay and then flew in as a group over the Welsh coast. The fleet wasn't cloaked, but that was the idea, to get the enemies' attention. And that wasn't all. On the bridge of the Arrow, Tarmal gave the order. In the Arrow docking bay, down on the tank deck, the head engineer Fass activated a wall of portals. Hundreds of tanks were waiting, both on the tank deck and also in a forward hold, engines running. The tanks themselves were compact vehicles, about the size of a mini-bus, with a main turret at the front and two smaller turrets on the sides. They were essentially hover-craft, but quite capable of operating in all kinds of terrain as well as underwater. Engineer Fass pressed the 'all go' button on her console, and the tanks shot with speed through the portals in front of them. The exit was deep underwater in Cardigan Bay, right at the submarine entrance to the Avalon complex.

Up on the Arrow bridge, Tarmal sent a short message, "Be safe." was all he said.

The fleet was still over Wales when the dragons began their first assault. The big dirigibles stayed hovering over Shropshire, instead initiating a huge volley of missile fire. Counter measures began immediately and the fleet gunners became incredibly busy. Other defences were available to the e.d.v's as well, such as tougher shielding fields and if that failed, venting core reactor plasma, which tended to incinerate anything clinging to the hull quite effectively. There were two cylinders of ships around the Arrow, shuttles and fighters forming two walls of fire power. Before, when the first engagement happened over Europe, the air crews had panicked and died, but this time they were ready and held on grimly as they flew into English airspace.

"We are entering Annwn." Fay announced to the tank crews, "Are we all accounted for? Check by the numbers people!"

The lights on her control board lit up. As tank commander, Fay was co-ordinating the insertion very carefully, using little known submarine courses into the British underworld of Annwn. But eventually they would have to surface and face the music. Somewhere deep under Wales, the first tanks surfaced, making a beach head onto a grassy field, which Fay's maps designated as Gwyn ap Nudd's Fields. Fay had been here before, once, with Tarmal, when they first came to Earth. She looked outside and could see the grass and occasional tree. There even appeared to be sunlight, but Fay knew that was only the natural glow of thermal gases up in the heights of the cave galleries. But there was no time to stop and admire the wild flowers, the objective of Avalon itself was still a long way off, and time was running out. There were courses for the different tank unit commanders to plot in. Three different battle groups would divide. Team one led by Fay would head 'inland' using a dry cave route. Team two would take a risky path, using some of the established roads along the northern bank. They had a good commander named Virey and his job was to head in fast and strike hard, drawing most of the attention of the enemy while the two other groups got into position. The third team, led by an Earthman named Weaver, would remain submersed and head along the waterways.

Over the English town of Shrewsbury there was now a massive air battle taking place. The big air ships guarding the town tried to push into the advancing fleet, but they were soon forced to teleport away. It then became a shooting match between the big ships, which was really difficult as the enemy air ships kept popping back and forth. But it was the dragons which were the biggest threat. Despite all the firepower aimed at them, some of them kept getting through. They were too successful at planting their mines and teleporting away. Eventually it created gaps in the wall of defenders around the Arrow, eventually a couple of dragons got through. They teleported into a gap and then appeared right inside the Arrow's hold! All hell broke loose. The dragons themselves teleported away quickly, with their pilots, but enemy soldiers remained behind carrying some rather big guns, with flame throwers!

There was at first a lot of damage, death and confusion as the unknown attackers rampaged about the docking bay. Tarmal got a report of fighting but little else to go on. The on-board garrison was already on alert and the heavy shields were already up over the bridge and tactical decks. Tarmal knew that he had to let his people do their jobs, he nevertheless opened the bridge weapons locker and armed all the crew, just in case, but they still had to fly the mission.

Down on the forward engineering deck, Grim Torgar and his Gorenge lizard guards could hear the fighting and so leapt down the forward grav lift into clouds of smoke and the chaotic noise of gunfire and screams. Somehow the three dinosauroids stumbled down the tank deck and managed to run into Fass and some deck mechanics huddled behind a girder. There were bodies nearby.

"Report." Grim cried.

"Down there.." Fass pointed with her blaster and fired again, "twelve or more with flame and heavy cal and body armour, big Anakim by their look."

"You're joking?!!" Grim replied, then was forced back as gun fire hailed all around them. They fired back. The lizard guards had missile launchers on their heavy blasters, which they used. There were noises of screams further down the deck, but too much smoke to see anything.

"How far.. the tank lift?" Grim suggested.

"Tried.. Some died." Fass replied, "We need help. Where is security?"

"Who knows ..but I can get us help. Cover me back to the lift."

Fass and her companions nodded, and with the lizard guards they opened fire with everything they had towards where they thought the enemy were. Grim ran fast back along the hull wall of the deck, dodging the return fire, leapt with flame right behind him into the grav lift, then fell out on the engineering deck, rolling to put his burning clothes out. He swore to himself, wincing with pain, but ran forward. From engineering he ran into some of the security troops suiting up in proper battle suits in the suit up area. Grim gave them a quick report of what was going on, then moved on past, leapt up a grav well and headed for the brig.

Down in the docking bay, things were getting worse, much worse. Emergency sirens were wailing and Fass was swearing over and over in frustration. The enemy had set up a mortar and were firing it upwards towards the primary reactors that powered the ship. The docking balcony above was gone. There had been security people up there and now they were dead. There were others wearing battle suits coming down the central lift over the tank lift. Despite their battle armour, the enemy kept blowing them away and some of the enemy had climbed up into the spine of the ship and had access to the transport tube train platform from where they could shoot anyone attempting to come down from above. The enemy armour was good. If they weren't stopped soon, they would destroy the ship!

More suited security troops flew out the forward grav lift, using their hover boots to attack quickly using force needles to strike at the different enemy positions. This should have finished the issue as they were using the most powerful weapons it was possible to use inside the ship. Fass and her companions hunkered down behind their girder and tried not to get in the way of any of the friendly fire. They were up against firepower that was too much for them now. Somehow, the enemy still fired back. Grim's two lizard guards, bravely or stupidly, were pretty well armoured and so they headed out into the smoke, hunting the enemy. The humans behind the girder saw one of them explode from mortar fire and the other disappeared into the fighting. Then they saw the enemy walk right past them! He was big, twice the height of a man, and very broad as well. He ignored Fass and her companions, although it was obvious that he must have seen them. Instead, he turned his large weapon towards the security troops and methodically began to kill them. Once the gruesome job was done, he turned to face those trying to hide behind him. It was the first good look of the enemy that anyone had. His armour was grey and looked smooth like mercury, although there were weapons packs attached to his hips and back. He wore a helm that looked strangely familiar, like something from Earth's history. It was bucket shaped and had a spike on top, the only noticeable adornment the huge soldier wore. There was a power cable, thick and articulated running from his pack to the chunky primary weapon he carried. His face was covered by a breather mask. He looked menacing and unkillable. Fass was wondering why they even bothered shooting at him.

For a moment, the Anak just looked at them, then dismissed them as irrelevant as he walked into the middle of the docking bay deck. There were others of his kind nearby as well. They appeared to be waiting, then there was a 'pop' noise and another dragon teleported onto the deck. More Anakim dropped out of their harnesses to join the others. The pilot and other riders on the dragon weren't Anakim, but a smaller possibly homo species, also heavily armed and armoured. The dragon itself was a modified pterosaur, large enough to carry the heavy load of troops and other ordinance. The creature also wore armour and possibly a shield generator, which is what enabled it to teleport.

Fass originally thought that the enemy was trying to destroy the ship, but apparently not. They were running around and the emergency sirens still blared. Then Fass did something that was definitely stupid, she stepped out and revealed herself.

"Ah... I can help fix things..." she offered and her courage was enough to bring the others out.

The big Anak that hadn't been bothered to kill them, turned to face her.

"Englander?" he asked in what sounded like a German accent.

"I'm an engineer." she responded, "The ship needs to be fixed or we die! Sprecken ze English dumkopf?!"

The Anak obviously understood what dumkopf meant and angrily pointed his gun and sprouted more German, this time including some insults of his own. The other intruders were seeing them too at this point.

"We kaput!!!" Fass yelled back and pointed up at the fires high in the docking bay.

One of the other Anakim, an officer obviously, gave some orders. The Anak pointed his gun again and spoke, his obvious meaning was "do something then because I'm going to kill you if you don't."

Fass and her mechanics led the Anak guard down to the tank lift and the nearby engineers console. There she activated the automated fire control and repair robots. There were some virtual reality seats and the mechanics hooked up to do the work.

"Alright crew," Fass said, feeling strangely calm, "we can fix this, it's manageable."

In the meantime, the other Anakim had headed off to whatever their mission objectives were. They obviously wanted to take the ship, but that wouldn't be easy, despite their formidable firepower and strength. The tank lift also had a personnel shaft that went right up to the bridge. If the enemy could get into the bridge, it would be all over. The Anakim had already begun to climb up.

Suddenly there was noise up high in the docking bay and Fass swore again. One of the repair robots fell to the deck. There was another explosion and Fass and her mechanics pulled off their virtual reality headsets to look. Big somethings dropped down to the deck or hovered in the open docking spaces.

"Take cover!" Fass screamed.

A powerful bolt of an energy weapon struck the Anak guard and he was incinerated.

Hiding in the lift this time, the engineering crew recognized the new arrivals. They were the Humdrid battle-wagons, now free from their captivity! There were about ten Humdrid battle-wagons. They were barrel shaped mechas with domed hoods, three legs and three articulated arms, one of which had a mounted weapon and blade. They also could fly, so now they proceeded to attack the intruders. The Humdrid were notoriously vicious and deadly warriors, mercenaries who fought for whoever paid them the most. They weren't picky about who their clients were, but they were always thorough. The fighting moved down the core of the ship as the Anakim retreated. The dragon in the docking bay was killed quickly and didn't have time to teleport away. The Humdrid landed upon it and used their nutronium blades to stab it to death. Tentacles from their articulated arms also thrashed out and grabbed the pilot, holding him captive and his swearing in German could be heard down at the tank lift. From the other grav lift, a squad of security troops entered the docking bay, accompanied by another Humdrid. One of the suited troopers led the way and met Fass and her crew, pulling off his helm. It was Grim Torgar. The security troopers headed towards the fighting, not so much to fight, but to mop up behind the Humdrid.

"Glad you could make it back and rescue us!" Fass grinned at Grim.

"An honour to be of service!" Grim replied, "Is all well with the ship?"

"Yes." Fass nodded, "We will still need some repairs and we are still in a battle zone."

"Apparently we are doing well there also." Grim reported, "But I need to supervise this battle for now and also find my bodyguards."

"One of them is over there." one of the mechanics said sadly, "The other one could be anywhere."

Grim looked stricken and briefly bowed his head but then he smiled and moved forward with the others, leaving Fass to find a communicator that still worked so she could report to the bridge.

Deep in the Avalon complex, the realms of Annwn and Albion, the three tank battle groups were right on time and still not detected by the enemy.

"Attack group, Fay, report." Tarmal's voice came from the tank communicator, "We have Intel for you."

"Doing good time." Fay reported, "No contacts yet. Signs of some battle. Villages abandoned and evidence of evacuation, but still no friendly contacts either. We are on schedule."

"Heads up Fay." Tarmal continued, "We just repelled boarders and nearly got taken out. Very formidable Anakim and heavily armoured. Regular suit armour and weapons were largely ineffective. Expect very heavy resistance. Change of plans. Use troops only as support for the tanks and focus upon getting to the portal ring. Forget the other objectives, at all costs, get to the portal and open the fifth gate. We will get you the help you need once the gate is opened. We've hired some well-armed mercs which were found relaxing in our brig!"

"The Humdrid???" Fay laughed, "Desperate situations demand desperate measures! Final contact my love, see you when it's over!"

"Protect the troops, come home and don't get shot!"

Fay smiled to herself and immediately contacted her tank commanders with the new plan. They all pulled up their tactical maps and Fay drew in the new courses and orders.

"Above all," Fay told them, "use the tanks as much as possible and protect the troops. When we get to the objective, the first in will open portal five and only then will we have to use troops on the ground. The rest of us ride to protect those troops so they can do their job. All green with that?"

The tank commanders all agreed and that was it. The tank group led by commander Virey in the water immediately surfaced and flew up over an area of trees. They were spotted by dragons flying further down towards Avalon itself, and were able to see the city on its island in the middle of the Annwn Sea. The other two groups, led by Fay and Weaver, broke cover as well and took more direct routes towards the Annwn Sea. Virey's group were already fighting. The two dragons that had spotted them teleported in for a closer look. The tanks fired a hail of plasma and sent the dragons down as charred and smoking ruins. The enemy now knew they were under attack.

In the air over Shropshire, the Arrow and her fleet of ships had regrouped and were heading for the small village of Wroxeter, forcing the big airships guarding the area to back away. Up to this point, the battle had been one of attrition, to see who could last the longest. While the Excalibur fleet casualties were higher, the dragons were nowhere near as numerous, and they were becoming a lot more cautious in their attacks because each time they teleported into the fleet, some of them didn't teleport away. It became a shooting match again, that is until something utterly unexpected happened. Underneath the Arrow the grav lift hatch irised open and small objects began dropping out like stones. Some dragons teleported in to have a closer look and got a nasty surprise. The Humdrid opened fire with their powerful weapons. One dragon got too close and the Humdrid mecha flew over and physically attacked the dragon and its crew, using mechanical arms, legs and bladed weapon to literally tear the dragon apart in mid-air! The Humdrid made a landing softened by electro-grav repulsors in their three feet right in the middle of the old Roman ruins, right in front of the remains of the palace walls. They were so quick that the enemy had no time to stop them. One of the Humdrid mechas opened, surrounded by the covering fire of a ring of protectors and a Humdrid pilot, and Grim Torgar leapt out. The Humdrid was naked, except for her weapons harness and ordinance. Like Grim, her ancestors had come from Earth a very long time ago. While Grim was a dinosaurian, the Humdrid merc was hominoid, small but with long arms now evolved into walking and running appendages, and short legs, now holding her weapon in feet that had become hands. She had a calm, broad, human face, and red hair, tied back to keep it out of the way. Grim himself was wearing a heavy battle suit which was much stronger and he carried a captured Anakim weapon, its power cable rigged into his power pack. Grim quickly found the stone shed behind one of the old walls. The armour less Humdrid used her gun butt to smash open the lock and she went inside.

Meanwhile, dragons had landed nearby and Anakim troops who had been in the village were arriving and began shooting at the Humdrid, who used force shields to deflect the fire. Fleet shuttles landed in fields as well and using their mounted guns, added to the fire. Heavy armoured troopers exited the shuttles using their side hatches, and they pulled large containers from the cargo pods in the forward arms of the shuttle. Suddenly a portal opened, a big one in the middle of the Viriconium ruins! The Humdrid merc ran out of the shed and leapt up into her mecha and pulled the hood down. The mecha raised an arm and gave a 'thumbs up'! At this point, the shuttles took off and circled the area, shooting at anything attacking the ruins, and the Humdrid, heavy suited troopers and their containers all went as quickly as possible through the portal, with Grim leading the way. The portal closed behind them and the shuttles flitted away as quickly as possible, leaving the enemy behind shooting at them in vain.

Avalon Island, home of the Seerlie Court, capital city of the A'sidhe and the realm of Annwn, was occupied by a deadly enemy. Scores of dragons either flew or were perched around the great city. The streets were swarming with the armies of the Pandemonium. Anakim shock troopers, accompanied by hominid goblins were the battle crews of the dragons, but the real horror were the Gorenge warriors waiting within the city. The Gorenge were reptilian relatives of the Torgar. These lizard warriors, though, served evil and were heavily armoured and armed with deadly weapons. Their armour and body shields were heavy power suits, but the Gorenge could still use their slashing toe and arm claws, as well as their teeth. They carried heavy blasters similar to those carried by the Anakim, but equipped with long razor sharp bayonets. Their tails and snouts were longer and more animal-like than the Torgar lizard warriors, and these Gorenge were larger as well. Also unlike the Torgar warrior caste, these Gorenge were genetically unmodified and were without anthropoid or human-like traits, but were true velociraptors. What made them dangerous though was that they were Pandemonium, in other words they were a Nephalim race, possessed by evil spirits, whose minds were very intelligent indeed. This data was being displayed on Fay's tactical computer and she sent the data to the other tanks via their intranet connection. All the different tank battle groups were in position. The final assault on Avalon would have to be very direct because they would have to cross the water in full view of the enemy. And all the enemy had retreated and were waiting for them there because the moment the tanks took out the first two dragons, the others withdrew to the safety of the island.

"Preliminary scans tell us that there are Human and A'sidhe hostages in the city." Fay told her people, "But the numbers are small. It seems that most of the people managed to avoid capture or they are somewhere off the island. These hostages may be killed if we attack, but we have little choice. We must retake Avalon. We all know what to do - by the numbers people and may the Great Spirit protect us!"

Three hundred hover tanks moved out onto the Annwn Sea and quickly accelerated to attack speed, coming in from three sides. Almost immediately enemy weapons mounted in the city began to fire at them. But the tanks were very heavily shielded and the plasma bolts just bounced off. A number of dragons flew up and then teleported to points just over some of the tanks, dropping large payloads. The explosions were huge and some tanks were taken out violently. But the shields were good and others fired back, and dragons crashed and burned as well! Shields and heavy cannon fire kept the dragons back and the tanks moved forward relentlessly toward the island. It seemed like an eternity to cross those small stretches of water, but it was less than five minutes. There were casualties, but that was to be expected. As they hit the island, it was a completely different situation. Anakim shock troopers were entrenched all along the shoreline and their weapons fire was far more effective up close. The first wave of tanks lost heavy casualties. Even Fay's tank copped some damage as the tank next to hers exploded! Her gunner was injured, forcing Fay to do some quick first aid and then take the gunners place. But everyone kept their cool and Fay fired their own heavy weapons back. There was no time to be tidy, so the tanks just flew over the Anakim entrenchments and moved on.

The enemy followed, some were picked up by dragons, but the tanks were faster. The city walls were just traditional architecture and no obstacle for the tanks weapons. The walls were smashed aside and the tanks were in the city. Enemy troops tried to attack, but they just couldn't make that much of an impact. The large guns of the enemy were still a big problem, but it was easy to hide in the streets of the city or even drive right through buildings, using them as cover. Ahead was the biggest, most dangerous ground to cross before getting to the portal ring, the city's space port. The area was a large open expanse of ground with some maintenance buildings, forming a ring around the portal ring itself. This was how the Excalibur fleet ships were berthed so when it was time to fly out they could open the appropriate portals quickly to the surface world. The centre of the city itself was up on the nearby hill, and when it became apparent that the city itself wasn't the target of the attack, the enemy did something utterly unexpected. At first it looked as though they were withdrawing to defend the portal ring, which was quite indestructible, then there was a huge explosion, or rather a series of many explosions all over the air field!

Fay swore under her breath, they were blowing up the fleet ships on the ground! Perhaps if they had people who had known how to fly the Order e.d.v's the enemy might have used them, but this was devastating enough!

"Plough through!!!" Fay yelled into her com, "We must get to the portal gate!"

The tanks entered the flames. There was no way of seeing where they were going. Alarms were soon bleeping inside all the tanks as the external temperatures rose. Some tanks detonated as they hit the flaming hulls of ships that got in their way. The reactors of the ships used electro-magnetic containment fields to hold the nuclear plasmid that powered each ship. It was as hot as the heart of a star in the middle of the flames.

"Fire ahead!" Fay ordered, "Destroy what's left of those ships or none of us will get through!"

The cannons fired into the flames, creating an inferno of exploding metal and earth before them, the temperatures increased, but a door was opened before them. Seconds later just over one hundred tanks ejected out of the flames and confronted the Pandemonium defenders barricaded within the ring of portal stones. There wasn't a lot of room around the ring, which like all the splinter rings, looked remarkably like the ring of stones at Stonehenge. The Pandemonium had taken the risk of blowing up the ships, hoping to stop the attack using blunt force, but now they were trapped within a ring of flames with the tanks.

Yelping with war cries, the tank crews fired at the Pandemonium barricades. Inside her tank, Fay, who was now driving, had to be very careful. They were forced to circle around the ring, firing their side cannons. Some of the others made a pass at portal stone five, trying to pull up, but the moment they opened their hatches, the enemy moved in and killed anything that tried to approach. Piles of tanks and bodies soon formed on the spot. It was also incredibly hot still as the wall of fire around them still burned. They were very quickly running out of time. More tanks were taken out as the enemy put up heavy resistance.

Fay called to her wounded driver, sitting in her command chair, "What are the numbers?"

"They will take us all out if we don't do something soon!" he croaked, "Most of us are about to break down! Shields will fail, we are being hit too hard! Ten minutes max!"

Looking back at the small team of soldiers in the back of the tank, Fay hoped they would live through what she wanted to do next. She pulled her own visor down over her eyes and powered up her personal armour. Everyone else did the same.

"Virey!? Weaver? You guys alive?" Fay called into the com.

"Only just!" Virey replied, "But ready!"

"We're struggling!" Weaver's com was full of static, "Engines about to shut down!"

"Ok, Virey, do what I do!" Fay yelled.

Fay turned the tank and ran straight at the line of trilithon stones before her. There was a dead tank in the way, but as she hit it, she accelerated and pushed the power boosters forward to full. Her tank bounced off the wreckage of the other, hovered over the top into the air, over the top of the ring of stones before her! She came down hard and Virey's tank dropped next to her only seconds later! Their cannon fired all around them as they popped the hatches using their explosive bolts. Fay dropped out the side and the others out the back, shooting as they went. The heat hit them like a hammer and then the enemy, who recovered from the shock of the attack remarkably quickly. Several other tanks began to drop in on top of the enemy, and it was these secondary attacks that saved their lives from the heavy blasters of the enemy. Fay was pinned down under the wreckage of her tank as it exploded, killing her gunner who was still inside. But she saw Virey and a few others reach portal stone five, narrowly dodging blaster fire and saved by the smoking tanks. The portal opened right in front of the altar stone in the middle of the ring, literally right next to an enemy gun nest. The Humdrid burst through like a swarm of scuttling spiders, tentacles and blades flashing, cutting the enemy down before them! Fay watched them go to work. In a few short minutes they killed every enemy within the ring of fire, efficiently and without fuss. There was little need for a lot of gun fire, the Humdrid tore their enemy's apart, limb from limb! In the middle of the fighting, Fay spotted Grim Torgar fighting alongside the Humdrid. He fought gracefully, firing single well aimed blaster shots that hit his targets each time. He remained in the ring as the Humdrid moved out to finish off the enemy. Other heavy armoured troops came through the portal behind him, this time carrying large crates with them. The portal closed behind them. Fay threw the wreckage of her tank off her and stepped forward. Virey and his companions had opened the portal, but they had also been killed in the seconds afterwards. There were a lot of dead bodies all over the place.

"Battle Commander Fay of the Aquani." Grim addressed her, "I see you were successful."

"What have you got for us Grim?" she asked.

"Heavy suit shielding and heavy blasters for the troops." Grim pointed to the crates, "We also have hover boots. The Humdrid are heavily armed as you can see and I have about ten heavy troopers here as well."

The fighting within the circle of stones and wall of burning ships had stopped. The fire itself, meant to destroy them, actually gave them some space to stop and prepare for the next stage of the battle. Weaver, his crew and troops had survived and picked their way over the wreckage of fallen tanks. Others were with them from other tanks which had broken down. Fay climbed up into Virey's old tank, which was miraculously still operational. She climbed into his command chair and checked the intranet data.

"We have fifty-six operational tanks, but only fifty of them will last to be any useful to us." Fay reported, "We have two hundred and twelve troopers and we can scratch up enough crew for our fifty tanks, plus a few extra. There are a lot of wounded and dead."

"I expected more survivors." Grim said sadly, "Alright, we must still work quickly, we have still got another battle ahead of us. The sixteen damaged tanks stay here with the wounded and as soon as we take the surface we will open another portal and evac them and send more reinforcements. But we need to get the others re-equipped. Weaver here can lead the tanks and have extra power packs and weapons, which will go to troopers riding shotgun on the tanks. You will lead the rest of us and we will fight on the ground. This seems good to you?"

"Let's do it!" Fay said.

Up above the ground in Shropshire, the air battle continued. The dragons were still flying and teleporting around, taking pot shots when they could, but preferring to hide behind the protection of the dirigibles. It was a big mistake. Arrow began to fire her primary weapon.

From his pylon fighter, Kit watched as the powerful particle cannon under the Arrows nose turned on the airships. Before, when the enemy were a cloud of attacking dragons and there were so many Excalibur fleet ships forced to fight them, the big gun was too dangerous to fire, and would have been too easy for the enemy to disable. Kit kept his position and kept firing at the dragons as before, and he kept moving. There was no dog fighting, that's not the way modern air warfare worked. The weapons were light fast or nearly so. Shields and pure luck was all that stopped one getting killed, or in the case of the dragons, the ability to literally leap out of the way and attack their enemy before they could lock onto the target. Now they were reluctant, now they hesitated and their numbers were too low. The particle cannon turned and fired six times in a matter of a couple of seconds. The enemy airships disintegrated explosively! The dragons, all as one, teleported away.

"Keep your eyes open!" Kit communicated to his wing, "They might just be hiding, keep alert! Begin mop up fire, support the ground troops."

Enemy soldiers on the ground suddenly found themselves being fired at. Any who were out in the open were killed almost immediately. The particle cannon took out groups and the shuttles and pylons used their computer targeting systems to scan and then shoot identified enemies where they stood. The high energy weapons simply vaporised whatever they hit. The Arrow began to open portals and land troops, at Viriconium, Wroxeter, in Shrewsbury and on the Wrekin, anywhere the enemy had troops of their own. This time the Excalibur troopers were much better equipped and armoured. They were using hover boots or sleds which looked a lot like thick ski boards. They hovered into battle, using their big weapons to take out the fleeing enemy. Not all the enemy fled though, and some stood to fight. The stabilisers on the boots were retractable, and the Order troops could walk as well as fly. Close combat was inevitable, including bayonet fighting (necessary in the medieval streets of Shrewsbury), but the main goals were to secure portal locations into Annwn. Both ground and air portals were opened once the portal stones were found.

The fires in the air field around the portal ring of Avalon were still burning, but not as brightly as before when the relief force came through newly opened portals. Ground troops wearing heavy armour and carrying portable hand cannons and plasma weapons came through. The Arrow's two drop ships came through portals opened over the Wrekin. They were large disc shaped vehicles with powerful cannons. They carried six more tanks in their undercarriages as well as troops, but their greatest usefulness were their big guns.

Fay had led her re-equipped tank force to attack the city. Avalon was crawling with the Pandemonium forces. There were a few of the dragons remaining, who were literally breathing fire, but the real enemy were the Gorenge raptors who were waiting among the buildings of the city. At the heart of the city was the main plaza where the prisoners were being kept, apparently still alive. Recovering the prisoners and destroying the enemy was the next objective.

But to have an objective and then have to fight to achieve it wasn't going to be easy in this case. Fay's tanks, accompanied by the now better equipped troops came under attack almost immediately and relentlessly by Anakim from behind and the Gorenge from the front. The Anakim carried weapons, or used cannons mounted upon the shoulders of dragons that could crack tanks open and vaporise troopers. The Gorenge were well armed and armoured, but were skirmishers, preferring to fight up close and personal. So Fay ordered Weaver's tanks and the troops into the protective cover of the city's buildings. Fighting with advanced Eldar and Zioronian weapons was only really possible because of shield technology. Fay left her tank in the hands of Weaver and the tank crew and went ahead with her troops, letting the tanks protect their rear as they advanced into the centre of the city. The tanks used ambush tactics to fire upon the attacking Anakim and then quickly moved back under cover, sometimes smashing right through buildings if they needed to. It was a deadly game of cat and mouse. The ground troops, supported by the formidable Humdrid and Grim's reinforcements and their heavy equipment, moved forward, block by block, on a search and destroy mission. The Gorenge were waiting for them, hiding and hungry for blood. Hand to hand combat was inevitable when shields were used. Blasters and particle weapons could break through weak body shields, but in close combat this was difficult. Up close though, the shields could be penetrated by powered hand held weapons. Ironically it had come back to the use of edged weapons like swords and blades as well as heavy maces, clubs and spears. These weren't flimsy things of mere wood and steel, but were formidable energy weapons in their own right. Heavy blasters were attached to the forearms, keeping the hands free to use the preferred weapon of choice. Forearms were usually protected by small corporeal shields called bucklers, but most of the Excalibur troopers preferred nutronium maces, made from super heavy nutronium that enabled the user to hit an opponent with great mass and inertia, or they used Aquani made solar swords or spears which used an energy beam to slice through any shield or enemy. The Humdrid mechas were equipped with talon-like manipulators, prehensile whips and a huge cannon with a mounted nano-blade that could cut through almost anything. Many of the Zioronians in the force carried personalised weapons, energy blades, power staffs, but everyone also carried grenades.

Using coded 'battle-speak', Fay was able to keep in touch with Grim and Weaver and control the tactics of the battle. Tank scanners could pick up enemy movements, but not always individuals and not always clearly. Fay had no idea where the enemy leaders were, nor did she have any real tactical targets, except for the central plaza of the city where the prisoners were being kept. The troops formed into teams of four. Fay led from the front, in her own team. This was the Zioronian way and one of the reasons why they were still leaders of the vast interstellar Aquani civilization.

Moving through the back streets, the troopers sent forward scanner globes which detected enemies in the next block. Using a house for cover, Fay, her team, and two other teams looked over a wide road.

"There's about ten of those raptors on the top floor." Fay said aloud, "Soften them up."

Missile and blaster fire saw the top floor of the building over the road blown apart explosively. But the raptors had dropped down to the bottom story and returned fire almost immediately, leaping out onto the street, with fire and smoke all around them. Fay was forcing the attack, which was part of the plan. Four of the raptors went down as they crossed the street, but then the rest were breaking through the front of the house, toe claws, slashing fore-claws and even teeth, tipped with razor sharp metallic diamond unsheathed. The twelve troopers were waiting, hand weapons ready. Fay's weapon of choice was the solar sword made from calibre elf blessed steel from the Vansadagaadian Corridor. Of course she was praying, but then a raptor kicked her over! Her shields protected her, but Fay's forearm buckler was hit hard and Fay felt her left arm break! Her suit internally splinted her arm and dosed her with a pain killer, but the creature was heavy and determined to cut through her shields. Fay watched with horrified fascination as the Gorenge's face visor retracted, revealing its teeth. Its face shield was still there, but it was hissing and pushing hard to cross through Fay's shielding in order to bite. Fay fought back, but let it drop forward. It opened its jaws wide and without hesitation, Fay shoved her right hand into the monster's mouth and fired her gauntlet blaster! The whole upper body of the Gorenge was vaporised in a shower of red liquid and gore! With a grunt and a thank-you to the Divine Being, Fay kicked the remains off her. Getting up, retrieving her solar sword, Fay lit its cutting beam and attacked the enemy nearest, stabbing into the Gorenge's side. The trooper that had been under the assault said a quick thanks and they both moved to assist others. The fight was short and bloody. The enemy were dead and so were four troopers.

"Keep moving!" Fay ordered, "The scanner globes are down, must be another wave ahead!"

Through the wreckage of the next block, Fay led the survivors into a park that was already on fire. Again, using covering fire, this time Fay led the troopers into the smoke. Using infra-red to see in the smoke and spot the warm blooded dinosaurian enemy, they were surprised to be confronted by a group of Anakim as well. These enemies were big and strong and smarter than the Gorenge raptors, but also slower, although their heavy blasters were mounted with long wickedly dangerous bayonets. Fay led the charge, yelling a bloodcurdling war cry! The best soldiers on Earth, indeed considered by many to be the best in the Galaxy, held a line and pushed forward, shooting, cutting and hitting whatever got in the way.

The Humdrid and Grim's team turned up, coming into the park from another side and other battles of their own. They used their flight engines to hover over the enemy, it was a good tactic, so Fay ordered the use of hover boots to give the troops height against the Anakim and pushing power against the Gorenge, who were great leapers. But there in the park, the two forces were facing each other, and the enemy greatly outnumbered the troopers.

"Just keep holding on!" Fay ordered over her com, "I think we are right on top of the enemies' main command area!"

Up ahead, through the smoke of a burning city, Fay could see the large dark outline of a huge dirigible. There was sudden heavy weapons fire from the top of the airship and the sound of screeching dragons flying nearby! It was going from bad to worse! Fay briefly pulled back from the fight to check her tactical map on the inside of her visor. She winced at the growing casualty rate.

Connecting to Weaver and the surviving tank groups, using battle-speak, Fay ordered them to move forward towards the park. It was a risky move as they were fighting enemies attacking from behind, but there was little choice. Fay returned to the fighting and could see a dozen dragons flying down to attack them! Cannons from the back of the park were returning some fire, but the dragons kept 'popping' back and forth using their teleportation ability to avoid the fire. They began to fire right into the line as they descended. There was a huge explosion right near Fay and she was blown to the side, with a white hot flash of pain! Unconsciousness overwhelmed her!

The Arrow hovered over the Wrekin and a ring of large portals were opened allowing ships to go in and out of Annwn and the ground portals in Shrewsbury and the Roman ruins (now a little bit more ruined by combat!) were open for the combat troops and others. Fire control ships had gotten the fires around the ring and in Avalon under control, and the wounded and dead were being brought down to a makeshift hospital next to the portal ring.

The battle in Avalon was still being fought, but now it was fresh troops cleaning up what was left of the enemy. Only a few minutes after Fay lost consciousness, the relief forces had swept onto the island of Avalon. Almost within seconds the Pandemonium forces withdrew without hesitation back to the big dirigible parked in the middle of the city and without even launching, the dirigible teleported away. Any who were left behind, were quickly taken out. There was no other option here, they simply refused to surrender, and fought to the death, to the last combatant standing.

Tarmal was on the bridge of the Arrow when a message came through from Grim.

"Tarmal, we have occupied Avalon and crushed the enemy, although their large dirigible was able to teleport away." Grim continued, "We need help here, there are lots of dead and wounded. Battle Commander Fay is badly wounded."

For a moment Tarmal was speechless, then he sighed, "Grim," his voice wavered, "I can't leave my post. I'll send help. Please, take care of my wife."

"It will be alright." Grim replied.

Tarmal changed com channel, "Newton, Rainbow!" he hailed the tactical room.

"We are here." Newton answered, "The battle is essentially over! What can we now do to help?"

"I need ground crews and medical down in Avalon a.s.a.p." Tarmal responded, "We also need to find any local survivors and secure the city properly."

"We're onto it."

"Kit?" Tarmal changed com channels again, "I need you down on the deck in Avalon to help Newton and Rainbow with securing the city. Your mum and brother are down there somewhere. We need the help of the Seelie if we are to get Avalon ready to launch a counterattack against this new enemy."

"On my way!" Kit turned his pylon towards the nearest portal entrance and headed in.

Landing at the space port, not far from the portal ring, Kit climbed from his pylon and he walked to the medical triage area on the other side of the ring. On the way he could see the busyness of the place, with lots of troops moving around, other ships landing and above all, the dead and wounded were being delivered to the ring. In the ring, Kit found Grim organising things.

"Ah! At last!" Grim reached out and embraced Kit warmly, "It is good to see you Kit Ryan."

"How is it going, Grim Torgar?" Kit felt a little worried, "What of the people of Avalon?"

"We have an interesting situation, a sad situation." Grim frowned, "It seems that there have been no A'sidhe survivors, not one."

For a moment, Kit was silent. It looked as though he was grieving the loss of his mother and brother, the loss of the people of his home, but Grim knew better. Kit reached out with his empathic sense and then opened his eyes. Looking around he could see them, the 'ghost balls' or spiritual traces of the Folk, hovering around the ring!

"I think I know what happened." Kit said, "And I know a way to make all this better."

"We need the skill of familiars and trace hunters to operate the more subtle functions of the ring." Grim nodded, "The replicators and incarnators."

"I can do that, but first I'll need to non-corporealize and check some things out." Kit agreed, "When I come back, we will begin the healing of the wounded and the resurrection process. We need to find the traces of the dead first."

Kit looked carefully at the inner trilithons and the altar stone in the middle of the ring. He knelt next to the altar stone and put his hand there. Suddenly Kit found himself in the virtual reality of the ring's artificial intelligence. Kit was standing in an orchard of apple trees. A Faerie Queen stood before him.

"Hello Mab."

"Hello Christopher." The Artificial Intelligence stepped forward and kissed Kit on the cheek, "I will guide you through the process of non-corporealization and re-corporealization when you return with the others. But I need to warn you that there has been another battle, a non-physical one that has played out at the same time as the one that has just been fought in Avalon by the Order and Zioronian forces. When the Pandemonium were killed on the battlefield, their spirits did not die, but they were only liberated to their non-corporeal forms. But you have been fortunate to have allies to fight that other battle for you. Your prayers have helped them."

Kit found himself kneeling by the altar stone, and he stood and turned to Grim. "Mab has talked to me. I'm going to dematerialize now."

Just then, Newton and Rainbow walked into the ring, along with a large medical team from the Arrow.

"What can we do to help?" Rainbow asked.

"Keep the wounded comfortable." Kit said, "I'm going to set up the healing and resurrection functions of the ring. Get the most badly wounded ready first. When I come back through, we can bring the wounded through, and the dead later on."

Kit went to the central trilithon and placed a hand upon the gate stone, opening a portal in front of him. Without hesitation, Kit walked through, to no place in particular. Normally a portal transition, the process of dematerialisation and re-materialisation was instantaneous, but now, Kit was fully non-corporeal. From his own perspective he was now standing on the top of the central trilithon, although it was obvious that he had no legs to stand upon. Looking around the ring, he could see the traces of the angels. Two hovered down and stood, taking on the naked likeness of their living bodies, one each on the two other trilithons.

"Mother! Al!" Kit exclaimed.

"Yes Kit!" Niamah Golden hair smiled at her son, "We are alive!"

Alaquandi Goodfellow was chuckling to himself, "More alive than most!"

Kit was looking at his mother's spirit. Strangely she didn't appear distinct, her features were changing, but Kit didn't think much about it.

"Look out there Kit," Niamah wagged a finger at her older son, then turned to her youngest, "there are the citizens of Annwn and Avalon. When the Pandemonium forces broke through the wards of the realm and attacked the city, many of us non-corporealized in the ring or we did the death ritual. Some of us were captured. But for those of us in our true elemental form we were ready for what inevitably had to happen."

Kit looked out around the ring and he could see the others 'walking on air' toward him. They were the Eldar in their non-corporeal form. Many of them were armed with weapons, not material ones but spiritual weapons, created from the minds of the bearers. Two Tuatha warriors each carried a grey sphere, about the size of a soccer ball. Kit knew what they were.

"War captives from the Pandemonium." Al laughed, "We've been bringing them here all day." The two warriors brought their captives to the middle of the ring and Mab, the ring's A.I. appeared, "I'll take them," she said.

Mab took hold of the grey spheres containing the Pandemon captives and the spheres began to shrink, until they became the size of marbles. Mab put them into pockets in her robes.

"Their traces are now stored in my memory banks in the ring." Mab gestured towards the stones below her, "Energy and information is what we all are, after all. The captives are contained until we can deal with them properly, later, on Tur Nan Ogg, in the Corridor."

"We have also been bringing the traces of the dead here all day as well." Niamah added.

Mab opened one of her hands and there was a small glowing sphere in her palm.

"This is a human named Virey." Mab pointed down into the ring, "He died down there, giving his life so that the portals could be opened. He's one of many who died today. Normally he would have to await the Resurrection, but today we can restore him."

"But first," Niamah said, "we will take care of the wounded. Re-corporealize and begin to take them into the portal that Mab opens. Take them in and then walk out and they will be completely healed and their youth restored to them. We need to hurry."

Kit could feel himself falling down into the middle of the ring. Suddenly he was walking out of the portal and back into the material world.

"Grim!" Kit cried, "Begin to bring the wounded into the portal! The healing process can begin."

Medical personnel already had the wounded on trolleys or stretchers and they began to immediately take them into the portal that Kit had exited from. On the other side of the ring, a second portal opened. The medics walked out, accompanied by the wounded individuals, now walking and fully restored to health. Not only were their wounds healed, but any other health problems were taken care of as well. Kit understood the process well, and of course he knew about his father's experience, who had died a hundred years earlier, and was then restored to life.

The replication technology of the portal rings meant that any person who used the portal system, were effectively given the potential to be immortal. Each time the ring portal system was used, those who passed through, if they were older than twenty, had their biological age restored back to their default age, usually twenty for most. It was something that was of great benefit to Order agents and Petra Alliance personnel. Some people preferred older default ages, but with access to perfect health, it didn't matter that much.

As the wounded were brought forward, Kit spotted Fay being carried on a stretcher by two medics. Most of her upper body was burned and covered in burn foam. She was also breathing with the help of a ventilator mask. Mercifully she was unconscious. Kit watched the medics take her into the portal. When Fay came out, she was carrying her stretcher and she was thanking the medics. There were no signs of burns, scaring and she even wore a new uniform.

"Hey Kit!" Fay grinned at him, "What a rush!"

"You have gate euphoria!" Kit laughed, "It often happens when a body goes through a big transformation as you just did."

"My injuries must have been worse than I thought!" Fay nodded, unable to stop grinning, "But it certainly feels good to be alive right now!"

"I think that a lot of people would agree with you!" Kit replied, "You up to helping ship the wounded through the portals? There are still a lot of people in the triage area."

Fay nodded enthusiastically. Rainbow, who was standing nearby, took her by the arm and led her over the nearby triage area. Grim and Newton, both carrying data tablets, approached Kit.

"We need to tell Tarmal that she's alright." Kit said.

"Already taken care of." Newton answered.

"Rainbow's taking care of the wounded," Grim added, "but the city here is badly damaged and we have lost a lot of equipment. The problem is logistics, and how soon we can get everything back up and ready for the next battle, which will have to be fought soon."

"Once the wounded and human dead are restored," Kit took one of the data tablets that Grim offered to him, "the A'sidhe will re-corporealize and then we can get on with the job of replicating the necessary equipment we need. But you are right, we don't have a lot of time. The enemy have only retreated."

"The latest report on the Order/Petra intranet is that the enemy has occupied London." Newton informed them, "They seem to be up to something. People are being moved around, but we don't know why. This battle is just the beginning of the war."

"Got anything back from your Dad?" Kit asked Newton.

"The world is a real mess right now." Newton was exasperated, "America no longer has a functioning government, but there are a lot of people being rescued. We are just teleporting the able bodied and the badly wounded. Most of the North Americans are going to Australia. It seems like the best idea for now. Tsunamis and earthquakes are still a problem around the ring of fire, and our rescue teams are totally overworked. There are no easy solutions. The enemy planned it this way... for now, they have all the real control."

"I have to agree." Grim nodded, "Even though we have this victory and we have the ring system to rebuild our numbers and losses, it will cost us a lot to fight this war, especially once we start fighting in the surface world. Up there, the dead, sadly, will have to stay dead. We can't recover traces outside of a Rath ward. The traces tend to wander off into the nether gloom. We can replicate new tanks, pylons and shuttles, but personnel who have the training to use them will be few. Even the wounded who have been restored today.... you saw Fay, she has the euphoria, they all will. Then there is the depression and psychic shock that resurrectees ALWAYS suffer. Even the Vansad will need to rest once they re-corporealize. We just won't have enough combat ready people to fight this war."

Kit had been looking at the numbers on Grim's data tablet, "It looks bad." he said, "This battle has cost us too much. There has to be another way to stop this enemy, before they take over the world."

"The problem is that there could be other waves of stasis bubbles 'rezzing up.'" Newton said, "More enemies to fight and no way to prevent them coming."

On hearing that, Grim lifted a hand to pause the conversation, "I'm thinking ....", he said.

Kit and Newton looked at each other, a bit confused, but anticipating Grim's words.

Finally, "We can prevent more waves of the enemy." he said, "But we are going to have to be quick."

"Are you thinking what I think you are thinking?" Kit said, "Causality doesn't work like that."

"No, no, no," Grim shook his head, "we can't change what has happened already, but there is a lot that hasn't happened yet, either here or in the past."

"You guys are talking about time travel?!" Newton asked.

"Yes." Grim replied, "We will need a very strong team, the right team, and we need to go immediately. We leave the battle in the present to others."

"What about things here?" Newton wondered, "We MUST get things up and running here."

"Let's get the A'sidhe re-corporealised, get the Arrow down here in Annwn." Kit said, "We go to Tur Nan Ogg and fly the strings."

Grim nodded, then quickly headed off to his work with the wounded.

"Newton," Kit said, "I'll talk to the Tuatha, you contact Tarmal. He needs to get the Arrow down here. It's no longer about fighting up above, but holding the ground down here. From here we can build an army."

Kit grinned, handed his data tablet to Newton, and he headed over to the altar stone. Newton nodded, pulled his com out of his pocket and dialled up the Arrow bridge.

Chapter Eighteen

Staging ground

An hour later, there were no more wounded, no more dead and the city of Avalon was crowded with citizens. The Arrow hovered over the Annwn Sea. As for the city itself, the A'sidhe were at work, replicating replacement materials at the ring and rebuilding. But the most important activity was happening in the city plaza.

At the ring end of the plaza, some of the A'sidhe had set up the King's Table. At the Table sat the Oberons and Morrigans of the city, the Dagda, Nuada, and Alaquandi, along with D'Anu, Badb and of course Niamah. Other members of the Council, like Finvara, Brigid and Lir were nearby. They all wore golden torcs and some wore only armour or mail, their only clothing. The humans stood before them, Kit, Newton, Rainbow, the Zioronians Tarmal and Fay, who was still recovering, was seated in a comfortable chair. Grim arrived accompanied by a red headed woman, his surviving lizard guard and one of the Humdrid. Other Arrow and Excalibur officers and Petra agents were there to watch. Many of the people present had been through the regeneration process and were sitting as they were still recovering from the euphoria. For the A'sidhe the process of re-corporealization wasn't so traumatic, but humans were always badly impacted, especially if they died and had to be bought back.

Kit was looking at his mother, sitting at the end of the Table. Al was grinning as well. As the meeting of the Council was about to start, there had been little time to catch up, but only momentarily. The amusement came from the fact that the A'sidhe, like all Eldar races were, unfortunately for Niamah, able to change their morphic field when they used the ring system. The ring had, for some reason re-corporealized Niamah with an older incarnation. Because the field had changed so had her appearance as a consequence. Kit, who was half human, Walter Ryan's son, had a strong human trace, but it was often seen as amusing among A'sidhe when the process didn't work. Niamah no longer had long golden blonde hair, but she now had much shorter hair, and other features which made her look quite different. She seemed quite happy with the result. It was nevertheless a private joke among those at the Table, a joke that Kit appreciated.

A portal opened in the Plaza, one from the Corridor world of Tur Nan Ogg, and I walked through. I'd been sent from the Realm to connect with the team that would be chosen for the mission that Grim Torgar was planning. I was surprised to see Niamah the way she was, but knew her immediately as we empathically connected. I wasn't bothered, it had happened to others I knew before and in fact I was pleased by her 'new look'. She could always change back later if she wanted to. I went up to the Table, shaking Kit's hand as I walked past, and sitting between Niamah and Alaquandi, I kissed her in greeting. Most of the folk were still having conversations, when Brigid, the leader of the Morrigans called for order. Behind her, Mab, the A.I. of the city's ring appeared. All the Tuatha de Danann turned and bowed to her, then they sat down again.

"We must press forward quickly." Brigid, whose hair was as white as snow began, "We have won a significant victory but should not be complacent. The enemy is numerous and cunning and has allied themselves with others against us. These strangers who invaded our city are Pandemonium from the ancient past, and they used stasis bubbles to transport themselves to our present day world. We believe that the Nephalim Baal named Enlil of the Anunnaki, also known as Graud, is behind this attack. Many of us are familiar with him."

I felt the back of my head. The memory of my own death at his hand was a painful reminder.

"This Council and the leaders of the Petra Orders are committed to working with fellow good hearted people of this world to battle this enemy and save this world from invasion." Brigid continued, "Their stasis bubbles were not only used as vessels of transportation, but also as weapons of mass destruction. Our world is suffering a cataclysm as a result. This enemy must be stopped. Grim Torgar of the Eldar has a plan."

"I must point out firstly," Grim began, "that the idea originated with Newton James, who wondered how we could prevent further invaders from resonating from the ancient past. Of course, the answer is to go back into the past and prevent them from coming in the first place. It isn't that time travel isn't common, because both the Seelie and Eldar have ridden the strings many times. It is how we travel around the Multiverse and occasionally Trace-hunters and Familiars use it for tracking down traces or for special missions. But time travel is difficult and dangerous. The main reason is that causality is complex and things can go horribly wrong, especially where we are ignorant of the past. We can go into the past, but the past has already happened, so we face a temporal inertia. In this case though, this inertia can help us have some hindsight, because it has indeed already happened."

Grim led the red haired woman forward.

"This is Mrorna." he introduced her, "She is one of the survivors from the stasis bubble that resonated in the Kermadec Trench, and which started this crisis. I have spoken with her and she has confirmed my suspicions.... that we did send a team back in time to attempt to stop the enemy. Mrorna knows this because she was there!"

Everyone began to talk all at once. Brigid stood and raised her hands to restore calm.

"Silence please! We need to listen." she cried, "Grim, what exactly has this woman told you?"

Mrorna turned to Grim and began to speak to him excitedly in some strange language. Grim replied in the same language. Some of the Tuatha got excited as well, as though they could understand the words.

"What is she saying?" I whispered to Niamah.

"I don't know," she shook her head, "but she's speaking ancient Neph."

Brigid stepped away from the Table and went over to Mrorna to look more closely at her. She took hold of Mrorna by her head and turned her head to the side. Brigid looked at Mrorna's wrists.

"She has the scars of a freed thrall." Brigid said softly, "Ask her who freed her."

Grim spoke again. Mrorna looked around the room and then she walked over to Kit and Newton. She led them over to stand next to Grim, then she pointed at

Rainbow, Tarmal and Fay, then looking at those sitting at the Table, she pointed at Niamah and Al. They all left where they were and went to stand with Grim as well.

"We will," Grim smiled, "or rather we did."

"Then you need to go." Brigid declared, "There is no choice, and perhaps, this will be a battle we will be able to win."

Afterwards I was talking with Niamah, Al and Grim.

"What if it's a trap?" I asked, "We are sending our very best into a killing zone. Can we trust this Mrorna?"

"Of course we can't trust her." Grim smiled, "She was a thrall, and even without her collar and bracelets, she was conditioned to obey her Baal lord without question. But her story is intriguing. During her medical scans we were able to sort through her memories. She suffered real disillusionment and she still has doubts about her conditioning. People who are moles are usually too good to be true, too convinced of their rightness. While we shouldn't trust her, I don't think she's part of a trap. The fact that she and her people are alive at all, that we just happened to find them, that couldn't be planned. They were condemned to death by Graud. They should have died, not end up here with us."

"We are going to need her, Walter." Niamah added, "We need her local knowledge, she can give us the language of the time and lead us into the heart of the enemy's lair."

"Alright then." I conceded, "So, why don't we just send an army of our own into the past and just nuke the bastards?"

"Because there is more at stake here than just our civilization." Grim replied, "We know from what historical reports we have of the time that the Nephalim civilization which rose up and then fell just before the establishment of the Sethani kingdom, fell when the main Nephalim fortress in Nod was destroyed in a massive cataclysm. Not a nuclear explosion, but rather a temporal displacement. Most of the fighting was using tech contemporary to the time but there were some odd exceptions. The Seelie were around that time too"

"What do we know for certain?" Al asked.

"Not much more." Grim replied with a shrug, "The time was confused. There were other combatants involved. The founder of the Sethani kingdom was of course Seth, son of Adam. He was a boy at the time. There is reference to a small band of heroes who helped him. It gives us enough to get there, but that's all."

"Not much." I said.

"I've time travelled before." Grim said, "It is best to not know too much. It gives us more freedom and choice in our actions. We don't even know if this mission will ultimately succeed the way we want it to. Even so, it looks good, that we can seriously hurt the Nephalim and Pandemonium forces, both in the past and the present."

"That sounds good to me." I responded enthusiastically, "We'll go to Tur Nan Ogg immediately and get things organised for the run down the strings."

In order to open the gate between Earth and Tur Nan Ogg, it required the use of the staff-like Gate Key. Our team gathered in the Ring, along with many others who wanted to see us off. Grim had been getting everyone organised. Bags of equipment, weapons and ordnance, some webbing belts and a small camera, to record everything, were packed. The team was to be led by Grim Torgar, and included Tarmal and Fay of Zioron, my Niamah and our son Kit, his half-brother Robin Alaquandi, Newton James and Rainbow, the Petrad scientist, and of course Mrorna who was to be our guide. As we were preparing to leave, a portal appeared high over the Ring and a Ren flew through, then descended to land nearby. As the Ren dissolved her flight field and folded her wings, I saw that it was Hilli and her pilot was Surreya. It was good to see her again.

"We are here from the Daedalus!" Surreya bowed to her old friends in greeting, "The rescue mission is going very well, but Grim Torgar sent orders for me to be here. We will be joining this mission!"

"I'm the transport!" Hilli exclaimed, "I've never run the strings before, and I'm looking forward to it!"

"Come and meet the team!" I said to them, "We need to get oriented before I take you to the Corridor."

"Are you coming with us?" Surreya asked.

"No," I shook my head, "I was sent here by Yeshua to make the arrangements for the cross over. But any chance to visit Terra-Avalon is always welcome. You have got to come over here, you'll never guess what happened to Niamah!"

I gathered the team in the middle of the Ring with all the gear piled up. They looked at each other. Grim and I also looked at each other and we could sense the feeling of unease that had come over everyone. There was some quiet talking, especially as old friends were reunited and everyone sized each other up for their roles in the mission. It was pretty obvious who would be doing what. Most of the team were highly trained Order soldiers, and Newton was a technology expert as well. Rainbow wasn't a soldier, but she was a scientist, and we would be needing her skills for certain. No one was really sure of Mrorna yet, and the language barrier would need to be dealt with soon. But I was pleased to see that Kit had taken to her and was trying to be friendly, although Mrorna herself still stood very close to Grim and looked terrified.

I cleared my throat to get everyone's attention.

"We are about to cross over to Tur Nan Ogg." I began, "We will get you oriented for the run down the strings. But you need to know that as we pass through the portal in a few moments, I have made some adjustments to the bio-morphic-genetic matrix in the Ring. Because you won't be able to openly use obviously advanced technology in the ancient past, in order to minimise our impact and prevent advantage to the enemy if we are captured, some implanted organic technologies will be added to your bodies to give you some advantages. These will include cranial implant coms, trackers, enhanced stamina, senses, lung capacity and muscular strength. Regenerative healing will be increased, but you will need to eat more for it to work. Niamah will get her wings again, and all of you of the Folk, including Kit, will have enhanced glamour. Most importantly, you all get the 'tongues' ability, meaning that you will be able to understand any language you hear and speak it, but it still takes time to process words and meanings, so once we get to Vansadagaadian-Avalon, practice speaking to Mrorna and Grim so you get some of the slang and other subtle meanings right. If you can sound like native Neph speakers, it will help. You will need to be able to blend in if possible. You will all have enhanced memory functions, so keeping alert, observing carefully, is going to be very important for your survival in a strange and unknown environment. When you get back we will be able to download your memories as part of the debriefing sessions. This is as much a fact finding intelligence mission as anything else. Anyway, we'll talk more about mission specifics in the Corridor and you are all properly geared up."

I sighed inwardly and paused for a moment in order to let all this sink in. They still looked a little unsure. For the humans in particular, going to the Vansadagaadian Corridor was a big thing. All the enhancements to their bodies also revealed that Vansadagaadian technology was even more advanced than they might have thought. In particular there were non-corporeal or 'spiritual' technologies that were going to be added here as well. They wouldn't be the same people once they were on the other side. One thing I had learned while living in Vansadagaadian-Avalon was that the Elohim never gave away the more advanced super technologies unless it was absolutely necessary. It was just too dangerous. Even the Eldar races from older universes understood this.

"Alright," I continued, "this isn't just another mission. I get it that you are all a bit stressed by this and also from the events of the last week or so. The war here will continue under the leadership of great generals like John James and the Oberons and Morrigans of the A'sidhe. But right now I think it is best that we pray before we go. Grim, could you do us the honour?"

Prayer, it is a strange thing, especially now that the Seelie and Angelic Eldar races and the other Elohim are revealed to Mankind more clearly. How does one pray to a man that one considers to be a personal friend? Over the last one hundred years, many of which were spent living in the Corridor, I have often spent time with Yeshua, and of course there were other members of his kind, the Logoi. El, himself, also known as Abba, lives on Tur Nan Ogg, and I had spent some time with him as well. I found Him to be a rather charming gentleman. Eloha, who preferred to go by the name Sophie these days, was a very feminine lady, and wise as her name declared her to be. Seeing these three as well as some of the Others together, revealed even more, that the members of the Logoi loved each other like family, and that they were asking us to be a part of that family. For a while after first living in Zion, I found it hard to pray because all the old religious traditions and rituals, well, most of them were just shadows of the reality I had seen. But Yeshua explained to me one day that prayer was still something we should all do. The fact is that the Divine Spirit, the Nephesh life force, flowed like a living river through the Multiverse, leading us, providing for us, and if we were able to listen with our spirits, speaking to us. It was another language, but we needed to pray nevertheless with our whole selves. Like a powerful empathic ability, prayer helps us connect into the Divine Life when we are on our own. The Transcendent Divine Being hears us. That was for certain. Prayer connected us all together. The Logoi were expressions of the Divine Being, living Avatars.

Grim prayed a simple prayer, brief yet encouraging. It wasn't just asking for stuff, but assumed a sense of certainty and hope. Not wishful thinking type of hope, but real expectation. We were on our way and the enemy had better be frightened!

I handed the Staff Key to Al, who was the one who best understood how to use it. He put it into the altar stone slot and I reached over and touched the sarsen stone on the right of the largest trilithon in the centre of the Ring. The portal opened with a flicker and the people around us cheered and applauded as we waved goodbye and went through. Standing in the other Ring, Al handed the Staff Key back to me with a grin. We were in the corridor. It was good to be home.

For Newton and Rainbow, Tarmal and Fay and Mrorna, this was the first time and their eyes were bulging out of their heads in wonder! We were literally standing next to the edge of the world. Before us, looking towards the sun-like brightness of the Strings, we could see the clouds of the sky-fall, like a carpet of wool. Behind us, looking outward, were the mountains of Prydain and the other Avalon city. Like a polished mirror, the stones of the huge cube shaped city shone in the light.

We were not alone in the Ring. The Rings were major transport hubs, and many peoples were constantly coming and going. Above in the air were sky portals. Air traffic was on the move. Mostly it was Renim, of different shapes, sizes and colours, but there were also some e.d.v's as well. The Ring was actually thronged with people, mostly waiting for the Ring Marshall to turn her Staff Key and open new portals so those walking could go to whereever they needed to go. There were all kinds of tribes and people, humans and aliens, and the Vansad tribes. In the warm climate, most were happy to go unclothed, but some wore traditional fashions from many different periods of history.

"Oh gods!" Mrorna declared loudly, "Is this Heaven?"

"Hey!" cried Kit, "I understand you!"

The two of them grinned at each other. I left our group to marvel at all the races and beings around them, and went straight to the Marshall. She was a Ren herself and a Familiar, presumably to make her job easier. Like many people living in the warm 'summer-lands' of Prydain, she was practically naked, except for some decorative jewellery and some attractive tattooing. Nearby I could spot the permanent guardians, who had been put there to guard the Ring. They were not just ceremonial guards wearing traditional dress armour, but were fully armed Host Warriors, equipped with full body shielding, particle beamers, disintegrators and wings. One of them wore red arm bands and a micro-equipment pack on her shoulder because she was a Ren. We were well protected then.

There were a lot of Renim around the Ring doing transport jobs, and warriors.

"A lot of the Host around." I commented to the Marshall, "What's going on?"

"This war of yours." she said, "The Faltionians have tried to run the blockade and so we are sending reinforcements to Pladan. Darmaekae super dreadnaughts are sitting out in the ort cloud. There is talk of sending Splinters to help the blockade. Even the Anunnaki are on the move. "

"Not worried about security?" I grinned, "Loose talk? Leaks?"

The Marshall laughed out loud! "It's old data!" she chortled, "This is the Corridor, not the trenches in 1918!"

"Maybe so...." I wagged a finger at her, "but in 1918, a Baal named Graud stood not far from where you are now."

"Ok Walter, I get the point." she nodded as Niamah came up behind me and put her arm around my hips. The others in our team gathered about us.

"We need to get to the Residence." I said.

"Already booked in." the Marshall looked at her data pad, "You are expected of course."

The Marshall turned her staff key in the altar stone. A portal opened nearby immediately.

"Thank you Terel." Niamah hugged the Marshall as we went past and through the portal, right into a lush tropical jungle.

The jungle was actually a beautifully planted garden. We were walking along a path. Along the path were these wooden poles, intricately carved with lovely plant and animal motifs. We walked into a glade, with grass as soft as the softest carpet. In the middle of the glade were some wooden benches, again, finely carved artworks in wood. Everything around us was exquisitely beautiful. The sound of running water could be heard nearby. A man and woman were sitting on one of the benches, looking very relaxed and comfortable together. They wore semi-transparent linen which seemed to glow. I recognized them immediately.

"Welcome friends. Shalom!" Yeshua beckoned us over, "Sit and relax a while."

He got up, bent over and kissed the woman, before turning to us.

"Do you want something to eat? Refreshments?" He waved his hand and a portal appeared rising horizontally from the ground, producing a table laden with food and drink, "I suggest you eat. You are about to embark upon a very dangerous mission, you will all need your strength."

He waved us all towards the seats. The woman stood as well. Those of us who had enjoyed the Master's hospitality before led the others to the seats, despite their uncertainty. Rainbow and Newton in particular couldn't help staring.

"Miri, could you pour some wine for our guests please?" Yeshua asked her quietly, as He began to lay out plates and broke out some unleavened bread, meat, cheese, fruit, vegetables and nuts. There were bowls of creamy dips, houmous and relishes. He passed the plates to me and I handed them around. Then came the food. Yeshua spoke a blessing in Hebrew as it was passed around.

"Eat!" He insisted, and then, as I was about to speak, He held up a hand, "No unpleasant business yet Walter! Eat, drink and relax first, talk war later!"

"I see that you've been carving some more furniture." I said, changing the subject made Him smile.

"My Lord," Grim bowed, "your work is very fine."

"Thank you Grim," Yeshua's eyes sparkled with mischief, "but you know that I won't have anyone using the L word around me. I might have to put on airs!"

"My L...." Grim was speechless briefly, then he laughed with Yeshua, who rolled His eyes at us. It was like a bubble burst and a feeling of comfort came upon us.

"Please, PLEASE!" Yeshua walked right up to Newton and Rainbow, put His arms around them and sat down with them. Miri passed around goblets of wine and Yeshua drank deeply.

We all sat together, there in the glade and ate and drank.

"You are the one they call Jesus?" Mrorna asked, "The one who was executed, but then was restored to life. You are Elohim, right? I have heard of you!"

"Yes dear lady," Yeshua nodded, "but I prefer the name my parents gave me, that is Yeshua. I am called Issa by some. Also, I am Logoi. The Logoi come from the Source. We are the First of the Elohim. And I have heard a lot about you. The Logoi, my family, have been watching after you for some time now. Did you know that?"

"I did not know, Yeshua!" Mrorna was astounded.

"Oh yes Mrorna." Yeshua nodded, "I know you very well. You are here because the Spirit called you. Despite your chains, you heard."

"All my life I have always desired to be free." Mrorna said, "Despite the collar and the bracelets, in my heart I never bowed to the Baals."

Quickly, Yeshua turned to us who were sitting and listening to this conversation and He spoke to us directly, "I guarantee this woman is trustworthy. You mustn't doubt it!"

"Mrorna," I wanted to suggest something, "why don't you tell your story to the members of the team so we can get to know you better. We want to know what your world was like and what we ought to expect when we go there."

Mrorna looked to Yeshua for reassurance and He nodded to her.

"What do you need to know?" she asked.

"We aren't here to interrogate you." I said, smiling, trying to be reassuring, "You are among friends. Tell us about your birthplace or where you come from."

Mrorna was quiet for a few moments. "I can remember my village and family in the time before Graud came and made us slaves. My people were Ashurim and we lived by the eastern sea. I was a daughter of Vrengr, of the Porma clan." Mrorna sighed, "They used to spike us if we mentioned stuff like that."

"Spiked?" Rainbow asked, "Who did what?"

"When Graud's army captured my village we were put into cages at first." she began, "But then the collars were put around our necks and bracelets on our wrists and ankles. If we said the wrong things, even thought the wrong things, the collars would put an electric shock right into our brains! If we were obedient or said the right things, we were given a different kind of shock, feelings of pleasure. We called it spiking, good spiking or bad spiking. It didn't take long for people to become completely obedient. We became Thralls."

"How did you resist something like that?" Rainbow looked horrified.

"Most didn't. Most even forgot who they were." Mrorna clenched her teeth and fists in remembered rage, "But somehow I was able to remember. That is all I did. Not everything at once, just one thing at a time. I'd spend an hour remembering my mother. The next, I'd remember an old doll I used to have, then I'd remember some other trivial thing. The collar couldn't pick everything up. Sometimes I'd get spiked anyway. Even so, one memory at a time was enough for me to know that I had not fully bowed the knee, that even if they made me do evil things, I was not choosing to be evil. The strength to do it came from somewhere else."

"So how did you come to be put into the stasis bubble?" Newton asked, "Was there able to be some kind of resistance?"

"There was never a resistance." Mrorna shook her head, "Once one was en-thralled, one obeyed. I only disobeyed once. I was working as a technician on the machines that sent Graud's army into the future. There was an electrical frequency that disrupted the collars. There were a few of us in the generator building when I turned on the disruption field. Graud sent in loyal Pandemonium warriors, those who no longer wore collars but served freely. We had to fight. I was attempting to set up the field resonance so we could escape to a time of our own choosing, but Graud had another generator building and he put us in stasis. Despite that, I was able to send a signal that changed the frequency of his own fields, sending the resonation date a hundred years further into the future, just before we were frozen."

"Wait ..Wait!!" Newton exclaimed, "YOU set the resonation date a hundred years further?"

"Yes." Mrorna nodded.

"Ah," Newton was grinning, "ok, looks like you inadvertently saved civilization! Yeah, if Graud's Pandemonium turned up one hundred years ago, right in the middle of World War I, he would have attacked the Allied forces, won the war for the Germans. That must have been the plan."

At that I reached over and tapped Newton on the shoulder. Looking across I could also see Kit, Al and Niamah all smiling as well.

"That is pretty obvious to some of us." I laughed, "We were there at the time! We fought that war. But you are right Newton. We always thought that Graud would be back. We expected him almost immediately, but as the years went by and he didn't return, we thought something must have stopped him."

"Something did." Kit gave Mrorna an encouraging squeeze on the arm, "It is something we can use."

"Definitely." Grim agreed, "Mrorna, you were right there. We need you to give us as much detail of what you know. We will need maps and other details, especially about Graud. When did you see us, for example?"

"I never saw you in person." Mrorna shook her head, "But it was while I was enthralled, just before we became free, that I heard the reports of strangers from the future. I was there when Graud read the reports. Spies had even sent pictures of your faces. Graud recognised some of you and cursed you."

As we were talking, Yeshua used the portal technology to remove the table with the leftover food and replaced it with a tactical table.

"Time to get to business." He said, "The table is identical in design to the one on the Arrow, so you should be able to use it." Yeshua smiled at Tarmal and Fay, who had already gone over to switch the table on, "There's a food and drink replicator built in, for coffee if you like!" He called to them.

"Walter," Yeshua beckoned me over, and Miri led me to Him, "we can talk while they do their planning. I have another task for you."

"I'd really like to do something helpful," I said hopefully, "something ah, military, please?"

"I was thinking that you would want into the fight." Yeshua nodded, "Although you do seem to enjoy it too much!"

"All for the Kingdom my King!" I grinned, "I'm a professional!"

"I don't question your effectiveness," He smiled, "just ask that you restrict the collateral damage."

"Yes Sir." I was completely serious.

"There are some among the Elohim who want to unleash the Splinters." He spoke quietly, "But I counselled restraint.....The world is not yet ready for Judgement."

"So instead you want to unleash me?"

"You are a formidable General and you have a formidable army. We need to get the Order units on deck and our Petra allies equipped and trained. John James and the Daedalus can only do so much. We have to fight a war, but we also have a lot of people who need to be rescued. The Pacific is one huge disaster area and Eurasia is about to become a war zone! The Seerlie Court is meeting at Terra Avalon right now and they are ready to follow your orders. You will be given the Cymbrogi, the White Regiment, the Djinni and the Danu."

"And my colonels?" I was feeling quite excited, "Arthun ap Meurig, Leonov Kurbatov, Anunnaki Namtar, and since Alaquandi Goodfellow and Niamah Golden hair are leaving on a mission of their own, the Danu war leader can only be one, Finvara."

"Exactly." Yeshua nodded, "They are gathering their forces right now in Annwn along with two Order units led by Vassilli Zabolotsky and Boris Rujansky and the Zioronian force, led by Fass with Virey and Peter Weaver her battle leaders. The Arrow will be at your disposal and the whole Petra e.d.v. fleet. Your main job will be to train Petra personnel first in the use of the advanced tech. I also give you authority to act for the Elohim and recruit allies whereever you can. We have spiritual allies in all sorts of places, but beware, it may surprise you who are the true friends and who will become enemies. Help defend free nations that resist the Pandemonium and fight those who join them. Take captives whereever you can. Put them in stasis if you have to. The less we kill, the less we are like the enemy.

But, I chose you because you can be ruthless when you need to be, my friend. I am the Prince of Peace, true, but I carry a sword too when I have to."

He paused for a bit, sighed, then continued, "I want you to know that I will turn up occasionally. I have a host of my own, Michael and some of the boys and girls..." He laughed then, "...to do a few strategic things here and there! Call me Joshua, as we have before when I visit the Earth. Call my host a Danu unit. I want to remain, ah, anonymous. I've instructed John James and the Petra Alliance to form new self-governing communities. The old national governments won't work anymore. The Nephalim are revealed to the world and we must establish what we are calling the 'Free States', in order to stand against them. Keep an eye on the Christians Walter. They are a silly sentimental lot, but they love me and I love them. I long to see them come to some kind of sanity during this conflict, get them out of that long religious rut they've been stuck in for so long." He sighed... "But don't let religious do-gooders screw it all up, ok?"

"Ok." I nodded.

At that, Yeshua reached out and drew me into a loving embrace. As we drew apart, I could see the tears in His eyes, which bore right into my spirit. He didn't have to say anything else, I was committed to fight.

Chapter Nineteen

Leap of Faith

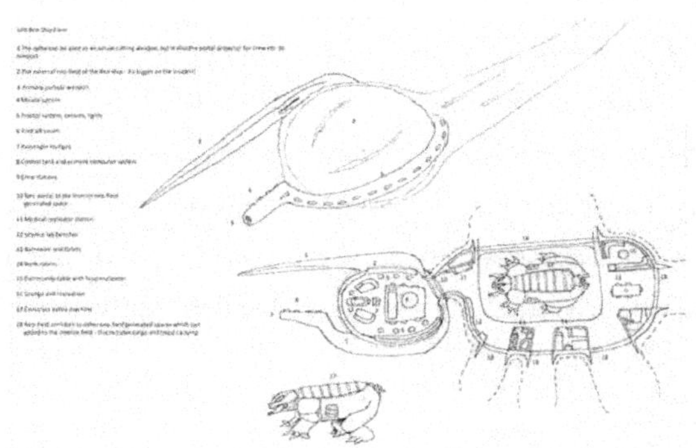

The great ring of Vansadagaadian Avalon was buzzing with activity. Engineers were busy re-designing and replicating new e.d.v. warships and battle equipment. Troops were being equipped with their advanced suits. My own units were on parade not far from the ring at a marshalling ground. Not only were we preparing to fight our own battles, but we were preparing to become military advisers. I was with my cadre of commanding officers at a desk as we worked out the last details. I was grinning as I watched Boris Rujansky putting the squads through drills in full kit, without the benefit of their power fields.

Our shuttles were already parked nearby, and the Renim pilots were waiting for us to board. Orderlies had already loaded most of our gear aboard.

"Looks like it's all sorted somewhat Walter." Arthur declared, "Our portal window is in about half an hour."

"Ok," I took a deep breath, "let's get this done."

I nodded at Leonov Kurbatov, who touched his com and contacted Boris, who was now a Major. The big Russian bellowed at the troops and they came to attention. There were four units, each with two hundred members. There were all seasoned warriors and most had fought as squad leaders before. As advisers, our job would be to train our own squads in the use of the new generation powered battle suits.

I personally shut down the tactical table as we began the boarding procedures. As I was walking to my shuttle, in full armour, I heard a Ren flying overhead, heading for the ring. I checked my helmet display and gave sub-vocal commands asking my suits A.I. who they were. It was Hilli, Surreya's Ren, transporting the team to the ring, and then to their mission. I said a little prayer for their safety and success.

Hilli flew down towards the edge of the ring platform, not far from the telescope deck. It was the very spot from where Graud had fled into the past, and the same spot where he had committed murder a hundred years earlier. Hilli closed down her flight field and the mission team found themselves standing at the edge of the precipice. A nice breeze was blowing in over the clouds from the core of the corridor where the cosmic strings glowed warmly. There were storms brewing out in one of the lower banks of clouds that would later bring rain to the inner lands of Tur-Nan-Ogg. But right now, the sky was open.

"It looks like a nice day for a secret mission." Al chuckled.

Grim came out of the nearby shelter accompanied by Yeshua and Enoch, who had come to see the group off. There were also a couple of dress guards, a male and female who accompanied Enoch as official guards to the Oberon.

All members of the mission team were wearing simple practical clothing, short shorts or briefs and a simple sleeveless tank top. Niamah and Al were wearing Danu style mail. Mrorna was wearing the same simple clothes as the others, but she had torn away the material around her middle and tied the strip in an X around her shoulders and breasts. Everyone wore walking boots and were also well armed with swords and small side arms. Hilli was wearing a large shoulder pack, with lots of extra internal storage and habitation space for travelling. This was all that the mission would need. Surreya and Hilli were both unselfconsciously naked.

"What if it gets cold?" Newton asked, noticing, "I feel kind of naked in this outfit!"

"I have a full wardrobe on board for prudes such as yourself." Hilli said happily, "We can also copy and replicate almost anything we need."

"As long as the mail and weaponry are in style!" Niamah straightened her hauberk.

"Attention everyone." Grim interjected, "We are about to embark on this mission and so I need to focus the telescope. We now have the right coordinates and resonation values for the run."

Grim moved over to the platform jutting out over the edge of the precipice and holding the handles of the telescope, he looked intently into the view piece. A second later, a laser fired down the corridor into the storm clouds below.

"There's a temporal rift down there." Enoch looked over, "We should be able to follow Graud's trajectory although he has a hundred years head start on you."

"It's time to go." Yeshua stepped forward and gently began to 'lay hands' on the members of the group, "Go with my full blessing and the protection of the Spirit and we'll celebrate when you return."

"When the mission is over," Enoch said, "return to the rift point and Hilli will bring you home. If for some reason Hilli can't fly, then any of you with Bene Elohim blood can send a message by scrying and we will come and get you."

"Now here's the fun bit." Surreya stepped out to the edge of the precipice, "First we have to jump, then Hilli collects us and we fly."

"Jump?" Rainbow asked, a bit afraid, "Can't Hilli just take us like usual?"

"No." Surreya shook her head, "Our bodies need to be moving along the trajectory before we can resonate. It's a fun part of running the strings!"

"I don't call jumping into bottomless space without a parachute or pressure suit fun!" Rainbow croaked, but she was still smiling, although uneasily.

"It will be fine!" Kit encouraged, "We will do it together."

The entire group moved to the edge of the drop. Mrorna looked over the edge and grinned. Newton and Rainbow looked uncertain, while for the others, it was a normal part of their jobs.

"Ready! Set!" Grim cried, "JUMP!!!"

They all leapt off the edge.

Grim, Kit, Tarmal and Fay, Niamah and Al, Rainbow, Mrorna and Newton were followed in their downward fall by Surreya and Hilli. They dropped down following the line of the trajectory laser fired from the telescope far above. Niamah, Al, Surreya and Hilli all had energy wings open, pulsing planes of force radiating from the organic generator organs in their shoulders. They flew to keep the others falling along the beam of light. Niamah had noticed that Rainbow was looking particularly frightened and so she flew closer and put an arm around her to reassure. Mrorna was actually enjoying the experience, and the others, including Newton (who wasn't enjoying it!), were all professional soldiers, silent and competent. Strangely, the air was warm that rushed past them. Kit looked to his right and could see the underside of the continent world of Tur-Nan-Ogg. Despite the wind blowing into his eyes, he had to look. He realised why the air was warm. Under the inner lands, the country that those living in Vansadagaadian Avalon called Prydain, there was a cloud of super-heated gasses. Kit knew what it was. There was a strand that had broken away from the string which was resonating hot in the atmosphere around Tur-Nan-Ogg, creating the superheated air under Prydain. That same air had blown a hole right through the crust of the floating continent, which the people of Prydain called the Cauldron.

Kit turned to look down along the line of the laser. Storms were brewing way down the line. He could see the clouds churning. He looked behind and spotted all the members of the team. Grim wasn't far away, he waved.

Hilli began to fly in rings around the falling team, using her wings to accelerate and control her descent. She spread out her arms and mentally activated her shoulder pack. The field began to grow around the group. Hilli's wings began to spread wide, forming loops of energy. There was a sudden snap noise of energy and Hilli's Ren sphere formed.

Within the sphere, the members of the team were still in free fall, but slowly Hilli increased the artificial gravity so that they soon were standing together in the main flight cabin. The way that Renim worked was complex, but simply put, they created a dimensional 'pocket' within which they could carry cargo and passengers. The outside of the pocket was a spinning electro-dynamic field, and the shoulder packet that Hilli wore, gave Hilli's Ren form some formidable weapons and armour. The Renim were not vehicles, the Ren form was an extension of Hilli's body, a living thing. Again they stood in the circle of light, looking out windows where clouds and floating rocks were flashing past. Hilli was still following the laser, but was now moving incredibly fast. Surreya sat in her pilot's chair, while Hilli was now invisible.

"Where are we going?" Kit looked forward, "How long before we enter the rift?"

"We have an eight hour flight along the strings to the rift that Graud's portal key opened." Surreya yawned, "Might as well relax."

"I'll open the door to the habitation section." Hilli's voice chirped.

Behind the pilot's couch, a section of the glowing wall became transparent, then irised open. Niamah was first through, followed by Rainbow.

"Where's the loo?" Rainbow asked, "That fall was so flippin' scary that I need to go!!!"

"End of the hall, I think," Niamah added, grinning, "I'm going to look at the armoury, see what we have."

"There's some period specific clothing and other stuff back there." Hilli's voice added.

"Can I go have a look?" Mrorna asked.

"We need you to have a look," Hilli responded, "you are most familiar with what we need."

Tarmal and Fay followed the others into the back area and Newton looked through the door.

"Hey, it's huge back here!" he exclaimed, "Kinda like the T.A.R.D.I.S. you know, bigger on the inside than on the outside!"

Kit and Al were grinning as Grim looked puzzled, "Tardis? What is a Tardis?"

"You need to watch some television to find out." Kit patted him on the shoulder. They all moved into the back and followed Niamah into the armoury.

Niamah was holding a sword and practising with it in an open exercise space surrounded by weapons racks. At the other end of the room there was a shooting gallery. She was moving beautifully, aggressively, her long hair flung out around her head. Suddenly, with an upward flick of the sword, Niamah cut through the air, making a victory cry! The others stared at her with surprise and Niamah grinned back.

"I'm sorry." she explained, "I'm feeling a bit strange lately."

"Mum…" Kit was uncertain, "are you ok?"

"I don't have gate euphoria," Niamah shook her head, "it's the biogenetic-morphic trace, my new one."

"I'll do a medical scan." Hilli said as Kit and Al stepped closer to their mother.

"No need." Niamah protested, "I've already been checked. It's new neurological patterns in my brain."

"Your personality has changed." Al nodded.

"It's alright." Niamah reassured everyone, "I'm ok for the mission. My memories are unchanged as is my love and loyalty."

Grim stepped forward, "Your new look is good Niamah," he said, "and we all need to pull together as a team and succeed in this mission. It won't be easy, but we are all here by Divine appointment. We all have specific gifts and skills, warriors, scientists, and an excellent guide. In less than six hours we will be somewhere on Earth, around twelve thousand B.C.E. Hilli has a lot of resources here in the Ren for us to use. It is time to be prepared, to sort out ourselves. Are we ready?"

For a moment, everyone looked at each other. Only Hilli and Surreya weren't present, but they could see and hear the conversation. Rainbow and Mrorna, Newton, Kit, Al and Niamah, Tarmal and Fay all nodded agreement.

Chapter Twenty

Heart of Darkness

The Yosemite caldera had made the biggest eruption in recorded history. At the same time, the South Pacific was a volcanic cauldron. Earthquakes still shook the ring of fire and the whole western side of the Pacific Plate was rising, creating a new landmass. Tsunamis had caused incredible damage around the Pacific, but the worst of the destruction was in the Western United States, which was utterly desolated. But that wasn't all. In the north, the caldera was spewing thousands upon thousands of cubic kilometres of superheated gas and ash. In the Eastern United States and Canada, millions of refugees were being ferried to safe havens and then aboard the Daedalus, which was hovering over New York. The Excalibur fleet were incredibly busy, but still, many more millions were dead after less than three days. The ash cloud was now totally blocking the light of the sun over North America. More ash, high in the atmosphere was darkening the sky of the entire northern hemisphere.

There was a similar ash cloud rising from the South Pacific, but it was nowhere as bad as the toxic cloud in the north. Rather, most of the volcanism was deep underwater. Most of the southern cloud was super-heated steam. Heavy rain was drenching the entire southern hemisphere.

Standing on the bridge of the Daedalus, Captain John James was looking at the data on the ship holo-tank. He shook his head, "The whole world is screwed." he said under his breath.

Much further south, out in the Caribbean Sea, right in the middle of the infamous Bermuda Triangle, the supercarrier USS Gerald R. Ford was sailing north towards home, or rather what was left of home. The mood of the crew, all over the ship, was morbidly depressed. They all knew what had happened and their compatriots aboard another, now melted and sunk carrier had sent film taken of events in the sea over the Kermadec Trench. In the ready room, the flight crews were watching the film of the rescue. Some smart crew member of the doomed carrier had used their phone and filmed the Arrow flying over the deck of the sinking aircraft carrier. They watched the big ship come in close, the docking lift lower and the Excalibur troopers come out. The pilots could only come to one conclusion...

"Not only is our nation gone to hell," one of the fliers said, "but we now have a bunch of guys using fucking anti-gravity ships! We're obsolete technology and pretty much useless in the water."

"Can it Simon!" the ship's wing leader growled, "We are going back home to see what we can do to help. The U.S.A. still has a working government and we will be needed. At least these guys, calling themselves Petra, are on our side. We've got orders to help with the rescue. Apparently there is a new alliance of states. The new President is calling it the Free States."

"Who knows," one of the other pilots said optimistically, "they may let us fly their covert tech! I'd go for that!"

"The Petra military arm is called the Order." the wing leader continued, "The captain has talked directly with some of their top people and he's talking about an integrated military for the Free States, so, yes, we will soon be flying on a whole new level. I don't know much more than that. Our job, once we get home, is to head for New Orleans and organise any rescue ops as well as gather people for evacuation."

"And where are we all supposed to be evacuated to?" Simon asked.

"I'm told Australia."

The pilot named Simon was laughing under his breath when the ships 'action stations' claxon began to screech all over the ship! Pilots were meant to scramble for their jets and other crew members to their posts all over the ship. The alarm meant that they were under attack. Simon and the other pilots ran up onto the flight deck where the crew helped them put their flight gear on and head for their jets, those already in position to launch using the electromagnetic aircraft launch system (EMAL). Capt. Johann R Simon, also known as 'Zealot' was first into the air, he was also the only one to make it.

He didn't see what was happening down on the ship, but right in front of his flight path was a huge island! 'Zealot' knew enough to know that the island wasn't supposed to be there, but somehow it was. Also, flying past him at incredible speeds were a small group of glowing, unidentified flying objects. They were disk shaped, classic German Haunebu III design, but with improved weapons and a slicker look. 'Zealot' had no time to think about it because they looped back from behind him without slowing down and one of them fired a particle weapon at his jet. The explosion flung his jet sickeningly sideways and Simon realised he was done and ejected immediately. It all happened in a matter of seconds, and then he hit the water heavily. At the same time there were some loud explosions on the flight deck as the enemy disks took out the remaining jets, then they flew in close and hovered over the deck.

From the island, at the rear of the flight deck, the commander and his crew watched as black armoured troops dropped in among the burning wreckage of the jets and under cover of the smoke, began to shoot at the marines that were trying to defend the ship. The enemy troops moved fast, inhumanly so, and were seemingly unstoppable. For the American sailors, instinctive combat training kicked in, along with a determination to not let the ship be taken. All over the carrier officers opened weapons lockers and led small groups of men and women to set up defensive positions around the ship. The commander himself led his bridge crew down to the flight deck where they were immediately under attack as the enemy rushed in through the main hatches. A fire fight was begun in one of the stairwells, but the enemy were using some kind of sonic weapon. Pulses of low vibrating sound punched up the stairwell regardless of whatever cover there was and sailors were knocked out cold. The bullets of the defenders just bounced off the black armour of the attackers harmlessly. Methodically the enemy moved through the big ship, firing their sonic weapons, even through walls and decks, there was nowhere for the Americans to hide. It took less than fifteen minutes to pacify the entire ship and every crew member was either unconscious or dead. Members of the attack group entered the island and shut the ship's systems down from the bridge. Out on the flight deck, three of the enemy E.D.Vs locked themselves to the deck using clamps attached to their landing gear and magnetic grapples placed under the deck by the attack group members. They then spun up their electro-dynamic drives and began to direct the carrier towards the island. As they moved the ship, the attackers began to bring the bodies up onto the flight deck and lay them out in rows. A box was brought out of one of E.D.Vs and opened. Inside were sets of grey metal collars and bracelets. Systematically each of the unconscious Americans were collared.

Still floating out in the ocean, Captain Simon watched the ship being towed towards the island. The enemy that had shot him down had apparently forgotten about him or assumed that he'd been killed. It was a long way to swim, but 'Zealot' was named appropriately and he was determined to follow. Relying upon his life jacket for floatation, Simon began to swim, following in the ship's wake.

London, Paris and Berlin were the main strongholds of the enemy. The battle in the English Midlands had shaken them. The Pandemonium forces had expected their arrival in 1918 not 2018 and so they were quite disoriented. We opened the portals from the Corridor and brought through the reinforcements, significant fleets hovering over Terra-Avalon, over the Raths at Olympus, Ararat and Shangri-La (which was in Tibet). Yeshua and his host of Malakim were doing something at the Zion Rath in Jerusalem. Pretty much we were able to move around as we wanted to, but this situation wouldn't last long. Eventually the enemy would come out of their occupied cities. For me, this lull in the fighting was frustrating because in my years of experience I knew what it meant. They were consolidating their position and gathering strength for the next big push. Just like in 1914, they were building entrenchments and rebuilding lost war-machines. Most horrific of all was the growing numbers of collared thralls we could observe doing all the manual labour. In the fight, they would be used as innocent shields. Some of the generals wanted to fight immediately, but I knew that would be a mistake. We had taken a pounding and our numbers were still low as we had to rescue the victims of the war. Getting citizens evacuated from North America and Europe as well as in the quake zones was the priority, and our enemy knew it.

Another thing concerned me. Back when the stasis bubbles first appeared, we faced the Humdrid and there was the Nephalim cloaked ship that we destroyed. Other than that, the Nephalim factions had been practically uninvolved, or at least it appeared that way. Some of us wondered what they were doing. I had sent out intelligence gathering teams into the occupied zones, but they weren't very successful. The enemy had collared almost everyone and once collared, the enthralled had no way to resist.

To make matters worse, the weather was getting colder, much colder. The volcanic ash cloud was blocking the sun all over Europe and much of Asia. Winter was coming early. The whole of Western Europe was still recovering from the e.m.p's and the huge storms that had destroyed so much infrastructure. A lot of communities still didn't have electricity and that was another reason why our Petra people were so busy. The biggest contribution we were making was power. Using the replicators in our Rath portal rings we were able to manufacture thousands of portable power generators, using advanced Corridor technology. But soon, we would also have to start replicating rations and other basics. Without the technological advantages of the Seelie, Europe would have descended into anarchy. That was probably what the enemy had hoped would happen.

I was personally involved in training new soldiers, with our biggest boot camp being set up in Shropshire near Terra-Avalon. A lot of the new people were Petra Alliance members, but the British military were ordered to co-operate, and God knew we needed their numbers. Lots of others were also volunteering from all over the world. This was made possible by something very special, the formation of a new international organisation called 'The Free States'.

Many world leaders had been horrified after the invasion by the Pandemonium and the battle for Terra-Avalon. The United Nations had tried to meet, but the ash fall made it impossible to do anything in New York. So, the UN called an emergency council in Geneva. I was there, along with other Petra, Order and Seelie representatives. Finvara himself, Al's father, came to me.

"The Seerlie Court are unanimous." he said, "They want you to speak on our behalf to the United Nations. You know what we need to do. The world is ready to know about us now, and we want to stand alongside humanity against the darkness."

I shook the tall Danann by his three fingered hand. None of them were cloaking themselves with glamour now.

"Thank you my friend." I nodded.

We had used the Arrow to go around the world and collect as many ambassadors and actual world leaders as possible during the time of crisis. Most nations were anxious to meet and so members of the UN Security-Council chose the logical place, the Palace of Nations (Palais des Nations) in Geneva. The Arrow was conspicuously parked in a clear space in Ariana Park, right next to Lake Geneva. The ambassadors were brought in, accompanied by their own security, but it was the Order that Switzerland had asked to provide overall security. Our best power suited special ops people were brought in, led by Weaver. A lot of our suits were Aussies, like Weaver, but there were enough Zioronians to cause a lot of the delegates to be curious. Virey and Fass had come with me into the Palace. Both were typical Zioronians of the Grenworlder ethnic group. They were fair skinned and blonde, yet looked Asian. But there were other things that made them look alien, their mannerisms and unusual accents. Though of course, it was the A'sidhe tribes of the Vansadagaadian Corridor that were the most alien of all. I would have a lot to explain.

The meeting was gathering in the main room of the old League of Nations building. This made me feel a bit strange. I was there when the League was formed, and I was there when it failed with the rise of the Nazis.

Our representatives gathered on the main stage, along with the speaker and the UN General Secretary, a Mexican lady named Maria Rivera. Seated on the stage with Finvara was Brigid, Fass and Virey. I was the lone Terran.

Mrs Rivera and the Speaker, an older Swiss man came over to me, "This isn't a formal UN gathering," she said, "that will follow later. For now, what I want you to do is to simply inform the body, give us some background. They want to know what has happened and they want to know who you and your people are and what your plans are. I have always been up front with people and believe in honesty."

"We do too." I replied, "There is no time to be deceptive with each other. Our planet is in grave danger."

The General Secretary and Speaker took their places.

The Speaker stood to introduce the meeting, speaking French, which would be translated for those who couldn't speak it, "This emergency crisis meeting of the UN General Assembly is called to order." he began, "By order of the General Secretary and the members of the Security Council, this extraordinary meeting has been called in investigate this recent crisis. Unprecedented catastrophe has occurred. There has also been a military attack by unknown assailants and large areas of continental Europe, including areas of both Germany, France as well as Southern England are presently occupied. Also, our world is experiencing rapid environmental change. We have with us representatives of ..." the Speaker looked over his shoulder and sighed involuntarily, "certain people ... who can explain this situation and help us to consider next steps of immediate action."

The General Secretary suddenly stood and moved up next to the Speaker quickly, stepping to the microphone, smiling at him as she interrupted.

"Ladies and Gentlemen," she addressed the body, "before Max introduces our guests, who have been so helpful in making this very gathering possible, let me begin with some very important considerations. Let none of us deceive each other anymore. No doubt all of you are aware that highly advanced weapons and technology is being openly used. Right now I want to declassify certain 'above top secret' realities that all of us here are generally aware of, yet which none of us want to admit to. Certain nations or alliances of nations exist, along with secret agencies."

For a moment the General Secretary stopped and looked around the big room. She knew who she was talking to and so did I.

"Some of you in this room know what I'm about to do. The code word is '*Aquarius 2691*.'"

There was a stirring among the delegates. I knew what she had done, we all did. The *Aquarius* Treaty was made back in 1991 and involved a number of world powers, those who used and had access to advanced covert technology. Petra was only one of a number of signatories, which included the American NORAD Operation Dreamland (Area 51), the NATO and European Space Agency 'Chevalier Project', Russia's (ex-Soviet) Red Star organisation in the Ural Mountains, China's Tao Agency, Japans 'Katana' and the Islamic League's 'Essential Fire Project.' The *Aquarius* Treaty was created so that in a global crisis, the different covert agencies could agree to work together against a common foe. It was obvious to everyone that just such an eventuality was now upon us.

With that, the General Secretary sat down. The Speaker, looking a little shaken, stood back up.

"Let me introduce our honoured guest," he said, "General Sir Walter Ryan of the Petra Security Corporation, known as 'the Order'."

As I stepped forward, looking over the large gathering of world leaders and diplomats, my feelings were mixed. All my life I had very little trust for politicians and any attempt at world government, like the League of Nations or the UN, was just more tyranny, more control. Nevertheless, I needed to talk to these representatives of the world, even if some of them had sinister motives. I wondered how many of these people took their orders from the Nephalim Baals. Still, the goal of the Kingdom to which I was loyal was to bring real peace to the world, not by force, but by giving people a chance to legitimately choose freedom.

"Ladies and gentlemen," I began, "leaders of the sovereign nations of the world, I have been asked to speak to you and explain the present situation which faces the planet, and also to make an offer of help. I have been given authority to reveal to you the true nature of this conflict."

I paused briefly, *here goes,* I thought.

"The enemy that have attacked France, Germany and Great Britain and presently occupy parts of those countries are time travellers from the distant past. The advanced technology they used to achieve this time travel was the direct cause of the release of huge amounts of electro-dynamic and gravitational energies in the atmosphere, causing the electro-magnetic pulses that has led to so much destruction. They call themselves the Daiesthai or the Shedu, but more commonly they are known as the Pandemonium. They are led by a ruler or Baal named Graud. Graud is a member of an ancient race called the Anunnaki or Nephalim, who have one goal, to enslave the Earth. You must understand the truth of our planet's history. Before Homo-Sapiens became the dominant sentient species upon our planet, other much more ancient races lived here. I am here representing another species. The Vansad have also been known by many names, like Angels, Elves, or Faerie. Members of the Vansad leadership, the Seelie Court are here with us now and they are our greatest allies. For many, many thousands of years, the Seelie have watched over and protected us from harm. Our human race would have been destroyed long ago without them here guarding us. Before each representative in this room we have left a dossier which gives details of both our enemy and allies. This is full disclosure. What I'm saying may sound like pure fantasy, but I want to assure you that this is deadly serious business. We face a deadly enemy who has inflicted a massive blow against us. The very existence of our species is at stake. I implore the leaders of our world to listen. The Seelie Court will always be our friends and will fight all who would seek to destroy us. We need to recognize who our friends are and work together for the sake of our children and our children's, children's future. I am a human being and I represent the Petra Alliance, an association of communities who are already working with the Seelie in the defence of our world. Our research and development corporation, PETRAD, and our security corporation, the Order, have free access to the advanced technology of the Seelie. We are going to use that technology to fight the Pandemonium with all our strength. The Seerlie Court, have asked me to present to the leaders of the world a Treaty for the formation of Free States, to be allies in this conflict against the Pandemonium."

At that point I stopped and stepped back. Finvara and Brigid came forward to join me. We looked out at the crowd before us and inwardly we prayed.

"Alright...." the Speaker named Max stammered, "it is time for questions, a chance then to review the dossiers given, and then after a recess, we will return and after further discussion we will vote on this resolution."

It took over six hours for the questions and the recess. During the break a lot of deals were done and secret alliances made. The fact is that the Seerlie Court were not the only Vansad faction playing the field and of course there were the Nephalim factions, the Atalanti who operated mostly in America and Unseerlie in Europe, who formed an alliance calling itself Medusa. The remnants of the Ouroboros were in Germany and Eastern Europe. The Immortals were in China, the Olympians in Greece and Italy. Our allies included the Djinni in the Middle East and the Malakim in Israel. The others were mostly self-interested and really couldn't be trusted, but that was the way it was with a lot of the Old Folk. All over the world there were a lot of Faerie Solitaries as well.

There was no doubt that some of these renegades would be working with or infiltrating some of the *Aquarius* groups. Nothing was simple, except that human survival was at stake.

In the end, not everyone returned to the Hall of Nations and a number of nations or rather blocks of nations were conspicuous by their absence. We wouldn't find out until later that new global power blocks were about to emerge. Of course the Free States Treaty was signed by what was left of the USA and Canada, Great Britain and Ireland, Scandinavia, the Netherlands and Switzerland, the new Caucasus Autonomous Region, Israel, the Southern African Block, and the Oceanic Block which included Australia, New Zealand and the South Pacific Territories.

After that the General Secretary called another full gathering of the UN, stood before the Assembly and declared that the Free States Treaty had been ratified. A significant part of the Treaty was that the member states recognized the sovereignty of the Vansadagaadian Nations. This included the recognition of renegade nations, but not those allied to the Nephalim. What happened next was expected and a part of the agenda given to the Speaker.

Three representatives stood, including the Ambassadors of China, Japan and India, but it wasn't any one of them who spoke for them. A fourth person stood, who looked obviously Asian, but then we could see the glamour flow away to reveal an Elder of the Immortals. He said nothing, he didn't need to. Across the Hall of the Nations, the representatives of the United States of Europe, (which included Russia and Eastern Europe) and the Latin Alliance were accompanied by two Vansad. As they removed the cloak of their glamour, there stood a Ring Maiden of the Ouroboros and an Olympian demi-god. Then to make matters worse the representative of the Islamic League stood with another cloaked individual. I winced inwardly when I saw that it was none other than Namtar, wearing a suit! The Djinni had shown that they wanted independence after all. I wondered what Surreya knew about this.

The first person to ascend the stage was the Chinese Ambassador, but he was introduced by the Speaker as the Representative of the Pan-Asian Zone.

"Honourable Speaker, Madame General Secretary, representatives of the United Nations, as this body has been aware for some time, there has been a growing relationship between the great nations of Asia. At this time of Global crisis the great nations of China, Japan and India have formed a regional alliance. As members of the *Aquarius* Treaty we have remained responsible in our co-operative use of advanced covert technology and have been working for many years with the Vansad Nation of Shangri-La, also known as the Immortals. Like other nations we are facing the consequences of the attack of the common enemy, the Pandemonium, and while we wish to make it exceedingly clear that we are determined to maintain our unique regional interests, we are also determined to remain an ally in this conflict against a common enemy. The Pan-Asian Zone recognizes the Free States and the Seerlie Court, but this recognition is conditional upon the recognition of all Vansadagaadian nations, including the Immortals, the Ouroboros, the Olympians and the Djinni as fellow members of the *Aquarius* Treaty. We expect this as part of the spirit of international cooperation and acceptance that is vital for the success of the United Nations and victory against our enemy. Thank you."

Next, it was a Spaniard who stepped up before the gathering.

"The United States of Europe and the Latin League have established a new treaty, the Western Global Alliance (or W.G.A.)." he said after making his formal introductions, "The W.G.A. was formed for the mutual security of our peoples. Europe is occupied by a dangerous and powerful enemy. The United States of America no longer exists as a global superpower, and is unlikely to be restored. While our European agencies are members of the *Aquarius* Treaty and we have the support of the nations of the Ouroboros and Olympia, the Latin League, indeed, all the peoples of Central and Southern America, need the support of Europe and we need them. While the W.G.A. is loyal to the goals of the *Aquarius* Treaty, and we formally recognize the Free States and the Seerlie Court as allies in both war and peace, without the resources of the United States, we are seeking a new global balance of power. So we have a vision for the future, a future beyond the defeat of an enemy."

Finally, the representative of the Islamic League came to the front. We all recognized him. He was one of the most significant spiritual leaders on the planet, his followers called him Mahdi, although he refused to accept such for himself, but preferred to simply be called Brother. He had finally convinced the Moslem world to stop the killing of endless Jihad. A lot of his success had been due to the final defeat of Daesh in 2017 and the League's anti-petroleum concordat that saw the end of OPEC and global oil. The Mahdi had personally invested his substantial personal fortune into renewable energy. The oil monopolies that were the reasons for so much war in the Middle East had been broken.

"Salaam. All my life I have been a man of peace." he began without any other words, "I continue to believe in peace. Yet, to understand true Salaam, one understands that it isn't just about the absence of conflict, but rather to find inner peace in the midst of life. This conviction that has been revealed to all good people of spiritual faith is that we fight Jihad not against one another, as though war can ever achieve anything, but hold as self-evident that Jihad is within our souls, where Allah resides. Let us bring peace within, then peace will come without. But now we face a time of crisis. The Shaitan is here to cause mischief among us and they come to enslave and kill. Is it possible to live in peace with the Pandemonium? I do not believe it is. With the help of the Djinni, we have come not to a new understanding, but a very old and true understanding. We will stand with the people of the world and fight, fight not for religion nor to tear down the west as foolish men did before, but to rescue the slave and restore life and freedom. As Isa said, we must love our neighbour as we love ourselves, and so we will fight to defend our neighbour."

Chapter Twenty-One

Captives

The crew of the USS Gerald R. Ford regained consciousness while still on the deck of the ship. The sonic weapons which had stunned them had left all of them with headaches, but it was something else which kept them paralysed and unable to move.

The captain of the ship and his officers and bridge crew were kept to one side, not far from one of the enemy e.d.v's. One of the black suited enemy troops stepped down the disk's ramp and stood over the captain. He reached up and unclipped the collar of his neck strap and then pulled his helm right off. The man under the helm was of Zioronian stock, with the same oriental features and fair hair and complexion, but his hair was in short dreadlocks and his face was marked with complex tattoos around his eyes. He grinned, revealing teeth that had been filed to points.

"Feeling comfortable?" he chuckled, "I expect not. You and your whole crew are now captive, oh captain of the USS Gerald R. Ford. We took you all in less than ten minutes without a single loss. So much for America!" the enemy laughed.

"I'm not talking to you now out of courtesy," he leaned closer, peering at the stricken captain, "but so you know that there is no choice but to obey me and my masters. Tell me your name."

"Cap..." suddenly there was pain, excruciating pain unlike anything that the man had felt before. It stopped as quickly as it came, and there was no after effect.

"I told you to give me your name." the captor said calmly, "No rank nor serial number. That does not exist anymore for you. You are not a captain. This is not your ship and you are now a thrall. Answer me your name if you understand."

"Anthony James Burgess."

"Very good Anthony, that wasn't too hard was it?" Feelings of sudden pleasure flowed into the ex-captain, then stopped, "I think you get the idea now. Stand up."

Anthony James Burgess stood up quickly and without hesitation. His captor just grinned at him.

"Stay there." he said, then moved onto another crew member.

Now that he was standing, Anthony, former captain, could see where the ship was. They had sailed into a harbour. The island rose up before them. There was a dock nearby towards which the large ship was being directed. The sound of the electro-dynamic drives powering down could be heard as the e.d.v's that were pushing the ship completed their task. There was no other obvious sign of civilization except for a road leading from the dock into the rainforest jungle that seemed to be everywhere. The ex-captain felt utterly numb and completely powerless.

Suddenly the carrier lurched with a crunching sound as it slid next to the long concrete docking area. The water was deep enough to accommodate the huge ship, but the dock was a long way below the flight deck or even the normal boarding gantries. The black suited troopers ordered their captives to line up along the deck. The e.d.v's were unclamped from the ship and they flew away.

"You thralls do not get to fly to the Rath." the enemy leader told the Americans, "You get to walk. We will get you down to the dock."

Black suited troopers began to 'unload' the captives by picking up individuals, two at a time, and despite their smaller size in comparison to the bigger Americans, slung them over their shoulders and then leapt off the flight deck down to the dock below! Orders to be silent had to be obeyed, but the leap down was a shock, even for seasoned members of the navy. The black troopers were obviously wearing powered suits and had repulsor units in their boots that enabled them to jump such a distance of over fifty metres. Down on the dock, the Americans were deposited like so much baggage and ordered to wait while the troops returned to collect more of their human cargo. Finally the job was done. There was no shouting nor pushing nor shoving. The Americans were told to follow a trooper who led the way off the dock and down the paved road into the jungle. They walked.

Walking into the jungle was like entering a living green tunnel. The only light was that which managed to filter through the canopy above, the only sounds were of marching feet and that of birds and other animals, unseen all around. In other circumstances the walk might have been pleasant, but the fact that the Americans had no idea of what their fate was to be, left them shadowed by fear. One of the crewmen suddenly fell to his knees, forcing others to walk around him. One of the black troopers ordered his crew mates to keep going and then turned to look at the stricken man. His face was contorted with pain and horror, not only because his collar was spiking him, but because he was almost catatonic with fear. The black trooper took hold of his head and turned it to the side, examining him. With a snort of derision, he made a sharp jerking movement and snapped the man's neck and he fell flat on his face, and then he was left behind. The group walked on and thankfully didn't see the man's body dragged into the jungle by something that leapt out quickly then returned, leaving no trace behind.

Up ahead the jungle was opening up a bit and letting in more light. The road itself entered a tunnel in a rock face. Standing guard on either side of the tunnel mouth were two more black troopers who watched menacingly as they walked past. Inside the tunnel the way was lit by glow globes in the roof. Occasionally there were side tunnels, but the lead trooper kept them on the main road, heading downwards under the ground. Finally, they came to the interior of the Rath. It was a huge cavern with the city itself located upon a table top plateau. The only way across to the city was via four bridges. The city was surrounded by a water filled moat and as usual there were tunnels leading out from the city into the Annwn realm that was even deeper underneath the city. The Americans had never seen anything like this before. Up above the city was the Raths power sphere, giving light to the Rath. As the group came to the first archway leading onto the bridge, about to cross to the city, there was a completely different kind of horror in the form of a simple red flag hanging down over the arch. There was a black swastika boldly emblazoned in the middle. The guards at the archway saluted the black troops as they passed with hands raised. Crossing into the city was depressing for the Americans. The city itself looked like a NAZI paradise. Swastikas hung from every window. Grey uniformed Aryan citizens glared hatred at them, but then the

Americans noticed the non-humans. All Raths had a dominant population. In this case there were Nephalim Baals and their bodyguards the Anakim. The Baals were tall, blonde and beautiful. Both males and females went unclothed although they were all armed with knives. The Anakim painted their bodies different colours and some wore chain or belts decorated with bone. They all bristled with deadly edged weapons as well as long blasters in shoulder holsters. The Anakim had typical Anunnaki features, but they were incredibly tall and powerful looking, and had the extra feature of having a long prehensile tail. There were also Nephalim Renim, known as Shrikes, many of whom were flying around the city.

But with the arrival of the Americans, everyone stopped to look. Some of the Nephalim actually growled, while the Nazis spat at them as they were led past. They were led into the centre of the city. As they came out into the central plaza, there was the portal ring, with the altar stone before the huge central trilithon. There were also three thrones, one in front of each trilithon. On the middle throne was a huge Neph. He was shaved bald and his cat-like eyes were glowing icy blue. Seated on either side were female Nephalim. One had her skin painted white and the other her skin painted black. Even their eyes were full coloured. They both had long hair, plaited and with a metal bar tied at the back of their heads. The Americans were marched before the thrones and told to sprawl face down. The two female Nephalim hissed at them like snakes.

The big Neph stood and he laughed to himself, "Ah, the gallant Americans, defeated by my Valorians."

He moved around the prone forms. They were still being brought into the plaza by the black suited 'Valorian' guards. The leader approached and bowed.

"How many?" the Baal asked.

"There are 4,660 crew members."

"That's a lot of new thralls," he nodded, "but not just that, they are a valuable resource, and so is their ship."

The Baal looked down at the bodies laid out before him. He spotted the captains uniform, walked over and picked the man up by the scruff of the neck, and stood him on his feet.

"You will obey me?"

The captain said nothing and fell suddenly into horrific agony, screaming and writhing on the ground. The Baal picked the man up again and the pain was replaced by pleasure. The captain sighed.

"You will obey me." a statement this time.

"Yes sir."

"My name is Baal Nimrod." he said, then pointed to the females behind him, "They are my Asherim, Ishtar and Lilith. You are old enough to be familiar with a particular science fiction program called 'Stargate'? Well, this is *NOTHING* like that show! I am not some self-deluded alien with a god complex. I am not a god. I am a Baal, I rule over the Nephalim of this planet and I am a very powerful person. We have one goal, a very clear one, to become the dominant species on this world as we once were. Also, I am not evil. I do not do evil things. Me and mine are the resistance against the true evil of the Eldar and the Elohim despots who DO claim to be divine! There is this Yeshua, the one you call Jesus, the one called the Son of God. A whole religious tyranny has grown up around him. Who is the self-deluded one? Listen to me and know the truth. Right now you and all your fellow Americans are thralls. It is a far more honest kind of slavery. Before you were under slavery, and now you are again. Before you did not know that you were a slave, but now you do know. I am offering to you the possibility to be truly free. There are many people here in Atlantis who were once thralls as you are now, but who now no longer wear their collars or bracelets because they are now trusted comrades, joining us in the fight against a false God and the tyranny of a world enslaved by religion."

Nimrod stepped back and looked at the American. "For now those collars are a tool to keep you co-operative. I have no problem with using considerable power to make my wishes come about. If you obey, you will be rewarded by the collar, and there are other rewards and freedoms as well. I have plans for you, but for now there are questions that need to be answered."

From behind Baal Nimrod came two other Baals. One of them was painted with red skin. He was huge as well, but muscular rather than tall. His companion was painted blue and he was as thin as his companion was wide.

"These two are my experts on training and interrogation, Baal Molech and Baal Dagon."

Nimrod turned and his two Asherim came to him. They walked away out of the ring. It was obvious that Nimrod had finished saying what he wanted to say. The two Baals nodded to the Valorian officers who stood around among the prone Americans. With a word nearly 4,660 sailors all stood obediently. The Valorians had the Americans march out of the Atlantis ring plaza and they were taken away.

Chapter Twenty-Two

Antediluvian Arrival

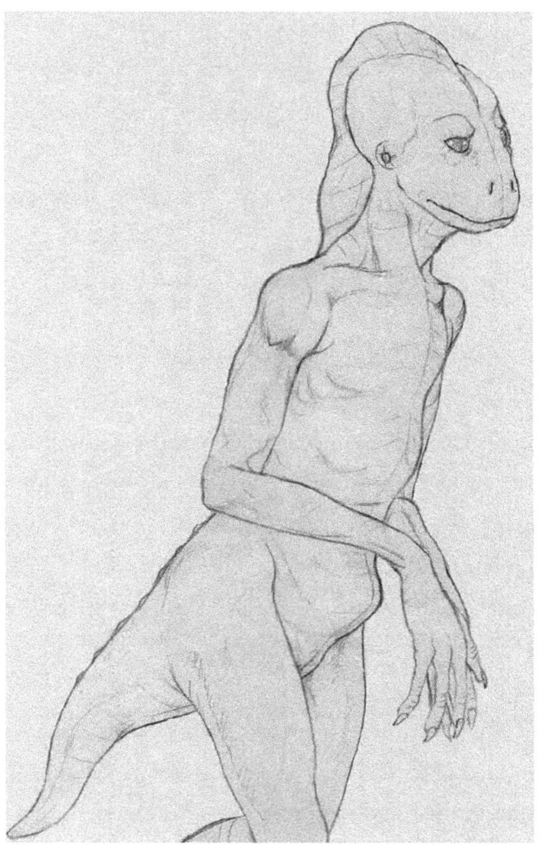

High in the atmosphere there was a flash of light and then the booming of the sound barrier being broken. Hilli dropped down and skimmed along above a body of water. Her Ren form was glowing with tachyon radiation dropping below light speed. She was flying at incredible speeds and trying very hard to slow down. At the same time, she was following the projected trajectory that Graud must have flown when he dropped through the hole in the time continuum. Like a stone being skimmed over water, so Hilli bounced over the water of the Eastern Mediterranean sea and then as she finally began to slow down, she shot up and over northern Mesopotamia, coming down somewhere in what is now Northern Iraq.

The impact caused a huge explosion and a crater, but Hilli hovered as a cooling ball of electric discharge in the middle of the burning hollow. It took a bit of time, but soon Hilli cooled down.

Inside Hilli's main cabin the whole team were together. Surreya was still in the control couch.

"Well that wasn't good at all," Surreya stuttered a bit, "but at least we are still alive. How're you Hilli?"

"A bit crispy but otherwise my systems are operating as they should." Hilli replied.

"What is our location?" Grim asked.

"I'll put up a map." Hilli replied.

On the wall before them there appeared a 3D map. It showed all of the Western hemisphere. Hilli moved the focus into a spot just to the west of Spain, over the ocean. In many ways the map looked familiar, in other ways things looked significantly different. In the middle of the North Atlantic Ocean was a huge landmass dividing the ocean in two. The north of Europe was covered by a blanket of ice, snow and cloud. The world was in the middle of an ice age and the ocean levels were lower.

"I'll mark our entry point and trajectory to where we are now."

The spot appeared over the ocean and a curved line moved eastwards, across the Mediterranean to their final landing spot. Grim stood closer to the map and looked carefully.

"Show me the local area please Hilli." he requested.

The map zoomed in.

"Ah!" Grim seemed ecstatic, "I know where we are! There is the Black Sea, reduced in size, to our north, and the much enlarged Caspian Sea to the north east.

We are just south of the region of Eden, in what was once called the land of Aratta. There is Lake Urmia, where the Garden is located! This could be no coincidence that we come to rest here, nor that Graud himself passed this way. We are not far from the Adamite tribal lands. We will have to seek answers among those people."

"So where do we go first?" Hilli asked, "What flight plan?"

"No flight plan." Grim smiled a reptilian smile, "We will need to walk."

"Now tell me Grim," Hilli said about an hour later, "why exactly are we walking?"

They had moved away from the burning crater their arrival had caused and Hilli had let them out in a clearing. They had seen what looked like a road while in the air and had headed through the forest looking for it.

"This is definitely a path used by humans." he said, "There is a hearth back over that ridge. We need to walk because we need to make contact with local people without causing too much alarm or disrupting their culture at this level of technology."

"We're carrying blasters Grim!" Newton laughed, "We'll disrupt someone's culture eventually."

"Only when absolutely necessary to do so." he replied, "Advanced communities, the Seelie, Anunnaki and others did exist in this time period, and they were able to coexist with the Neolithic culture of this time."

The path that the group were walking on soon cleared and they stepped out into an open area. To everyone's most startled surprise, there standing right on the path in the middle of the clearing there was a dinosaur! Not just any dinosaur, but a large carnosaur! It was just standing there, all bold and not doing anything in particular. The group all stood as though transfixed to the ground. Grim raised a hand to his mouth to signal silence. The big creature turned its head and looked right at them! It snorted derisively and without any other sound began to walk towards them!

"Run for it!" Grim ordered, "Into the thick scrub!"

So they scattered into the scrub land behind them. The large theropod moved quickly down the path and to the spot where they'd been standing. Kit watched from behind a large tree and could see the beast sniffing at the ground.

"So much for being dumb and having a visual acuity based on movement!" he grumbled under his breath. The big carnosaur looked right at him, "Oh shit!" Kit turned and ran as the beast ran after him!

Most frightening of all was the way that the beast seemed so intelligent. There was no loud roaring nor was there much noise at all. Kit had run into a grove of trees and met up with Mrorna and Al. The creature seemed to have disappeared.

"Where is it?" Kit asked, breathless, "Have either of you seen where it went?"

"It's a leviath!" Mrorna lamented, "It's wearing a control cap! Someone is seeing and hunting for us!"

There was a sudden crashing noise and the trees behind them seemed to explode as the leviath smashed through violently. Kit led Mrorna back the way he'd come and Al leapt up, flashing his flight wings and took to the air, narrowly avoiding the beast's snapping jaws. The group met together further up the path, called together by an implant com message sent by Grim. Hilli, Surreya, Niamah and Al were all flying by now.

"We have to fight it!" Grim cried, and they all drew their hand held blasters, pointing down the road.

"It's coming around behind you!!" Niamah suddenly screamed, and the creature barged out from among the trees and was upon them. The group scattered, but the flying Seelie quickly opened fire. High energy particle weapons arched into the dinosaur, blowing considerable holes in its body! Still, now enraged with pain, the creature finally roared, spraying blood fleck from its mouth! On the road, Newton and Mrorna pulled Rainbow into the cover of the trees while the others formed a line and began to fire as well. It didn't take long and the creature fell over and shuddered in its death throes. The smell of burnt flesh was overpowering. Everyone exhaled in relief. Rainbow, despite the protests of her protectors, broke free and wanted to get a closer look at the now dead dinosaur.

With weapons still drawn and carefully, they moved in for a closer look. Mrorna though was shaking her head.

"This isn't good!" she said anxiously, "Leviath scouts always precede a war band! We need to move on quickly!"

"No time to check this out." Grim agreed, "We need to move on. Not on the road, but along the tree line. Let's move!"

Rainbow wanted to protest, but she realised that safety had to come first. They'd made a lot of noise, and Mrorna looked mortified! The group moved quickly into the cover of the trees. Keeping low and spread out, they moved carefully, keeping to cover as much as possible. Under the tree cover, their clothing took on the colours of the surrounding vegetation.

Looks like we are right in the middle of something. Grim sent a soundless message using his implant com, *What can you tell us Mrorna?*

The leviath was capped and riderless. She began, *there will be others along the road, probably looking for us. If they saw our arrival, there will be a war band. But we are in Eden, this is way outside their territory.*

No large parties? What can we expect? Grim asked.

Pandemonium perhaps, but more likely we will meet Gorenge in a pack.

Gor-en-gee, Rainbow pronounced the word sub-vocally, *what are they?*

Lizard warriors. Mrorna replied, *Very smart, well-armed. Their leader is usually a Neph.*

Velociraptor type dinosaurs, Newton added, *but genetically engineered to be as smart or smarter than humans. The Neph leader is possessing one of them. Very, very dangerous.*

Al, Grim sent, *scout ahead of us on this side of the road. Surreya, cross the road, be careful, and*

scout ahead. We need to find out what is ahead. Niamah, lag behind a bit. Keep your eyes open people, weapons drawn all the time.

While the main group moved along, both Al and Surreya, who were fit and fast runners (and fliers!), moved ahead on either side of the road. Thankfully the tree cover was good and there were lots of ferns and rock outcrops to hide behind. That Grim had asked the three Vansad members to be the forward and rear scouts was logical because they were faster runners, light in their movements, and had much keener senses than the human members of the team. Hilli remained with the group as back up, and as quick transport if needed.

Fay and Tarmal, the two Zioronians, ran on the left and right. They were almost invisible in the undergrowth and moved with almost Seelie stealth. They both carried small bags on their hips, containing spare grenades, just in case. In the rear, Niamah did her best to remove the tracks of those ahead or leave behind deceptive markers. She had her sword out, her preferred weapon. In particular, she was on the look-out for large reptiles!

After some time, Surreya came upon a clearing. The road itself was climbing upwards and the hills had little cover. So she moved along a higher ridge, drawn there by some noises she could hear, noises that sounded like battle. The road ran between two hills and from her higher position Surreya could see what looked like a caravan of large animals with baskets and passenger gondolas on either side. More dinosaurs! This time they were large long necked sauropods, being used as beasts of burden. These dinosaurs were huge, and the passenger gondolas slung over their broad backs contained at least several passengers each, as well as cargo. Seated on the creatures necks were drivers, holding onto a chord that was attached to their mouths high above. The people were definitely humans. The drivers were bare chested men wearing short linen kilts with their faces covered in turbans. Surreya could also see bare breasted women in the gondolas, along with children. There were warriors armed with long spears walking along the ground next to their large animals. Looking across the small valley to the hill on the other side, Surreya suddenly saw reptilian forms running along the ridge. With her excellent sight Surreya could see the Gorenge warriors clearly. They wore uniforms, of a kind, including some body armour and helms, as well as metal toe claws on their feet. Their bodies were painted with symbols in different colours. Some of them carried edged weapons, but for most, their long fore-claws were looking formidable enough. They were rallying, obviously preparing to attack. Surreya drew her blaster in one hand and her sword in the other.

We need to move quickly! Grim alerted the whole team, *Surreya has spotted a group of humans about to be attacked by a Gorenge war band! I propose that we help them!*

The team soon caught up with Surreya on her hill and Grim signalled them to positions.

We all fight. Grim said bluntly, *Don't get killed! Go!!*

The four Seelie Vansad, Hilli, Surreya, Al and Niamah all took flight and with weapons drawn, they swooped down into the valley where the Gorenge raiders were already attacking the rear of the caravan. The human warriors were fighting valiantly, but the Gorenge were much bigger and more powerful. Without help, the humans wouldn't last long. The others in the team ran down the hillside and using their blasters began what would become a very one sided battle. The Gorenge tried to leap against them, but against the rapid fire of the particle blasters, the enemy fell one after the other as smoking corpses! The humans in their caravan drew close to each other and watched the fight going on around them with surprise and stunned amazement. There had been about fifteen of the enemy that needed to be dispatched. They had no idea what hit them, and while a couple of them needed to be finished off, most were ended cleanly. One of the Gorenge, a large female, was the Neph leader and the last to die. Niamah took her on in particular, shooting her in the leg to disable her as she roared defiance, then killing her with a sword stroke to the heart, and a sacred killing word! While the others finished killing, Niamah sat down next to the still twitching body and went instantly into a deep trance. Al stood guard over her, while the team gathered near the startled members of the caravan. The warriors were already bowing down upon the ground and many of the passengers and the drivers were making trilling noises in victory, the drivers waving their spears in the air. One man though stood by silently, nor did he bow. Mrorna went immediately up to him and bowed, kissing his hands. The man pulled his turban aside and kissed her hands in return.

"Greetings Elder," Mrorna began formally, "peace to you and your tribe."

"Peace to you and yours as well." he replied. At first the team members didn't understand the words, but as he spoke more, their 'tongues' ability kicked in and they could understand his particular dialect, which Mrorna already spoke, "I am Rom." he said.

"I must apologize my lord," Mrorna presented her hands to him again, "my companions do not know the ways of your tribe nor are they aware of the protocols, please let us continue to serve you."

The man named Rom smiled and again kissed Mrorna's hands. She turned and smiled at the team members.

"We need to introduce ourselves." Mrorna said.

"My name is Grim Torgar," Grim stepped forward, "I am the leader of this band of explorers."

"You are obviously not Pandemonium, since you have helped us," Rom responded, "but your species is unknown to me, and I have met many beings as my tribe are traders."

"I belong to an alliance of races called the Eldar which serve the Elohim."

"If you serve the Elohim," Rom was smiling, "then we are definitely friends. You and your warriors have the hospitality of my tribe. I notice you are also in the company of the Seelie. We are honoured to have met you here on the road to Manhome."

"You are going to Manhome?" Grim asked, "Who rules there at the moment?"

"You cannot be ignorant of that!" Rom laughed, "My father Awdame still rules the people."

"I thought he would be the ruler there." Grim nodded, "We have come this way to see him. We are aware that this is a violent time and we want to help the people."

"Are you warriors for hire?" Rom asked, "What cost for your services, hmmm?"

"No.." Grim shook his head, "put it this way, that we have a common enemy and that it would benefit both of us to see that enemies' downfall."

"Then I will introduce you properly."

While Grim and Rom were making their introductions, Niamah was busy doing something else. After she had killed the Gorenge leader, Niamah had sat down next to the body and entered her tracer trance. Almost instantly her spirit had left her body behind and she'd floated away. Niamah looked around quickly and spotted the trace of the dead Gorenge hovering to one side, looking disoriented, writhing in death agony. Smaller traces were nearby of the other dead Gorenge, but these were quickly losing energy, floating off into the forgetfulness of the ghost realm. Some had already formed into ghost balls and their fate was to fall into the earth and sleep. But the dead Neph was different. She was beginning to wake up, freed of her mortal body.

Niamah, glowing with life force, formed a sword in her hand and attacked the trace before it could wake up! For those who were talking nearby, they had no idea of the invisible battle taking place, but it was something absolutely necessary. Niamah drove the sword into the non-corporeal energy trace of the Neph. There was a popping noise and the reptilian form began to shrink, forming into a ball of light. Niamah had to exert herself, drawing the life energy into herself through her sword arm. Finally she drew the sword out and grasped the ghost ball in her other hand, squeezing more energy out until it was only the size of a small marble. Then Niamah let the small ball drop. It was now grey in colour and it fell into the earth, unable to cause any further harm.

Niamah dropped back into her physical body, feeling exhausted, yet also extremely pleased with herself. To make more poetic justice, that night, as the team settled for the night with their new friends, the Romany, they butchered and cooked the carcasses of the dead Gorenge, and ate the roasted meat!

Chapter Twenty-Three

Manhome

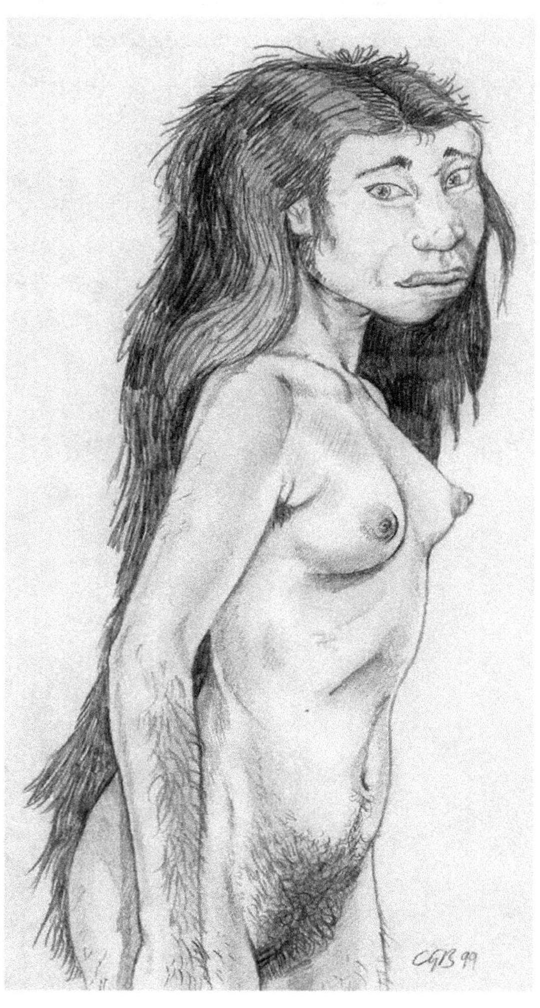

For the next five days the caravan travelled northwards, then passed eastwards by some snow covered peaks.

"Over that ridge of mountains is the Garden." Rom had told them, "Ahead of us to the east is the headwaters of the Pishon river, and then the land of Havilah. Beyond that is Nod and the Eastern Sea and Greater Nod, the Cainite lands and Manlore. The only way into the Garden is through a pass between the mountains. The Cherubim live upon the Mountain of the Lord and they block the way! But we will not be going that far. Before us is the Pishon, which flows into the Eastern Sea. The city of Manhome is a day's journey away. The Enemy have been raiding up the Pishon Valley from the east. We have been called in to help defend Manhome. We are glad to have your help. Your weapons are very effective!"

The days of travel were very informative. It was a chance to talk to the Romany and learn about the world they were now exploring. Around the campfire at night, the Romany loved to tell stories, to dance and sing, and like their distant future descendants, they liked to play skilful tricks for amusement. Both men and women were keen dancers, but one thing remained, the turbans which covered their faces, which were never shown. Only their eyes were ever seen.

The world through which they passed was incredibly beautiful, and it made some of the team wonder what the Garden on the other side of the mountains must be like. One night, Rainbow asked about the Garden and Rom told another of his stories.

"My father Awdame was not born in the Garden," he began, "but was born in another land a long time ago. In that lifetime Awdame was not his name, he had another name, Ish Adamu. The world at that time was ruled by the Anunnaki. The Anunnaki god Enki Ea and his consort Ninhursag ruled the Apsu deep ocean and there the Igigi mined gold for the Anunnaki. But the Igigi rebelled against the gods and there was war. In the end, it was Enki who brokered a peace by creating a new kind of worker. All I know is that men were made by mixing the blood of the gods with that of beasts by some strange magic. The first men were called the Adapu and they were not very smart, but they made good workers. Then Enki and Ninhursag made a new better kind of man. Some say that Enki himself was their father – a son and a daughter, my father Ish Adamu and Titi my mother. But this was a forbidden thing and ruler Anu sent Enki's brother Enlil (may he forever be cursed) to destroy the new race of men. There was war again and this brought down the wrath of the Elohim and their Eldar against the Anunnaki. It was the Elohim who humbled the gods and built the great Edens where men could live and be safe. The Garden, it is said is a wondrous place, and men lived there in peace with the Elohim. But it was not to last. It was Enlil, the Great Dragon(may he be forever cursed) who came into the Garden and turned against the Elohim. Enlil and his Nephalim and Dragon army were massing to destroy everything. Again, the Elohim and the Eldar led by Enki, the Serpent came against the enemy and defeated them. For their safety, my parents were sent out of the Garden and settled by the Elohim in Manhome. Since then, we have lived under the protection of the Seelie Occupation. The Kerubim Serpent Brotherhood have guarded the entrance of the Eden so no-one can enter. That is the way the world is today, that is the story the people tell. But things are changing. It is said that Enlil (may he forever be cursed) returns and the enemy stirs. Those Gorenge who attacked us and which you defeated are further proof of that."

The team members sat looking stunned at the story, all except Grim who nodded knowingly and Mrorna, who just showed a satisfied interest. It seemed so familiar yet fundamentally different.

After most of the people had gone to sleep, Grim, whose species didn't need to sleep, was sitting keeping watch by the fire. Fay and Tarmal were also awake, not because their species didn't sleep, but because they were on guard.

"Brother Grim," Tarmal sat on a log next to the Torgar, "That story that Rom told, that is a version of the Yahwistic creation story, the original version?"

"Yes." Grim made a sound, Torgar laughing, "But different, yes?!"

"What is the truth?" Fay asked.

"Ah, the truth." Grim sighed involuntarily, "For most Terrans the story is a very old one, and here we are not long after the actual events. Even so this world is already incredibly old and the Multiverse even older. Essentially the Garden of Eden story is a true one. Adam and Eve are real people. There really is a Garden. But what exactly is going on here? It is a war between two brothers, Enlil the Dragon, who claims to be the true god of Earth and his brother Enki, the Serpent, who raised humankind up from slavehood to freedom. As a member of an ancient Eldar race, my people, the Torgar, existed even before this universe came to be. You need to be aware that we Eldar have a very long view on things. We see the big picture. The Edin or Eden was one of a number of compounds used by the Anunnaki and the Elohim for trade and as a safe place. Enlil laid claim to Earth for the Anunnaki, while Enki wanted Earth to be protected. That was why the Eldar and Elohim had to intervene."

They were all quiet for a bit, just thinking that one over.

"The truth is that the Elohim are also divided. The Unseelie and Pandemonium support Enlil while most of the Vansadagardians support Enki. Ea is an old name for Enki, the Sumerian creator god. He was also known as the Serpent, not because he was a literal reptile, but because the snake is a symbol of wisdom and renewal. Enki's enemy is, Enlil, his brother, that is, our old friend Graud. Some people theorise that Enlil, Graud, Satan, the original Lucifer are one and the same. Others say that Lucifer is still in the Pit, waiting to come forth some time. Others claim that Anu is Satan. Who really knows? But this story has Ea Enki in the Garden. Ea, pronounced ay-ah, is the root name from where the Akkadians and later the Hebrews get the infamous Name. It comes from the sounds of breathing, literally the breath of Life."

"Yahweh." Tarmal said quietly.

"Yes." Grim momentarily bowed in respect. "Actually pronounced 'Yahveh' is a personal name for the member of the Elohim that the Hebrews and Canaanites knew as El. El is the leader of the Elohim in this Creation phase. Enki was called Ea because he served the Elohim. Enlil has wanted to rule over the Elohim for a long time, so he stole the name Yahveh and is an imposter who claims to be the god of this world. The story is complex and most of it has been kept hidden from humanity. This species of Homo-Sapiens Sapiens, beginning with Awdame and Haveh, the progenitors of the Messianic bloodline, really know nothing much about the being that they so rudely refer to as God. Awdame wasn't created from the dust of the Earth on the sixth literal day of creation. The Elohist creation story, with its internally consistent structure pattern of evenings and days, is beautifully profound, speaks volumes and is more true, spiritually speaking, than any crude literalist could ever hope to understand. Awdame had a whole other life, living in what some ironically call the Pre-Adamic Age. There was indeed a war, a really big one. I know this from personal experience because I was there, in what is now the Sahara desert in Northern Africa, when the war was fought. It nearly all ended right there, everything could have died. All life, extinct. We came close. The Humans were as usual, caught in the middle. So many died in the destruction, a time called the Purge, which made the violence of the Deluge look like a minor event. The event took place around seventy seven thousand years BCE, while most humans were still in Africa, although some migrations were spreading out around the world. Lots of things happened including huge volcanic eruptions. When it was all over there were only around one thousand humans left. The human race had to start over. It was a man named Ish, whose body was found by the Elohim in the aftermath of the Purge that was taken to the Garden. The Elohim built a great portal gate there. This was before the time of the Splinters. The Elohim established the Kerubim garrison who also lived in the Garden. At some point Ish was restored to life, this time with little memory of his previous existence, and given the new name of Awdame. Haveh was cloned yet modified from his bio-morphic field. She is essentially his twin. It was Enki and his partner Ninhursag who engineered Awdame and Haveh, against the wishes of Anu. Enlil is called the Dragon because of his use of Rahab and Gorenge saurians as his troops. The leader of his Gorenge is a shapeshifter named Lillith. She claims to have been a former wife of Ish, but she is now a general of the Dragon's army."

"How long until the Deluge?" Fay asked.

"About five thousand years from now." Grim replied, "There's a lot of history still to go, but the Sethani Kings will be long lived and you know the rest."

"The Aquani Migration." Tarmal nodded, "This world."

"One thing we must continue to have faith in," Grim continued, "is that the Source of All loves us and is totally committed to our eternal lives. There is a big picture, to be sure, but right now our job is to love the people we meet and do our best for them. I've lived and died many times for the sake of others. It is still worth it. But right now, you two can sleep. I'll stand guard."

The next day began with fog covering the land. The Pishon valley lay before them and they descended down towards Manhome. The hills were covered in forest and full of wildlife. Birdsong and the distant sound of running water brought a feeling of serenity. Even so, everyone was on the watch. The road came down the side of the valley in a series of switchbacks which made it difficult with the large dinosaurs in the caravan, but when they finally reached the river, the road widened and was easy to use. Down by the river, there were people in the shallows with fishing lines or nets. They weren't Romany because they weren't wearing turbans. Rather the people were all bare headed, with long dark hair tied back. They wore short kilts or lap laps, with their tools attached to belts around their waists or across their shoulders. A lot of the people turned around and waved as the caravan moved past. Standing on the shore were guards here and there, armed with spears and wooden shields.

"Not much of a defence against Gorenge." Kit said to the others.

They moved along. Eventually, up ahead, they could see a wall. Getting closer there was an open space and a wide gate. In the side of the cliff face to the right of the gate was a large cave with an annex over the entrance. Under the annex there were large bales of hay and piles of gourds that looked like odd shaped yellow pumpkins. The Romany drivers directed their beasts towards the cave. People came out to greet them. Rom went forward and spoke to a young man, who then ran through the gate. Others helped the Romany dismount and unload the caravan. A lot of the baggage was taken into the cave. The team helped them carry stuff in as well. Inside the cave, the dinosaurs were watered from a large stone trough or they were fed some of the hay and gourds. They were big noisy eaters, and they made big noisy smelly droppings! Further in the cave there were other beasts of burden and another exit cave beyond. Rom had disappeared briefly during all the busyness but came back.

"Come with me!" he said excitedly, "Father and Mother want to meet you."

The Romany left their animals in the cave, still eating, and they followed Rom out towards the gate. The team members followed as well. At the gate, some children came out with wooden bowls full of water and Rom nodded to the team members that they were to drink. Then, the young man that Rom had spoken to before returned. Walking behind him was a man and woman.

The only way to describe the man and woman was that they were perfectly beautiful. Not like supermodels but rather that it was as though someone took all the best things that humans can be and put it all into twin packages. They were similar to each other in some ways, but the man was breathtakingly masculine and physically powerful, and the woman, who was dark and powerful like her husband, was wonderfully feminine and attractive. Whoever Ish may have once been, Enki and Ninhursag had made improvements and Awdame and Haveh was the result. They were indeed, the most perfectly designed humans. The young man who stood between them was a younger mirror image of his parents.

The Romany stepped forward and kissed the progenitor's hands. Some of the women took the children through the gate and beyond, but most of the adults remained to hear what was to be said.

Grim stepped forward first, with Mrorna beside him and greeted first Haveh then Awdame by kissing their hands.

"We are servants of the Elohim, come to aid the people of Manhome against our common enemy." Mrorna spoke the introduction.

"The people of Manhome have heard of your coming and stories have come to us ahead of you." Haveh replied.

"You save the lives of our kindred," Awdame continued, "so let there be no formalities between us. You are friends and welcome to share the Cave of Treasures with us."

"My loyalty is to Life." Grim bowed, "We gratefully accept your hospitality!"

At that, Awdame and Haveh both grinned huge smiles and then laughed cheerfully!

"This is our son Shet." Awdame introduced the young man, "Come in and find rest! All of you!"

They went through the front gate. Other villagers were also coming and going and they greeted the visitors with friendly smiles. The gate was just the first step to enter the city. On the other side there was a wide open area. Lots of people were there, bringing in produce from along the river. There were large granaries at one end of the compound, full of grain. Near them was a baking area and there was a slaughterhouse at the other end of the compound. The actual entrance to the city was a cave mouth in the cliff face and there was a ramp leading up to a ledge protected by a barrier. There was a big wooden door that could be slid across the mouth of the cave by those inside. Out in the compound there was a lot of activity, the kind of business that took place in a busy Neolithic community. Climbing up the ramp, they met some flint nappers at their work stations, making sharp cutting tools by striking the stones against each other. Awdame and Haveh led them up into the mouth of the cave.

Inside the cave, they walked along a narrow tunnel and finally came out into a large gallery. The gallery was surprisingly well lit from light coming through a hole in the ceiling. But the thing that was the most noticeable was a large pool of water in the middle of the space. It was obviously the main water supply for the community. There were some girls there carrying clay jugs, filling them and heading back out into the cave. On the other side of the cave was a side gallery formed with pillars of stalactites and stalagmites. In the middle of the gallery there was a circle of seats made of wood and wicker. Around the walls of the little gallery there was light reflecting off the cave walls. Awdame led the group, including Rom and his wife, into the gallery and to the seats to sit down. Looking closer at the walls, it could be seen that there were gemstones forming a seam in the limestone. The stones seemed to be radiating light, glowing with an inner fire.

"This is why we call this cave the Cave of Treasures." Awdame explained, "There are lots of little galleries and grottoes like this all through the big cave. There's more water holes as well, and a hot spring. This is the perfect place to live. We have never run out of water and we are protected and warm in the cold times. We have secret ways in and out of the cave and the main entrance is easy to defend. We have had to defend ourselves a few times from some of the wild folk and once before from a Gorenge raiding party about a year ago."

"Now the Gorenge have returned, Father." Rom said.

"We have come here to help you fight the Gorenge." Grim added.

"I have a question." Haveh leaned forward to look closely at the guests, "It is obvious that some of you are Seelie, walking openly too, some of you are humans, but all but one of you are different, and you, leader, are Eldar. You helped my children, so we are grateful, but who exactly are you? Please tell us the truth."

There was an awkward silence. Grim was about to reply when Awdame raised a hand. He looked right at Mrorna.

"You tell us." He said.

Mrorna looked at her teammates hoping for some reassurance, but Grim squeezed her hand and nodded at her.

"I am Mrorna, daughter of Vrengr, of the Porma clan."

"I know Porma." Awdame nodded, "You are a descendant of my son Ashur. But your clan no longer exists. I'm sorry."

"We were made into Thralls, my Father." Tears began to well up in Mrorna's eyes.

"It is alright daughter." Awdame reached across and touched the side of Mrorna's face, "You now are part of this tribe. You belong to my family. But who are these friends of yours?"

Mrorna smiled through her tears and shook her head.

"It is a very long story," she began, "but the basic truth is that our enemy sent me into the distant future and these people brought me back."

Awdame, Haveh, Rom and his wife looked visibly shaken, but Awdame nodded again.

"Tell me more."

Mrorna told the whole story, trying her best to explain in simple language. It wasn't too hard because she barely understood herself. Rom found it hard to understand how it was possible to prevent events by going to the time before they happened, but Haveh shushed him for being stupid.

"So what does this mean for us?" Awdame finally asked, "We are already fighting the Gorenge, and the Pandemonium, well, we have heard bad things. Even so, we will do our best to help you."

At that moment a young child came into the grotto.

"He's here," she said, "at the pool."

"Ah!" Awdame stood quickly, "Come and see! There is someone you must meet!"

They all followed quickly, back the way they had come to the main gallery. The pool in the middle of the cave was churning quite vigorously. They watched curiously as a form rose up in the water, a man, no, a Malak, one of the angels.

"Hello everyone," he greeted them, "Thought I ought to check up on you."

Grim, Kit, Newton, Niamah and Al recognised him immediately and stepped forward to shake hands all around. Hilli and Surreya knew who they were looking at, but only by reputation. Rainbow, Fay and Tarmal had no idea. Awdame and Haveh moved forward as well.

"Welcome to our home, Melki." Awdame patted the angel on his shoulder.

There was no doubt, the Malak was none other than Michael, although Awdame had called him Melki, which was essentially the same name. The way he wore his hair and his kilt was different from the western clothes he would wear in 1918 and in later years, but he didn't look different otherwise, even though he was many thousands of years younger. But for Eldar races, that wasn't a problem.

"Hello Grim," Melki began, "and my other friends from the future!"

The archangel looked at the other members of the team.

"You may not believe this Kit, Al, Niamah," he laughed, "but I haven't met you before. But I still know you. My future self has sent me a message. It is hard to explain, but time can be bent a bit when you leave behind the corporeal aspect. So, I know who you are and why you are here."

"You are a far seer?" Niamah asked.

"Some of us have the gift." Melki nodded, "It has been very useful for me many times."

"So can you tell us what to do so we don't get killed and go home as soon as possible?" Newton asked, chuckling, "Be nice to have an edge."

"The far sight doesn't work that way." Melki shook his head, "But I'll join the band and help."

"I remember you." Mrorna said, "You were there when I saw.... what I saw."

"Or rather I will be." Melki smiled.

"I hate time paradoxes!" Newton grumbled.

"Try being a far seer." Melki sighed, "What is a memory and what is a future sight? Still, the important thing is what is going to happen next? What I'm seeing right now is war."

"It doesn't take far sight to know that." Awdame said, "Gorenge forces are growing in strength."

"We didn't actually come here to fight the Gorenge as such." Kit pointed out, "The Gorenge are just a part of the problem. A Baal named Graud is behind these attacks you've been suffering. He leads a whole Pandemonium army."

"How do you know this?" Haveh asked.

"Because we have already fought them." Niamah added, "They have weapons that are very advanced and large numbers."

A very serious look came over Melki's face. He looked at Awdame and Haveh, Rom and his wife.

"I need to talk to our visitors privately." He said, "Is that alright Sir?"

Awdame nodded and led his family members out of the grotto. When they had gone, Melki confronted both Niamah and Grim.

"Why are you here?" he demanded, "You do realise that these people are tribal primitives? They are wonderful and they have a lot of hope, but they won't be able to fight a full blown Pandemonium army!"

Mrorna stepped forward quickly and put her hand on Melki's arm.

"Please," she begged, "Do not be angry. They are here because I saw them here. I do not know if we will win this war, but I was a captive thrall at Graud's fortress. I heard that Graud had captured some strangers. I heard rumours of war and fighting. I was a technician, one of the workers who controlled the machines that sent the time bubbles into the future. I know that these people set me and others free. I am here because of them and because of them, there is a chance. That is not all. I have a warning to give. Graud thinks that he can change history. He wants to kill Shet and so prevent, well, everything."

"It's not possible." Grim said hesitantly, "We are all here. He failed. We are here to stop him from sending more troops, we can't undo time."

"That's not what he was trying to do." Mrorna had tears in her eyes, "He was experimenting. His time bubbles were just the beginning. His plan is to ..... it is hard to understand, to open a rift, that's what he called it. A rift in space/time. He's going to capture Shet, put him in and that will cause a paradox. The future will be erased and he will change everything."

"It isn't possible." Grim asserted.

Melki sighed. He was shaking physically.

"It is possible." He stammered, "I know, because it has been done before."

"When?" Grim was incredulous.

"I'm older than you Eldar." Melki said bluntly, "There is Ancient Darkness that you know nothing about. In other realities we are still fighting wars to undo what was done a thousand Creations ago."

"I'm sorry." Grim was weeping, "I do not deserve to lead this mission. I didn't take Mrorna's warning seriously enough."

"You knew about this?" Rainbow cried, "When were the rest of us going to be told?"

"I'm sorry." Was all that Grim could say.

Melki stepped forward and picked Grim up and set him down again, forcing him to look forward.

"Look!" Melki roared, "I accept the remorse you have, but with remorse must come repentance and then forgiveness. It is right to be angry, but we should direct our anger towards Graud. There is likely to be a greater evil working behind him too! We have no choice but to fight."

"Then how much intervention do we use?" Grim asked.

"I give full discretion in this case." Melki nodded, "But the people of Manhome need to be completely protected. There are a few people here, Awdame and Haveh as well as Rom and some of the other first sons and daughters who I personally trust with the technology. Awdame and Haveh are personally familiar with Vansadagaadian technology we use in the Garden. But the rest of the people are subject to the non-interference policy of the Seerlie Court. My people will protect the tribe within the Cave of Treasures, while your team will be free to use full discretion outside to fight the Pandemonium, when they arrive. We need to make plans."

There were nods all around. Melki led them all back out into the main gallery of the cave to where Awdame and his family members were waiting.

Less than an hour later, Hilli and Surreya were flying in Ren-form eastwards from Manhome. In the main cabin, Surreya was scanning ahead. In particular she was looking for spatial and temporal disruptions, the kind caused by flash portal technology.

"There's definitely something popping out there over the sea." Surreya said, "They are moving quickly towards us."

"These guys took out Order e.d.v.s" Hilli sounded a little uncertain.

"You're a Ren, not an e.d.v." Surreya chided, "That gives you a distinct edge."

"O.k. then." Hilli giggled nervously, "I'll prepare to engage seeing you have such confidence in me!"

There were three large zeppelins, surrounded by formations of flying dragons, about twenty four of them. They appeared suddenly above the coastline of the Sea of Nod (which would one day be called the Caspian Sea). With a flash of light, they all portal jumped again, appearing further inland to the west.

"I think I can predict their trajectory." Surreya said, "It's obvious that they are at least aware of us."

"I suggest a direct probe attack." Hilli suggested.

"Couldn't agree more!" Surreya exclaimed.

The zeppelins appeared over the eastern Eden Nod border along with their dragon formations. Hilli and Surreya were already there waiting for them. They had already fired off some guided missiles, which exploded almost instantaneously! One of the zeppelins exploded spectacularly, venting flame over the others as it fell. The air was then filled with gunfire as the other airships retaliated. The dragons wheeled away, as though to get a better view of what was going on. Then they popped away again.

"Dragons are on the move!" Hilli cried.

"I know…" Surreya was looking all over, trying to spot the enemies, "I'm attacking the other two zeppelins."

"No time!" Hilli warned as the dragons suddenly appeared all around them, trying to grab onto the hull of the Ren.

Hilli flooded her hull with electricity, and fired all her weapons as she spun among the grasping and screaming reptiles. More missiles were fired, and dragons fell in burning ruin, but there were too many.

"I'm getting us outta here!" Surreya screamed, and they made a sudden reverse, heading back to the west, leaving the much slower dragons behind. As they fled westwards, Surreya was laughing!

"We got what we wanted!" Hilli was delighted, "Full detailed scans! We know everything they have."

Down on the ground at Manhome, the people were preparing for the attack they knew was coming. Most of the people were being directed into the Cave of Treasures, to the safety of the lower galleries. Melki, Awdame and Haveh gathered a small group of trusted family members, including Rom and his brothers and Melki gave them Vansadagaadian weapons. They were not going to fight outside, but guard those inside.... Just in case.

Grim, Kit, Newton, Niamah and Al, Mrorna, Tarmal and Fay and Rainbow would remain outside, alone. They were all kitted out with helms, collars, utility belts and gauntlets, and of course, hand blasters and full body shields. It didn't look like much, but they were wearing some of the most advanced weaponry in existence. Down from the sky, Hilli dropped, landing beside the river. She glowed briefly and then she closed her Ren field. Both Hilli and Surreya stepped out as the light dissipated. Behind them were a number of strange looking figures. They looked like advanced robots, with smooth looking metallic bodies. But while they resembled men in some ways, they also were inhuman – faceless and they carried large particle weapons on their backs. There were four of them, which was enough.

Melki was chuckling when he saw them.

"You have four constructs!" he shook his head in wonder, "You brought them with you?"

"I'm a class twelve Ren." Hilli nodded, "I have room for lots of things."

"Very good then." Melki smiled, "We are going to need them shortly."

"In about five minutes." Surreya added.

"Then there's no time to waste." Grim said, "We need to prepare for battle."

Kit, Newton, Niamah, Al, Tarmal and Fay all knew what to do. Newton had Rainbow stand with him. He was to be her babysitter. Likewise, Mrorna stood with Kit. He would help her in the middle of the fight. The members of the team took up places around the compound and they switched on their blasters and power systems. Melki himself stood by the door to the Cave of Treasures and he pulled the door shut, then switched on his own weapons, which also included an energy sword.

"Why don't we take cover?" Mrorna asked, "Behind the barriers perhaps?"

"If it makes you feel more comfortable." Kit replied, "But our body shields are good protection. Do you remember how to fire the weapons? It's simple, you remember, point and shoot!"

Mrorna nodded and grinned.

Hilli and Surreya used their wings to fly down towards the main gate to the city compound. The four constructs took up positions of their own around the walls, with their particle cannons hot and pointed up at the sky. Everyone was looking upwards. Using their helmet heads up displays and scanners, they searched the skies for the enemy.

Suddenly there was a loud pop noise and three zeppelins appeared in the sky above, surrounded by dragons. The constructs immediately opened fire, targeting the middle zeppelin. The dragons screamed and scattered when the airship exploded in gouts of flame. The other two zeppelins teleported a second later. On the ground, everyone else joined the constructs, shooting at the dragons who were desperately trying to get down to the cover of the ground. About half of them made it, while the others were destroyed.

For a moment there was a strange couple of minutes of silence.

Then, "There are eleven dragons surviving." Hilli informed the group, "The two zeppelins have landed in nearby valleys. They are deploying their troops. We probably have about ten minutes before they get here."

"We have to hold our ground." Grim cried, "Let them come to us. Our job is to defend the city and protect Shet. This spot is the only way in. We stop them here."

A strange sound could be heard from outside the city, a loud wailing noise.

"What the hell is that?" Newton asked.

"It's the dragons." Mrorna sounded frightened.

"Don't be afraid." Kit told her, "You are well protected and we'll get our chance to fight back soon."

"I won't be happy until Graud and all his horde are all dead." She smiled uncertainly.

Through his helmet, Kit grinned back.

Down at the city gate, Surreya was taking a peek.

"Is this the only way in?"

"The main way in," Melki replied, "but they can climb down from behind us."

"O.k." Surreya nodded, then she pointed at one of the constructs, "You, deploy along the ridge behind the city. Observe and report, then withdraw to that point and defend."

Surreya pointed at a spot up above the city entrance. The construct turned and leapt across the compound and then again, up to the ridge over the city entrance. It moved very quickly and was gone in a couple of seconds.

"Keep me informed construct two." Surreya tapped the side of her helmet.

"Will do so." The construct replied, "Already detecting movement in the forested area below the ridge, a small force only. Will observe and report."

"They're coming!" Hilli called, "They are just outside the gate!"

"Thought we had ten minutes!" Grim called, but then there was a loud bang!

They appeared all around the rim of the compound, ten dragons who immediately vented fire right into the cauldron, burning everything! The fire was like a flood, destroying anything combustible. Anything stored in the compound, any wooden structures all burst into flame. Down in the inferno, the team were all busy, not burned or dead, but protected by their shields. The fire kept coming, but safely shielded, they could use their scanners to see and the team members returned fire for fire! The three constructs used their cannons to blow huge holes into the dragons, and then to make sure they leapt at the enemy, firing again as they attacked.

"Let the constructs take the dragons!" Grim ordered, "Look to attack from other quarters! They will be coming!"

Grim was right. The front wall of the compound exploded inwards and Pandemonium forces swarmed in, the eleventh dragon shooting fire over their heads. Rock shrapnel was exploding everywhere, and the enemy troops were carrying heavy projectile weapons. They were also wearing fireproof armour and ventilator masks. But the well trained members of the team were up to the task, firing their advanced particle weapons.

"Hold your positions!" Grim fired at the wall of attackers, "Let them come to you!"

The enemy fell in large numbers. The constructs had taken the top of the compound and all the dragons and their crews were dead. They then turned around and fired upon the enemies attacking on the ground. Even so, some of the Pandemon attackers were good soldiers. They found footholds and fired back. Two of the constructs received serious damage and fell down, unable to function. More enemy troops were pouring through the gap where the gate used to be. Despite their formidable shields, the team members were struggling against the sheer force of overwhelming fire. The compound was hot and there were lots of explosions. It was obvious that the enemy were intent on wearing the defenders down with numbers.

Where Kit and Mrorna were standing, they could see that the enemy had shields of their own, which they carried with them. They used their shields as cover as they crept forward, firing as they went. Kit was very tempted to break rank and attack, but Grim's orders were clear. Mrorna was doing well, keeping her position and rate of fire going.

"Pull back to the cave entrance and hold it!" Grim cried, "Let them come!"

Carefully, the members of the team retreated back towards the closed doors of the Cave of Treasures. This was not to escape though, rather it was to force the enemy to expose themselves as they attacked. More of the enemy did just that, more fell before the relentless fire of the particle weapons used by the defenders. Despite that, Kit could see them still coming, and his helmet computer was telling him that his shield power was running dangerously low and his internal environment was heating up, around 47 degrees. They were all feeling the heat, and the enemy who were smart, knew it. They were close enough that Kit could hear their calls to each other, and their taunting.

Don't get angry. Kit thought, *Keep focused, pray.*

Soon they were standing together on the landing near the door of the cave. The one remaining construct in the compound moved to the position in front of the defenders and extended its shield, giving those behind some relief from the gunfire. It also used its heavy weapon to send the enemy scattering in retreat. Inside their helmets, most were sweating heavily, but they were still grinning that they were prevailing.

"There are too many of them." Hilli noted, "If they are bringing reinforcements in, we could be here a long time."

"That would be a losing game." Kit added. He used his scanners to look over the compound and wasn't happy with what he was seeing either. The enemy were regrouping inside one of the side storage caves and Kit swore that he hadn't rigged some explosives to blow them away.

Grim was looking too, and thinking. *What were they doing?*

The second construct that Surreya had sent behind the compound was practically invisible, having turned on its camouflage function. It was watching some members of the Pandemonium approaching from the west. They were carrying something.

"Construct two reporting." Surreya heard in her helmet radio.

"Report." She responded,

"Small enemy force are delivering a package to send coordinates......."

A huge explosion violently rocked the hillside! In the confusion, there were suddenly two zeppelins over the compound and an open portal in the middle of the space. Heavily armed Pandemons rushed out, accompanied by huge Anakim wielding maces and hand cannons! The construct standing before the attackers ran forward and physically began to tear into bodies on all sides. There was very little room and weapons fire was difficult and dangerous. There was no room to stand holding the high ground, the fight was on!

"Swords!!!" Grim cried, and all the team members switched their particle blasters to energy blade mode and ran forward into the mass of attacking enemies.

It wasn't just a wild rush, but Grim barked orders as they moved down the steps from the gate into the wall of approaching enemies. The construct, accompanied by Surreya and Hilli, formed a point at the front with Al on the right and Niamah on the left. The combined shields formed a wall of energy which sizzled with enemy gunfire. At the back Kit, Tarmal and Fay formed a triangle of protection in front of Rainbow, Newton and Mrorna who were the weaker fighters. Right at the back, still standing at the top of the steps was Melki, holding the higher ground, using his hand weapon to pick off any enemy soldiers trying to slip in behind them. But they all knew that they were trapped in the heart of a cauldron of fire. Eventually someone's shields would collapse, and then they would start dying, despite the formidable technology. But the enemy were Pandemonium and they were using some advanced weapons as well as huge numbers. They wanted to overwhelm the defenders. Standing back to back, a combination of blaster fire and sword play as enemies moved within striking distance was the main tactic. The enemy continued to pour out of the portal which remained open nearby.

They got a sudden surprise as an Anak, nearly three metres tall, used a heavy mace to smash into their defensive shields, knocking a hole in the wedge! Both Kit and Mrorna were thrown clear and the Anak and a number of his Pandemon companions moved in for the kill! There were just too many of them for the others to reach the pair, and Kit was hurt, he felt his ribs were probably broken. Mrorna let out a wild battle cry and launched herself along the ground, sliding underneath the giant, who was puzzled but a moment, when Mrorna fired her blaster point blank up from underneath. In agony and crying with frustration, Kit forced himself to sit up and he began to fire at the other enemies. Some fell, but Mrorna, still screaming like a banshee, turned on her blade and began to slash into the wall of Pandemons before her! Kit watched with some admiration as she fought, slipping around like a gymnast among the attackers. He forced himself to stand and was helped up by Tarmal and Melki who had just arrived. The wedge they had formed was broken, and now they were forced to fight individually. The enemy had shield-edged weapons or power maces as well as their automatic rifles and shields. Their numbers were still growing.

Then there was another surprise. Behind them, Kit looked up and could see the door of the Cave of Treasures opening up! Maybe the enemy had already taken the city within and were now coming from behind! Despite the thought that death and failure of the mission was immanent, Kit gritted his teeth and kept fighting! But through the door came Shet! Behind him was his father Awdame, Rom and behind them, the other construct. Awdame and Rom began shooting using the weapons Melki had given them, but Shet, followed closely by the construct ran quickly down the stairs and right into the fray.

In the minds of those fighting in the compound was that the one they were there to defend and protect was about to get killed, but the young man looked very determined! He was carrying a shielded sword, one of those owned by Melki, held high as he attacked. Shet leapt as he hit the wall of enemy bodies and as he brought his borrowed sword down, he moved into the blurred movement of one in a battle trance....

"He's in the trance!!!" Niamah cried.

Enemy bodies began to fall quickly before the slashing blade as Shet drove himself into the heart of the enemy. He was briefly among the defenders, weaving among them and dispatching enemies on all sides. He was almost impossible to watch as he moved so quickly.

"Keep fighting!" Grim bellowed, "Use the advantage!!!"

Some of the enemy were retreating and Grim led them in pursuit, while Shet himself ran through the enemy lines, leaving a killing zone as he went, but he was heading towards the portal itself. It happened very quickly indeed. Shet leapt right over the enemy who stood before the portal, cutting off the head of an Anak to do so. He dropped into the event horizon and vanished. He wasn't gone long before he was back. In that very moment, the two zeppelins hovering overhead exploded, raining fire as they veered to the left and right, smashing down in destruction!

"Finish it!" Grim yelled joyfully, "We have won the day!"

The enemy knew this was true, but one thing they were prepared to die for their cause and refused any further retreat. There would be no prisoners and as the fight came to its conclusion, no quarter was given from either side. But with two constructs, Shet and the team now reinforced by Awdame and his fighters from in the Cave of Treasures, it was inevitable, a few minutes later, the Pandemonium forces were all dead.

There was only a bit of mopping up, and the two constructs headed out the city gate to see if there were any others. If there were, they had left in a hurry.

Back in the city compound, everyone stood as though numb. Those wearing their shielded armour switched their shields off and stood there cooling down, sweat and steam rising from overheated and exhausted bodies. Kit, Mrorna, Shet and Newton lay on the ground. It felt good to be alive!

Chapter Twenty-Four

Shet

In the quiet time after a battle there was always the danger of becoming complacent. Everyone was exhausted and many wanted to sleep, and there were the children to consider, but it was agreed between Grim, Awdame and Melki that the enemy would be back in greater numbers.

"We have to get the people to a safer place." Grim said.

"There is only one thing to do," Melki nodded, "the people must be taken to Cherubim for safety. From there we can gather an army to make a stand. This is a very difficult situation. The enemy have advanced weapons and we have been forced to use weapons that are even more advanced just to defend ourselves. These people here are stone age primitives..."

"Primitives?" Awdame raised his eyebrows.

"Sorry," Melki grunted, "you know that's not what I mean."

"No offence taken Melki." Awdame nodded, "I used to live in the Garden and I know how far we have fallen. You want my people to grow and develop by themselves. I get it."

There was a moment of awkward silence. The others nearby turned to look and listen.

Awdame sighed.

Shet got up from where he was sitting and stood before his father.

"The Spirit is testing us." he said, "We will serve the Elohim. That is all we need to know."

"My son is wise." Awdame grinned, "We will do whatever must be done. We will take the people to Cherubim for safety and will gather an army of warriors, the right people, the best fighters. But we will need help as well, we will need to gather allies."

"That's a good idea." Melki nodded, "We'll send messages out to the tribes to gather at Cherubim as well. But I can think of one group that would be very helpful to us. The enemy will be back in force and they need to be stopped with a strong force."

"You are talking about the Shile." Grim realised, "They were here at this time."

"They have been helpful allies in the past and they are excellent warriors." Awdame agreed, "But what do we do to protect Shet? The enemy wants to kill him."

"Who told you that?" Grim asked.

"I had a vision, a dream a few nights ago." Shet explained, "I saw a deep darkness that swallowed me, and then, like a great beast, the darkness swallowed the whole world. I could see the one called Graud laughing at his victory, but the Spirit spoke to me and told me that I would cast Graud into the darkness he intended for me."

"God works in mysterious ways." Newton said to no-one in particular.

Everyone looked at Shet. The young man was a mystery.

"I will go talk to the Shile." Shet said.

"I don't think that would be a good idea." Tarmal interjected.

"No...no..." Grim shook his head, "It might actually be the best thing. If Shet goes with the tribe to Cherubim and they are attacked, well, that would be it. But if Shet came with us and we could protect him personally, he would be safe."

"And the Shile...." Kit added, "are they a threat? We've been dealing with the Shile in the twentieth and twenty first centuries too. They are scoundrels."

"The group here is a different faction." Grim reassured him, "This lot are more civilised. They are True Shile. Those in the future are Grey Archons, who served the Anunnaki in the Igigi. "

"As long as they don't try to probe us!" Newton laughed nervously, "I don't mind meeting them."

Grim gave a disapproving look.

"Despite some reservations," Melki said, "I think this is the best thing to do. We have to prepare to leave quickly."

There were nods all around. Awdame and Haveh as well as Rom and some of the other people of Manhome had gathered around. Many of them reached out and embraced Shet quietly. They then turned and went back into the Cave of Treasures to gather the things they needed for the coming journey. They had to bring out the behemoths as well from where they were being kept. It was time to leave.

Surreya and Hilli approached Shet.

"Where do we go to find the Shile?" Hilli asked.

"There is a mountain to the south where we meet for trade." Shet told her.

"Can you show us from the sky?" Surreya wanted to know.

"No, no." Grim said, "We will be walking."

"More walking." Newton grumbled.

"Why walking?" Kit asked, "I assume it's the best solution to keep us safe."

"That's right." Grim nodded, "If we fly, the Pandemonium will spot us and we don't want them to know anything about where Shet might be. We can still move fairly quickly and will be faster than the Adamites, who will be travelling in a big band."

Melki stepped forward, "I'll go with the people to Cherubim. I'll also put shields on the behemoths and have advanced weapons we can use if we need them, similar to the ones you used in the last battle. We will be safe enough."

"I will accompany Shet." Rom said, "I have spoken with the Shile before and know their ways of trade."

"This Shile faction hates the Pandemonium." Mrorna added, "If the Pandemonium try to enter Shilean lands, the Shile will fight them."

"That's the idea." Kit agreed, "The Shile have formidable military strength. What faction are we talking about?"

"How about we talk about it on the way." Grim suggested, "The quicker we move the quicker we get the job done."

"Do you need food or supplies for the journey?" Rom asked, "We can provide food and water."

"We have what we need." Hilli said, "Shall we sort things out?"

"The day is nearly over." Fay pointed out, "The sun is going down. We are still leaving now?"

"Yes." Grim answered, "The people are also on the way too, in the dark. We need the cover of darkness. The Pandemonium don't have night vision goggles, and we do."

"But we are exhausted." Rainbow said, "I'm not a soldier. I'll need to sleep tonight sometime. I'm not complaining, just putting it forward."

"Good point." Kit said.

"We have the constructs." Surreya said, "We can modify them to carry a couple of passengers each. We can travel and take turns sleeping. It will be ok."

In the meantime, Hilli had moved to one side and had switched on her Ren field. She began to glow and an oval of light formed around her, becoming her Ren-form ship. She opened a hatch and lowered a ramp. Her Ren-form ship hovered silently about a metre above the ground. Niamah, Al and Kit led the way up into Hilli's hold, walking past the pilot's cabin and through the inner door.

Rom and Shet followed, full of wonder at the space within. Everyone went in and put their gear down.

"We will need a quick change of clothes, something to eat and drink, and recharged weapons." Surreya told everyone, "That ok Hilli?"

"No problem."

There were replicator platforms against one wall of the hold and Hilli switched a couple of them on. The portal windows moved up then down, leaving behind water bottles, food containers and folded clothing behind.

"Here's what we need." Niamah told everyone, "The food looks like high energy protein bars and we have water. There are some shorts and vests and belts. Weapons are already charged in the gun bins on the other wall behind us. I suggest we all use the toilet as well."

Niamah, Kit, Al, everyone except Newton and Rainbow began to undress and put on the new clothes and gear. Al looked over at Rainbow and Newton and grinned.

"Just get yourselves sorted." he said.

Rom and Shet didn't get changed, but Tarmal and Fay helped them put on the webbing belts, water bottles and helped them stuff some food bars into pockets. Tarmal showed Shet how to rip open the food wrapper and eat the bar. Getting weapons, knives, swords and energy weapons belted on came next.

"We have body shields if we need them," Grim added, "but I'll put them on the constructs for now."

Soon, everyone was finished and they exited back into the city compound. Hilli turned her Ren-field off and stepped out of the light, along with the two constructs. Seats for two passengers each had been added as well as storage buckets for extra equipment.

Grim looked at the group.

"Rainbow, Newton, Mrorna and Tarmal get to sleep first. We will swap a bit later." he said, "Let's get moving."

Kit made a quick prayer as they walked out of the compound and away from Manhome. At the same time, there were loaded behemoths heading up the north road. Awdame, Haveh and some of the others were waving as they walked away.

Chapter Twenty-Five
2018 World War

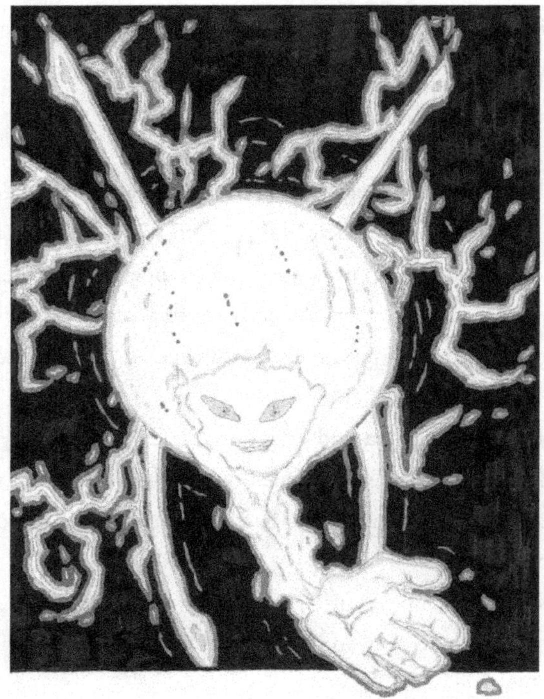

I was visiting Hopetown, Petra 18, with my battle-group. The town itself was really only a small village, with about five-hundred people living there. But Petra 18 was more than just the village. Over the mountains hovered a number of big ships, including the Arrow, and next to her was my ship, the Eagle, a Seelie Capital Battle-Ship. We were on the ground, with open portals to our ships and troops grounding to the school sports oval. I brought only a small contingent with me, just an honour guard really. Most of the people who had gathered at the school were Petra members or other volunteers, some from the local Tasmanian population, including some army units who had just turned up. They all wanted to wear our powered suits and fight the invaders.

God help them.... I thought.

Boris Rujansky and Peter Weaver had come with me and they were both ordering people into lines. A Tasmanian army colonel was there with about one hundred eager infantrymen. The civilian volunteers were led by Petra 18's head of security. We were here to collect them, train them and get them into the battle. We would be collecting a lot of others at lots of other locations all over the world. Training would not be a simple process.

"Here's what we are doing..." I told the two leaders standing near me, "We will be taking you through the portals into the Rath within these mountains here."

"You," I turned to the Petra Security officer,

"Officer Terry Braun." He shook my hand.

"And,"

"Colonel Warren," he saluted, "Tasmanian Army Reserves."

"Good," I saluted back, "Braun, you will be familiar with the Rath. Warren, you may not be aware that beneath us under the Tiers here is an ancient subterranean city built here by the Seelie after the time of the Deluge when they established a Splinter portal complex here. This spot is one of the gates into the Rath of Mu. You can enter on foot via the power station tunnel up the road or through the waters of the Great Lake above or via an underwater tunnel that comes in under Tasmania from the Tasman Sea. The Daedalus that was here a few days ago is usually based at this Rath. At the moment the Daedalus is doing rescue operations all over the world, but mostly in America. The main job we will be training these volunteers for will be rescue work based aboard the Daedalus. This will release more of our more battle experienced people to get into the fighting that is ramping up in Europe right now."

"Rescue operations?" Warren asked.

"I know you want to fight." I grinned involuntarily, "But using the powered suits is one thing, and fighting another. You need to get used to wearing and working in your suits. You need to get used to the weapons under supervision. Rescue ops is the best way to do this. Don't worry, you will get to actually fight probably sooner than you think. Enemy forces are turning up in all sorts of awkward places. Not only are the Pandemonium Antediluvian forces around, but their present day allies are getting involved as well. Medusa and Atalanti forces are in America as well. You both would have been briefed on this."

Both men nodded. They didn't have a lot to say so far.

"Alright," I tried to sound encouraging and cheerful, "we'll get your people through the portals into the Rath and my people will get yours suited up and we'll do some exercises in the local terrain ok."

"Yes Sir!!" Both men replied.

I watched as Boris and Peter got the volunteers through the portals. Within the Mu Rath there were teams of Petra advisors waiting to receive the new troops, get them equipped and give them some basic training. Later in the day they would be practising using their suits in the rocky landscape around the highland lakes. I would have to leave them to it because another portal was waiting open for me to return to the Eagle. I had other things to take care of today.

The enemy had been strangely quiet after the first big battles. We were glad of it. So far there had been no more time bubbles, but the Petrad techs were all saying there would be at least another wave, although the readings they were getting were difficult to locate. But there were a lot of small raids by enemy battle units dropped by dragons that would teleport into a target, do a lot of damage and then just as quickly teleport out again. Petra Intelligence were telling me that the enemy were surprised to find themselves in 2018 rather than 1918 and so they were gathering as much intelligence as they could. They weren't expecting to have to face such advanced technology. We tried to infiltrate behind their lines too, but they had captured a lot of civilians who were then quickly enthralled and put to work. We couldn't do much about that.

The most disturbing trouble was coming from contemporary Nephalim activity. The Atalanti in America were on the move, taking out American military assets including an aircraft carrier, which just vanished. I wondered what happened to them.

We had a strategy though, and we weren't going to just wait around and see what the enemy were going to do next. Some people, despite our warnings, had tried to contact the enemy and work things out diplomatically. It would never work. This Pandemonium horde were the real deal, true Satanists, and so unable to be swayed by mere talk. They were determined to stay and wouldn't stop for anything.

There were two obvious battle fronts. The main forces of the enemy were in France and Germany and there was a second horde in Southern England. Their airships were everywhere. A third horde was just north of the Black Sea. We were worried about that because they were in good striking distance from some of the major Raths, including Utnapishtim, Sinai and Zion, which was no co-incidence. We were determined to take out those two forces outside of mainland Europe first. But I wasn't so concerned about the enemy we could see. It was the not so obvious that worried me. The Pandemonium often turned up when least expected.

Capt. Johann R Simon, also known as 'Zealot', swam ashore. He had been floating in the sea for hours and was exhausted, thirsty and hungry. He knew that he was now in enemy held territory and that he had to do something, get help or resist in some way. But he was too tired right now. So, still wet and shivering, Simon went looking for fresh water. It took a while but he was happy to find a small creek further inland. He drank deeply, but was careful to keep his wary eyes open. After filling his water bottle, the next thing was to find shelter. The forest around him was thick and closed off the light. There were lots of strange animal sounds so Simon kept his side arm handy as he searched. Finally he found a large fallen log with a dry patch underneath. He pulled some ferns around to form a barrier and other dry branches were used to make a simple bed. Despite being a 'Zealot', Simon was too exhausted to want to do anything more this day. He could hear the sounds of animals waking up as the sun went down, big animals, moving through the jungle. Simon was terrified but didn't care if he got eaten tonight. He curled up in a ball and instantly fell asleep.

We had just started getting the troops into their training when I got a message from my ship's bridge. I opened a portal from the Rath and stepped out on the teleportation deck aboard Eagle. It was a quick turbo lift ride to my bridge and I fronted the tactical tank. My communications officer tapped the side of her nose and pointed. Holographic projections appeared in the tank of two men. One was Arthun Ap Meurig and the other was Finvara of the Tuatha De Danann.

"The enemy just tried to nuke Manchester." Arthur reported, "They teleported the damned thing right into the middle of the city. Thank God we had a jamming signal on the place or it would be glassed right now."

"Shit." I swore under my breath, "What are they up to?"

"I think they were just trying to break the stalemate in Britain and perhaps it was just out of spite." Fin added, "If they are trying to provoke us, it's working! I want to kick some heads in!"

"Very tempting old friend!" I laughed, "But let's not be too hasty. We are a bit understaffed for a full scale invasion right now."

"You are gathering recruits?" Arthur asked.

"Got some newbies just today." I scowled, "They're as raw as hell and would only get killed."

"What do we do?" Fin looked determined, "Lead us, by the Spirit, we have to do something!"

"We do indeed." I thought briefly, "Perhaps a surgical strike is more in order. We have to set the enemy straight. We cannot allow them to use nuclear weapons. We need to find out where they launched the strike from and see if we can hit their base."

"Good idea." Fin nodded, "We can track nuclear weapons easily enough."

"They were using captured nuclear weapons." Arthur explained, "I thought you would want to have some intelligence. Apparently the Americans had a bomber squadron based in Germany."

"With nuclear weapons..." I was angry, "Europe's been a nuclear free zone for five years, it's reckless of them. Do we know where they are?"

"The enemy have three other warheads." Arthur nodded, "We can set up a strike."

"They will be expecting us." I said, "But let's do it anyway!"

"Sounds good to me!" Fin laughed.

"Overwhelming force this time." I said, "Three capital ships, we dust everything. Take out those bombs and those who launched them. We need to send a message."

"I'll send you both the tactical stuff." Arthur said.

"Let's get going immediately." I nodded vigorously, "No waiting, let's just do this and get it done quickly."

The two holographic projections of my co-commanders vanished. I ordered "All hands" and claxons sounded in the ship.

"Get Boris back aboard." I told my second officer, "We'll leave Peter here with the trainees. He won't mind being left behind this time, but Boris would be offended!"

The tactical data just then came through from Arthur's ship. I looked carefully.

"Ok…" I thought it through, "we have three direct trajectories to the target. There's going to be collateral damage, but this has got to be done."

The two other ship captains could hear me.

"We do a direct strike," I detailed using the control desk near me, "Very quick. Then we look for secondary targets."

We were already moving. Our ships were accelerating out of the atmosphere, Eagle from Tasmania, Arthur's ship, Lady Guinevere, from Terra Avalon, and Fin's Selki which had been hovering over central Asia. We plotted our courses to get us to target simultaneously. I watched the tank carefully.

"Boris." I used my com, "Prepare troops, we may need you."

"Already done." He replied cheerfully, "Suited up and armed."

"Tactical coming." My second officer said, "Enemy dragons are teleporting. They've seen us."

"Punch through." I said.

They were trying to latch onto us, but we were going too quickly at supersonic speeds for them to catch us easily. We stopped dead over the captured American air force base and my gunners fired our primary weapons. The base was utterly destroyed in only a moment. The nuclear threat was gone.

"Now we are for it." My usual understatement.

Enemy dragons were all over us, but our shields were holding well.

"Targeting." My second informed me, "We have multiple secondary targets."

"Take them."

"We are taking damage."

Outside, our three ships were rocking with explosions as the enemy dragons clustered around us, dropping payloads then teleporting away. They were hard to target, they were learning how to more effectively evade our weapons. But we were collecting good Intel while we were here. I looked at the scanner readouts.

"What's that?" I pointed to some buildings near what was left of the base.

"It's a caged compound." The scanner tech replied, "There are people in there, appearing to be civilians, about fifty individuals."

"Boris," I touched my com, "we have a rescue."

"On it."

Boris and his squad got the tactical data and our teleportation deck opened a portal into the middle of the compound. There wasn't time to convince anyone to come. Besides, these people were enthralled, so Boris and his troops moved around the compound quickly, stunning anyone, friend or foe. They picked up the civilians and carried them back through the portal under heavy fire from Pandemon guards. We closed the portal and I gave the order to bug out. Just as quickly as we came, we accelerated back up into space and away. The enemy couldn't follow us. It looked like we had a successful and effective mission.

We took our ships back into an orbital position over England, just to keep a watchful eye. I would have to return later to Tasmania, but that could wait for now. But my immediate attention was focused upon the people who had been rescued.

My second officer, a Danu named Paq, and I, headed to the teleportation deck where medical had set up a triage for those who returned.

"There are fifty-two civilian captives." Shara, the chief healer told me, "One was injured by enemy fire during the escape, but the others are all in reasonable health by the look of them."

Boris was standing close by and he raised his visor, "We all got back intact." he said, "We did this in under five minutes."

"We did well under the circumstances." I punched the big Russian on his shoulder, "But we'll need to keep alert just in case the enemy try anything else."

"By the book." Boris grinned and turned to start barking orders at his troops.

I turned back to Shara, who was a petite blonde Ren, yet very tough and strong and she reported further, "We will need to quarantine them until we can get the collars and bracelets off. I'm not sure how to do that. It won't be easy I guess because the collars are meant to never come off, not unless a Baal orders it. That requires a neurological trigger. If I try the wrong trigger, it will probably kill them. If we wake them up, they will probably fight against us. They will be fully enthralled."

"Best to keep them unconscious then." I suggested, "Try your best Shara."

"It's all I can do." she sighed.

I returned to my bridge and sat in my command chair, looking intently at the tank. I was always looking at the tank lately.

"Paq." I asked, "Let's look at the global situation."

My second officer used the tank controls himself and then joined me, standing behind my chair. We looked carefully. There were all our big capital ships, the Daedalus in America, Eagle, Lady Guinevere and Selki over northern England. Arrow was still in Tasmania. Leon Kurbatov had a battle platform, the Juggernaut, with a fleet of drop ships over the North Sea. Our other capital ship, the Seraph, under the command of "Joshua" was over Israel. Namtar had ceded his Djinni forces, along with another capital ship, the Saladin, to the Islamic League. He was over Arabia, the bastard. At least he was still an ally, Allah be praised!

"Where are the others?" I asked.

By 'others' I meant the Aquarius Alliance forces. Most of them were limited to small class E.D.V fleets in their own regions. Some were flying missions, which was good. But there were some big ships. The Chinese Tao had three battle platforms, big cylindrical ships over Asia. We knew they had them, but didn't get a good look until now. The Japanese Katana had a capital class ship, looking like a huge wedge, conducting rescue ops over Japan. The Europeans had a combined Chevalier/Redstar fleet of cigar shaped destroyers. Six were hovering over the Alps and another ten over the Urals. The W.G.A. also had destroyers, three of them, over Mexico. The Americans had a similar fleet of medium wedge shaped destroyers, twenty-five ships as well as a significant fleet of disk shaped drop ships and e.d.v fighter bombers, but they had chosen to operate alongside of the Daedalus. I was glad to see them out there as an obvious presence. The enemy would hesitate before doing anything big. We were all on edge, watching and waiting for what would happen next.

"Sir.." my com officer got my attention, "we have messages coming from a number of the Aquarius allies. They want to know what the hell we were doing just then!"

I sighed. I suppose I better talk to them.

Chapter Twenty-Six

Shile

They had been travelling for two days, moving quickly. Hilli had been able to repair the two damaged constructs and having them to carry the slower members of the group or those taking shifts sleeping made the journey a lot easier, now there were four. But even so, Rainbow and Newton discovered that they were fitter than they thought. When they went through the last ring cycle, they had their bodies "improved" and so were able to cope with the pace. It was almost sundown on the second day when they crested a hill and Shet pointed towards a mountain before them. It was a plateau really, with a flat area on top.

"There is a stairway carved into the rock, and a cave that leads up to the top." Shet explained.

"My people have come here to trade at times." Rom added, "But we prefer not to trade with the Shile, although sometimes we must."

"How long to climb it?" Kit asked.

"Not tonight." Shet shook his head.

"Do we walk up in the morning?" Rainbow asked.

"We could risk a short flight up." Tarmal suggested, "Will the enemy spot us now that we are this close?"

"No," Grim replied, "Shet and Rainbow are right. We will camp here. It could all get very bad if we were confronted by the enemy now. How many times did we see enemy flights today?"

"Ah," Surreya thought, "Hilli and I spotted two zeppelins and there have been lots of dragons."

"I saw at least twenty six dragons." Hilli nodded, "We had to hide five times they got so close."

"Good point." Tarmal agreed.

The group climbed down into a small hollow under the cover of a grove of trees.

"Why don't we climb up tonight?" Fay asked, "We've been running for two days, what's a couple more hours?"

"You've led troops into battle." Grim smiled, "Think tactically."

"We need real sleep." Fay nodded, "And a warm meal. Tomorrow might be a battle and we need all our strength."

Under the protection of the grove of trees, Hilli and Surreya unpacked supplies from the construct's baggage and camp was set up. Surreya, Niamah, Kit and Al took a construct each and did a bit of petrol and then set the constructs as guards, forming a perimeter.

As they sat and ate self-heating meals around a camp heater, they were quiet. Everyone was tired after the running.

"Shame that I can't rig up the Ren field as a habitat." Hilli sighed, "We could sleep in real beds rather than hammocks."

"You can do that?" Rainbow exclaimed.

"Yes," Hilli replied, "But my field gives off a lot of visual and other radiation. The enemy would see us, even from a distance."

"Oh."

So they put up hammocks and slept. Even Grim, whose species didn't sleep, took the chance to rest his body. The four constructs kept watch.

In the morning at dawn, they set out to climb the plateau. Rom and Shet quickly found the stairway up and the tunnel that had been carved through to the open space above.

"This stairway is very old." Rom explained, "Even older than father."

"Who built it?" Rainbow wondered.

"It was carved by people from before the Purge." Rom explained, "Back then the Shile ruled over this entire area. Now they only have control over the land to the south, down where the rivers enter the sea."

"But they still come up here sometimes." Shet added.

Finally the tunnel came out on the plateau. The area was covered in grass. There were no trees, no cover at all except to retreat back to the tunnel itself.

"What do we do now?" Newton asked.

"We wait." Rom answered, "They won't be long, they always come."

"They must watch this spot." Tarmal commented, "The Shile might have scanner devices here somewhere, or perhaps a satellite."

Indeed they didn't have long to wait at all. Soon there was the sound of a sonic boom and a very fast moving e.d.v. could be seen approaching from the south. As it got closer, they could see a glowing "manta-shaped" vehicle. They could also *feel* intense sound waves probing them.

"It's a space-whale!!!" Kit cried out, "A living creature genetically engineered into a spacecraft!"

"What is that vibration?" Newton asked, "It's very disturbing."

"The space-whales emit a scream which they use like sonar to scan their environment. It's only good at subsonic speeds, but it is also a very effective weapon. Raise the frequency just a bit and our bodies would boil from the inside out."

"Like a microwave." Niamah growled.

"Wonderful." Newton complained, "I feel very safe now."

"It's coming around!" Fay cried.

And indeed it was. The space-whale flew overhead and then came to a dead stop only as an e.d.v. can. It hummed for a bit and descended as its flight generators spun down. Landing pods, like feet, extended underneath and the living ship landed. As its field was cooling down, the team could get a much better look.

The ship was quite large, drop ship sized large. Its upper surface was black and the underside a nice light blue with flecks of grey. On either side of the mouth were large flaps. Weapons ports could be seen around the creature's eyes, but there was a bit of a shock as the long tail of the space-whale flicked forward, with a tip glowing with the energy of a powerful particle weapon!

"Not very friendly at all." Newton grumbled.

Within the space-whale's mouth they could see an iris hatch open and figures walked out and came down a ramp which extended from the creatures' lower jaw. Grim led them forward to meet the Shile.

"Be very careful." Rom advised, "There is a Pigrian guard, a Bardel, and Chipperwaal accompanying the Shilean Herder."

"Herder?" Rainbow asked.

"A Herder is what the Shile call their leaders." Grim explained, "They have a ruling caste that are genetically designed to control the Humanimal servant castes. Their commands cannot be disobeyed by any Humanimal servitor. It gives the Herders incredible power. Only one in every hundred or so Shile is born to the Herder caste."

"So," Rainbow realised, "The Humanimals have no choice? That's not much different from the enthrallment collars."

"Hmm," Niamah touched Rainbow's arm, "not quite the same. I've met the Shile before. The Herder is more like the heart of a symbiotic relationship. The Herder and their servitors are telepathically and empathically linked. They need each other. If the Humanimals are hurt, the Herder feels their pain. The symbiosis relationship makes them formidable as a team."

As the Shilean group got closer the three servitors moved in front of their Herder. The Herder was a small, hairless being with large black eyes.

Newton couldn't help grinning, "It's a classic grey." He said to himself.

The Chipperwaal approached them first. He was a large grey male wearing a tool utility harness.

"I speak for my collective." he said, speaking the Sethani language, "Have you come to negotiate with the Shile?"

Rom and Grim stepped closer to the Chipperwaal who stood in front of his Herder. The Pigrian and Bardel moved to flanking positions on either side. Niamah, Al and Kit stood to face the Pigrian while Tarmal, Surreya and Fay tried to face off the imposing Bardel. There was a lot of tension. Shet moved forward to join Grim and Rom.

"I am the patriarch Rom of Eden." Rom introduced himself, "It is my honour to speak to your collective. With me here are representatives of a people who are at war with the Pandemonium forces that have recently invaded our territories, I ask that they may speak with you."

Grim moved further forward. All the members of the Shile collective looked alarmed, although they were all, especially the Chipperwaal, trying to look un-emotional. Even the Herder was blinking involuntarily.

"We do not recognise your species." the Chipperwaal said, which was a big admission.

"I am a Torgar of the Eldar." Grim replied, "My species have served the Elohim from before the existence of this space time continuum. I bring with me human and A'sidhe representatives, as well as people of Eden to speak with you because we have common cause against the Pandemonium. We recently fought against the Pandemonium at Manhome and defeated a large force. Despite that, it was decided to send the people to Cherubim and to gather our warriors to fight more effectively. A large Pandemonium force, including Anakim and Gorenge are being prepared to invade the heartlands. Will you stand against them?"

"We will."

With that simple statement, the Chipperwaal turned around and headed back towards the others. For a moment the Herder just looked across at everyone, but especially at Grim and also at Shet. The Herder nodded then turned away, leading the others back towards the space-whale. No-one spoke. The Shilean collective re-entered their space-whale and they rezzed up and moved off quickly.

"That was brief and to the point." Newton said.

"Very Shilean." Tarmal nodded, "They never waste words."

"What will they do?" Rainbow asked.

"They will attack any Pandemonium force that tries to land this side of the western shore." Grim turned and began to lead the group back towards the stairway down.

"I'd like to see that battle." Fay grinned, "The Pigrians in particular are formidable."

"I too would appreciate seeing that." Niamah agreed, "But we need to get to Cherubim as soon as possible."

"Another forced run?" Rainbow said unhappily.

"We'll ride the constructs as much as possible." Grim reassured her.

"That's good." Newton agreed.

"But I think I'll scout ahead." Kit added.

"Me too." Al slapped his younger brother on the shoulder.

"Can I come too?" Mrorna asked, "I'll keep up!"

"Let's get moving then." Niamah started down the stairs.

Chapter Twenty-Seven

Manlore

Later that night, as the three beloved members of my family, and Mrorna, ran tirelessly ahead of the constructs carrying their other team members, little did they know but the Pandemonium were already on the move in huge numbers. A massive flotilla of ships floated off shore on what would one day be the Caspian Sea, but which was now the much larger Sea of Nod. Not far away, further south along the Nodin coast was the mouth of the Pishon River and the Cainite city of

Manlore. The Manloreans had already come out of their city to face the enemy. Also not too far away, to the north, another army of Cainites had lined up on the beach, also waiting to see what the enemy would do. At the head of the Manlorean army was their king, Lahmech. He was a huge bear of a man with a shaggy mane of pure white hair, characteristic of all the people of his race. He was after all one of the 'marked ones,' a descendant of Kayyin who murdered his twin brother Hebel and was cast out. The great patriarch, Kayyin himself, first born son of Awdame, led the Nodin. These people, like the Manloreans, were also white people, but more so. Like Kayyin, they were albinos, a people with no pigment and so no tolerance of the sun at all. They preferred the night and so had long ago abandoned agriculture for the hunt and the making of tools. Kayyin ruled over the wild lands of Nod. Although close relatives, Kayyin and Lahmech watched each other with hatred and suspicion. Lahmech had established his own line in defiance of his patriarch and built his own city. The younger clan had declared war against their own ancestors. Lahmech had ensured that he intermarried with some of the darker skinned people, and he married two wives of Havillah and Koosh and made alliances with those tribes. It was those alliances that had most angered Kayyin and driven him to war with Lahmech.

Beside Lahmech were his own clan leaders, his sons, Vulkayyin the ironworker, Jahbaal the herdsman, Jubil the musician, his brother and Hecate, Vulkayyin's sister. These children, like their mothers, were not under the curse of Kayyin. Lahmech boasted of this often! He waved his spear high in the air and his army yelled a war-cry. To the north, Kayyin heard it and he was full of rage.

But it was rage that for this time had to be put to one side. A bigger enemy was there to deal with. But once that was done, then things would be taken care of.

Kayyin looked across the sea coast at the enemy fleet that seemed to cover the ocean as far as the eye could see. Would they live beyond this night and so see vengeance fulfilled? At least the night was dark and cool and it had begun to rain.

There was a sudden flash of lightning and Kayyin briefly shielded his eyes, but not before he saw the dirigibles hovering overhead. There were hundreds of them! Kayyin, full of fear, contemplated a hasty retreat, but a second surprise was to follow.

Down on the beach, the front row of landing ships ran aground on the beach and landing ramps were lowered and Gorenge and Anakim warriors began to wade ashore. These warriors were well equipped and heavily armed. The Gorenge were wearing camouflage armour and helms with claw blades, energy rifles and grenades. The Anakim were even more heavily armed, carrying heavy plasma guns and rocket launchers. The armies of Nod on one side and Manlore on the other began to withdraw from what amounted to certain death.

But even as those on shore retreated, sudden confusion fell upon the enemy. Gigantic explosions rocked the ships in the water!!! The noise and light shattered the night as ship after ship erupted in flames! At the same time, missiles were fired from under the water and also from above, the airships began dropping in flames as well!

The troops on those ships closest to the shore began to force those in front of them forward in panic as they desperately sought the safety of land. Confusion dominated the scene. Up out of the ocean and down from the sky above came waves of space-whales. Even the Cainites who were retreating could hear the sonic-cry of the whales, but for many of those on the beaches it meant death. The powerful soundwaves not only ruptured ear drums but disrupted internal organs and even caused some to be literally cooked alive!!! Enemy forces in the hundreds were falling and screaming in agony! Some of them, though, had sonic protective gear and were able to pull down their helms and visors in time to save their lives. These fled up onto the shore, seeking to reform their forces and strike back.

Gun nests were quickly set up and they began to fire at the attacking Shile. Likewise, the Pandemonium were fighting back in the sky against the space-whales, sending their dragons forth in their hundreds. In the water, the Shile were continuing the attack on the landing ships. Not only were the Space-Whales launching torpedoes from underwater, their aquatic troops were holding boarding actions. It was the Pigrian Tuskers, in bio-mechanical diving suits, swarming aboard the landing ships and fighting the crews and warriors aboard. Others were coming ashore as well, attacking the Pandemonium forces waiting there. At this point the fighting was getting up close and personal. Especially on the ships, there was a lot of hand to hand fighting. Despite the size of the Anakim giants and the viciousness of the reptilian Gorenge, the Pigrian Tuskers held their own as fighters. Their bio-mech armour enhanced their strength and protected them as well as the best shielding. Once they had taken ground, they were joined by Bardel, similarly armoured, but much larger. The enemy Pandemonium were beginning to panic.

Those on the beach were in the best position and they had a good Gorenge commander. Survivors from the ships were making it to ground and they rallied to the banner of the unit commander. She was a Gorenge Neph and very smart and Rah-hab in a former incarnation. This made her very dangerous and her warriors, even the Anakim, trusted her with unfailing loyalty. She knew that staying put wasn't an option, so, when she realised that there wouldn't be many more survivors off the sinking ships, she led her warriors inland. On their escape route, they ran into Kayyin's Nodin army.

In that fateful moment, Kayyin made a choice. He openly approached the Pandemonium force and then he ordered his warriors to lay down their weapons and bow on the ground.

The Gorenge commander ran forward ahead of her horde and postured a threatening hissing pose. "Mammals!" she said it as an insult.

Kayyin remained silent as the Gorenge stalked forward.

"Why should I not just kill you all?" She demanded.

"Because you need us."

She grunted, then released a soft hiss.

"We will alliance with you."

"Good." Kayyin and his warriors all stood. They then turned and led the way forward into the Pishon valley.

Down on the beaches, the fighting continued as stragglers from the Pandemonium forces tried to fight the Shile. The fighting was brutal. The Space-whales had forced the enemy airships to teleport away or they had destroyed them. There were dead dragons floating in the sea or dead on the beach. While many of the landing craft had reached the beach, those in the water were mostly sunk or on fire. Most of the Pandemonium forces had fled into the forests, but the Gorenge general had left forces behind to protect their retreat. These had managed to dig in and hold their ground. They had set up shielding and large calibre weapons and the Pigrians were forced back into the sea. But this wasn't such a problem. The Space-whales had long range weapons and just hovered beyond the range of the enemy and began to bombard them with high energy particle cannon, the ones mounted on their tails. Other Space-whales just flew overhead and began a search for the fleeing Pandemonium forces.

Lahmech and his army were watching all this taking place from a hill to the south.

"Jubil." Lahmech called for his son, "Blast a horn. I wish to speak with the Shile."

Jubil took a rams horn and blew a loud blast. His brother Vulkayyin lit a torch and waved it in the air. They did this for some time, until a Space-whale turned from the battle and headed towards them.

Lahmech did not bow as the Chipperwaal steward and his Pigrian guards approached. The Pigrians pointed their weapons right at him, but Lahmech stood tall.

"You are an affront to the Shile, Manlorean." The Chipperwaal spoke with disgust.

"Be that as it may," Lahmech laughed, "but I know where the remaining Pandemonium forces have gone, and you do not."

"Tell us so we may destroy them."

"They have gotten help from an enemy of mine." Lahmech replied, "If I lead you to the enemy, I must have freedom to destroy my enemy as well."

"You have that freedom," the Chipperwaal beat his chest with a closed fist, "We will both destroy our enemies this night."

The Chipperwaal stepped forward and gave a round, egg-shaped object to Lahmech.

"This will help us to track you." He said, "You can also speak to it and we will hear your words. Pursue our enemies and when you find them, we will come to you and we will fight together."

"You speak quickly." Lahmech grinned, "Do you speak for your collective or for yourself?"

"Many members of my collective have died tonight. I speak alone among others." The Chipperwaal bared his teeth, "I seek blood."

"As do I." Lahmech nodded, "As do I."

The Chipperwaal grunted and turned back to his Space-whale with his guards.

"Let's get down into the valley." Lahmech told his four children. Jubil blew on his horn again and the warriors cheered, beating their shields with their spears, and began the march inland.

Lahmech knew exactly where to go. He sped up and began a run as they came to flatter ground. Kayyin was not far away and he would be leading the Pandemonium into the Nodin hills on the northern side of the Pishon River. The Manloreans found a ford across the river near its mouth and they continued northwards.

Fleeing northwards as Lahmech expected, Kayyin and his Nodin army ran alongside the Pandemonium through the forest. Kayyin was a good runner and was easily keeping up with the large Gorenge general.

"We give our service freely." Kayyin called to her, "We are to be free people. No enthrallment for my tribe. If you try it, we will resist you."

"Fair enough." The Gorenge barked at him, "But if you betray us, I will ensure that your whole tribe is exterminated." She hissed a reptilian laugh.

"Also fair enough." Kayyin ran ahead.

Kayyin's oldest son Enosh ran in from the side to his father, "The Manloreans follow us." He was panting with exertion.

"Good." Kayyin said, "It is my plan to die tonight."

"What if Hecate is wrong about this?"

"Then it will be up to you to avenge me," Kayyin laughed, "and if The Elohim keeps Their promise, then you will have Divine power and not fail. We go to the valley ahead and stop there and wait for them to come to us. The Shile will be nearby as well. It is a good clear night now that the rain has stopped. A good night for killing."

"Yes father." Enosh ran back to pass on the message to the other warriors.

As for Hecate, daughter of Lahmech, she ran with the Manloreans. But as she ran, she whispered occult words under her breath in an ancient language and stared at the back of her father's head. Shile Space-whales flew overhead.

About half an hour later, Kayyin led the two armies into a narrow valley. Again he caught up with the Gorenge leader to speak to her.

"We will have to stop up ahead." He told her, "We have a fortress and caves and can defend ourselves. We are being pursued and need to fight. I also have allies among my enemy who will fight for us. We can crush those who pursue us here."

"And what of the Shile?" the Gorenge demanded.

"I am the first son of Awdame." Kayyin said, "I am not ignorant of your technology as my descendants are. I know how to fight the Shile."

"You had better be right," she said, "or we are all dead. But we will make this stand where you say so."

They continued to run and soon entered a closed area, through a gate in a thick wall. There in the middle of the space beyond the gate was a single crystal standing stone. The walls of the fortress were beautifully carved.

"This is an 'Old Stone'!!!" The Gorenge's mouth gaped open in shock.

"And I can use it." Kayyin touched the stone.

Behind them a portal shimmered open.

"Through there is my city of Enosh, named after my son, and protection for us all."

Kayyin opened other portals.

"These portals I can open to places behind our enemies." Kayyin continued, "I can open portals underneath enemy troops and send them into the sky so they fall to their deaths. I can move portals like nets to capture the Shile Space-whales and send them wherever I want. I can send them to nowhere."

By this time, most of the Pandemonium and Nodin armies were inside the fortress.

"Shall we flee or shall we fight?" Kayyin asked.

"We shall fight." The Gorenge said.

"Excellent." Kayyin grinned.

Kayyin waved at three of his warriors and they went through the other portals. Shortly they returned and whispered in Kayyin's ear. They and others returned through the portals.

"I have planned this battle for some time." Kayyin told his new ally, "That you get to benefit from this is to our mutual advantage. I shall keep the escape portal open until we all retreat through it. Send your warriors forward and attack those who are coming towards us down this valley. Draw them in and kill as many as you wish. I will take care of the rest. Kill everyone but I ask that you do not kill Lahmech, nor his children. As for Hecate, she fights for us. I have a special treat for my traitorous child and his sons. Kill anyone else but not them."

"As you wish." The Gorenge bowed and hissed with anticipation. With a bark, she ordered her troops back out through the gate. As he saw the Pandemonium army running to battle, Kayyin smiled because she to whom he had bowed in submission had now bowed to him! Kayyin put his hand back onto the stone and he concentrated upon what he could see within his mind, that which the spirit of the stone showed him.

Lahmech spoke to the stone that the Chipperwaal had given him. The Shile told him that the enemy had fled into a valley and that there was a fortress there. Some of the enemy were within the fortress, but others were coming back down the valley to fight. Lahmech felt a bit uneasy, but the Shile told him that they would use their superior weapons to destroy the enemy. Lahmech saw and heard the screaming Space-whales fly overhead and he was reassured. Lahmech raised his spear high over his head and Jubil blew on his horn! The warriors all cried a war cry and ran down the valley. Up ahead the Space-whales had begun a bombardment. It lasted but a little while and then abruptly stopped, it was as though the Space-whales had vanished. Little did he know, but they had.

As they ran, Lahmech could see the dust of the bombardment ahead. They ran forward into the haze. Little did Lahmech know, but Hecate and her daughters had pulled back and had withdrawn from the battle to the mouth of the valley. From there Hecate looked up into the sky. She could see the flashes of the portals that Kayyin was opening and closing, sending the Space-whales into oblivion. It had all been accomplished with deep magic and very old technology that no-one knew was still there. She grinned and one of her daughters gave her a bag of salt. Hecate began to pour out the sacred circle upon the ground.

In the dust haze of the valley, two armies met each other, the Manloreans and the Pandemonium! With the Manloreans, Lahmech could see that there were some Pigrians and the occasional tall Bardel ready to fight alongside of them, but where were the Space-whales? Where were their superior weapons? But now the fight was on and Lahmech had other things to worry about, as a huge Anak appeared before him.

The Anak carried his rifle, with bayonet fixed, and Lahmech was forced to use his spear to parry and then stab. The Anak died and then a pair of Gorenge took his place. Lahmech pulled out his blow pipe and downed one with a poison dart while he pulled his spear out of the dead Anak. The second Gorenge leapt with toe claws extended and Lahmech met it with his spear. All around there was the sound of Pandemonium gun fire. The Manloreans were wearing good armour and had their blow pipes and darts. These they used to good effect because the darts long needles pierced the Pandemon uniforms. Lahmech was confused. He had expected Shile firepower. But there was almost none of it. And where were the Nodin warriors? They were nowhere to be seen. Lahmech's sons were nearby, as well as shield bearers and archers. The archers had explosive arrowheads which were very effective. Lahmech drew back behind his shield bearers for protection from gunfire and let the dart-men and archers do their job. As enemies came close, it came down to spear fighting or long knives against bayonets. Lahmech kept his army in order, forming up ranks, keeping the line against the enemy. Pandemonium forces ran against them and again and again there was brutal fighting until the enemy pulled back and tried a different angle in the narrow gorge. Then, unexpectedly there were cries from the rear! They were under attack by the Nodin!

The Nodin pushed hard and Lahmech led forward, deeper down the valley. Ahead, through the dust, they could see the fortress wall and the gate standing open mocking them as enemy troops moved in and out to face them. The Gorenge were roaring near the gate, taunting the Manloreans to attack them. But Lahmech knew better than that. He also knew that he had led his warriors into a dangerous place with no way out except to fight and kill everything that they could. He looked around carefully and thoughtfully. Two enemies had him between them. The Shile reinforcements were nowhere to be seen. Had the Shile betrayed him? He didn't think so. There were a thousand Pigrians and Bardel among his number. The Shile collective wouldn't sacrifice such a large number so recklessly or painfully. Something or someone had destroyed them. It was then that he realised that something was seriously wrong. There were flashes of light among the battle lines and whole groups of warriors just vanished! There were no screams, they just fell and were gone! Lahmech screamed at the line to stay together, but as they were swallowed again and again, the warriors began to panic! Even Lahmech himself knew there was nothing for it but for every warrior to flee for their lives! Evil magic was at work here. Jubil blew the retreat horn and the line collapsed. Enemy troops from front and back flooded in the gaps. Lahmech and his sons retreated down the valley, refusing to stand. Many of those who surrounded them were mercilessly gunned down or forced to fight. Small groups of warriors formed bands and hand to hand fighting continued. Lahmech noticed that he wasn't attacked, but his warriors were. They were being systematically exterminated! It was all happening so quickly. Soon Lahmech realised that himself, his three sons and about a dozen shield bearers were all that were left. Blocking the way out of the valley was a group of Nodin warriors. Behind them in the valley were the Pandemonium forces holding their position. From among the Nodin stepped forward two men. A young shield bearer and behind him, Kayyin himself. Lahmech noticed that Hecate stood among the Nodin as one of them. Lahmech spat on the ground and hoped she saw it.

"Come and fight me!" Kayyin taunted.

Lahmech took his spear, pushed those around him aside and full of hot focused rage, he ran towards Kayyin and his shield bearer. The shield bearer confronted him first and Lahmech smashed the shield aside. In that moment, the young man used his knife and made a cut at Lahmech, drawing blood from his side! Lahmech grunted with surprise and he used his spear butt to smash the young man's head in. He fell like a sack. Then Kayyin was there and the two rivals were striking at each other, each howling angrily! Kayyin was obviously the better warrior, and all of those watching could see it! Yet Kayyin looked grim and in a little moment just raised his arms. Without hesitation Lahmech drove his spear into Kayyin's chest, yelling with victory!! He looked up and there was no other noise. Strangely, all the others, the Nodin warriors, the Pandemonium behind, they had all suddenly vanished into the dust haze. There was nothing but Lahmech, his three sons, Kayyin's dead body, transfixed by the spear, and thousands of dead bodies filling the valley. Lahmech stopped his war cry and a chill shook his entire body. He turned to his sons. They had looks of horror upon their faces. None of them had expected him to actually win, if this carnage could be called that. It was a hollow victory gained at a huge and unacceptable price. Yet there they were.

"Let's go home." Lahmech said quietly, "Bring his body and my spear."

Chapter Twenty-Eight

Cherubim

On the journey north to the sacred city tree of Cherubim, the travellers had to stop sometimes to rest. At these times, Mrorna, Kit, Al and Niamah would visit some of the local villages for news. There were stories of Pandemonium forces landing along the Nodin coast as well as rumours of a great battle in the south.

It was incredible how quickly the news spread. Many of the people they met were preparing to retreat to Cherubim and a lot of villages were empty as the people had already left. The people of Manhome were gathering as many as they could as they headed north.

Looking north from the heartland of Eden they could see the ring of tall snow-capped mountains that ringed the Garden. There were only two ways into the Garden. From the west, one could cross the Crystal Sea which blocked the western side of the great valley in which the Garden was located. But crossing that sea was fraught with danger. No-one crossed the water without Seelie permission, and those who tried were never seen again. It was a sea full of portals to other worlds, so it was said. The other entrance was a narrow gorge on the eastern side of the valley between the mountains of Koosh in the north and the Havilah Mountains to the south. Where these two ranges met was a narrow gap and standing blocking that gap was the Cherubim Tree. It was THE Tree of all trees, they were told by the people they met. Long ago, these Great Trees grew in many places, but now there was only the one.

Kit, Niamah, Al and Mrorna listened to these stories as they headed north ahead of the rest of the travellers. It was decided that having better intelligence was important. Although they had to run on foot, Mrorna managed to keep up the pace alongside the other three. The tribal people they met spoke with such confidence and awe – despite the danger of imminent invasion, that the Seelie garrison of Cherubim would protect them.

Despite this seeming confidence, Kit could also sense unease. His mother and brother could feel it too. Mrorna got to speak to a lot of people who were fleeing for their lives to Cherubim, but even then, they were uncertain. The Pandemonium invasion was unprecedented in this age. Rumours of whole tribes being enthralled caused panic to rise. One question was asked again and again to Niamah and her sons, "Why doesn't the Seelie just go out to fight them?"

Kit's own growing unease came from the same question. His mother's people were notoriously detached. Would they leave the humans to their fate? Kit was determined to try and convince them to help if he could. While resting and eating in one village, Kit took Niamah aside, and Al listened in. Mrorna had gone to catch up with some distant relatives.

"Mother, I wonder…"

"….if Cherubim will actually help." She finished his sentence for him.

"Yes." Kit nodded, "Will they take the people in? What of the people of Man-home?"

"The children of Awdame they will certainly protect." Niamah reassured him, "The other tribes, I'm not so sure. There will be a big encampment when we get there of refugees, no doubt."

"Who will we be talking to when we do get there?"

"Gabriel is Morrigan of the Tree, but the Daughters of Hebel rule."

"Hebel?" Kit wondered, "Is that Abel? The son of Adam that was murdered by Cain?"

"Yes." Niamah nodded, "We know the story."

"Hmm."

"Abel, that is Hebel, had no sons." Niamah explained, "So his daughters, led by the eldest sister, Maia, went to Cherubim and they were welcomed into the city. Maia rules there still. We will talk with her, as well as to Gabriel and other leaders of the Seelie council. I think in coming back in time we have bitten off more than we can chew by ourselves. We will need all the help we can get. The council will want to talk with Awdame and Shet as well. The bloodline must survive."

"Could Graud really do what Michael said he was trying to do?" Kit was horrified, "Can he actually destroy this time stream and create another?"

Niamah and Al looked at each other briefly. There was a moment of frightful silence.

"I think that is a nightmare we will discuss when we see the council." Niamah finally said.

"I agree." said Al, "We should keep on our journey."

"Let's run then." Kit sighed, "The physical exercise will keep me preoccupied."

Silently, they drank from their water bottles and then ran quickly out of the village. They met Mrorna outside the gate and she joined them. An hour later, as

Kit, with Mrorna beside him and his mother and brother, ran along the road to Cherubim, Kit still felt very unsettled.

A few hours later, the four runners came to another village. It was a large walled settlement. Like all cities of the time, there was a gate and large compound for the animals and storage of crops. While the people of Manhome had lived in a cave, these people had built a city for themselves. Unlike the post-deluge Iron Age cities in Mesopotamia, these cities had no streets. Instead, there was a ramp (in this town at least) or ladders, leading up onto the roofs of the buildings, which were all built together without any gaps, like one really big house. The citizens would walk from house to house across the roofs and enter each room from above. Inside the city there were also interconnecting doors. They filled their water bottles at the well located in the middle of the city compound. There were a lot of people coming and going. The locals stayed up on the roofs of their city and watched those below. They seemed content to stay up there and it was obvious that was where they spent most of their time living anyway. Kit noticed the cooking fires and could smell unleavened bread being baked on the domes of the ovens. He realised he was very hungry.

Mrorna was hungry as well and she suggested that she go purchase some bread from the villagers. That was the way they had to do things, through her. She spoke the language as a native and most importantly knew the culture well. She would be accepted by the people a lot more than the three Folk, and people talked to Mrorna and she was a good listener. Kit watched her as she went over to a group of children nearby. As she spoke with them Mrorna turned and looked back briefly, smiling at Kit. He waved back and Mrorna went with the children, presumably somewhere to buy food. Kit had the sudden realisation that Mrorna was incredibly beautiful. He sighed inwardly.

As for Mrorna, she was grinning as she followed the children up a ladder. She looked back again and could see he was looking at her. The children led her up onto the roof of their city and along to a shelter nearby. There was a woman there with a large stack of unleavened bread. There was a group of men standing with her. As Mrorna and the children got closer, one of the men turned. He was wearing a head turban, but despite that, Mrorna recognised his eyes immediately.

"Rom!"

The tall son of Awdame put his hands on his hips and laughed.

"I see we have caught up with each other." He said.

"Not quite all of us." Mrorna corrected him, "I'm here with Kit, Niamah and Alaquandi. We have been scouting ahead. Where are the others?"

"My nephew and the rest of your group are not far away."

She nodded, "I think that the Shile will be very helpful allies."

"The Shile can be helpful." Rom said, "I have made good trade with them many times, but they are never allies. They do only what serves their own purposes."

"As long as they kill Pandemonium!" Mrorna pointed out, "That is all that matters!"

"They will certainly do that." Rom told her, "Where are your companions?"

"Down there." Mrorna pointed behind her, "I came up here with the children to buy bread."

"So did I." Rom looked at the children who were sitting near their grandmother, holding stacks of unleavened bread, "Also, the people of Manhome are just north of this city, encamped in a clearing. We are a day's journey from Cherubim."

"Good!" Mrorna said, "We can all reunite and travel together."

"I will pay for the bread." Rom opened a bag and drew out some herbs. The woman's eyes grew very wide and she nodded vigorously.

"Is that what I think it is?" Mrorna's voice croaked with surprise.

"Yes." Rom whispered, "It's ambrosia plant."

The bread was collected and they went back down the ladder to the compound below. Kit was waiting at the bottom of the ladder.

"Rom paid for the bread with ambrosia plant." Mrorna told him.

"That's a bit of a risk." Kit raised his eyebrows at Rom.

"It's alright." Rom's eyes sparkled, "I've been trading with that family for many years. She's one of the Stone people."

Kit looked a little puzzled.

"The Stone people are the people who lived here before the coming of Awdame and Haveh. Those of us who are children of the Progenitors are much longer lived than the Stone people, whose lives are so much shorter than ours."

"And the ambrosia gives her people longer lives." Kit nodded and smiled, "Fair enough."

"More than that." Rom said, "Trading ambrosia keeps the peace between the two peoples and the Seelie give us the plant from the Garden."

"All the more reason why we must go to Cherubim and keep the alliance with the Seelie." Kit said, "We need to keep the tribes protected and united."

"The Romany have always worked to do that." Rom nodded, "Ambrosia and brides."

"Brides?" Kit asked.

"The tribes are bound together by marriage alliances." Rom began his explanation, "The sons and daughters of Awdame and Haveh marry the children of kings and so our tribe has been enlarged and become a kingdom of its own. Our gardens and animals feed the people and those who marry into the family have access to the ambrosia which prolongs their lives beyond that of the stone tribes."

"Does that mean that as a son of Awdame and Haveh that you have married as an alliance and not for love?" Kit wondered if the question would even make sense to Rom.

Rom laughed.

"I am the exception to the rule." Rom chuckled, "First of all, Haveh isn't my mother. Awdame is my father and my mother is or rather was a Stone woman from outer Cush. To keep the blood true I was able to marry my cousin. So I was able to choose love. Myst is the matriarch of my tribe. My other wives, Tiva and Fornel are also grand-daughters of Haveh and so we have no alliances with any one tribe. It's for that reason the Romany can travel and trade with all the tribes without difficulty. We transport ambrosia and brides to their destinations."

"That makes you very important in keeping the peace then." Mrorna said.

"Yes." Rom nodded, "All my brothers are bound by alliances, but the Romany are not."

By that time they had met up with Niamah and Alaquandi outside the city gate. They greeted each other cordially. The conversation was only just started when along the path they could hear some strange noises. People on the path were talking or crying out and moving aside as four large forms came into view. It was the constructs still carrying their passengers. Shet was riding on the shoulder of the lead construct and he called out when he saw the familiar faces up ahead. The Stone tribe people along the path and in the nearby city were all gathering around and looking in wonder. They had never seen anything like the constructs before. Many of the people knew Rom, and a few recognised Shet, but they were also surprised by the appearance of Grim, who was riding in the basket on the back of the second construct. Everyone was waving and talking at once! Newton had jumped down from his construct at the rear and ran forward to embrace his friend Kit and the others.

"Finally we are all together again!" Newton was grinning.

"Rom tells us that the people of Manhome are encamped just up the road!" Niamah told him, "We will indeed all be together tonight and tomorrow we reach Cherubim."

"Fantastic!" Newton exclaimed.

That night there was a reunion around a large fire only a day away from Cherubim. Awdame, Melki and Haveh sat down with Rom, Shet, Niamah and Grim to one side and talked quietly together. Kit, Mrorna, Newton, Rainbow, Tarmal, Fay, Al, Surreya and Hilli sat near the constructs and a large group of Manhome children who wanted to hang around with them. Manhome and Romany servants brought food from the camp fires around and everyone ate meat.

"You know what," Rainbow said, "my grandmother told me that before the Flood that no-one ate meat, that they were all vegetarians. She said it was in the Bible. She also told me that it never rained. Well, since I've been here, it's rained rather heavily at least twice."

"She was a creationist?" Newton asked, "One of those literal six day people?"

"Yup." Rainbow smiled.

"Some in my family too." Newton laughed, "I asked them how did they know since they didn't have a time machine to come back and look!!"

The others were grinning as well, but Mrorna was bewildered.

"Oh!" Kit noticed her look, "Mrorna, in the distant future this time has become legendary and many people believe odd things about how things were or rather are in this time. To make matters worse, it's religious teaching, and some religion is difficult."

"I still don't understand." Mrorna sounded offended, "If people don't know something for certain, why pretend that they do?"

"The religious like certainty." Newton said.

"But you are followers of Yeshua, the one called by some Jesus?" Mrorna asked, "Isn't he your God?"

"Yeshua is one of the Elohim, a Logoi." Kit explained, "The Elohim, are, for a better word, Servants of God. Yes, and we are followers of God. But you have met Yeshua. Not only is he a Logoi, an Avatar of the Source of All Being, he is also a man, a man very full of Spiritual power and eternal life. He is a man but he also has true transcendent consciousness. But he is also a wonderfully humble man. He served you food and drink with his own hand did he not?"

"Yes." Mrorna said, "I could tell he loved me."

"Certainly!" Kit smiled, "And we Eldar peoples, the angels, the A'sidhe, the Elves, we know him by many names and he was before in other incarnations known as Adonai, or Melkizedek or older names such as Logos, even Aslan and Eru Iluvatar. If we Folk become myth to mortal humans, then religion has made something of him as well. We and you have seen the Corridor and we have seen him face to face and we know him, but most people only know him from holy writings about him. His teachings though are true and that is what really counts, that and eternal life. I know because I am a Halfling – my mother is A'sidhe and my father is Human."

"What then is the purpose of religion?" Mrorna asked insightfully.

"Religion can only ever show us a shadow of what is real." Kit said, "But for forgetful humans a shadow is better than no memory at all. For those who are spiritually mature, they know the difference between the shadow, which is merely symbolic and the truth, which is reality."

Just then Grim appeared to them and he coughed.

"We've talked." He said, "Tomorrow we reach Cherubim and speak with the Morrigan there. It's a very important meeting so we need a good rest tonight."

With that it was time for sleep.

The next day they climbed up the valley towards the Tree of Cherubim. It was quite a trip because it was all the people of Manhome, with Awdame leading out front as well as the team from the future, riding their constructs, keeping watch for the enemy. To get to the Tree, the big throng had to climb steps up into the mountain pass. Not only did the people have to traverse the narrow path, but so did their rather large dinosaurian pack animals, who protested with bellows constantly! Even at the lower levels of the "stairway to Heaven" as it was known, the roots of the tree could be seen and the ambrosia plants were growing there as well. The higher they went, the more the Kerubim warriors appeared watching them from rock ledges along the way. These Seelie warriors wore feather head-dresses and mantles and carried beamer weapons, known as 'lightning sticks'. The fact that the mountains rumbled with storms, thunder and lightning made things even more intimidating for the people of Manhome as they climbed.

Eventually they climbed out of the narrow passes and came out on a flat area. Ambrosia trees were growing everywhere and the roots of the Great Tree formed gnarled walls all around them. Above were the huge branches and the leaves which gave shade over the whole mountain top. The Tree itself actually sat in the cleft of two mountains, blocking the pass into the valley of the Garden beyond. The only way through was to pass over the branches of the Tree and past the Kerubim who were its guardians.

The eyes of the Kerubim were watching. From the branches above a single Ren could be seen flying downwards using his wings. He seemed to be floating down like gossamer using his force wings almost like a parachute. Finally he landed and shut down the force generators in his shoulder-blades. Like the Kerubim watching from nearby, this Ren wore the feathered mantle and carried a weapon. He walked boldly up to Awdame.

"Hello Raph." Awdame greeted him.

"It has been a long time as humans reckon." Raph said, "We have been expecting you."

Raph, who was tall, wiry and stern looking, walked in among the people and began pointing.

"You..." he pointed at Shet, "and you..." he pointed at Grim, "bring Rom and the others from the future. The rest of you will need to wait here for a bit before we bring you up."

That was all he said and then he reactivated his wings and flew up into the tree again. For about a minute nothing seemed to be happening. Then out of the foliage above a large platform was lowered with ropes. It was like an elevator, but big and open to the air. It was obvious what it was for. The ones Raph pointed at were to go up into the Tree.

"Can't we just fly up?" Hilli asked.

"No." Melki said, "That's not allowed. You must use the lift."

So, Shet and Rom climbed in followed by Grim, Niamah, Rainbow, Mrorna, Hilli, Surreya, Fay, followed by the men, Newton, Tarmal, Al and Kit last. There was plenty of room on the platform. It was probably big enough to hold one of the fully laden behemoths and seemed strong enough to lift the weight. As soon as they were on, the platform began to rise rather quickly.

Up in the foliage, they continued to rise past larger branches until finally there were signs of habitation. The Living Tree itself had been formed and shaped. Branches became actual hollows and flat areas where people could live. It wasn't that the tree had been carved or that structures had been built within the branches, no, the Tree had been grown into dwelling spaces and pod-like growths became rooms. Finally the upward movement stopped and Raph led them off the platform onto a branch. The top of the branch was flat and as wide as a wide road. There were some more Kerubim guards waiting there and Raph led them all along the branch towards the centre of the Tree. Moving through the branches, the visitors realised they were in a wondrous place. Despite the green darkness of the leaves, fluorescent moss growing on the branches gave a soft and cool light. Branches both big and small formed a tangled maze around them, yet there were obvious pathways and every now and then they passed dwellings within the pods or in hollows in the Tree trunks around them. Some of the pods hung down from above like great tear-drops and Renim lived in them. Some of the forms reminded Kit of Ren homes in Utnapishtim. Where branches crossed over each other or met with a trunk of the Tree, there were large flat spaces, often filled with soil formed from leaf litter. Ambrosia trees grew in those spaces. They also saw birds and monkeys in the higher branches.

Sometimes, there were tunnels through the trunks and huge hollow spaces within, filled with dwelling hollows. Within one of these living tubes there was a spiral stairway, again, grown and not cut, climbing upwards. Raph led them higher.

The stair eventually came out to another wide branch. Raph pointed from where they stood. They had passed into the heart of the Tree and they could see the primary trunk. Only the largest of key branches grew out from it, branches which were incredibly wide and strong. Looking where Raph was pointing they could see a collection of large pods, dozens of them.

"We are going there along this branch." He explained, "The Morrigan lives up there."

The branch Raph led them out on was a virtual highway. There were a number of pod homes forming little suburbs and the roads ran around them. Here in this part of the Tree, many of the residents were humans. They were a blonde and slender people with fair almost white skin from living in the shade of the Tree. Most of them were women and there were only a few men.

"These are the Daughters of Hebel." Raph explained, "They are the only humans allowed to live in the Tree permanently. Hebel and his primary wife Gaia had no sons and his daughters in turn took husbands from among the Kerubim, and they also only had daughters. Only recently have sons begun to be born and these are few."

While Raph was talking, Niamah moved forward in the line. She looked very concerned and her empathic senses were going crazy! Kit and Al noticed, but before they could say anything, their mother had pulled out her power bow from her belt and activated it. From the grip the arms of the bow rapidly extended and Niamah let the bow string release and an arrow automatically formed and notched. Niamah drew and loosed immediately up towards a nearby branch. A body fell. There was sudden movement along the nearby branch as arrow flights replied to her action! Raph took off in flight as did other nearby Renim, with weapons drawn. One of Raph's companions fell dead with a spear in his chest! Tarmal and Fay pulled out their energy weapons and Raph yelled at them!

"No energy weapons!" he called, "You'll damage the living Tree! There are too many people around!"

Niamah and the Kerubim as well as some of the women nearby ran over to the body which had fallen further along the branch. Looking up they could see shrouded figures fleeing along the other branch, with the Ren Kerubim flying after them.

Niamah got there first and rolled the body over, pulling aside the light green shroud that covered them. It was a woman, a blonde woman, but not a Daughter of Hebel. This woman had much lighter hair, and the features of a Daughter of Kayyin.

"She's of Lahmech's Tribe!" Mrorna declared, "One of the Hecate."

Raph returned, landing nearby. He came over to look at the tattooed body of the woman.

"Yes, you are right." He said, "She's Manlorean. What is a Manlorean doing here?"

"What about the others?" Niamah asked.

"Our warriors are pursuing them." Raph sounded a bit shaken, "This is very, very, troubling. Armed strangers have never penetrated the Tree like this before, and this is a bad omen, especially at this time of war."

Another of the Ren Kerubim landed and spoke to Raph.

"Another of the intruders has been killed." He said, "Another Manlorean. Why would Lahmech send spies here? Let's go to Maia right now and report this."

Kerubim warriors with spears or bows were busily looking around the Tree habitat looking for the remaining intruders who had escaped. In the meantime, Raph led the group up the central trunk to the level nearest to the pods where the Morrigan lived. Here again there was a platform similar to the one that had raised them into the Tree. Like the one before, it was alive, made out of living parts of the Tree. The cable that raised and lowered the platform was a living vine that would constrict upwards or relax downwards and so raise or lower the platform.

The platform not only moved upwards, but across right towards the pods. It moved smoothly and quickly, right up to the landing of the largest of the pods. This bulbous pod was as large as a palace, and that is what it was.

Lots of Kerubim warriors got onto the platform as the group, led by Raph and his guards, were quickly moved off. Renim were flying all over the place. Kit and the others couldn't help noticing that they were now armed with advanced equipment including shoulder pack harnesses for Ren flight. Hilli turned to Surreya and winked.

They were led along through living corridors until they came to what felt like the middle of the pod. There, right in the centre of a large round room was a stone monolith. There was no doubt about it, the monolith was a Gate Stone. It was a bit of a surprise. Raph produced a short staff that had been hanging off his belt, under his feathered mantle. There was a key hole at the base of the stone and he activated it. A portal opened.

"Go through." He said, "I will be staying here."

The whole group went through the portal and found themselves on a large open to the sky area. They were at the top of the Tree, high up in the sky. The flat surface underneath them was living wood. Next to them was another Gate Stone. The portal closed itself behind them. Here and there were stairwells going back down into the Tree. Kerubim warriors and Renim were coming up and forming ranks nearby. The Renim pilots were human women, Daughters of Hebel. Standing before the group was a woman. She watched them quietly and intently, but in particular she looked at Shet. The woman looked young, but she was a Granddaughter of Awdame and that meant she could be any age. She had the fair hair of a Daughter of Hebel.

"Come with me." She said, "I am Maia, oldest daughter of Hebel and Morrigan of this City."

She led them across the flat space, heading west towards the now setting sun.

The edge of the flat area had a lip, like a fence or rail that protected people from falling off. Maia took them right to the edge and they looked westwards.

"Few people see this." She said, "That's the Garden down there. You can see the source of the rivers and the Crystal Sea beyond. Also down there are the Two Trees, the Tree of Life and the Tree of the Knowledge of Good and Evil. "

Maia turned around and smiled a wonderful smile, "But it is hope that the Tree of Life is there in the Garden. Death will take all of us, even the so-called Immortal Eldar races. But the Divine Life will bring us all back. Death is defeated by Life. This is why the people, especially the Stone People, bring their dead and dying to Cherubim. They all come here to die and so the faithful enter the Garden at last and find true rest."

Maia walked over to Shet and she reached forward and kissed him on the lips.

"In the meantime," Maia smiled again, "Adonai will send us a deliverer, Son of Awdame."

Shet jumped a bit right then with surprise.

Maia laughed. She walked back through the group, leading them back the way they came.

"We need to talk about a lot of things," she said to Grim as she passed him, "But we also need to eat."

Maia led them all down one of the stairwells and into a room set for a meal. There were lots of cushions for sitting on and a long table set with platters of food and drink. There was also a hollow in the wall of the room flowing with water. Maia went over to the hollow and she disrobed. From a nearby table she took a cloth and first washed herself, her face and hands and feet in the water and then she dried herself off. She then beckoned Shet over and she carefully washed him and then each in turn had their feet, hands and faces washed. For some, Rainbow and Newton in particular, it was a bit awkward, but they submitted to the ritual politely.

Servants helped pour drinks and they sat down to eat. Maia said a blessing and then she explained the meal. There were individual bowls for each person and the platters of food could be passed around. Most of the food was vegetarian, although there were eggs, milk and cheese.

"I've already been told a lot of things." Maia began as they continued to eat together, "You ought to know that the Shile have fought and defeated a large

Pandemonium force on the shore of the Eastern Sea. Still, members of the enemy were able to escape with the help of an unknown ally. We sent Renim to investigate and they barely escaped with their lives. The skies are full of enemy aircraft and the Shile are also about in large numbers. But we did find the bodies of a large army – Manloreans in their hundreds, slain. The Shile did not do it. We have another unknown enemy."

"Again it is the Manloreans who seem to be at the heart of things." Rom said, "They send assassins into the heart of the Great Tree and they are slain on the battlefield. Perhaps Lahmech is someone we should speak with."

There was some murmuring at the table until Maia raised her hand.

"What do you say Shet?" she asked.

"I agree with Rom, we need to speak with Lahmech. Something is going on."

"I can have him brought here." Maia nodded.

"What can we do to help?" Grim asked, "We came here to fight Graud, but we are also here to help as much as we can."

"You have a Ren and her pilot." Maia pointed at Hilli and Surreya, "Perhaps you can transport a team of warriors to bring Lahmech here?"

"Only if Kit, Al and Niamah come with us." Surreya added, "We are an experienced team and have fought many battles together."

"Raph and some of my Kerubim will come with you." Maia said, "We must find out as much as we can. In the meantime we must talk about the Pandemonium threat. Shet, Awdame and I will talk and we will all make plans together, with you visitors."

"We are glad to serve." Grim nodded.

"You have our gratitude Eldar." Maia bowed to Grim in respect.

Mrorna stood and bowed, "I ask that I come as well." She asked, "I have a feeling that I need to be there."

Grim searched within his spirit and sighed, "Alright." He nodded, "I think you need to be there too."

The mission was prepared quickly and Maia led them all back up onto the roof of the Tree. Some of the Kerubim Renim were there to have a look at Hilli, the Ren from the future. Hilli was glad that they were suitably impressed. She was appropriately proud of her shoulder units and her skill at the transformation of her Ren field. Surreya gave her a stern look for being arrogant.

"This will not be an easy flight." Raph explained, "We will need a group of Renim just in case there is an attack."

A formidable looking Ren stepped forward.

"This is Torq." Raph introduced her to Hilli and Surreya, "She is my personal Ren. We will fly wing for you this time. You will carry the passengers."

The Kerubim were equipped with light body shields, hidden discreetly under their cloaks. They had spears with particle weapons concealed within – the idea was to look primitive without actually being primitive, and so give them an edge over the Manloreans, *when* they resisted.

Similarly, Grim suggested to Niamah, Kit, Al and Mrorna to go light as well. Shield belts only and regular shielded blades and power bows like the one Niamah had used earlier. Only Mrorna didn't have a bow. She carried a blade instead.

The flight was south east to Manlore. For the small fleet of Renim, it was a quick journey at supersonic speeds, but there was still trouble. Crossing the mountains of Nod to the coastline of the Eastern Sea they entered airspace that was now contested between the Shile and the newly arrived Pandemonium forces. While they spotted some space-whales flying formation over the sea, it was a wing of Pandemonium dragons who teleported right on top of them that saw them see combat. The Kerubim Ren tried to manoeuvre out of the dragon's sneak attack, but the dragon's just teleported on top of them again. The dragons were dropping high explosives and then flashing away. It was impossible to predict where they would turn up next. That was the main idea behind that tactic. During the journey Surreya had been talking to the other pilots, and now she was angry with them!

"I told you!" she yelled over the com, "We have to form a closed circle! Also, electrify your fields!"

"Pull into a circle formation!" Raph ordered the group, "Form around Hilli!!!"

"Now, rotate randomly," Surreya demanded, "Don't hit each other!! The moment anything appears, full concentrated fire!!! Keep your guns hot, people! It's the only way to stop them!"

Surreya had Hilli flying tight random loops and the others were flying circles around Hilli. The effect was something like a hive of bees in swarm! The dragons returned and the Ren swarm attacked and fired all guns! Dragons burned before they could get a purchase. They flashed away quickly. The Renim flew on, holding the flight pattern, but the dragons were cowards and didn't return.

"We've flown against the dragons in our own time!" Surreya scolded them, "We know what we are doing! Looks like there will be more battles with these guys! In bigger engagements we have got to hold the line or they get in and blow us apart!!!"

"We bow to your experience and wisdom, Surreya." Torq apologised.

"No need for bowing," Surreya growled, "just flying."

Hilli giggled to herself.

The city of Manlore lay before them on the coast. Like all cities it was a single big structure, but that structure included large towers and pavilions on the roofs of the core temple structures. Manlore, as the name suggested, worshipped no gods, but instead worshipped the will of man. In this case that man was Lahmech.

And Lahmech was on the roof of his temple home, under the shade cloths of his personal pavilion, making love with his two wives, Ayda and Zillah. They were so preoccupied they didn't see the approaching Renim, who quickly braked, falling out of their battle formation. There was a sonic boom as they dropped over the sound barrier and then a wind as they decelerated over the city.

Lahmech swore and leapt up, tossing the women aside, so he could see.

"Get below!" he ordered them, "Get what's left of our warriors to arm themselves!"

Lahmech ran out onto an open part of the roof as his naked wives quickly ducked down a roof hole to the others below. Lahmech wrapped his king's cloak around his shoulders and took up his spear as the Renim descended upon the roof of his city.

Hilli rezzed down and let her passengers onto the roof of Lahmech's city. Their shields were on and weapons ready. The other Renim remained in flight overhead, ready for anything. Lahmech stood before them in all his proudly semi-naked glory and defiance. Up out of the roof holes all around his pavilion came his wives and also a disconcerting number of warriors, both male and female. Not all of his warriors had been killed in that last battle, and Lahmech wouldn't let anyone suspect such had happened.

It was then that the members of the landing party noticed the bier located in the centre of the roof. On the altar lay a body covered in a shroud. Niamah stepped forward with Mrorna and her sons and the Kerubim forming a rank behind. Everyone was eyeing each other suspiciously and weapons were drawn. Kit looked at these Manloreans and realised they were either incredibly brave or incredibly stupid. It was spears and blow darts against shields and blasters. No contest, and yet they stood their ground.

"Get out of my city foreigners." Lahmech told them.

"Your presence is required at Cherubim Lahmech, king of Manhome." Niamah told him back.

"And why should I come with you?" He demanded, "You come here with weapons to force me?" He put on a tone of moral outrage, "Is this the way of the Kerubim and the servants of the Elohim?"

"These weapons are not for your benefit!" Niamah retorted, "Do you not know that there is war in the Earth?"

Lahmech flinched a bit at that.

"I see you do know." Niamah nodded, "We have heard reports of your warriors slain on the coastal hills by an unknown enemy. We have cause to know, for the security of both peoples, those of Manhome and those of Cherubim and all of Eden. Come with us."

"I will not come." Lahmech insisted.

"Then answer some questions." Kit stepped forward.

Niamah put a restraining hand on her son, "It's ok." She said quietly.

"Tell us," Niamah asked, "Who is this dead one on the bier?"

Lahmech's eyes sparkled with pride and he turned to his wives and all his people, then spoke.

"Yes, my warriors lay dead upon the hills," he crowed, "but they died hon-ourably. Wives of Lahmech pay heed! People of Manhome listen to your king! If Cain is avenged in blood sevenfold, then Lahmech shall be avenged seven times seventy fold! For I have killed a young man for attacking me and slain this man who wounded me!! But for these deaths we shall be avenged even more!!"

One of the Kerubim moved towards the shrouded body to get a closer look, his face looked ashen with shock.

"Dear Elohim!" he gasped, "*WHAT* did you do??!!"

"Here is Kayyin my ancestor and my deadly enemy." Lahmech pulled back the shroud.

There lay the body of Kayyin.

All those who had flown in, even Mrorna, the only human among them, had felt the feeling of dread as they landed upon the roof. Now they knew why.

"You killed Kayyin?" The Kerubim warrior asked, horrified, "Let us leave this cursed place and these cursed people right now! Don't bring this man with us or we will only bring it all down upon us. The wrath of the Elohim is upon them!"

The Kerubim were unable to resist their impulses as they deployed forward and pointed their weapons at Lahmech and all his people. The Manloreans had spears and blow darts ready. It seemed all about to go pear-shaped, when Niamah ran to Lahmech and grabbed him by the shoulders.

"Don't provoke the Kerubim!" she shook him, "We will leave you, we have what we came for and you can live with the consequences of your actions on your own."

Niamah gave Lahmech a little push as she backed off. Lahmech just grinned back at her.

"Let's get out of here." Niamah turned her back on Lahmech.

They could hear him still laughing as Hilli reformed her field and they ascended. Lahmech thought he'd won, but Niamah had the benefit of knowing history. Now she understood a mystery.

"We will return tomorrow." Niamah said to the others once they were flying away, "We must know more. We will know for certain tomorrow."

Down in his city, Lahmech looked down at the body of Kayyin lying before him. He reached out and touched his patriarch's arm. It was cold, almost ice cold to the touch. His body should have started to decay by now, but it was still whole.

Lahmech wondered what strangeness this was.

Chapter Twenty-Nine

Kayyin

As night fell over the Eastern Sea and the city of Manlore, Enosh, son of Kayyin, led his warriors through the forest around the city. Although Lahmech had suffered a great defeat and lost most of his warriors, his city was heavily fortified and he still had enough armed warriors to defend himself effectively. But Enosh was not there to attack the city. His dead father Kayyin had told him to just come to the city this night and to wait. With Enosh was Hecate, Lahmech's oldest daughter. She had betrayed her own people, but for Enosh, that was good.

"My daughters have set up the sacred pillars." Hecate told him, "The spirits are with us and the moon is full."

"Good." Enosh smiled, "Now we wait and see."

Inside the city, most of the people had fallen asleep. Lahmech himself though was unsettled and was pacing in his pavilion. He looked at the body and wondered if he shouldn't just burn it. He went over to one of the torches burning in its niche and went back to the bier. He pulled back the shroud and stared in horror! The body was gone!!!

Lahmech was utterly speechless. He looked around wildly, seeking futilely. He didn't see the form of a man rise up behind him. There was no time to scream. With incredible force, a hand drove in from behind. The pain was an explosion in his chest, but he couldn't cry out! Lahmech was lifted up and then suddenly dropped down, his heart and spine were ripped physically from his body! He fell, dead, like a sack.

Kayyin stood over him. He wasn't gloating, nor was he enjoying his revenge. This was his manifest destiny, his grim purpose. He looked across. Lahmech's wives were still asleep in the pavilion. They hadn't woken up. Kayyin went into them. He opened his mouth and bared his teeth, which had now become animal-like fangs!

The next day a larger fleet of Renim left from Cherubim and flew south to Manhome. No enemy dared to confront them, but they watched from afar. Most of the fleet hovered overhead, but a number of larger Renim, including Hilli, landed in the city and dropped their passengers. Grim gathered his team together near Lahmech's pavilion and Maia was with them. The Kerubim, led by Raph and Torq, moved out, armed and ready for anything. Up near the pavilion, Maia was first to see the blood. They found Lahmech's body.

It wasn't long and Raph also appeared.

"We've searched the entire city." He said, sounding a bit unsettled, "There is no-one here, no bodies, nothing. The front gates are open. What happened here?"

"Something terrible." Maia responded. She walked around the top of the city for a bit and then turned back to the others.

"Here's my orders." She told them, "We are going to destroy this city, burn it utterly and leave nothing but scorched earth."

The people on the ground gathered around their Renim and they rezzed up and ascended. Once high in the sky, the Renim heated up their particle cannons and rained fire upon the abandoned city of Manhome. It wasn't just a bombardment, the city was vaporised! It didn't take long, only a few minutes. There was no fire, it had been too hot for that, and all that was left was a black crater of scorched glass. The Renim returned to Cherubim.

There was a gathering of the Elders of Cherubim on the roof of the Tree. The Kerubim were there, as well as Maia and her daughters. The people of Manhome had also been invited. Other leaders were there as well, including many of the sons and daughters of Awdame and Haveh, leaders of the great tribes, and chieftains of the Stone People too. Melki and Maia stood on a raised platform before the entire congregation. Gabriel, who was Morrigan, stood to one side. It was probably the largest gathering ever of the People of Eden. A portal suddenly appeared between where Maia and Melki stood. Out stepped three people.

The first was a mature man. He was tall and powerful looking, wearing a simple white tunic. His hair was white also, long and tied in a plait and his skin was the colour of black ebony. The second was a woman. She was similar to the man, dark and as tall as He, yet the embodiment of feminine beauty. Her hair was loose. Last of all was another man. He was like the others, but appeared youthful and full of happiness, and there was a sparkle in his eyes.

"You are seeing something few have the privilege to see." Grim told the members of his team who stood with him, "You see before you three representatives of the Elohim, the Logoi of this universe together."

While the Elohim looked amazingly human, normal even, they were also perfectly beautiful and there was a spiritual light that flowed over them. There was a feeling of irresistible awe that swept over the entire assembly. People began to bow down on their faces. Even those from the future found themselves bowing.

Kit and Mrorna were next to each other when a pair of bare feet appeared before them.

"Rise, Kit Ryan and Mrorna." They stood and the second man was there, smiling at them.

"I know you and have been with you." He said, addressing Mrorna, then turned to Kit, "Take care of her."

Kit had the feeling that he was familiar with this man, that they had met before, then he realised....

"Shhh!" He whispered, "That revelation is yet to be. Not yet, not here, my friend."

The man hugged both Kit and Mrorna, then He re-joined His companions.

All the people stood.

"This man, the Father of All, is Elyon." Maia intoned.

All the people said, "We are your children."

"This woman is the Mother of All, Hochma, the Spirit."

"You are our Mother." The people replied.

"This is Adonai, Lord of all the Earth and Sea."

"Adonai is Lord!"

The whole assembly clapped and then sat down. While Elyon and Hochma sat on the platform with Maia and Melki, Adonai, still smiling, walked among the seated people. Sometimes He would sit down with them.

For the visitors from the future, this felt very strange. Very strange indeed. Mrorna turned to Kit and whispered, "Adonai is Yeshua!" She gasped.

"Yes." Kit grinned at her.

"Does he know?"

"I think he does." Kit squeezed her gently, "They are about to talk."

"I speak for all the people." Maia began, "We find ourselves at war with the Pandemonium. Enlil has sent his troops, the Pandemons and the Gorenge to invade Eden. Many of the people have fled before them and come here to Cherubim for safety. Already the Shile have fought a great battle against the enemy and defeated them, but this will only delay the enemy for a time. More of them are coming. We also have another enemy. The Nodin defeated the Manloreans in battle as well. Kayyin was killed, as well as all the people of Manlore."

The people made restless sounds, some moaned in grief for the horror of it all.

"We know that the Pandemonium are at war with us," Maia continued, "but we are not sure what role the Nodin will have in the fight ahead. One thing is for certain, we will need to fight and the enemy are using advanced weapons."

"What of the visitors who have come among us?" someone called.

"I will let Grim Torgar of the Eldar speak." Maia beckoned him forward.

Grim stood and moved up next to Maia.

"It is important for everyone to know the truth." Grim spoke loudly and firmly, "Enlil, who is also known as Graud, has built a huge army and equipped them with new weapons. My warriors and I have come from a time in the future. There he has caused huge amounts of damage and killed many people. He has found a way to transport entire fleets of airships and large numbers of his warriors and dragons into the future. Not only is he determined to invade and conquer this world, but he also wants to invade and conquer our world as well. We came here looking for a way to stop him only to find that the enemy is strong here as well. Also, we have discovered that he plans to use his power to destroy everything and utterly control the whole world forever. He has the means to erase history. We have got to stop him."

"Who will lead us against this enemy?" one of the Stone chieftains asked.

"Shet will lead." Elyon said.

Shet stood up, and although the eyes of many saw only a young man, everyone accepted the statement. Shet was to lead.

As he stood, Hilli stood and with a big grin she cheered, "Harrah!!!" At first, everyone just looked at her, but she looked right back, "Come on!" she rolled her eyes, "Harrah!!!"

People stood up and began to cheer and clap. Her fellow team members laughed and joined in the cheering too. Shet looked around in wonder and he bowed his head, with tears in his eyes. There would be more talking to come, strategies to consider, a war to plan. As people began to talk, the Three stood together, not involved, not physically involved, in the conversation. Kit looked over at them at one point and could see the light of Spirit around them, their eyes glowing with an inner light. He knew what that was. They were now in gestalt union, as one Being, the Three as One, staring into the transcendent and seeing eternity.

What did the One see?

Kayyin. Alive? No and yes. And he wasn't alone. Others were with him, his blood children. They were full of the hunger. Hecate was there too, with her daughters and they were decidedly uneasy in the company of the killers they had created with occult power. Kayyin could sense the unease of the Hecate.

"Do not worry," Kayyin told her, "the Bursar will never feed on the Hecate. After all, you brought us to birth, so to speak. But you will serve us, you will be the mothers of a new race."

"Not as servants." Hecate corrected him, "As partners or not at all."

Not far away stood the Rah-hab and her Gorenge. She too looked uneasy. This was a dangerous and regretted alliance, yet she could see the potential for great power. The only problem was Graud. She didn't even consider the humans as a problem, just a minor obstacle.

"We are all partners here." The Rah-hab said, "But what do we do now?"

"I will turn us an army." Kayyin said, grinning and baring his fangs, "We will hide during the day in the caves of Enosh and come out at night to feed. Some I will turn, others can be yours. We will grow strong and watch."

"What of this war between the Pandemonium and the Elohim?" The Rah-hab asked, shaking with fear, "Do you know what you are up against?"

"I have seen the face of Death." Kayyin laughed, "He marked me this way and the curse exists and because of this I have this power of vengeance. I am a tool, a weapon in the hand of Death!!! So, in this war between lesser beings, it is I and I alone that will prevail. I will bring the Baals low, and the Seelie will not be able to stop me."

At the top of the Tree of Cherubim, the Three members of the Logoi sighed simultaneously.

Chapter Thirty

Alliance of Darkness

Atlantis Island. That was the codename for the place. Baal Nimrod stood in the middle of his throne room. There was a scanner console on one of the walls. The airships had arrived at last.

There was a sudden flash of a teleportal and a group of well-armed warriors just appeared there. Nimrod turned and laughed at their World War I styled uniforms.

"Do you realise what you look like?" he waved a hand at them, "You need new uniforms."

One of the soldiers stepped forward. He was a Pandemon, one of the Nephalim hybrids.

"My name is Captain Kruug." The officer introduced himself, "Graud sends his greetings."

"I have been watching this war you have started, Kruug." Nimrod replied, getting to the point, "You have an alliance already with the Medusa cabal."

"Yes." Captain Kruug nodded, "I assume you know most of the intelligence about us."

"I know that you have occupied large areas of Europe and southern England. Our competitors, the other Nephalim and Vansad factions have moved to consolidate themselves. World powers are revealing the covert electro-dynamic technology they were forced to keep secret under the Aquarius Treaty. But most concerning is the Petra Group and the new Free States. They are our biggest problem and they have already dealt your forces some big blows. Big battles in England and Germany. So we need each other."

"Your Atalanti cabal is well known to be powerful in the Americas." Kruug said, "What is left of the Americas."

"No need to be a smart arse Kruug." Nimrod said menacingly, "Your electro-magnetic pulses have done us a great favour. The United States no longer exists and we will shortly own what is left. With your co-operation, we will be able to strike a heavy blow against the so-called Free States."

"The enemy control important splinters in Eurasia." Kruug pointed out, "The Daedalus is operating in North America."

"And the Order has Vansadagaadian Class fleet ships and an alliance with the Zioronians." Nimrod added, "Very formidable. You have low level tech in comparison, dragons and teleportation. The enemy are finding holes in your armour. But the Atalanti can plug those holes. Atlantis Island is a Rath and we have a portal ring. We can replicate whatever we need."

"Graud anticipated that we might have to face much more advanced technology." Kruug responded, "Even in 1918 we understood Vansadagaadian advances. Graud is now aware of our misplacement in the time stream. New, more advanced weaponry is being prepared for the next deployment of time spheres. We have a limited number of Shrikes, but more will be coming soon, as well as troops, dragons and a new more advanced zeppelin with enhanced shield technology."

"But in the meantime you are outmatched by Order forces." Nimrod smiled, "You need better technology now – which I can provide."

"It is to our advantage..."

"No need to convince me." Nimrod interrupted, "I already considered all this. We must destroy the Seelie power on this world. There's nothing more to it than that."

Nimrod beckoned Kruug to follow him. They were joined by Nimrods Asherim Lilith and Ishtar and his Baals, Dagon and Molech. From the Throne Room they went into the central plaza of the Rath. There was the portal ring. The plaza was a huge place and it was very busy. The ring was activated and replicator portals were working. Nimrods people were replicating weapons and incredible electro-dynamic vehicles. The Atalanti were all wearing Nazi Swastikas. There were humans and Nephalim working side by side at the ring, using the portal controls and then groups of thralls carrying replicated weapons and equipment away. To one side of the plaza they had just replicated a light cruiser. It filled the whole cavern above and was dropped with a clunk into a holding cradle.

"We are replicating one of those every six hours." Molech said proudly, "We are also replicating weapons, body armour, tanks and equipment. If you bring your ships here we should be able to fully refit them with modern equipment."

"What about troops?" Captain Kruug asked.

"Troops we can't replicate." Dagon replied, "But we have been doing some recruiting from among the wraiths in what is left of the United States."

Wraiths. These were the disembodied Pandemons and other spirits that existed on the spiritual plain.

A personal portal opened up nearby and an Anak stepped out. She was huge and powerful looking around with interest at the world around her.

"Shit!" she swore loudly, "It's been a long time since I had a body, I miss it!"

Nimrod stepped forward. The Neph standing at the portal stone stepped aside. Nimrod struck the Anak with a closed fist, knocking her to the deck.

"You have been given corporality for a reason Anak!!" Nimrod roared at her, "You are now a member of the Atalanti, and a soldier in the Medusa alliance. If you are loyal you will be able to recorporialize in the advent of your death. If you fail, you will never see flesh again."

"Yes Sir!"

"This one doesn't have a lot of discipline." Captain Kruug sneered.

"She will after training." Nimrod grinned, "We will kick the new ones into shape."

Nimrod turned to the Neph officer standing nearby, "Take her to the training unit immediately. Obey and fight hard Anak, or I will kill you myself."

"Teleport your, ah, ships here and into the vault above." Nimrod pointed up towards the Rath power sphere hovering above. "We will refit them with new weapons and E.D. stabilisers. No more need for hydrogen as liquid fuel for the nuclear power plants. We can organise new uniforms and armour for your fighting units. Just give Molech the insignia and design specs you want to keep – but I do insist that your forces modernise."

"You are insisting a lot." Kruug growled, "While I see the necessity of quick action and co-operation needed for our forces to unify, I insist that we retain full autonomy in our own battle theatres and with our own troops."

"Of course." Nimrod nodded, "We Shedu are learning to co-operate more and more lately. The Medusa Alliance is forming as we speak, where before we were constantly at war with each other. We can divide up the spoils after this war is over. We need each other. Besides, I have a plan to deal with the Daedalus."

"To destroy it?" Kruug asked.

"No," Nimrod grinned an evil grin, "to capture it!"

Nimrod led Kruug out of the plaza and down a corridor to a dock. There in the water was the USS Gerald R Ford Super Carrier. Standing along the dock were six thousand United States sailors and marines all collared and enthralled.

"We just installed a portal lock beacon in her hold." Nimrod said.

Kruug laughed out loud as he understood what Nimrod planned.

Not far away, among some generators standing at the end of the dock, Captain Johann R Simon was watching. He had managed to sneak right into the heart of the enemies' lair. He was now wearing a Nazi uniform. He felt quite uncomfortable that it had come to this. But the uniform had meant that he had been able to walk right back into the Gerald and see what was there. He'd overheard enough to be very concerned. He had no idea what the Daedalus was but he could guess that the enemy were up to some serious no good. Worst of all though, he knew he was way in over his depth. The tech here was way beyond anything he was familiar with. There would be no stealing an enemy plane and flying out, no stealing a boat. They had spaceships!

He'd tried to talk to his enslaved shipmates but they didn't even seem to see him. They were like zombies. At least they hadn't given the alarm. Zealot had no idea what he was going to do, but he needed to be ready to act when the opportunity appeared.

Chapter Thirty-One

Elementals

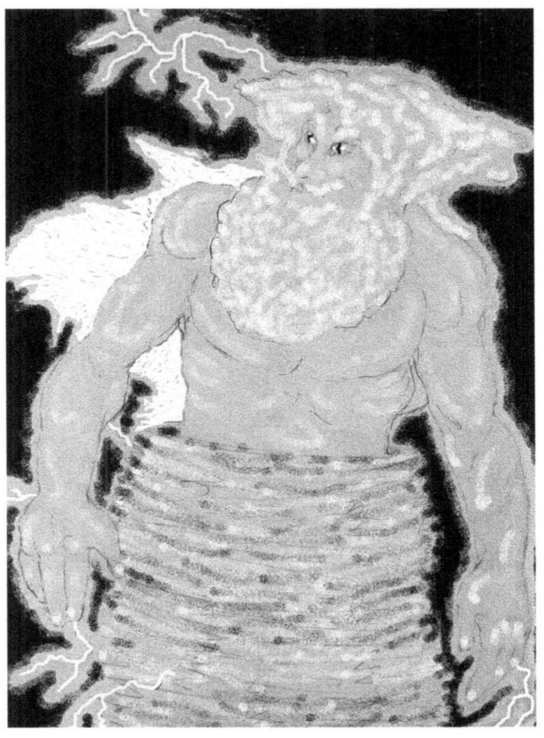

Shet had been talking with Elyon for some hours and then he returned to the council.

"We are going to gather an army to fight the enemy." Shet announced. "The staging ground will be at the foot of the Tree below the Ladder. We will be equipped with what we need to fight and we shall also have some allies fight with us. Our enemy are numerous. The Gorenge and Pandemonium have again landed upon the shores of Nod and they are gathering to attack us. But we shall instead attack them first. Our Renim will attack from the air and our army will attack from the earth. We will also strike at the Nodin and drive them from our lands. Once we are free, we will cross the sea to the east and strike against Enlil's capital of Magog. The Logoi are with us! We have the victory!!!"

Hochma stepped forward with Adonai and with a gesture they opened a series of seven portals.

"We step through and they will equip us for battle." Shet told them.

Shet stepped forward through the middle portal, beckoning others to follow. Those gathered at the top of the Tree stepped forward through the portals nearest them.

The members of the team from the future watched this process with interest.

"It's incredible." Grim said, "I haven't seen anything like this for a long time. Most of these people are New Stone Age tribal farmers and they have such faith."

"What should we do?" Tarmal asked, "Do we join this army or just observe?"

"The warrior in me wants to fight." Fay, his spouse, elbowed him in the ribs.

"I say we go." Rainbow agreed.

There were nods from everyone.

Melki, Maia and Adonai were heading towards the group.

"Shet invites you to come too." Melki told them.

"Now it's official." Newton grinned.

"Time for war." Kit added, giving Mrorna a squeeze.

They moved to the central portal, with Adonai leading the way, and went in.

The portal had opened on a large flat plain at the base of the Cherubim Tree. An encampment was set up with many tents and camp followers preparing food and organising things. They could even hear music being played somewhere nearby. But the plain was mostly a gathering of warriors. The seven portals had delivered the gathered tribes-people, but they now wore powered shield armour over Danu style chain mail. The individual warriors carried energy lances, which included a long blade, but were primarily an energy blaster. On their helms they bore coloured plumes representing their individual tribes. Nearby they could see hundreds of behemoths, including some of the big sauropods and triceratops all decked in powered armour. The bigger dinosaurs were effectively outfitted as weapons platforms, carrying big shield generators, capable of deflecting even the most vicious bombardments and a pair of energy cannons slung on each side. Members of the Kerubim were moving among the humans giving instruction on the use of the various weapons. The tri-horns were fitted to carry two riders, a driver and a gunner and were obviously meant to be used as fast attackers. Other very large behemoths were fitted out as cargo carriers, still shielded but devoted to carrying equipment and supplies. In the middle of the field stood the Renim, with Gabriel there, along with Hochma. They all wore upgraded shoulder harnesses as well as personal shield armour over their naked skin. Hilli and Surreya turned to Grim. Hilli was similarly equipped and Surreya had a pilots armour on.

"Go join them." Grim nodded at them.

Melki and Adonai were standing at the centre of a group of tribal leaders, talking to them, but Shet was with Elyon, and they approached.

"I see Hilli and Surreya have joined the Renim." Elyon said, "Hilli is going to be the lead wing for this fleet. We have some heavy carrier Renim here, but Hilli has a huge containment field. It will make her the command Ren. I have given Shet instruction in the Seelie way of war and Melki has trained him in sword play. You have seen him fight in battle trance. He knows what to do."

"I want you guys to stay with me." Shet said, "It means that we will be in the front of the fighting most of the time, but I've seen you fight and we need you. I need you all to fight alongside of me. I may have the battle trance, but I'll still need you and Melki to form the attack wedge we need to drive into the enemy. But I need some of you for a special mission."

Just then the portals flickered. This was a sign that they had changed location origins. New people were about to come through. Melki and Adonai went over to wait. Everyone turned to watch. Through the portals came five glowing forms. They were representatives of the most powerful Eldar races – an Aesir air elemental, a Triton water elemental, an Astari fire elemental, a Terrestrial earth elemental and a Gaean life elemental. They were obviously spiritual beings, and VERY powerful. They originally came from the Vansadagaadian Corridor. Some say they are born along the strings, where time and space are warped and causality does some very strange things. But the material world draws them like flies to honey. They seek corporeal form. Some of the first Elementals were drawn to the raw power of the elements – the power of the air, water, fire and earth. These powerful Elementals literally clothed themselves in energy, visible as light, but then covered that light in the elemental substance. The Aesir looked like a cloud. The air around him constantly moved, drawing up dust detritus. The air that formed his body wasn't insubstantial though, it was pure force. Likewise the Astari, she glowed with burning fire. The Triton, her body was formed of water. The Terrestrial had built around his spiritual core a body of stone. He was huge and formidable. The Gaean came last. Her species was the first of the Elementals to achieve organic life. She looked almost human but her skin was coloured green and she was obviously plant-like. Her long green hair was leafy and flowers literally grew there.

Those who saw them gasped. Elementals such as these were rarely seen. Sometimes their very presence was dangerous, but these Elementals seemed to reduce in size and they contained their power so not to harm those around them. But this power, everyone knew, could also be unleashed.

"We have come to wage war." The Terrestrial spoke for them, his voice booming like rocks cracking against each other.

The portals flickered a second time. More were coming. They flew through the portals, winged beings. There was a loud humming noise filling the air, but also the thump thump of great feathered wings as well. There were two kinds of flying beings here. They filled the air. The first through the portals were the Debora, bee-like creatures, but as big as men and carrying in their hands, their weapons. One of them, their Queen, flew down and landed before the Elementals. The second group of flying creatures came through the portals after the Debora. These were feathered beings, bird-like and even larger than the Debora. Their leader descended with a screech and landed next to the Debora Queen. He was a huge bird with steely eyes and a vicious hooked beak, but when he folded his wings, from under the feathers can long pale arms with clawed hands. Under his wing was a holster containing his blaster.

"Those bird creatures are the Ziv." Grim explained to the others, "They are an ancient and noble race that have always supported the Elohim. The other race are the Debora, the Hive Kin. They are usually accompanied by their symbiotic partners, the Tecorah."

Just then from the portals came a third group. These were walking creatures, again, they were insectoid and ant-like, so these must be the Tecorah.

The arrival of the Elementals and their allies the Zoel races caused quite a stir among the people. These beings were legendary and at times in the past falsely worshipped. But here they were.

"If the Elohim have brought these to fight beside us," Grim commented, "then we must be up against a very formidable enemy."

Mrorna stepped forward, "I was on the Island of Magog." She said, "I have seen the forces that Graud has there. The Pandemonium and Gorenge forces you have met so far are but a small part of his huge army. He too has gathered ancient ones to do battle. We will need all the help we can get!"

Shet and Elyon had gathered together with the generals of the different armies and the troops were being formed into their ranks, along with all their equipment and supplies. Among the Renim, Gabriel Morrigan of the Kerubim was giving orders to the pilots and Renim so that all the army could be gathered up for transport.

"Time to go." Shet said when he returned.

All the warriors watched as the Renim formed up near those they were to carry. Hilli and Surreya stood next to Shet and then they both activated their wings and Hilli rose up and turned on her Ren Field. Simultaneously, all the Renim, with a flash of light, gathered up their passengers and then the fleet flew up into the sky. Thousands of Renim flew eastwards towards the enemy.

Among the Renim, the Ziv and Debora also flew, carrying their Tecorah passengers, and the Aesir carried them all within a mighty wind.

The destination for this mighty force was directly eastward. After the battle further south between the invaders and the Shile, and then the defection of the Gorenge forces to the Nodin, who were now led by the vampiric Kayyin, the Pandemonium had landed a second, much larger force further north. They had moved into the Nodin hinterland quickly and had set up a fortification in the hills.

The whole northern coast of the eastern sea was shadowed by Graud's airships and dragons in their thousands.

In the south, the second enemy, who were calling themselves the Bursar, had retreated to the Nodin city of Enosh. They too would have to be met, sooner or later.

But now it looked like an impending air battle. The Aesir and the Debora and Ziv flew ahead of the Renim fleet. In the east, a wall of zeppelins could be seen waiting. Great bay doors opened underneath in the cabins and the dragons flew out like a black cloud, all wings and talons, their cries shrieking with rage.

The dragons teleported. At the same time, a fire appeared in the midst of the windstorm that the Aesir had created and the Astari appeared, flashing like lightning across the sky. The clouds formed into dark thunderheads and the Astari sent lightning bolts in all directions! In the main cabin of Hilli's Ren-ship Shet and his companions watched as the dragons reappeared in the middle of the clouds. The wind caught many of them and they found it almost impossible to maintain controlled flight. The lightning struck others, sending them to their deaths. The lightning also seemed to be acting as a net, the electrical fields preventing the dragons from teleporting away. Within the storm, the Aesir and Astari were tearing the dragons apart. Those that escaped were attacked by the Debora, who fell upon their enemies with great violence, grappling and stinging and using their weapons to blow them apart. The Ziv remained in flight, fighting any dragons that remained. Some of the dragons teleported away, but within minutes, most of them were dead. The enemy airship commanders must have seen this, or realised what had happened and they opened fire with their particle cannons. The high energy particle beams cut through the storm, but with it being so dark, the air-fleet behind it were safely hidden, so they quickly flew forward to engage each other. The airships flew into the storm boldly, using their cannons to supposedly clear a path, but the storm and electrical discharges coming from the Astari was blinding them even more. Out of the storm, the Debora descended upon the airship flight decks, blasting their way in and dropping their Tecorah troops who swarmed inside. It then became a battle of hand to hand combat inside the airships.

At the same time, the Renim flew downwards, under the storm, towards the enemy ground position. In Hilli's control cabin, Shet was giving his orders. On the ground, the enemy had their big guns and they opened fire at the attacking Renim. A lot of them were hit and their fields ruptured explosively! But most got through. Below was a line of fortifications, gun nests and trenches protected by shield walls. This was the most dangerous part of the attack. The Renim fired their own weapons at the shields, and they looked for weak points. It was a bombardment like no other in human history and must have been terribly loud and shocking for the Pandemonium forces under the shields. Holes were punched through in some places and Renim flew through, closed their fields down and deposited their passengers. In this case, not troops but armoured Triceratops with their heavy weapons suddenly appeared atop the trenches and with great violence began to demolish and smash everything around them. Their main targets were the enemy shield generators, which fell one by one, opening huge holes in the shield and letting more Ren in to land! Hilli and other Renim carrying troops now flew down and landed, and they found themselves in the middle of a chaotic fight to the death. Shet entered a battle trance and almost immediately set out to clear a space of the enemy. At first that was the main strategy, just to fire weapons and clear an area.

Melki put up the command standard, which included a beacon for the other surviving attack units. They were all wearing helms with visual cortex displays, which made it easy to know where each fighting group was. Shet, his voice breathing hard as he fought, shooting a blaster with one hand and cutting down an enemy with his other sword hand, gave his orders.

"Set up beacons!" his young voice roared, Hold and clear your positions then link up! Push them! Take out the main nests with the Behemoths, troops, move in!"

All across the battlefield, the different chieftains and other battle commanders got their warriors into a fighting order. They were surrounded by enemies on all sides, but the battle commanders quickly identified objectives and where successful, some groups were able to join up and create a bigger force. Flying above, some of the Renim continued to bombard the enemy shields, but those carrying the big behemoths had landed outside the shielded position on three sides, and were making their own attack. The Ziv had also flown down but were flying low over the battle, doing what damage they could.

Each member of the expedition from the future were fighting their own individual wars, yet working together with the other Kerubim warriors, led by Raph and Torq to push the enemy back and flush them out of the trenches and weapons nests. The Kerubim were very good at this kind of close quarters fighting and were experts at using the advanced energy weapons and body shields. Some of the human tribal warriors were not so confident and skilled, but with sheer bravery they fought methodically and well. Grim had taken Tarmal and Fay down a trench and killed about a dozen Pandemons hiding there, while Kit, Niamah, Al and Mrorna went the other way. Rainbow, Newton, along with Hilli, Surreya and the constructs held the beacon position and cleared the open upper spaces. Shet and Melki led the Kerubim in an attack against a large gun position. The same position was being attacked at the same time from the other side by a group of Triceratops and their support troops. The constructs used their heavy cannons to provide cover. Bit by bit they fought their way across the enemy position. Sometimes Shet had to withdraw from the battle and he would return to the beacon where he would look at the battles progress in his helm display and give new orders. They had managed to open huge wounds in the enemy's side, but the enemy still prevailed in some places. The main concentration of the enemy was atop a flat topped hill in the middle of the ridge. It had a second set of shields under the first set and was obviously where the commander of the Pandemonium forces was located.

Up in the sky, the enemy zeppelins were done, their wreckage having fallen to the earth below. This left the Debora and Tecorah free to fly down through the shield breaches and join in the ground battle. It made a huge difference. The big behemoths with their weapons platforms, cannons and shields were able to break through from the outside in some places and were driving into the enemy lines very quickly. Everyone had landed and the battle was going well, all except for the attack against the main citadel of the enemy on its hill. While a lot of fighting continued, it looked to Shet that the battle might grind to a halt.

Shet and those with him had destroyed the big gun nest and Melki had picked up the beacon and they all moved to a safe trench not far from the main citadel of the enemy. Shet ordered everyone to hold their positions in a ring around the hill. The enemy looked down at them from above.

Then the Elementals came to Shet. The Aesir, the Triton, the Astari, the Terrestrial and the Gaean had all taken on their battle forms. They had already been single handedly responsible for causing a lot of damage to the enemy and it was obvious why. The Elementals were huge.

"We are going to create a storm." The Triton told Shet.

"I will cleave the earth asunder!" The Terrestrial added.

"But I will enter first and make the way possible." The Gaean grinned.

"Once the shield is down, we will attack." Shet nodded.

At least that was the idea. From upon the hill, they could now hear war-drums. Portals suddenly opened on all sides and a horrid black and filthy mist flowed out in a rush over the battlefield. Within the mist were things, evil things.

"Wraiths!!!" the Aesir cried, and he put his hands out either side and with the Triton taking one hand and the Astari the other, these three took to the air, becoming a storm to face the darkness. The wraiths themselves had the appearance of spectres, but there was something else flying with them in the mist. There was the sound of insectoid wings. With cries, the Debora and Ziv also took to the wing. What happened next was even worse than the fighting that was before! The black mist soon covered everything along the ridge. It was like night. Warriors were suddenly attacked by the wraiths, who with a touch seemed to drain the lives from their victims! If that wasn't bad enough, great giant flies, the evil race known as the Zeebub were flying in the darkness. Big like the Debora and equally well armed for attack in the sky or upon the ground, they fell upon anyone they could! The Debora and Tecorah were their ancient blood enemies and they fought viciously with each other. On the ground everyone was fighting for their lives!

New portals opened, this time great spiders, the Nagda, emerged. These monsters were huge and also intelligent. Upon their backs rode Gorenge warriors, shielded and carrying heavy mounted cannon. A lot of the battle was in the sky again, so many of the Renim, including Hilli with Surreya took flight to do battle.

The sky was full of terrible storm, black and thunderous as the gods above tore at each other.

The Terrestrial and his Gaean companion were earthbound, yet also incredibly powerful. They both strode forward towards the nearest attacking Nagda with their Gorenge. The Terrestrial was pure brute force. With fists like massive boulders he took to smashing anything that dared to attack him and he left death and carnage all around him! The Gaean was more subtle. Her limbs became long vines and branches and her hair seemed to form a great canopy. Green living terror flashed toward her foes and she engulfed them, tore them apart and absorbed them. Their bodies enabled her to grow and inflict more damage! She also called to the trees from the nearby forest and they uprooted themselves in obedience and went to war as well!

Shet began to bellow orders via his helm communicator, rousing the warriors and they pushed against the attacking forces. Shet still had his eyes upon the fortress.

"Melki, Grim, Raph!" he called, "Gather your warriors! Bring the constructs as well!! Follow the Terrestrial! He's heading for the hill!"

Forming a wedge, with the constructs leading the way and punishing all who stood before them, they moved quickly through the throng pushing aside any enemies who tried to intercept them. The Terrestrial had come right up to a cliff face in the side of the enemy citadel. With a loud cry that sounded like an eruption, he rent a crack in the solid rock, ripping it open! He then stepped into the breach and literally tore the hill apart! The Gaean stood to defend Shet and his warriors as they followed the Terrestrial along a path that would take them up and under the enemy shields.

Up in the enemy fortress, the Pandemonium General was a massive Anak, supported by his own Anakim bodyguard and a good number of Gorenge. They had been watching the battle using remote viewers and so far had been very happy. But suddenly from underneath, the earth began to quake and with a violent rending was shoved aside, crushing anyone standing too close! Out of the hole in the middle of the citadel came the Terrestrial, who threw huge slabs of stone and rolled forth like an avalanche! Behind him followed Shet, in another trance and behind him, warriors armed with blasters and shielded swords.

For Kit, the battle had exhausted his body, but he had prayed, as they all were trained to do and his blessed weapons cut even deeper. With his family on one side and Mrorna on the other, along with Fay, who was always formidable and her husband Tarmal, they spearheaded the attack deep into the citadel. Shet and the constructs and Grim were attacking the Gorenge host but Kit could see the General withdrawing. They could feel the static charge of a large electro-dynamic field starting up. He had an airship and was trying to escape!!

"No you are NOT!!" Kit bellowed in anger.

Rainbow and Newton had crawled out of the hole by now and were looking around.

"The shield generators are over there!" Rainbow pointed.

"Let's take them down!" Newton grinned.

The General was running and he ordered his guards to stay and fight. Kit and Niamah with Al and Mrorna, Tarmal and Fay just behind came upon the giants as they ran around a corner. With surprise Kit cried a war-cry and without hesitation he leapt upon the Anakim! It was all flashing swords then and blood as the Anakim fell back. A moment later they were dead and Kit led the way as they ran on. They came out in the middle of an open space and the General with two of his guards were nearly at the airship.

"Gorjard!!! You bastard!!!" Kit heard Mrorna screaming next to him. She dropped to a crouch and fired her particle blaster at the fleeing Anak and shot him right in the middle of his back! Niamah fired her bow blaster and dropped the other two. They ran forward, but the airship crew began to lift off. Just then there was a huge explosion behind them as Newton and Clarissa detonated their mines and destroyed the shield over the hill. As the shield fell apart, Hilli flew in from above. She fired a single bolt from her cannon. The airship blew apart like a popping balloon!

The battle was essentially over at this, but the fighting continued as the enemy still resisted.

Mrorna began to cry. Kit and the others didn't need to ask, it was personal, so he just held her in his arms as she wept.

Chapter Thirty-Two

Battle of Mount Ararat

The enemy were certainly on the move now. We had all been building up for a big push and they had consolidated their power. Now they looked poised to strike against Utnapishtim. There had been a number of significant skirmishes in Europe and Russia, and the Shedu had been equipped with new gear by their modern Nephalim allies. From POWs we had discovered that the Nephalim had formed a powerful and disturbing alliance with Graud's forces. The Medusa in Europe and the Atalanti who were somewhere in America were co-operating to equip Graud's armies with all the best stuff. There were even new uniforms and refitted airships that were now as good as anything else fielded. Almost every power on earth was involved in fighting of some kind and new empires were forming. Somehow I had to make sense of it all as leadership in this war had fallen to me.

My ship, the Eagle, along with Arthur's ship, Lady Guinevere and Finvara's Selki, we all hovered over eastern Turkey. Paq and Shara stood with me on my bridge.

We were watching the holographic tank in the middle of the bridge. Ship movements weren't always easy to track, especially with an enemy that could teleport their ships instantaneously. We hadn't been able to capture one of the airships. They all evaded us or self-destructed if we tried. If we had one, we would have been able to reverse engineer the technology. Our scientists still couldn't figure it out, how Graud had achieved the ability.

"There's a newscast coming through on the European channels." My communications officer announced.

"Put it up on the tank." I ordered.

A familiar face appeared on the tank. It was Jeremy Hood, the new "Prime Minister" of the "British Sector" of the "New European Union" and Chairman of the Union Assembly.

I couldn't help it, "Bastard, traitor." I said under my breath. Hood wasn't wearing a thrall collar and was wearing an open shirt to prove it.

... "and we of the New Union put our full support behind the New Guard Forces. More and more individuals are giving their allegiance to the Union. Enthrallment remains a necessity in some of the occupied territories, but more people every day are freely accepting citizenship. It is the repeated message of this office that the present occupation by New Guard Forces is for the good of global peace and prosperity. Global citizenship and a New World Economic Order has been the hope of many nations, willing to give up national sovereignty for the greater global good. It has long been recognised that environmental collapse, global climate change and the continuing violence of international terrorism, perpetuated by rogue anarchist elements of the newly formed Free States and their ally the Petra Group has forced our hand. This present occupation is for the good of the world! With new advanced technologies and economic restructuring, we call upon the remaining nations of the world to accept membership of the Global Union. Our war is with the so-called Free States, who must be stopped. We are about to engage in new military actions against the Free States to put an end to global disunity and chaos."

What followed then were some interviews on the street, in London, Paris and Berlin, with citizens, all without collars, happily espousing the goodness of the new government and the evils of the Free States. There were even representatives of the Pandemonium forces, in their new black and red uniforms, being mobbed by happy young girls.

"In further news," a reporter stood before people receiving injections at a health clinic in Paris, "voluntary sterilisation clinics all across the New Union are receiving large numbers, all willing to do their bit for population reduction and saving the planet!"

"Turn it off." I growled, "Inform the fleet that we are going to action stations."

I had a feeling that something was about to happen. Hood had been putting out announcements and making threats ever since the Union was formed and his puppet government was set up to run things for the Pandemonium. But open threats of imminent military attack was a new one. I knew Hood well enough to know that he meant business this time. Besides, enemy ship activity the last few days had increased dramatically.

"Show me the fleet positions." I asked the scanner tech.

The tank showed the globe with all the important tactical data. There was the red zone of enemy occupied territory over Europe, Southern England and Russia. There were a lot of their ships in guard positions in southern Russia. That was easy teleport range to Utnapishtim and also the two splinters at Jerusalem and Sinai. The thing that bothered me was that anything could happen. It was a whole new world now. Our ships could flick into space and then back to any location within minutes. The enemy could teleport just as easily. Even so, I was concerned. Tarmal and I used to discuss these kinds of situations. He was an experienced space fighter and had led huge fleets into interstellar battles against formidable enemies. Defending and attacking planetary positions was a very different matter. We had three capital ships and we had control over the Free States only because of our Splinters. We occupied Albion and so held most of Britain. We occupied Asgard and so held Scandinavia. We held the Zion Splinter and so had Israel. We had full occupation of the Mu and Lemurian Splinters in Tasmania and at Uluru and so were able to hold our position in the South Pacific. We held the Caucasus because we were in Utnapishtim. But the Islamic League controlled Sinai, and the Immortals controlled Shangrila. We had cordial relationships with those powers and we were cooperating against the Pandemonium but the enemy held Splinters of their own. The Ouroboros and the Olympians held Olympus in Greece and so effectively held Europe because they had joined Medusa. Just recently the Pandemonium New Guard Forces had taken the two Splinters in Africa. It had happened very quietly. Somehow they had broken the wards protecting the Splinters of Atlas and Kilimanjaro and overwhelmed the garrison tribes guarding them. The Djinni had held Atlas and so their defeat meant that the New Union now effectively controlled North Africa. It was this defeat that made me think that Utnapishtim was next. The New Union wanted global control. To get that control, they needed to take the Splinters. The fall of Kilimanjaro was a real shock for the Free States. It had come as a sneak attack and they had gotten through the wards.

This time we hadn't been able to take the Splinter back. The New Union now effectively controlled Africa and we were in trouble. Even more disturbing was the fact that we knew that the Atalanti held Atlantis Island, the American Splinter, but we had no idea where that Splinter was. Its wards were particularly powerful and they remained well hidden. The situation in America still wasn't good. The Daedalus and Arrow were still evacuating victims of the destruction. US Military still occupied cities along the Eastern Seaboard, but there were few civilians left. The United States still existed and had a provisional government in Washington DC, but it only existed under the support and protection of the Free States. There were now more Americans living outside America than in. Most of the survivors were now living in Australia.

Now I was looking at the tank and thinking about the last few weeks. I also was thinking about Niamah and our sons and the others. If they failed to stop Graud in the past, we would be in serious trouble. One thing the POW's told us that I believed, was that more of them were coming, a lot more.

The bridge crew were all busy at their tasks as we headed for action stations. They called to me as the different crews became ready.

Then, suddenly, right on time it seemed, the tank lit up with new objects.

I was right, there were now one hundred enemy airships just teleported into attack range. They were already firing upon us. Without hesitation I ordered, "Return fire, launch all attack ships."

The immediate tactic we had discovered that worked was to pretty much fire a screen of everything we had. We fired plasma weapons, missiles and needle particles as well as a spread of lasers. The idea was to keep the enemy at a distance and stop the dragons from leaping into our holds as they had done before. The faces of Fin and Arthur appeared in the tank before me.

"Enemy are forming a wide net." Finvara informed me, "Think they're trying to hit me first."

"Let them try." I responded, "Draw them in closer to Utnapishtim."

Outside, over one thousand Renim and three thousand E.D.V. attack fighters, including Pylons and our own Petra Wedge fighters and Platforms, flew out forming a mist of cover and protection. There were no dragons in the counter attack, they would be used later, but rather Medusa had given the New Guard their own fleet fighters, including the disc-shaped Haunebu platform fighters and Foo fighters. But there were also Shrikes in the mix as well, the Pandemonium version of Renim.

I watched the battle and Eagle shuddered as our shields took a big impact from an enemy missile. We knew what we were doing. Fin was letting Selki take the bulk of enemy attack as Eagle and Lady Guinevere pulled back towards Mt. Ararat behind us.

Other enemy airships suddenly appeared on the northern side of the Mountains. I smiled to myself.

Up from the Rath of Utnapishtim came thousands of Renim, like a cloud. The snow on the top of the mountain and Parrot Glacier itself was melting. The rock under the snow was opening and the Raths Power Sphere was emerging.

This was something we hadn't been able to do before, but it had been discussed. The Sphere was glowing like a small sun!

"Ready here!" the voice of Atra came from the com.

"Let's do it!" I cried.

Down in the Utnapishtim Plaza, Brigid had the Portal Ring activated and portals were opened. In the Plaza itself were our troops. Boris, Peter and Terry from Petra 18 with Warren's reservists, now fully trained and ready for first blood, were all suited up with the best gear. They hovered wearing their boot sleds, ready to head to wherever the fighting needed them. Atrahasis, the A.I. stood next to Brigid, who controlled the portals, along with a number of other Danu warriors.

It was Boris who opened a force wide channel and said these immortal words,

"He who dwells in the shelter of the Most High will rest in the shadow of the Almighty.

I will say of El Elyon, "He is my refuge and my fortress, theElohim in whom I trust."

Surely He will save you from the fowler's snare and from the deadly pestilence.

He will cover you with His feathers and under His wings you will find refuge.

His faithfulness will be your shield and rampart.

You will not fear the terror of night, nor the arrow that flies by day,

nor the pestilence that stalks in the darkness,

nor the plague that destroys at midday.

A thousand may fall at your side, ten thousand at your right hand,

but it will not come near you.

You will observe with your eyes and see the punishment of the wicked.

If you make the Most High your dwelling even the Source, who is my refuge

then no harm will befall you,

no disaster will come near your tent.

For He will command His Bene Elohim concerning you, to guard you in all your ways.

They will lift you up in their hands, so that you will not strike your foot against a stone.

You will tread upon the lion and the cobra, you will trample the great lion and the serpent.

"Because he loves me," says El Elyon, "I will rescue him, I will protect him for he acknowledges my name.

He will call upon me, and I will answer him, I will be with him in trouble,

I will deliver him and honour him, with long life will I satisfy him,

And show him my salvation. Psalm 91, Amen."

The whole fleet and battle group heard the prayer. It was as though a bolt of energy went up my spine. I was grinning like a mad man. These enemies were doomed!

Atra fired the Power Sphere. Huge bolts of energy flashed across the sky like lightning, striking the enemy ships! One after the other they fell in flames, their shields unable to stop the strikes. Our air fleet broke their defensive cloud formations and attacked enemy fighters directly. The battle was now truly on.

Down in the Utnapishtim Plaza, Atra cried out, "We have enemy contacts within the Rath!"

Brigid, who being connected via the control staff to Atra's central processor, could see the locations of the enemy dragons and troop deployments. Local Danu and Djinni loyal to the Free States were already engaging them in Irkalla and along the Hubur. Enemy troops were in the Rath itself, near the Torbor.

"Phoosh-ee." Brigid opened the portals, The Petra Order troops made a single battle cry, "Yah!" and they flew through the portals and to battle.

Boris and his troops came out firing right in the middle of the Great Hall between the two parts of the Torbor. The place was crawling with New Guard troops in their new distinctive red and black uniforms. The Petra Order troops went camouflage, almost but not quite invisible and began to hunt.

In Irkalla, Weaver did what he was best at and came out underwater, attacking enemy positions all along the Hubur!

Braun's troops and the reservists ended up in the tunnels and faced some Dragons that were trying to claw their way into the Rath, along with some Anakim. It was going to be the hardest fighting, in the dark and wet bowels of the Rath, and the enemy were very determined.

Dragons had turned up in the Netherworld as well, blasting fire everywhere, destroying homes and gardens. Many of the Anunnaki and Djinni living there were forced to flee under the protection of the Order.

Outside, the Power Sphere had decimated the enemy ships and most of them that survived were forced to flee by teleporting away. Some stayed to pick up surviving fighters, of which there were few, and the ships that picked them up were taken out shortly after.

I knew what this meant, that the enemy had landed their battle troops and had put their hope in taking out the Rath quickly and so use the portals and perhaps the Sphere itself against us. Their airships would then return to finish the job. Their plan might just work, except they hadn't taken into consideration the faith of those fighting below.

In the Rath and in the Netherworld below that, our troops were fighting with a prayer on their hearts and no thoughts whatsoever of defeat. The enemy fell back from their attack and died where they stood. Dragons were taken down and hacked to pieces by warriors with maces and blades. In the tunnels, the reserves never backed down but pushed forward and downward where Warren's troops finished them off.

The enemy had utterly underestimated those they dared to attack. Not one of the enemy gave themselves up for capture. They all died to the last. The men and women who had done the killing stopped and rested, satisfied, not happy, but content that they had done what had to be done.

Up in Eagle I looked at the casualty reports with amazement. Not one of our ships, not one of our troops had died!! It was a miracle! The enemy that remained in the sky, seeing the utter destruction of their forces, fled.

Chapter Thirty-Three

Battles

Shet gathered all the battle leaders together in the middle of the ruins of the enemy encampment. All the cleaning up had been done and people were now able to look after the wounded, bury the dead and rest a bit. But not for the generals, not yet.

"I've sent scout Renim out along the Nodin coast lands." Shet told those gathered, "We can expect reports soon about what the enemy are doing. But most importantly, how are we all doing right now?"

Shet listened carefully as he heard the reports from the different chieftains and war leaders. He was particularly concerned about the wounded and that they be cared for. The supply caravans with their mounted support were in place. Shet was pleased.

"We have two enemies before us." Shet began, "We don't yet know exactly where they are, but they are out there. I need advice." Shet looked right at Grim and his future companions.

"We really can't fight two fronts against the Nodin and the Pandemonium at the same time. The Nodin are just down there on the plains, the closest enemy. Normally we would fight the closest foe before moving onto the other. The Pandemonium have airships and can move troops quickly. We have destroyed their position here in Eden, but they will return. They are the greater threat to both this world and the world of the future. They also specifically want to destroy my future, and with me, the whole future of both our worlds. This is the case?"

"Yes," Grim nodded, "that is the case."

"I need to lead this fight." Shet said determinedly, "I am not a coward to hide from the enemy that would try to kill me."

"Not kill you." Melki pointed out, "They seek to contain you and your future, and ours. You are the origin of all future history. We cannot afford to lose you. You need to be protected."

"But we also need to destroy Graud's ability to send his armies into the future." Shet protested, "Do I lead this attack from the back like a coward?"

Kit, Newton and the others looked at each other knowingly. Leading from the back was a modern tactic.

"Just do what your heart tells you to do." Maia told him.

"My heart tells me to lead." Shet nodded, "My heart also tells me that we must finish this quickly and attack Graud in his fortress, and do so tomorrow."

A short time later, Hilli was flying eastward in her Ren form. Surreya was piloting and with them on board were Niamah, Al, Tarmal, Fay and Mrorna too. They flew alone and cloaked, heading towards Graud's island fortress of Gog Magog, located in the middle of the sea.

"There's the target ahead." Surreya told everyone, "You can see the fleet of ships."

Hilli put the image up on her main screen so everyone could see. The island itself was quite large with a line of mountains in the middle. At the top of one of the tallest mountains was the fortress itself. Graud had built a portal ring and had a power sphere hovering above.

"Does he have a Splinter?" Tarmal asked.

"No," Mrorna answered, "Not a Splinter, but he could tear the island up out of the sea if he wanted to, maybe that's his plan."

"There are a lot of big ships there." Niamah pointed out, "What exactly is he doing with all those ships?"

"Graud is about to create new time bubbles around those ships and then send them to specific locations to wait for resonation." Mrorna explained, "I was trained as a technician down near the ring and I controlled some of the portal equipment. It was how some of us got to escape."

"That's a lot of ships." Fay said.

"Can we get in closer for a better look?" asked Al.

Hilli flew in closer.

"They are scanning for us." Surreya said, "They know we are here but haven't locked onto us yet."

"Just want to record a bit more...." Hilli replied, "then we get outta here ok!"

Hilli let Surreya pilot her closer into the fortress. They flew over the island itself and could see how the whole place had been turned into a huge industrial complex. There were also impenetrable battlements and shield generators as well as large numbers of troops. There was a port full of troop ships, constantly coming and going.

"This isn't going to be easy to crack into." Tarmal said, "The technology is anachronistic but still formidable, even by 2018 standards."

"We have the full backing of the Elohim and Seelie of this era." Niamah told him.

"True, but we might get a nasty surprise."

Just then there was a massive crack, like the loudest thunder ever and Hilli was screaming! Everyone was in shock as Hilli began to tumble uncontrollably to the ground. Surreya tried to control the flight and she could see that the power sphere over the portal ring was glowing and sparking with power.

"They got us with a needler!" she called to the others, "Full suits everyone, we are going to crash!"

Hilli was in agony as the sphere over the fortress fired another bolt of lightning-like energy at her and Surreya had to force her hand to make Hilli fly over the fortress to a forested area beyond. Hilli couldn't hold onto her field much longer and it collapsed over a small lake. Those within the field fell into the water, Hilli, her five passengers and the three constructs.

Within moments there were Shrikes flying all over the place. The Pandemonium version of Renim, the Shrikes were heavily armed and slick. Their weapons harnesses included a long scythe as well as particle cannons. Although Hilli was unconscious, one of the constructs put her onto its back and they all climbed out of the water and fled into the nearby forest. From above the Shrikes began a systematic bombardment, blasting trees into splinters and chips of hot flaming wood! In their shielded battle suits, those on the ground were protected from the shrapnel but not from the concussion of the blasts and they were often knocked off their feet as they ran. Even so, under the trees there was some shelter and the Shrikes were unable to detect the shielded intruders. While a few of the enemy remained airborne, some of the Shrikes de-resonated, landing crews on the ground. Big Pandemons and Shedu warriors, along with their Shrikes began to search.

Niamah, the most experienced fighter in the group, gathered them under an overhang of rock covered in vines. Hilli was passed in and Al took a careful look at her.

"She's ok." He said after checking her, "She's suffered from an electrical shock, but her field resonators were able to discharge the energy. But her harness is dead. Hilli won't be able to fly, even if she regains consciousness soon. We have to walk from here, sorry."

Tarmal swore under his breath. It wasn't good.

"We are in the heart of enemy territory." Niamah said the obvious, "The question is what do we do? A futile fight will only get us killed and Graud doesn't believe in the Geneva Convention for the treatment of prisoners of war."

"We complete our mission." Said Fay, "We remain free for as long as possible and gather information."

"And if we do get captured?" Tarmal asked.

"It will be when we get captured." Mrorna responded, "I'm not being pessimistic. They will find us pretty soon. It is inevitable."

"We won't make it easy for them though!" Al growled.

"No, we won't." Niamah nodded, "We are wearing camo-armour and have three constructs with us. We try to get into the fortress and keep away from enemy troops."

Surreya had been outside keeping watch and she came in.

"We have company approaching." She said.

"We run silent." Niamah told everyone, "It won't be easy but we need to go stealth and stay close enough to follow my lead. I will have a passive beacon on for you to follow."

"Be careful." Al was concerned, "If the enemy get close enough, they will detect you."

"If they get me, they get me." Niamah grunted, then she turned on her cloak and went out from under the cover of the overhang. Al put Hilli back onto the construct and the rest of them went out, following the quiet beacon that Niamah switched on. She led them back the way they had come towards the lake into which they fell. Niamah carefully led through the enemy search line and they went undetected. They moved quietly but also quickly. Eventually they came to a small hill overlooking Graud's fortress.

Looking down across the small valley, the fortress rose above them. The platform with the portal ring and power sphere was high above. All kinds of energies were being manipulated up there and large numbers of airships, dragons and Shrikes were filling the skies.

"If they can see us down here, we're screwed." Al said, still cloaked.

"Screwed?" Mrorna said.

Al just chuckled to himself.

Niamah was looking around carefully. Tarmal and Fay were on either side of her, and the three of them, perched on the edge of the hill, were practically invisible.

It was then, quite without even noticing it, that everyone in the group realised they couldn't move. No-one could even talk. The constructs had shut down. Then the cloaking fields of their suits switched off. It was a moment of utter horror. A group of Pandemons simply strolled up over the face of the hill. They had rather smug looks on their faces. Niamah saw them first, and unable to move or cry out, she resolved herself. They were captured and there was nothing they could do about it.

Captain Simon, called "Zealot", had snuck onto the Gerald. He personally thought that was a miraculous achievement under the circumstances. There were his crewmates all around but they all wore those damn collars, turning them into robots. There were also a lot of the black suited warriors. That's how he thought of them. Not soldiers, but barbarian warriors. They creeped Simon out. But Simon had managed to stay hidden. The super carrier had been refitted and the aircraft hangers modified to hold the disc-shaped craft of the enemy. They had put in big generators and done things to the guns. From the outside, the Gerald still looked like a carrier, but it wasn't any more.

But the Gerald still sailed like a ship and they were underway. It was difficult, but Simon was able to find out that they were heading back to U.S. waters, the east coast. He'd managed to find an enemy communication device and used it to listen in on some of the chatter going on. Most of it was in German, which fortunately Simon understood. Some was in another language he couldn't understand. It was ancient Neph, the language of the Nephalim. Other than listen, there wasn't much more Simon could do but wait. He had a nice collection of weapons and ordnance, including some explosives, and he hoped it would be enough.

As they came closer to what used to be the United States, the skies got darker and it was often raining. Simon knew what had happened. The United States had been struck a death blow and the aftermath of the eruption of the Yellowstone caldera was still darkening the whole northern hemisphere. Before they were captured, they had seen the footage on the news.

"Fuckin' anti-gravity ships." Simon said under his breath. What could he possibly do against these new enemies?

Then one day, Simon was looking outside from one of his hiding places. He saw the big ship flying high in the clouds. It was the Daedalus. It was also HUGE! Simon had McGyvered a radio and the enemy communicator and set up a small directional dish which he pointed at the big ship. He then pressed a button and fired a short encrypted message. Simon hoped it would be picked up by the right people, but he didn't want to take a chance either. Simon inflated a life-raft and dropped it down into the sea and he jumped in after it.

The U.S.S. Gerald R Ford was a big ship, but tiny compared to the Daedalus that now hovered above it. On the bridge of the Daedalus, Captain John James, Newton's father, was looking at the visual display of the super carrier.

"Zoom in there Con." He ordered.

The image showed American sailors and deck crew on the deck of the ship, looking up at them. There were a couple of helicopters on the deck and all the usual busyness that was normal for a United States carrier. Normal. Hmm.

"The scans show nothing unusual." The com officer reported.

"Recheck the bio scans." The Captain told the con officer.

The result appeared on the screen. James sighed.

"Ok then," James nodded, "I'll talk to them."

"This is Captain James Burgess of the USS Gerald R Ford," came the voice only contact, "To whom am I speaking?"

"I am Captain John James of the Petra EDV Daedalus." James replied cheerfully, "It is good to see some more Americans alive and well. We need all the help we can get with the rescue and reconstruction process."

"Thank you Captain James." Burgess replied, "What is the procedure for us now? Can you put us in contact with remaining US Armed Forces?"

"US Department of Defence no longer exists but has been incorporated into the new Military Command Headquarters of the Free States. All US Military forces, including the Navy are now under the command of the North American Provisional Taskforce and President Taylor."

Burgess didn't reply immediately.

"President Taylor?" he finally replied.

"I'm sad to inform you that President Clinton was killed in the destruction of the Yellowstone eruption. Vice President Roman Taylor is now President of the United States." Captain James told the American.

Again there wasn't an immediate reply.

"To which port do we sail and to whom do I report for further duty?" Burgess asked.

"No need to sail anywhere." Captain James said, "We will tractor your whole ship up into our docking bay. The NAPT and President Taylor are here on board the Daedalus."

"That is good news." Burgess said.

The Daedalus turned to face the oncoming aircraft carrier. From underneath, out of the flight bays came a number of Renim and as well as Arrow and her compliment of Pylons. They all flew wide to either side of the Gerald. Down the front of the Daedalus were the large hemispheres of the electro-dynamic generators. The spheres began to glow with electro-magnetic energy and the supercarrier suddenly lifted up out of the water.

The super-carrier was a huge thing, the biggest warship ever, but nothing as big as the Daedalus that hovered overhead.

Up in the con in the Daedalus, Captain James looked at the data screens anxiously, looking for any spike of energy or sign of unusual movement.

"We know it's a trap." one of the deck officers said aloud.

"Of course it is." James replied, "Pull her in anyway. Get me Fass on the Arrow."

The face of the acting captain appeared on the big com screen immediately.

"John," the Zioronian nodded in greeting, "just so you know, we have troops ready to go. Also, one of my Pylons picked up the American airman."

"Now it's time to spring a trap of our own." James replied, "Send them in."

"My pleasure." Fass was grinning.

Suddenly there was a frozen moment. The Daedalus electro-dynamic generators hummed a different frequency and the air became like treacle. It was a partial stasis field, and no-one was moving. On board the Gerald, Captain Burgess was roughly pushed aside by Dagon, who was in full glamour and wearing the uniform of a US Navy lieutenant.

"Shit! Shit! SHIT!" Dagon cursed, "They are onto us! Damn you Nimrod, I said this wouldn't work so easily! Get the troops ready! We are about to be boarded!"

Dagon's Nephalim officers worked frantically, while the Americans stood there doing nothing. As Dagon moved around the bridge he just knocked them over viciously.

"We use the portal lock NOW!" Dagon screamed, "Teleport us in!"

There was a sudden sickening lurch and the big super carrier was no longer floating in front of the Daedalus, but was now deep inside the main hold, hovering within sight of the floating platform of the Daedalus' bridge. Within the Daedalus there was plenty of room for big ships, and the Gerald wasn't alone, surrounding her were fifty of the new refitted airships of Graud's fleet.

"Launch the Haunebu attackers!" Dagon ordered.

In the central hold of the Daedalus, the air was full of fighting ships as well as troops carrying dragons, launched from their airships and heading for the main decks of the big ships. The flight deck of the Gerald opened up and twenty disc shaped E.D.V.s could be seen resonating up. But none of them were to launch.

Down under the decks of the super-carrier, the portals opened and the Humdrid spilled out. They had orders to take the ship, preferably without killing any of the Americans, so the Humdrid were armed with weapons capable of being set on stun. But the black suited Nazi troops they were facing as well as the Shedu officers were another matter. The Humdrid were unstoppable and utterly merciless as they attacked using their battle chariots. They used combinations of particle weapon, pushing the charge to kill levels when required and those they clearly identified as not having collars, and tentacles and their scythes on their gun arms. They attacked the Haunebu E.D.V.s still in their cradles and killed the enemy troops trying to board and escape.

On the bridge, Dagon was receiving a battle report, "They are coming here and we cannot stop them."

Then, they arrived. The bridge hatchway had been bolted shut. Death screams could be heard on the other side, and then the hatch itself was twisted and wrenched free. A Humdrid war chariot climbed in through the hole it had made and its faceless dome seemed to stare at Dagon, who held up a collar control device in his hand. The Humdrid stopped with a clunk.

"If you do not leave this ship immediately!!!" Dagon cried shrilly, "I will kill all the enthralled hostages!!!"

"Orders were to take the ship." The Humdrid monotoned, then swiftly, faster than the eye could follow, a razor sharp tentacle slashed out from one of the Humdrid's arms and sliced up through Dagon's body and then his wrist, sending the device flying. The Humdrid caught it as Dagon's body fell bloody and lifeless to the deck. The Zioronian battle leader Virey, in full armour, came into the bridge then. The Humdrid passed the enthrallment device to him and Virey switched the device off.

All around the ship, the Americans woke up as though from a long slumber. They were disoriented and tired, but the hostages were saved.

Virey got a good look at things going on outside in the heart of the Daedalus through the windows of the bridge. The airships were fighting hard, dragons were being set loose to descend upon the strategic areas of the Daedalus. It was clear that a primary target was the floating bridge platform of the Daedalus herself. If they took the con, they would be able to control the ship. Virey knew what had to be done next.

He opened a channel to the Daedalus bridge, "We have the ship and she's floating safely in the tractor net of the harbour." He quickly reported, "I'm heading by air to the con. You guys need us!"

"Indeed we do!" the com officer cried, "We are under heavy attack!"

Virey spoke to the Humdrid chief, "New orders," Virey pointed upwards to where the Daedalus bridge was hovering in the middle of the main hold, "the Daedalus bridge is under attack, we must stop the attackers."

The Humdrid chief seemed to look upwards. The shadow of the Humdrid pilot could just be seen moving within the hood of their battle wagon.

"We accept the orders." He said, "We will accept the usual remuneration times four. This task requires greater risk. There will be casualties."

"You have a deal." Virey nodded, "I will come with you."

At that time, Weaver turned up, he had a number of American sailors with him, including the ship captain.

"Gotta go fight some more." Virey told Weaver, "You ok with this lot?"

"No problems," Weaver answered, "God go with you."

"And with you."

Virey nodded at the Humdrid chief. The other Humdrid battle wagons were now assembling on the main flight deck. Virey and the chief went out to join them. Within moments, the whole group leapt upwards into the open space of the main hold. The Humdrid fired their inertialess drives and Virey pulled his hover sled down onto his boots and took after the Humdrid mercenaries.

Captain Burgess had a bandage on his head, but he was no longer enthralled. He turned to Weaver, who removed his helm.

"You're a human." Burgess almost looked surprised.

"Name's Peter Weaver," he smiled, "I'm a battle leader for the Terran Petra Order forces. I'm Australian."

"We want to help." Captain Burgess asked.

"Ok mate." Weaver nodded, "We'll get your boat put down somewhere, and then we'll see what we can do."

Virey and the Humdrid flew up towards the Daedalus bridge. Virey himself broke away from the others and flew to the bridge itself, but the Humdrid had other ideas. Virey grinned inside his helmet, the Humdrid were notorious for their storm and board tactics. They were attacking the enemy front on. The Humdrid were hard to stop. Dragons appeared and the Humdrid just climbed onto them and began to fight relentlessly.

Just as Virey got to the bridge, a dragon teleported on top of him! Virey could see the Nephalim troops near the beasts head, but in the troop containers on the flanks, there were black uniformed soldiers, not Graud's army, but wearing the same uniform as those down on the big aircraft carrier. He could see swastikas on their uniforms, he also recognised Zioronian tech. But there was no time to think about this strange incongruence, it was time to fight! Forearm blasters were not going to cut it with this lot, so Virey pulled his heavy blaster off his thigh and leapt onto the dragon's back and began blasting!!! His shields were coping a pounding from particle weapons, but there were black armoured soldiers climbing out at him with energy blasters! Underneath them all, the dragon screamed in agony as the shots into its side made it lurch sideways. Virey was thrown clear and kept up firing his heavy blaster. He could see the angry black soldiers scrambling to bail out as their dragon began to fall in its death throws. The black suits had flight capacity and they were heading for the bridge. Virey also flew over to the side of the bridge. He found a lock and used an encryption to unlock the hatch and climb in. He came out on a lower deck, got his helm AI to give him a way forward to the bridge itself proper.

Scanners came up as did heat sensors. Inside the bridge there was a lot of smoke from the fighting and almost no visibility. Virey's helm display told him where the friendlies were and there were also a lot of red markers for enemies. The troops from the dragon were boarding. Virey ran forward. He pinged his location to the other Daedalus Order troops.

"We have boarders at the main lock to the bridge." Captain James' voice came over the helm com, "Anyone left outside?"

"Virey here." He replied, "I'm looking for others to make a stand."

"All troops to Virey."

He came across a group, about fifteen Order troopers on the next deck. They looked a bit beaten up.

"We've been fighting all over the place," the ranking officer reported, "got boarders coming in everywhere."

"I just met some of them coming in." Virey told him, "Ok, we get to the main door to the bridge and hold that."

"Yes Sir."

They moved quickly along the corridor towards the bridge deck and came to a T intersection. The enemy were already there. Virey led them forward firing his cannon in the confines of the corridor, heat flashing the air before him. In the flash, the enemy turned and fired back, but they couldn't see. The Order troops had their scanners and were able to target better, they fired a wall of energy. The enemy pulled back. As they went after them, moving by the numbers, Virey noticed that the helm of one of the enemy who had been killed had blown off. He recognised

Zioronian features immediately, the Asian features, but with white blond hair and blue eyes looking up sightlessly. Virey had to look more closely, turning the dead man over. He had tattoos on the side of his neck.

"Shit." Virey spat, "Fucking Valorians."

Some of the others must have heard him, they hesitated.

"What are you doing?" Virey roared, "Who cares if they are the Devil himself, we kill them ok!!!"

They pressed forward.

Valorians were from Zioron too, but they had a different history. While the escaped slaves and Grenworlder guards who settled Zioron about 7000 years ago went onto become the great Aquani Federation, the Grenworlders who remained loyal to the Nephalim went to the Valor system and the Hell world of Cootac, from where they fought against those they thought of as rebels. They were the most vicious and best fighters, after the Humdrid. This wasn't going to be easy.

But what were they doing here, on Earth and fighting now?

The door to the bridge was just ahead. The Valorians were already trying to cut through and they had set up a barricade in the corridor. Virey set up a fire-team in the corridor and they quickly pulled panels from the walls and then shielded them. They moved forward and began to fire at the enemy. Virey himself led another group down a deck. As they headed for the area just under the bridge, they ran into a group of Valorians and they began firing at each other.

Outside in the main hold, the airships of Graud's fleet were not doing as well as they had hoped. The Arrow and a lot of small fighters had come back into the hold and were putting up a hard fight. The E.D.V. and Renim fleets of the Daedalus were also out in force. They had been prepared. On the bridge of the lead airship, Kruug watched the battle. The Daedalus bridge hovered not far away. They had been pouring troops into that, both Shedu and Valorians, to take it, but there was heavy resistance. There were also reports that the same Humdrid that had destroyed Dagon's force on the aircraft carrier, were now attacking airships. So, it was going to come down to troop fighting. It was impossible to move within the hold of the big Daedalus, but troops and small ships could move around freely. The Order forces were everywhere, including both humans and Vansad fighters.

Kruug realised that the enemy must have been warned just before they attacked. They were too well prepared for the attack. But the plan had to be put into effect anyway.

"Alright," Kruug sighed, "we do phase three."

It came very unexpectedly. The airships were resonating their teleportal fields again.

On the Daedalus bridge, they could hear the enemy outside the main door trying to cut through. Then John James looked at the screens and was surprised to see that the enemy ships seemed to be readying to flee. But there was a sudden lurching feeling as the E.M.P. flashed. The airships were still there in the main hold. The enemy were still trying to cut their way in.

"Captain..." the scanner technician spoke up, "... Captain, we have moved."

"Give us an outside view." James asked.

The screens showed an island and above it was the power sphere of a Splinter. All around the power sphere were hundreds of enemy ships.

Chapter Thirty-Four

Gog Magog

They woke up in agony. All but one member of the mission were stretched out, with their arms pulled up over their heads and bodies pulled tight. Energy couplings held wrists and ankles. Surreya, Niamah, Al, Tarmal, Fay and Mrorna were naked and utterly powerless to move. As for Hilli, she was also, and held in a cage, forced into an uncomfortable squatting position. This was to stop her from using her field generators in her shoulders. The room they were in was quite dark, except for a small lamp in one corner. They were not alone because there were guards, two large Shedu Anakim in full World War I German style uniform. The only difference in the uniforms, which included the old spiked pit helm, was that their packs included very advanced full body shields, which were switched on. They weren't taking any chances with these prisoners.

A door opened and Graud walked in, with more guards following behind.

"Oh lookee!" Al growled, "It's shizer kopf himself."

"Charming as always Alaquandi." Graud sounded bored and he pressed a modified collar controller, and Al's body was suddenly hit with electricity, contorting in excruciating pain, so intense that his jaw locked shut. He couldn't even scream. Moments after that, Graud did the same to all the others. Graud switched the electric torture off and watched their bodies momentarily relax, and then and only then he hit them again. The torture went on like this a few more times. When he finally stopped, they were shuddering with remembered agony. Tarmal's mouth was bleeding from biting himself, Fay had defecated involuntarily and Mrorna and Hilli were whimpering. The others had been trained better to withstand this sort of thing, but they were all in a bad way.

"That was just to impress you." Graud said casually, "I gather that you were the forward scouting party." It wasn't a question but a statement, "The attack will come shortly I think."

"We won't tell you anything." Niamah gasped.

Graud walked over to her, reached over and squeezed one of her breasts cruelly, "I always liked you Niamah, shame we are on different sides. But I'm sure you realise how enthrallment works."

Graud illustrated it by twisting Niamah's breast, inflicting pain, with one hand and reaching between her legs with the other hand and softly fondling her there. Graud alternated between pain and pleasure. Niamah gritted her teeth and just stared, saying nothing.

Graud tired of it, "I can get data from you just as you do from those you capture. It is in your heads and enthrallment is easy, even with the Vansad mind. In some ways it's easier to break one of you."

He walked over to Tarmal, "Humans are mentally fragile things, they sometimes break beyond repair." Graud lashed out with a powerful punch, hitting Tarmal right on the jaw! Teeth broke and Tarmal spat one out, with more blood!

"Enough poetry." Graud sighed, and walked past Hilli and just for fun he juiced her, leaving the power on as he went to Mrorna.

"You will all be enthralled," he said, "I'll find out what I need to know and then when your allies attack, I'll capture Shet and change history. Pointless really."

Graud looked at Mrorna and laughed a little laugh.

"I know you," he turned Mrorna's face to one side, "I'll have to think up something creative for you."

Graud turned to leave, he gestured at one of the guards, "Get that shit cleaned up would you. Then process them. I have more important things to do. You know, fight a war, take over the world, change history." He laughed as he left.

Hilli's torture stopped and she wept in her cage as Graud walked out. One of the guards took a hose out from a nearby alcove and turned the cold water onto the captives, rinsing them all clean. The second guard returned with a hypodermic device and put them all to sleep.

Graud and his elite guards left the dungeon and walked up to a landing at the top of the tower. There was a bridge that crossed the keep to the central tower in the middle of the city. It was Graud's private walkway so he and his guards could get to all the important parts of his fortress quickly. Graud liked to take a personal interest in the conditioning of his thralls as he liked to have their personal allegiance rather than that of one of the conditioners. Graud wanted to go back later to see these captives in particular. He felt confident, with Niamah and Alaquandi as thralls, he could do some serious damage to his enemies.

But now, Graud had more work to be done in his control room. He had only just sent off the first wave of time spheres into the future and he had been very upset that they had ended up 100 years too late. Nevertheless, things had worked out, alliances had been made and they had occupied most of Europe. Getting messages back from the future wasn't easy and the timing of receiving those transmissions required careful monitoring of the portal matrix that Graud had set up. The control room was a wide platform at the very top of the tallest tower. Gog Magog wasn't a splinter, but it was the next best thing, it was a portal junction. From this one place he could manipulate time and space in new ways that no other Baal Lord had ever been able to achieve, nor any Vansadagaadian Oberon either.

The bridge entered underneath the control room. The main fortress was a huge building. Graud had built it to contain massive generators that probed deep into the earth. The generators created the vast amounts of electricity needed in two ways, with the thermal heat of subterranean magma, but more importantly from the electro-dynamic shell fields of the earth itself. Graud's Shedu had built the world's largest Ring Gate complex. The Gate stone pillars went down deep into the earth and then towered high over the fortress into the sky. Compared to the Stonehenge sized Gate Rings of the Splinters, this Ring was five times larger in diameter and at the top of the fortress, there were twelve layers of the Ring lintels climbing high above. At the centre of the Ring, as usual was the altar stone and the primary control Ring, identical to those in each Splinter. On the altar stone was the portal stone and the staff key that he had stolen from Utnapishtim in 1918. Those two items that Graud had stolen were the literal key to the whole complex because he had found a way to use the whole Splinter complex to connect his portal matrix together, using their own system against them. The Portal Stone was one of the original Vansadagaadian Seeker Stones. Graud could draw power from the Corridor itself. He used the Staff Key in new ways as well, finding subtle frequencies and other dimensions, pocket dimensions that enabled him to create the time bubbles. He hoped to create the bubble dimension that would enable him to banish Shet son of Awdame forever and so close off the present time continuum and create a new one. He was nearly there.

When Graud walked into the centre of his main control Ring, all his guards saluted and the Gate controllers, all wearing their white robes, bowed. The only one who didn't bow within the Ring was Graud's personal Shrike. She was the same one who has gone with him to Vansadagaadian Avalon with the stolen Stone and Staff Key and they had run the strings together into the past, right after he caved Walter Ryan's head in.

Graud looked up. Hovering outside of the Ring Tower were many airships of Graud's fleet. Dragons were flying overhead as well, crying out to one another. It was dark this night as clouds covered the sky. Graud already knew about the defeat in the west, and he was expecting this new attack to come soon. Some of his Pandemon generals were standing nearby, waiting to talk to him. Well, they could wait a bit longer.

Instead, Graud inspected the lower tier of the inner Ring. The Gate controllers had their hands on the Portal Stones, in deep trance as they manipulated the energies of the Ring using their minds. He then headed back over to the Altar Stone and took hold of the Staff Key, pushing it down into its slot. While Graud's consciousness entered virtual space, his hand carefully turned the Key, very gently seeking the frequencies he wanted, building connections to other dimensions. Graud grinned to himself as he saw the energies and electro-dynamic fields fall into their right shells. It wouldn't be long and he would have enough time spheres to send the next wave, an even larger fleet of ships and troops into the future, to crush the Petra Alliance and the so-called Free States.

While in his trance, Graud saw a window opening before him. The message was coming through. It was Kruug standing on his bridge with his airship crew.

"My Lord." Kruug bowed.

"Report Kruug." Graud ordered.

"We are in the process of taking the Daedalus as we speak, and have drawn the ship to Atlantis Island, where our Atalanti allies are joining us in taking the ship back for the Nephalim."

There was a massive explosion that rocked Kruug's airship. The general tried to look unimpressed by it, but failed.

"It seems that you have not yet occupied the Dreadnaught." Graud stated the obvious.

"There is still resistance." Kruug understated, "We are fighting the Order as well as a small force of Humdrid."

"I need the task finished soon Kruug." Graud warned him, "We can't have the Daedalus as a loose cannon when the second wave comes through. Act quickly. Get the Atalanti to help you."

"We already are my Lord." Kruug reported, "The Atalanti have made great improvements to our ships and we are being aided by the Valorians who serve Baal Nimrod."

"The second wave airships are improved as well." Graud replied, "I have withheld nothing we could use this time. The full effectiveness of Nephalim technology is being unleashed this time. We will shortly conquer the whole world."

"Victory is assured my Lord."

Graud closed the window and stepped back out into the real world.

For a moment things seemed normal. Graud could see his grand fleet overhead and his generals waiting to be given their orders, but from a shadow behind one of the nearby trilithons stepped a man.

The guards near the man acted suddenly to kill or capture the intruder, but the man, in a dark cloak, turned and moving like lightning, he dispatched the guards with brutal force, ripping out one guard's throat and the other, he snapped his neck. The bodies dropped. The man turned his hooded face to Graud who could see eyes glowing with a pale light staring at him. Another guard fired his blaster, but the man, like a blur, seemed to simply step out of the way. A knife was thrown and the guard died.

"I'm not here to kill you Enlil." Kayyin pulled back his hood, revealing his new visage. Kayyin was albino since the time of his curse, but now his eyes glowed with a demonic fire and as he smiled, he revealed his new fangs. Graud shuddered. "I am here to tell you why."

"Why???"

"In a short time you will know." Kayyin stepped forward. He reached down with one hand and picked up the guard whose neck he'd broken. With a lunge, Kayyin bit down on the neck and he seemed to inhale the blood, and not just blood, but Graud could clearly see life-force flowing from the nearly dead guard into Kayyin. When he was done, Kayyin dropped a husk to the ground. "Hell no!" Graud cursed.

"Hell," Kayyin turned his blood stained face to the side and hummed to himself, "perhaps, or perhaps not. I don't know for certain. No deal was made with the Dark One, but a deal was made with the Light One. Perhaps I am his Angel of Darkness?"

"Leave here." Graud was clearly shaking with fear, "What are you, but an abomination?"

"Coming from one such as yourself, such is a compliment." Kayyin laughed, "But I'm here so you know."

Kayyin looked up into the dark sky, "They are late." He said to himself.

Looking right at Graud Kayyin said, "You know that you cannot twist time and I and my Bursar will not allow it. We have a purpose in mind in this world and also to find and colonise other worlds out there." Kayyin waved a hand in the general direction of the stars, "I have made an arrangement to end your little attempt. The Bursar shall prosper and you shall not. The Sethani will be, because even the Bursar needs lambs, in time."

"Who are the Bursar?"

"We are..." from the shadows they came, Kayyin's blood children, marked like him and hungry.

Kit Ryan followed the fugitive through the forest. He was hard to follow despite the enhanced functions of the battle suit that Kit wore. One word kept rising in

Kit's mind, the word was "vampire." The creature called itself a Bursar, a blood child of Kayyin. Then it ran, calling to Kit to follow. This was stupid, really stupid. What if it was a trap? That strangely seemed unlikely. The full force of the Kerubim and the Elementals were flying above and there was only one of them, leading Kit through the forest.

Kit knew where they were. It was the same valley where Lahmech's army was destroyed by the Nodin, before Kayyin turned into his new incarnation. Not far away were the wrecks of Pandemonium ships and dead space-whales, along with rotting corpses on the shore of the sea. Kit could see the enemy running ahead as the trees vanished and the valley opened up. There was a gorge and a narrow path through. Kit followed.

Kit entered the end of the valley and he was astounded with what he saw there. The Bursar was gone, but there at the end of the valley were Gate Stones, a dolmen structure, more ancient than the Gate Ring of the Splinters. The Stones were active and there were portals there, quite large ones, shimmering in the darkness. The portals were large enough for Renim to fly through.

Kit had butterflies in his stomach as without hesitation he leapt through one of the portals. He was dropping briefly, then found himself landing on a bridge. Kit looked around. There were Pandemon bodies nearby, exsanguinated. The Bursar had already been here. Here turned out to be a Pandemonium stronghold and Kit realised with Shock that he was on Gog Magog.

Kit aimed his communicator beam on his forearm through the portal he just jumped through and sent a message.

"The portals lead to Gog Magog and are good for a fly-through attack." Kit knew that Grim was listening, "For some reason the Bursar want us to attack Graud here and now, Kit out."

Kit ran along the bridge looking for more intelligence. Grim and the others in the team back with Shet would be seeing everything on their helm monitors that he was seeing.

"We lost contact with Hilli and the others." Grim told Kit, "See if you can find out what happened to them."

"I'll do my best." Kit entered one of the towers, "There are blood drained bodies everywhere here, no resistance as far as I can see. Kayyin has been here already."

"We are coming through." Grim said, "Shet is coming with us."

"Fly through," Kit reminded, "the portals are up high."

Kit used his cuff blasters to cut through a bolted door. As soon as the door was down there was gunfire from the other side. Not all the enemy were dead. Kit didn't hesitate, he ran into the smoke of the burning door and into the corridor beyond.

Outside, the fleet of Renim were swarming through the portals that the Bursar had opened for them. There was no sign of the enemy fleet, no sign of enemy troops. There were ships in the harbour below and the fortress itself seemed quiet. But it was obvious that there had already been a lot of heavy fighting. The transport Renim flew in for landing patterns both within and outside of the fortress, dropping their cargoes of troops, and beasts of war.

With the Renim also came the Elementals and their companion races. They descended upon the central keep of the fortress itself, where most of the troops should have been. What they discovered were bodies, both Graud's army and a few Bursar.

The Tecorah and Deborah swarmed into the interior of the keep. The Kerubim led by Raph and some Stone People warriors followed after them. The big behemoths and tri-horns were dropped outside the fortress. Shet himself, along with Grim, Rom, Newton, Rainbow and also Melki and Gabriel, were riding one of the larger behemoths. Other behemoths and their tri-horn supports went out into the surrounding area looking for enemies. The flying Renim were searching around the island.

The helms of all the warriors who were moving forward were connected to Shet's helm computer. He could see a full display of the entire battlefield, including all the scanner data coming in, seemingly floating before his eyes, but actually in the visual cortex of his brain.

The scanners showed it clearly, there were large numbers of some enemy force in the forests surrounding the fortress. They had formed up a defensive line and were slowly moving back towards the fortress through the trees.

Similarly, while it seemed that the fortress had been abandoned, this wasn't true, there were large numbers of enemy troops held up within, again, looking as though they had just been fighting a defensive battle. Both Grim and Shet looked at the battle images.

"Where is Graud?" Shet asked the obvious and most important question, "And where has Kayyin and his Bursar gone?"

"There is nothing for it but to go and look." Grim replied.

"Let's go into the fortress." Shet said, "Rom, you lead the warriors here outside the fortress. Many of them are your people."

"Certainly!" Rom leapt off the back of the behemoth and down onto a nearby tri-horn. The driver turned the beast away towards the trees and the approaching enemy line. Rom gave a great battle cry, returned by both Romany and Stone People warriors. They knew what they had to do.

"The enemy fleet is missing too." Melki said.

"My Renim are out looking for them." Gabriel replied, "I would expect them to return soon. But the reason they teleported away rather than defend the fortress is a mystery."

"We have already shielded the entire area." Melki added.

Shet's behemoth was moving quite quickly towards a breach in the wall of Graud's fortress of Gog Magog, preceded by a wall of tri-horns and large numbers of troops.

"If the Bursar can do this," Melki commented as they pushed through into the keep of the fortress, "what would it be like if we had to fight them?"

"We may still have to." Grim admitted, "The Bursar let us come here using their own portals. Kayyin will have a reason for letting us be here."

"All the warriors know that we might have to fight both enemies." Shet said, "It is just hard to plan in this situation. There is no way to work out battle strategies. This is a battlefield where it is up to the courage and skill of individual warriors."

"The Kerubim are trained in this kind of warfare," Melki nodded, "but the Romany and Stone Tribes aren't. Rom is a good war-leader though. He has won many battles."

Kit was joined by a group of Kerubim warriors and some Tecorah as well. They fought their way through the prison tower. The survivors of Graud's army were just beginning to dare to venture out of their hiding places when Kit and his warriors turned up. They were easy to subdue as they were already paralysed with fear. Kit let the Kerubim and Tecorah go ahead of him as he searched the prison cells. Most of the cells were empty. A couple had dead prisoners in them, their throats cut by guards as they retreated. But one cell was locked and Kit melted the lock and kicked the door open. They were there, left where the guards had thrown them in, unconscious on the stone floor. Kit reached Mrorna first and he used his scanners to check on her. She was alive, but in a bad way. Kit pulled his helm off and bent forward and kissed her forehead.

"It's going to be alright." He said to her, "I have you safe now."

Kit checked the others too, Niamah and Al, Fay and Tarmal and Hilli. Kit injected each of them with the stimulant torashaan and it had an amazing effect as they began to wake up. Only Hilli remained unconscious, so Kit carried her.

"What's happening?" Niamah asked, "Is there a battle?"

"I'll give the Readers Digest version," he responded, "the Bursar, Kayyin's vampires, have attacked Graud already and then opened portals for us to get here. We think they are helping us, but not sure why. Most of the killing has been done before we even got here. Now we are finishing the job. We have to find Graud and I need to get you all to medical help."

"We don't need medical help," Al said, putting a hand on Kit's shoulder, "just get us some weapons and we can help."

Hilli began to stir in Kit's arms and she woke up, "I agree," she said, "put me down and give me a gun."

Kit nodded and grinned at her, "Follow me then."

They went back the way that Kit had gone in. Kit and his naked companions turned up in the centre of the keep and found Shet's behemoth. Shet, Grim and Melki were talking with some of the war-leaders, Raph, the Deborah Queen and her Tecorah war-chief, and the Aesir. When Shet saw them he ran forward to meet them, asking questions.

"We were tortured." Fay said, "We want weapons. It is time for some payback."

"I'll get you what you need." Melki turned away.

"Food and water too!" Kit called after him.

"There is a report that Graud is in the main tower." Shet pointed in the right direction, "We've tried to land Renim up on the top but they get shot down."

"I might be able to get us up there." Hilli said.

"But you were badly electrocuted," Niamah protested, "does your Ren-field even work anymore?"

"No." Hilli nodded sadly, "My shoulder packs are dead. Nor do I have enough energy reserves to resonate up. But some of us here have our wings."

Hilli, Surreya, Al and Niamah all flexed their shoulders and their energy wings unfurled. Hilli gave hers an experimental flap.

"Mine still work," she smiled, "we can carry you others up with us and we can sneak in all quietly."

Just then, Melki returned with some Kerubim warriors carrying an equipment chest. Newton and Rainbow were with them, already fully harnessed up.

"We are coming too!" they said together.

Niamah, Al, Surreya, Fay, Tarmal, Hilli and Mrorna went over to the equipment chest and began to pull out helms, belts, power-packs, boots, forearm gauntlets and weapons. They began to help each other harness up. Niamah, Al, Surreya and Hilli needed special power-packs for their backs that were worn low so that their shoulders could be left free for their wings. Fay, Tarmal and Mrorna found flying sleds to attach to their boots so they could fly too. None of them bothered with clothing as such, just the weapons and shield harnesses went on. They checked their heavy blasters were at full charge and so the whole group were ready to fight. Grim looked at them.

"Are you sure you want to do this?" he asked those who had been captured, "You will be weak."

"I gave them torashaan," Kit explained, "enough to keep them going for several hours."

"Here's some food." Melki passed what looked like cakes to them, then also bottles of ambrosia. The cakes were made by the Kerubim and were highly nutritious and gave energy. The Ambrosia gave healing and alertness.

"Ambrosia," Al sighed as he drank, "better than torashaan."

"We are not sure what you will find up there." Grim told them, "If you meet powerful resistance, come back down. We can climb up the tower, fight our way through that way."

"In the meantime," Newton stepped forward, tightening his harness, "Graud could be up there sending the next wave of ships to 2018. We can't let that happen at any cost. If he has already put them in their stasis bubbles, we will need to see if we can pull them back out. Rainbow and I know the physics, we think. Al, we need you to control the key."

"I'm coming too." Shet announced, "I can help fight off the enemy and believe me, Graud himself is someone I must face."

"Not a good idea." Grim shook his head, "That might be precisely what Graud wants you to do. He wants to cut you off, destroy the future."

"I know that." Shet nodded, "But Graud would have to kill us all to get that kind of victory and I think our Bursar friends have given us the advantage. I said that I will fight and lead, so that is what I intend to do."

"Alright," Melki lifted a heavy blaster and his sword and gave them to Shet, "But I will come as well."

"That leaves you, sir Grim," Shet clipped his blaster onto his harness and strapped Melki's sword onto his back, "to lead the warriors down here. We need to keep the fighting pushing forward on all fronts. Graud must be kept occupied so we can get in and face him."

"Then may the Lord of Light and Love guard you all." Grim blessed them, "May we see victory."

In other parts of the fortress of Gog Magog, the fierce fighting continued. Graud was remembering how a female thrall named Mrorna, daughter of Vrengr of the Porma Clan of the Asherim, along with a lot of other thralls, suddenly discovered that they were no longer enthralled. In fact, the whole thrall population in the fortress had become suddenly free. There had been a brief battle. He had quickly put the rebels into stasis and then sent the time sphere to the bottom of the ocean in the Pacific. He had thought that would have been the end of them, and yet she was back. Only later did he realise that she was the one who had so disrupted everything and sent the Pandemonium forces one hundred years further into the future. But right now there were more pressing concerns. The vampiric Bursar had withdrawn to the forests or they had portal jumped away, but then the others had come. Shet was leading them. Hate rose up within Graud.

Kit, Melki, Fay and Tarmal were forming a wall around Shet as they faced the attack. They had flown up cloaked towards the top of the tower. Along the way there were ledges and the numerous bridges that connected different parts of the fortress. The cloaks on their suits didn't work for long as there were disruption fields higher up. The Pandemonium had a stronghold in the middle and top of their main keep and were using advanced shield and disrupter technology to hold it. The German style uniforms were no longer a joke as proper shielding and energy weapons were being used effectively. Still, because the A'sidhe members were flying with their own wings, the E.D. disrupters didn't work although their cloaks left them open to attack. They had been forced to quickly land on one of the bridges. The bridge itself was damaged and couldn't be crossed, but they landed on the side closest to the keep and ran under full blaster attack, with only their personal shields for cover. Up on the tower was a gun emplacement, just above where the bridge entered the keep. The bridge was shuddering from weapons impacts, but return fire sent the enemy under cover enough for Shet and his companions to get into the keep itself. It was Shet who ultimately saved their lives at that moment. Entering the keep, the warriors faced a wall of enemy troops and a concentrated line of fire. Shet leapt over his supposed protectors and was among the enemy and fighting in his battle trance! Sword in one hand and blaster in the other, Shet wrecked havoc among the enemy, cutting them down. It was enough for Kit, Melki and the two Zioronians to get in and finish the job. They now had a solid foothold with most of the enemy below them.

"Got to move quick! Quick!!!" Melki called to everyone.

Shet knew enough to stop for a bit as Niamah, Al, Surreya and Hilli literally flew forward, laying down a lot of fire down the corridor. Enemies hiding inside rooms were taken out. Scanners in their helms gave them all a good idea of the layout ahead, but enemy troops had shielding that prevented them from being seen clearly. The twelve attackers were now in enemy territory. Newton and Rainbow followed along, taking out door locks and throwing heavy grenades.

Everyone had a job to do. Mrorna led the way deeper into the corridors of the keep, with Kit right beside her. She stopped near some large pipes that ran up through the building.

Newton and Rainbow joined her.

"Those are main power conduits that run up to the roof and power the defensive shields around the Ring Tower." Mrorna told them.

"Put remote charges here." Kit said, "We can blow them if we need to."

Newton set them and then they moved forward. For a bit, Niamah, Al, Hilli, Surreya, Tarmal and Fay spent some time clearing the entire floor of the keep they were on of enemy troops and they blocked the lifts and stairwells also with booby traps.

"It is interesting." Shet said to Kit and Mrorna as they watched Newton and Rainbow looking in some of the rooms and placing more explosive charges, "Those explosives look different from the ones they put onto the power conduits. The tactic is to blow holes upwards and attack the next level that way?"

Melki was off doing something else. His eyes were closed and Kit knew that he was astral travelling, either taking on the traces of dead Pandemons or having a spy around.

"There are only five floors above us to the main control area of the Ring Tower." Mrorna said, "We are very close. Graud knows we are here though. He will be waiting for us."

"I think we get that." Kit responded with a smile, "Melki will have a plan."

Even as they spoke, it was obvious from the explosive impacts from below and above that Grim had the full force of the host attacking on all fronts to keep the enemy busy and give them a chance to succeed.

Melki came out of his trance and called everyone to him.

"Ok, we blow the conduit and all the explosive charges," he said, "but we go up together here as one group en-mass. But we don't stop, we keep going, blasting holes all the way to the top. We attack Graud at the heart of his nest as quickly and violently as possible. Alright, ready to go?"

Everyone nodded.

"Lock and load." Said Al, grinning and patting his blaster.

It was meant to be quick and it was. The whole floor of the keep rocked with huge explosions and in the middle of the fire, they flew upwards through the hole they blew open, dropping grenades behind them as they continued upwards. The enemy had almost no time to respond as their shielding inside the building was inadequate. Melki led the way upwards. The concussive force of each punch through the floor above was massive and nerve shattering, but necessary. Suddenly they were through to the roof and the Ring Tower that was above. At each floor, Newton had fired rockets at certain key points, not to kill enemy but to take out technology, especially the technology that kept Graud's portal system going. They were doing damage that was really hurting the enemy and they knew that once they stopped at the top, the troops would be upon them like a swarm of angry hornets! By now, the whole keep was shuddering and likely to collapse! Graud stood on top of the altar stone holding the portal staff key in one hand and the original portal stone he'd stolen from Utnapishtim in his other hand.

Pandemonium warriors were everywhere, but they were confused and uncertain. All around the Ring, the big trilithons were flashing electrical discharge as the system was crashing. The twelve blasted at anything that moved, but with Melki in front and Shet just behind him, they pushed right at Graud. Enemy troops fell like flies or hid behind standing stones or nearby consoles. Newton and Rainbow, guarded by Surreya and Hilli got to one of the outer sarsen stones and immediately they attached an interface device and connected to the A.I. of the Ring. Al, Niamah, Tarmal and Fay were killing anything that moved. Graud himself was screaming, not with fear but rage! He punched the Portal Key Staff down into the altar stone and twisted it. The stone in his other hand began to glow with a powerful blue light. A portal began to form in front of him, but not like other portals, it was more like a spinning vortex.

"It's a pocket dimension!!!" Rainbow cried, "He could swallow us whole!!"

Kit, Melki and Mrorna were howling war cries! Melki picked up a Pandemon and threw him into the vortex. But the vortex was also sucking things in as well! Graud watched with anguish as his personal Shrike, who was nearby, got caught in the gravitational forces and sucked in, screaming! The forces were too strong and Kit, Melki and Mrorna pulled back behind nearby Trilithons. But then, it was Shet, not pulling back, but running towards Graud, that let the forces catch him and as he passed one of the central Trilithons, he pushed off with his legs, with all his strength within his battle trance state. The mighty leap pushed him up and over the top of the vortex and down, right on top of Graud where he was standing! Shet brought his sword down, cutting off Graud's extended right hand holding the portal stone! Hand, still clutching the stone, flew upwards and into the vortex! Graud was screaming now in agony as Shet crashed down behind him and using both legs kicked Graud off the altar stone. Shet pulled the Staff from the altar stone and as Graud stumbled forward he brought it up between Graud's legs and lifted! Graud rose up and the gravity well of the now dying vortex caught him and sucked him in, doing to him, what Graud had hoped to do to Shet. The vortex itself lingered briefly, but no longer sustained by the Stone nor Staff, then simply winked out of existence.

But the drama wasn't over yet. There was a loud grinding sound. The whole fortress was swaying and the Portal Ring Tower was erupting great electrical bolts of energy into the sky.

From down on the ground, Grim and the others could see the energy discharges, but they could also see that it wasn't just the fortress that was swaying, but the entire island they were on with a huge earthquake! Out in the forest, Rom and his warriors watched the Bursar open portals and teleport away. One of the leaders, perhaps it was Kayyin himself who actually waved at Rom, just before he stepped through the last portal.

Rom screamed at his warriors, "Back to the fortress!" he beckoned, "We need to evacuate now!"

At the fortress itself, Grim, Raph and the Elemental leaders were gathering their troops and preparing to escape. What was left of the enemy were fleeing either into the forest or down to the harbour and to their boats. Grim knew from what he was seeing that they wouldn't escape what was about to happen. Some enemy Shrikes could be seen fleeing, but most of the enemy were stuck on the ground. Or so he thought, as looking up at the lightning above, Grim could just make out spheres of energy and within the spheres were the missing second fleet that Graud was preparing.

"Shit! Oh SHIT!" Newton bellowed as he worked with the interface device. Rainbow too looked horrified.

"What is it?" Kit yelled above the noise of the growing earthquake, barely able to stand.

"We've done too much damage to the Ring system and it's destabilising. There are all sorts of random portals and other crap opening everywhere. The A.I. can't shut down the programs and so has gone into a self-destruct sequence! So bloody typical!" Newton cried.

"We have to get out of here!" Melki called.

"There's no doing that!" Newton shook his head, "When this Ring goes, it will send out an electrical shock wave that will not only destroy the island, but render all electro-dynamic flight impossible! We won't be able to escape it!"

"We have to find another way!" Shet cried.

For a moment it seemed hopeless, but then Rainbow saw something in the interface screen.

"There's one program still running!" She cried, then she looked up, "Look up there!!!"

They all looked up. There above them, within their field bubbles were hundreds of enemy ships, just hovering there. The big airships had been refitted and upgraded but when the Bursar had attacked, their crews and dragons had gone to fight and left the big ships unguarded, except for their shields and a few crew.

"Why are they still there?" Kit asked the obvious question, "Why not fight or teleport away?"

"It's because they were programmed by the Ring A.I. to stay in position until Graud put them into stasis and then placed them where and when he wanted them. The stasis fields switch on in about ten minutes."

"Ten minutes!" Kit cried, "I think we can do it! Grim, are you there?"

A few minutes later, all the Renim with their passengers were flying up towards the awaiting airships. The skeleton crews on board the zeppelins gave up without a fight and were quickly secured. Some of the warriors were unloaded aboard the enemy ships, but most remained within the holds of the Renim, who hovered next to the airships or on the empty dragon decks.

Down on the top of the Keep, Newton and Rainbow were busy working with the Ring A.I. through the interface device, while Al had the captured staff at the altar stone, doing some work to control the Ring as it was quickly self-destructing.

"The rest of you get up to one of those airships!" Al told the others, "I'll stay here with Newton and Rainbow until we are finished and I'll fly them up before the stasis fields switch on and the whole place destroys itself!"

"Ok my friend," Kit told him, "but don't be late!"

"You know me!"

"Yes we do!" Niamah came up and kissed her son, "We will see you up there soon. We will bring us all home."

The others flew up to the airships and joined those waiting there. The three remained behind to finish the program and keep things from falling apart.

Shortly, "It's done!" Newton cried, "Let's get outta here!!"

Still holding the staff, Al flew over to Newton and Rainbow and they flew upwards.

Then, not long after that, there was a flash of silver light as the stasis fields around the big airships came on, and they vanished into time. This was followed, only moments later by the Ring Tower itself glowing with a hot blue light and sending great waves of electrical discharge into the sky! Then there was a huge explosion.

Kayyin was standing on a peak on the Nodin coastline to the distant west. He saw the explosion rise like a second sun in the east. He smiled to himself and waited for the sound of it to reach him.

Chapter Thirty-Five

Atlantis Island

The Daedalus had simply vanished off our screens. My two deck officers Paq and Shara, immediately began a global scanner search, while the communication channels were searched.

"We have a faint signal," Shara reported, "but it is being jammed."

The location came up in the middle of the North Atlantic.

"The scanners are detecting atmospheric displacement," Pac added, "two large objects. It's the Daedalus and a landmass."

"Looks like we've found something." I said to them, "I think I know what it is. Shara, contact Selki and the Lady, it's battle stations."

The Daedalus was under heavy attack, both from within and from without. Captain John James could see things clearly on the ship screens, but he and his deck crew could also hear the enemy right outside the door trying to cut their way in. All of them were fully suited up and armed, just in case the enemy broke through. Barricades were up and the deck guards were ready, but John and his crew also had to fly the ship and fight the enemy outside. The enemy ships that had jumped into Daedalus' hold and then teleported themselves, along with the Daedalus were now trying to get out of the hold to the outside. Fass had brought the Arrow around and was blocking their way. There was a full blown scrap going on. There was no room for using the big guns, but large numbers of troops from both sides, along with E.D.V.s, Renim and Shrikes were dogfighting in among the deck structures.

But from on the Daedalus bridge, they could also see the big airships hovering outside and the Sphere rising above the island nearby. Dragons were flying towards them in their hundreds, perhaps thousands, both from the airships and from below. Haunebu saucers were also flying up from below.

"We are being jammed," the communications officer reported, "but I think we are still detectable by the scanner grid."

"We are going to need all the help we can get shortly." The Captain growled, "Prepare to open fire, all defensive batteries, fire at will."

Within the hold of the Daedalus, the Arrow was moving in for the kill. Fass stood on the bridge and she was looking intently at the remaining enemy airships that continued to fight them.

Flying up from below were all of Arrow's Pylon shuttles, about twenty of them. They were loaded up with hundreds of American marines and sailors, newly equipped with power-suits and blasters and ready for some payback.

The Arrow had a big gun under the front of the ship, and although probably a bit powerful for the interior of the Daedalus, Fass had decided to use it. They fired at the airships, causing desolation. The enemy ships would normally teleport out, but it was too tight inside now and they couldn't while all their troops were engaged.

Fass knew that she had them dead in her sights and she was grinning. The shuttles reached the Daedalus bridge and Weaver led the Americans as they boarded. There were dragons and their Anakim guards waiting for them. The Americans, with no experience in using the advanced technology, nevertheless held up very well and their officers led the charge to take the landing deck. Weaver got a group of marines, mixed with a few Petra troopers into the landing deck control centre and there they confronted some Gorenge who attacked viciously!

"Trust in your shields mates!" Weaver encouraged the Americans through their helm coms, "Just keep pushing forward!"

And they did, using their blasters to shoot down the Gorenge as they came forward. The Petra Order troopers pulled out their edged and other assorted blunt weapons when the Gorenge got too close and Weaver led them in the hand to hand combat. The fighting was violent and bloody and shields on both sides could only take so much and with shield failure there followed death. The Americans did their best to keep up and their blaster fire cover saved a lot of lives. It didn't take long and the Gorenge were dead. Others were still fighting the Anakim who were out on the flight deck, but Weaver had to move quickly and deeper into the bridge platform.

"We need you Weaver!" Virey was calling to him via helm com, "We can't get to these guys in here, there's too many of them and they have nearly cut through to the bridge itself!"

Within the bridge, they could see sparks coming through the main door where the cutters were burning through.

Weaver, his troops and the marines, including Captain Burgess himself, came upon the large group of New Guards that were guarding the underneath approach to the bridge. Pushing forward with concentrated fire along multiple corridors, the enemy found themselves quickly overwhelmed, although at a price. Virey and his force renewed their own attack at the same time, using support and new grenades brought in by the American relief.

The enemy near the bridge door suddenly broke through with their cutters, and pushed from behind, they kicked the door down and threw grenades into the bridge. The barricades held, but some guards died. The enemy pushed in through the smoke. The deck crew and the remaining knights fought back desperately. Normally they would have been quickly defeated by the superior numbers coming in, but Weaver and his troops came up from behind and took the enemy attacking down.

Virey came in shortly after and Weaver brought Burgess forward to meet John James. They were all grinning through their helm visors and shook hands together like old friends.

As for the airships, they were unable to stop the Excalibur and Humdrid boarders. Like pirates of old, the Humdrid landed on the dragon decks or the gondolas underneath and then cut their way in, then fighting hand to hand with the enemy troops and crew members they found there. The Humdrid were merciless and vicious fighters and their arsenals of weaponry were formidable for this kind of close quarters fighting. Many of the New Guard soldiers leapt to their deaths rather than face the Humdrid.

Meanwhile, enemy dragons were landing on the outer hull of the Daedalus. Many were on the dome that covered the top of the huge ship. The top of the Daedalus was covered by a clear roof underneath which was the ship's environmental zone. Daedalus was large enough to have a fully landscaped habitat under that dome, including hills, rivers, lakes, plants and animals and three distinct climates. There were ten towers spaced along the spine of the big ship, rising up from within the habitat zone below and acting as docking stations where they came out above the dome. The enemy dragons attacked these docking towers. The Daedalus' powerful weapons batteries were fired at the enemy until their crews were killed or the guns disabled. Enemy troops, mostly Anakim and some New Guards managed to board the Daedalus from outside and descend into the habitation zone.

On the Daedalus bridge, James got his bridge crew back to their stations while the Order and Americans helped clear up some of the mess. One of the Americans who arrived at the bridge right then was Captain Johann R Simon. Burgess introduced him to Virey and Weaver as Zealot.

"We have boarders in the habitation zone." Captain John James told everyone loudly, "Sorry that there will be no rest yet for you guys."

"Download the specs then." Virey replied.

"The quickest way to get there is to fly the bridge up to one of the zone entry points." The bridge crew were already making it happen according to their captain's wishes, "We will need the shuttles for combat outside very shortly. In fact, we are facing imminent attack from outside by enemy fleet ships and it looks like we've found the Atlantis Splinter."

"We were all captured and taken there." Zealot said, "But I was free and managed to have a good look around before I stowed away on the Gerald."

"Very good that." James nodded, "We will be able to use you I'm sure when we go down there. We can also use any intelligence you have right now."

One of the Daedalus bridge crew led Zealot over to the main scanner screens and immediately began to look at the exterior scans of the island below. Zealot began pointing and telling the scanner tech what was what.

"We are coming up on zone entry four, the Plazashan tower." The helmsman informed everyone.

"Get your troops to the flight deck." James ordered, "You will deploy directly onto the lower landing platforms."

Details of the layout and scanner readings of the Plazashan tower were already being fed into the helms of the Order troops and the Americans coming directly from the A.I. and the Daedalus tactical officer. "The enemy have infiltrated via towers five and six. We have people already fighting them there."

Virey, Weaver and Burgess led their people to the flight deck. Zealot wanted to go too, but James asked him to stay, "We need you in tactical for now." he explained, "When we send troops down to the island we need to know everything you know and I'll need you to lead them. Are you up for it?"

"Yes Sir!" Zealot saluted.

"Get me Fass on Arrow," James ordered, "Open a channel to all remaining wings. New orders. All wings, bar refuelling, all squadrons are to immediately deploy to defend the Daedalus from attack by enemy ships from outside. We are under imminent threat."

Fass' face appeared on a screen, "What about the Atlantis Splinter Sphere?" she asked.

"They aren't targeting us directly because they want to capture us." James said, "That's what all this drama has been about. But we managed to upset their plans quite a bit. Still the enemy might decide we aren't worth it if things don't go their way soon. We have to engage those airships and there will be an attack from the ground too no doubt. Fass, you need to hit that Sphere. It won't be easy."

"On the way." Fass nodded and her face disappeared from the screen.

"All our squadrons are away." The scanner officer said, "The bridge is docking with zone four entry port one."

"God go with you all." James prayed as the troops deployed from the bridge flight deck onto the entry port deck and squadrons of pylon fighters, E.D.V.s and some Renim, along with bigger platforms and the Arrow left the hold.

As soon as Virey, Weaver and Burgess got their people across, the bridge pulled away into the relative safety of the open space of the hold.

"We need all remaining units, including the reserves and trainees to be assembled for ground deployment via a portal drop." James looked at a screen with remaining personnel numbers and casualty lists, he wasn't happy with what he saw, "And I want to make a further contract with the Humdrid, we are going to need them too."

The Daedalus was a huge ship, really huge. She was something like fifty kilometres long and a lot of space within the big ship was still left empty. When the enemy dirigibles entered the hold, there was a lot of space to manoeuvre. The areas where people lived and worked on the Daedalus included a forward dormitory area, the small craft fighter and shuttle bays in the middle port side and the large ship bays, engineering, and a section on the middle starboard they called the academy, which was where troops trained, assembled and were deployed from. During the battle, the Humdrid had basically stormed and boarded the enemy ships and New Guard troops that attempted to cross over to the main deck areas were tracked down and eliminated. There had been fighting all over the place. The fiercest fighting of course had been on the bridge, but the Humdrid had been keeping themselves very busy. Eventually the enemy airships, or what was left of them, had been tractor beamed and then dry docked and medical and engineering personnel got stuck into the cleaning up, while the Order hunted down any remaining enemies in the lower decks. Now, most of those troops were being assembled at the academy. The bridge was flown over to its docking station at the academy and Captain James, accompanied by Zealot, went to speak to them. The Daedalus Danu first officer and bridge crew, with the help of Zealots' local knowledge, began to face the enemy in the skies.

Captain James met with the battle leaders in the academy citadel. There was a wide window overlooking the wide open colosseum-like space they called the red deck, because of the red sand there. The battle groups were being assembled, including a large number of war constructs. The battle leaders included a Behan Sidhe Dwarf-lord, a tall Tuatha Danann woman, a dark skinned Lemurian, three human Order officers, of whom one, a woman was a reserve leader, and of course, there was the Humdrid battle chief, his battle wagon was outside, so he had come "in skin".

"I don't have a lot of time here," James addressed them, "but this is going to be a tough one. Our intelligence is that we are going to be up against Anakim, Gorenge and Valorians. There are Baal lords down there too. Our usual target for any Splinter is to take the Portal Ring. There will be thralls there. Most of the time they don't fight, but sometimes they do. We are downloading scanner specs and intelligence into your helm A.I.'s now. We need to do this quickly so that we can drop over the horizon, just in case that Splinter Sphere is used to take us down. But if we can take the island, we will have another Splinter and will have defeated the Atalanti. It is time to pray for the troops."

Below the window facing the red deck was a stairway down to the deck itself. As Captain James and the battle commanders stepped out, the whole assembly cheered. James raised his arms. The Humdrid returned to his battle wagon, watching with interest the proceedings. James prayed, "To the Sovereign Divine One, we give ourselves as living sacrifices and lay our lives down for the cause of light! Give us victory this day against the enemy that we may not only defend but prevail. Give us courage and defend us as we fight, in the Name of Yeshua."

Thousands of voices as one said, "Amen."

At the bow end of the red deck the big portal generators started to hum. A line of portals opened, and with a loud cry, the troops ran forward.

James quickly led Captain Simon over to the reserve battle leader.

"Reserve Battle Leader June Harvey," James introduced them, "Captain Simon former United States Navy wing commander, called Zealot. Zealot has been there before and knows the terrain. Use him Harvey to help you get to the Ring quickly.

The quicker we take the Ring, the better it will be. Zealot, Harvey's team are good people. You will do well together. Time to go."

Everyone shook hands and Zealot joined Harvey and her battle group as they went through the portal.

James returned to the bridge. It didn't take long to see that it was worse than he's thought. The enemy were incredibly numerous and their big airships were moving in close, forming a wall of fire before them. Both the Daedalus and the enemy fleets had good shielding, but it would give out eventually and then it would begin to hurt for real. The Daedalus had one thing going for her, she was big and had big guns. The air wings from the Daedalus, led by the Arrow, didn't fly forward between the big ships into the fire zone between them, which was suicidal, but instead fanned out in a wide net hoping to fly over or under or around the big enemy ships, avoid getting blasted and so take on the wings of dragons and enemy Haunebu E.D.V.s and Shrikes.

The enemy ability to teleport made the battle extremely difficult. Dragons were constantly teleporting close into the Daedalus hoping to breach the shields and drop boarders or fire weapons. The big enemy dirigibles kept moving too, making it difficult to target them. The line of heavy fire kept changing and the smaller fighters and battle platforms often found themselves caught in the middle. The Arrow faced particularly heavy fire and damage, but also gave as good as she got. With advanced Zioronian technology, better weapons and manoeuvrability, Fass had her crew push the ship to her limits. Surrounded by a wall of Pylon fighters and shuttles, the Arrow threw herself at the big enemy ships and used her primary weapon to inflict terrible damage. One of the enemy airships exploded violently and fell burning into the ocean.

Despite the bravery of the fighter pilots, and those aboard Arrow, the enemy ships were just too numerous and more and more of the enemy were getting past the defenders and aboard the Daedalus.

Virey, Weaver and Burgess had already met the enemy in the habitation zone. Automated security systems helped stop a lot of them, but more and more of the enemy were getting through. They now controlled three towers and they were bringing dragons down through the docking cores to the interior of the big ship.

The defenders divided into three groups, with Excalibur officers joining with the Americans to provide technical aid. It was a steep learning curve for the Americans to get used to the powered battle suits, the flight sleds and energy weapons that they now were forced to use. But they did excellently, and having escaped from their own thraldom, they were determined to prove themselves. The cores of the towers were for small ships to fly through and now there were enemy dragons and their crews inside, trying to cut down through the docking doors. Pandemonium and Valorian forces in their black uniforms had occupied the lower levels and had spilled out into the habitation zone. It was there in the forests and fields of the habitation zone that the defenders counter attacked the occupied towers. Virey, leading mostly Zioronians, held position under the fourth tower, where they had entered, while Weaver took his Order troops to the fifth tower and Burgess headed for the third tower. They moved quickly, using flying sleds on their boots and were cloaked when they attacked the enemy sentries. Virey's forces climbed up through the fourth tower, opening doors that had been locked to the enemy. They struck first and with complete surprise and success. Moving quickly, Virey had his Zioronians find their positions first and then attacked simultaneously, entering the occupied levels of the tower and also the core. They killed whatever they found there, whether it was men or dragons. Ten dragons were caught in the core of the tower and killed, along with their crews and the troops they had carried in. As Virey's knights climbed up the tower, they locked the doors behind themselves, leaving sentries. There were five dragons and their passengers found, just landed on the top of the Daedalus and about to enter. They were attacked without hesitation and before they could teleport away, the enemy were taken down.

Similar battles were going on in the two other enemy occupied towers, with very similar results. Enemy forces were just not large enough to put up an effective fight. But that was still just the beginning. Retaking the towers and repairing the defensive systems that had been damaged was the first step. More dragons were making it past the shields and landing. The three teams divided again, occupying all the towers and preparing to defend against any further attacks.

Zealot and the reserves came through the portal right in the middle of the main hanger of the Atlantis Rath. Battle Leader Harvey led her troops forward and formed a line against enemy forces who were already returning fire. Zealot got his bearings and realised that they were actually very close to the main passage that led into the main plaza where the Rath Ring was. But then it became very obvious who their opponents were, they were Gorenge, with a few Valorian officers. Zealot remembered them from when he was hiding on the island, before stowing away aboard the Gerald. He pointed this fact out to Harvey, who simply nodded, then she pulled out her battle mace, "We'll have to fight them up close." She grinned.

Zealot had also been given a mace, which he hefted to get the feel of it, "We actually fight with blunt weapons?"

"Our shields mean that we have to fight up close," Harvey said, "Just stick close to me."

Harvey called to her troops, "We hold the line!"

"We hold the line!" they shouted in reply, "Faith is power!"

With that the line began to run forward toward the enemy down the wide corridor. Both sides were firing their energy weapons at one another, but as Harvey said, their suit shields largely protected them from major harm. Being hit though was like a punch and exploding shrapnel and blaster fire would eventually deplete even the best shields.

Moments later they were among the enemy. The Gorenge had gauntlet blasters and their clawed feet and hand talons were sheathed in long shielded blades. Their helms had jaw guards that enabled them to open their mouths and although shielded, they could use their teeth to grasp and crush. Zealot didn't know what to expect, he just ran headlong and collided with the Gorenge that rose up before him! Screaming with rage and determination he swung his mace again and again!

Like an unstoppable force, James brought the Daedalus relentlessly forward towards the island. Getting in close meant more protection from the power sphere over the Rath and the island could be used as a shield against the enemy airships. The Atlantis Rath of course had shielding of its own, but this close, the guns of the Daedalus were still devastating. But enemy dragons were still teleporting under Daedalus' shields and putting warheads into her side. Protective gun turrets were unable to stop all of them. Virey, Weaver and Burgess were still busy securing the towers and resisting boarders. It was obvious though, this couldn't go on indefinitely, the enemy were just too numerous as they poured up from the surface of the island.

Then suddenly and without warning there was a massive E.M.P. The Daedalus since her repairs had shielded electronics, but some systems still failed and the big ship shook as the electro-dynamic drives worked to adjust.

"What have we got?" James asked his bridge crew.

"Collapsing stasis fields!" the scanner tech officer reported, "Hundreds of them! The resonation frequencies are the same as the first wave of attack!"

"Another enemy fleet?!" James looked at the big screens as the scanner data appeared.

There they were, hundreds of new airships. There was also a weather report coming in, a super storm was forming around them and the sky over the island was already going dark as the clouds gathered. But there was something about the formation of the airships that made James take a second look.

"They're not doing anything." He said.

"Incoming coded message." The communications officer announced.

"Open it." James ordered.

"Greetings Daedalus from the Antediluvian mission team," A cheerful voice said, "Hi Dad, it's Newton, and we have brought friends with us!"

"Newton!!!" James cried, "Was the mission a success??!!"

"Most certainly!" Newton replied, "We are prepared to give assistance."

"Assistance would be most appreciated right now!!!"

"On the way!"

Immediately the new airships teleported and then reappeared right among the enemy. They opened fire without any hesitation.

"Mark those ships as friendlies!" James told his crew, "Tell all our people to not open fire on the marked ships."

The launch doors of the airships gondolas opened. This time is was wings of Renim that flew out, with Hilli and Surreya leading the way!

"Newton," James sent a message, "we have combat forces down on the ground."

"We have forces of our own." Newton replied, "We will deliver them."

The Order inter-ship security codes switched on and the ship A.I.s talked to each other. On the control screens of the Daedalus, what had been red markers signifying enemy ships turned the green of friendlies.

"We are scanning other friendly markers," the scanner officer reported, "coming in from space. It's Eagle, Lady Guinevere, Selki and Two Trees."

Chapter Thirty-Six

Facing the Darkness

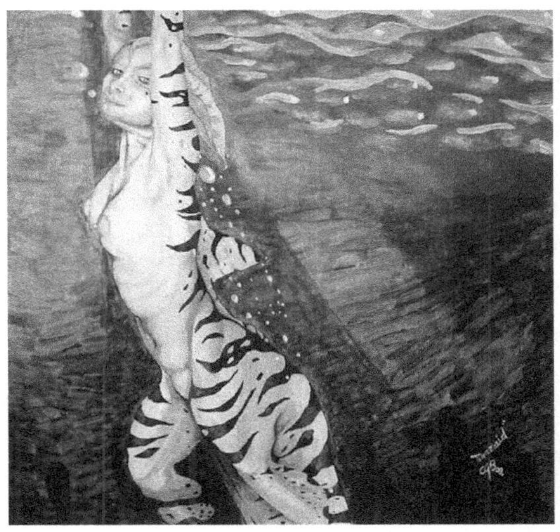

E.D.V. Two Trees was another capital ship that guarded the Zion Rath at Jerusalem. Her captain was Michael. He had with him a force of Danu and Malakim knights.

Not long after we went to full alert and battle stations, the Two Trees joined our group and I immediately gave the flag to Michael. We cloaked and headed into orbit over Europe, then came back down over the North Atlantic. From high in the atmosphere we still couldn't clearly scan what was going on below, but when the E.M.P. happened, our scanners suddenly had clear sensor readings. Looking at the Holo-tank aboard Eagle, I could quickly see the situation below. Red and green markers were lighting up before our eyes. Ship A.I.s talked to each other and Michael's face appeared in the holo-tank.

"We go in shooting." He said, "You three put your troops on the ground, I'll send mine over to the Daedalus. We are facing the full might of the Atalanti as well as Graud's forces here."

"This is where they were doing the refits on the big ships and the new arms and gear." Finvara added, "We need to take the Rath intact if we can."

"There are marked units already on the ground." My first officer Paq reported ship scanners were giving details and the A.I. sent the data, "We should have communications shortly."

Fass' face appeared in the holo-tank. The acting captain of the Arrow looked tired.

"Greetings friends," she smiled, "sending encrypted data to your A.I.s. It's so good to have some more help. Those other marked airships, that's our people, the mission has returned."

I was grinning. I would have my family back shortly, once we won this battle.

John James appeared beside Fass in another viewing window in the holo-tank. Data streams were running as we connected into the Daedalus A.I.

"John!" Michael cried, "How can we assist?"

"We have a problem with boarders," the Daedalus captain replied, "and we need air support really badly."

"Launch all wings." Michael ordered, "Arthur, the Lady and Two Trees to guard and support the Daedalus. Walter, you and Fin help Arrow disable the sphere before they decide to fire the primary weapon. We are on the way."

From the Eagle and Lady Guinevere we launched our Wedge fighters while the A'sidhe and Malakim launched swarms of Renim. Our four capital ships descended into the fray. At the same time I had Paq and Shara prepare the troops. James had sent tactical maps of the island and we used our own scanners to quickly plan drop points. Paq did most of the tactical work for that, just before he and Shara left the bridge for the portal room, putting their helms on and barking orders to their troops. Shara wore a red cross on the top of her helm and shoulders, and would lead medical teams to the ground. On the holo-tank I watched the Lady and Two Trees swing up beside the long hull of the Daedalus. They flew down the length of the big ship, using needler weapons to strike at the enemy dragons and fighters that buzzed around them. Portals opened on top of the clear canopy over the habitation zone near each of the towers and Michael's Angel Knights went in. My own people went in shortly after. We opened portals down on the island and I sent them to battle with a prayer.

Down in the Rath, Harvey's reservists had joined forces in support of the Humdrid, who had quickly taken on the Gorenge, literally cutting them to pieces using their formidable scythe blades. Zealot heard the new orders in his helm coming from the Daedalus. Help had come and fresh troops, more of these Petra people were coming. Despite getting into the Rath itself, the inner areas had powerful wards placed over them, which meant that no-one could use portals to get into the heart of the island. Enemy forces were numerous and well equipped and they were fighting back viciously. Zealot saw the portals open up behind him. The troops who came through were unusual, with armour styled like Ancient Roman plate, but also with neck torcs and decorative tartan trims and patches over their armour. These were the Cymbrogi, and their battle leader was Arthur himself, who preferred to take the fight personally, leaving his ship in the hands of his first officer. With the Cymbrogi was also a small force of Pigrians. Zealot didn't know it but Finvara's Ghost Warriors were deploying in another part of the Rath, while outside the Rath, Renim were landing and opening their fields to drop their passengers. My own troops formed four units, the main group led by Paq, demolition and engineering led by Boris Rujansky, lancers riding battle constructs led by Vassilli Zabolotsky and the medical team led by Shara.

Overhead, the dogfighting was still happening, and the two fleets continued to shoot at each other. Before, the enemy just had to deal with the Daedalus, the Arrow and their small ships, but now they were outnumbered. The sphere over the centre of the island began to glow ominously. With sudden violence, the sphere spat three great bolts of energy, one after the other. The first destroyed one of the captured airships, the second struck the Daedalus in the bow, opening a huge gaping wound and the third struck the Lady Guinevere, sending her down in flames!

The sphere was powering up to fire again as I brought Eagle in to attack, with Selki to my right and Arrow between us. We wouldn't have a second chance this time, it was do or die. Our two big capital ships flew wide, while Arrow flew low and straight. Smaller guns on the rim of the caldera below the sphere were firing at our big ships while the Arrow flew an avoidance pattern,

Fass putting the Zioronian warship into a random spin end over end. The muzzle of the primary weapon on the sphere's surface turned towards Eagle and was glowing and about to fire, just as the Arrow straightened and flew underneath the sphere! With a single shot of their main weapon, Arrow fired almost point blank at the sphere. There was a horrible sound, almost like a scream and electrical discharge flowed over the sphere. Then the sphere lurched sideways and fell heavily into the caldera below. The sphere crashed down into the main docking area, destroying the landing cradles and setting the whole docking bay area alight. There were some huge explosions as power generators overloaded and plasma containment conduits were broken.

Inside the Rath and indeed, the whole island was shaken by the explosions. Fortunately for the enemy, they had closed the heavy bay doors that led down into the main Ring plaza located immediately below the sphere. If those doors had been open, the sphere would have fallen down and destroyed the Ring, which would have been a big loss.

Hilli and Surreya had landed not far from the main entrance of the Rath, along with a lot of the other Kerubim Renim. They had shut down their fields and the armies of Eden along with their armoured war animals were deployed. Others had deployed down near the port or on any large open area they could find. The Order forces that had entered the Rath with their portals had quickly occupied and opened the main doors into the interior of the Rath. They had only been able to do so because of the intelligence that Zealot had been able to supply. Shet was still riding in his war behemoth and in fact had never left it once Hilli had picked it and her team up from Gog Magog, before its destruction, which had taken place many thousands of years before. There hadn't been a lot of time from then, relatively speaking, for the passengers aboard the captured airships to take control and work out how to fly them. When the stasis fields had activated, they didn't immediately reach zero resonation but had to resonate down as the stasis field stabilised. There had been room in the docking bays of the airships for some of the Renim to drop some of the troops. The Kerubim had quickly taken over the airships, subdued the crews and using deep empathic mind techniques learned what had to be learned, just as the stasis fields reached the point of zero resonation. Around 12,000 years had gone by in an instant. Then, before the stasis fields had fully collapsed, they began to resonate, venting huge amounts of kinetic and magnetic and gravitational energy. By the time the captured fleet had resonated to the same frequency as the world around them, they had control of the ships and all the Renim and their passengers were in the docking bays or hovering between the gondolas.

Shet looked up, along with a lot of others, as the storm quickly intensified. Lightning was spiking down onto the island and tornadoes were forming out over the ocean. The sound of the wind and thunder was ear-splitting!!! Rom, riding on the shoulders of a tri-horn and leading other Romany riders forward approached the entrance to the Rath. The Order troops on guard there looked at the ancient warriors on their dinosaur mounts with great unease, but also relief.

Boris Rujansky and Shara had set up a headquarters under a huge overhang of rock. The big Russian engineer got a message in his helm and ran out with some guards into the wind. It had also started to rain, the torrents falling like great waves! He could see three constructs approaching. Boris activated his boot sleds and hovered up to see the riders in the first construct. Riding in the seats, it was Kit, Mrorna and Al. They opened their helms in greeting. Niamah, Tarmal and Fay were in the second construct. Surreya, Melki and Hilli were riding the third. Grim was riding with Shet in the lead behemoth, while Newton and Rainbow had remained aboard the lead airship.

"Welcome back to 2018!" Boris yelled over the wind, "We are thankful you are here!"

"How can we help?" Kit called back, "These uniforms still don't have interface with the tactical computers."

"We have battle-groups inside, Order infantry, lancers, and Humdrid mercs." Boris replied, "The Rath complex is huge and there just aren't enough of us. There are other entrances to the Rath around the island as well as enemy bunkers, gun emplacements and we need troops out here to secure the island. Your big beasts and some of your force can help with that. But we need fighters inside too."

Boris reached into a pouch on his tool belt and produced what looked like a small mobile phone.

"Got a router here for helm interface." He explained as he tossed it up to kit, "It should just scan the frequencies and connect you in."

"Thanks," Kit plugged the router into a connection on the side of his helm, "we will need language translation for most of these people."

"The ship A.I.s will have all the ancient languages on file," Boris nodded, "and we can bring all the forces under one command."

"Good." Kit knew who that meant, "Thanks Boris, we will get it sorted."

Boris and his guards turned back to the command post, while Kit led the three constructs back to Shet's behemoth. The construct Kit was riding helped him up to the carriage and Kit climbed in out of the rain to speak with Shet and Grim. Melki also climbed in and so did Raph and his Ren Torq. Already with Shet and Grim were the Deborah Queen and her Tecorah battle commander. The Ziv leader stood with them. Rom was there representing the Stone Tribes, and the Elementals were there too. The Elementals had all taken on physical forms that were more human in appearance, although their bodies flowed with elemental power. The Aesir was a pale grey colour, the Astari glowed with an inner fire, yet gave off no heat. The Terrestrial had the form of a huge man, stooping low in the cramped carriage. The Gaean had a green tinge to her skin.

"We have a data link to the Order ship A.I.s" Kit said to Grim, then turned to Shet, "We can now receive orders from my people."

"Then we will serve and fight." Shet replied, "What is the will of the commander?"

"Our forces are outnumbered and fighting hard inside the Rath." Kit explained, "The island itself needs to be occupied and any enemies in the jungles hunted down and destroyed. The Rath has a number of entrances that need to be found and occupied so the enemy do not escape or find ways to attack us from behind. But help is also needed inside the Rath."

"My people are already leading the Stone Tribes to guard our position." Said Rom, "We have tri-horns ready for battle."

"We need to act quickly and get into the fight." Grim added, "We are already in the air battle, joining our captured airships and our Renim to the fight."

"Rom." Shet took Rom by the hand, "Take your Romany and the Stone tribes, find these other entrances and hold them. Fight and kill any enemies you find outside the Rath. Use the behemoths and tri-horns to destroy any enemy strongholds."

"I will go immediately." Rom bowed, then went out into the storm.

"Most of the Deborah and the Ziv are flying the airships with some of the Renim of the Kerubim." Shet continued, "But some of you and all of the Tecorah are here. Melki and Raph, you are leading most of the Kerubim. The rest of us, including the Tecorah, need to help within the Rath."

"And what of us?" the Aesir asked.

"Grim has told me that we need to secure the power sphere of this Rath, which contains the Rath Artificial Intelligence and so the means by which we can control the Ring." Shet told him, "May the Deborah and Ziv who are here with us go with the Elementals to secure the sphere?"

The Deborah made clicking sounds and swaying movements with her body. The Ziv bobbed up and down and hissed.

"They both agree." The Aesir translated, "We will also go immediately."

"We all have work to do." Said Shet.

The Daedalus was badly damaged and on fire. I watched the holo-tank with interest as some of the enemy ships moved in for what they thought would be an easy target. But we had them. The Daedalus was limping but not crippled, and she fired her big guns. A few more enemy airships went down in flames. The Lady Guinevere was destroyed and we could see what was left of her in the shallow water near the island. There wouldn't have even been time to abandon ship. No-one would have survived that. Still, Arthur and most of his Cymbrogi were on the ground. Arthur wouldn't be merciful.

About half of the remaining enemy airships were being boarded by those captured by our new allies. They would just teleport right in close and before the enemy ship could teleport away, hundreds of flying creatures would tie lines across between the ships and storm aboard. I would find out later that it was the Deborah and the Ziv doing most of that fighting. The captains of the other enemy airships that remained realised that the air battle was lost. They began to teleport away, defeated.

A lot of enemy Shrikes and Haunebu discs were still resisting us, but almost all the enemy dragons were dead. Fighters against capital ships, the Arrow and the Daedalus was a one sided battle now. We grimly began to clear the skies.

In the Daedalus habitation zone, Virey, Weaver and Burgess and their troops were still fighting enemy boarders when the Malakim from Two Trees came to help. With Michael leading them, the Angels systematically moved down through all the towers, killing any enemies they found. Down in the Habitation zone itself, they searched through the various habitats carefully. Eventually, Michael came across the American captain Burgess.

Burgess commented as they shook hands, "It is so good to see you guys," he grinned, "how many have you got?"

"I have twelve hundred in my host," Michael told him, "and two of me!"

Burgess didn't know what he meant by that last comment.

Melki was leading a group of Kerubim and Tecorah into the Rath. He could feel the psychic presence of his future self aboard the Daedalus. It was a strange sensation, but it explained a lot of things when it came to his natural prescient ability. Melki wondered what would happen if he actually met himself later.

Orders were coming through from the Two Trees. The A.I.s had finally connected to the helms of all the troops on the ground and the fight was being properly coordinated. There were good scans coming through from those who had gone in before them. They came into a large gallery and met up with some others. A section of the corridor ahead had collapsed. The Humdrid were there trying to cut and blast their way through. Melki approached and asked for the battle leaders. An Order officer took him and the Tecorah leader to them.

Harvey and Zealot were talking with Arthur. Melki raised his visor and Arthur looked over and gasped with surprise, "You look just like...." He began to say.

"I am called Melki and come from many years ago in the past." He felt the need to explain, "We have come to help you fight our common enemy. And yes, I can feel the presence of my future counterpart. He is here somewhere nearby."

"You are known as Michael in this time." Arthur nodded, "I am Arthur, this is Harvey and Zealot. As you can see, our way ahead is a bit blocked."

"We will clear the path." The Tecorah leader stepped forward, "We Tecorah are good at such work."

"I will take you forward," said Zealot.

Zealot, feeling quite astounded by his new companions, led them forward to where the Humdrid worked, who were also astounding.

"Zagrad!" Zealot called to one of the working Humdrid.

"We are preoccupied, Zealot." Came the reply from one of the battle wagons.

"We have help."

The Humdrid stopped working and turned around, "Ah, Tecorah." Zagrad said cheerfully, "I have fought the Tecorah before. You are good warriors. You may help."

The Tecorah didn't say a word but just led her fellows forward. They looked around the area where the Humdrid were digging and then chatted among themselves for a few seconds. They then got their weapons out and used them to start digging a hole to one side. They worked quickly in teams, blasting the concrete floor, then removing rubble and moving forward again. The Humdrid seemed almost annoyed, but they began to help clear away rubble too.

In another part of the Rath, there had been a pitched battle between the other Daedalus battle groups and a mixed group of Valorians and soldiers wearing what looked like Nazi insignia. At first, the enemy had prevailed and the Valorians in particular were formidable fighters. The Nazis had fought fanatically, but were not as cool or detached as the others. But in the end it was the Order constructs that won the battle. While the enemy had armoured vehicles, the constructs from Daedalus and the troops and constructs from Eagle, led by Zabolotskys Lancers, were just better war machines. Most of the enemy retreated deeper into the Rath, into the subterranean regions.

The Three constructs with Kit, Mrorna, Al and Niamah in the first, Fay and Tarmal and Surreya in the second, Hilli, Grim and Shet in the last arrived after the battle, along with a large force of Kerubim led by Raph and Torq. Some of the soldiers were Zioronians, who crowded forward cheering when they spotted Fay and Tarmal. Others then began cheering and clapping too! The battle leaders came forward. Grim and Shet got down off their construct to meet them.

Shet and Grim listened patiently as details of the fighting was explained to them, with Shet using his helmet translator to understand. There were only two ways into the centre of the Rath. The main corridor had been blocked, which was where the Tecorah were helping to dig through, along with the reserves, the Cymbrogi, the Humdrid and Michaels Kerubim force. The other way was open, but it led down into a maze of subterranean corridors and caverns before ramps rose up into the centre. The Ring itself and the plaza around it was protected within a walled cylinder with only those two entrances.

The fighting up to this point had been hard. From now on it would only get worse. Scanner readings were transmitted to Shet and Grim's helms and they had a good look at what they were facing.

"We can't use portals to get in." One of the officers said, "There are powerful wards over the Rath. Whatever we do, it looks like we are going to have to fight our way in."

"Maybe not." Shet raised his visor, "I have an idea. Is there any way to know what is actually inside?"

"Our scanners don't read in there." The officer shook his head, "But we have someone who's been in there."

"We should talk to them then." Shet nodded, "We also need to talk with some others too."

The air battle was effectively over. All the enemy airships had either been destroyed, captured or they had teleported away. Captain James wasn't happy that so many had escaped and he wondered where they actually went. The big ship, although badly damaged, was flying well now. The fires had been put out and the worst of the damage was being repaired. Ship crews were busy and the enemy boarding parties had been eliminated.

The flagship, the Two Trees as well as the other capital ships, had all docked with the Daedalus at the towers. The Arrow and the smaller fighters, shuttles and platforms, along with the Renim had flown close to the island and had been put to work searching for enemies lurking in the jungles. The storm had done a lot of damage and it was still raining heavily, but the wards of the island had largely protected them. It could have been a lot worse. In the Daedalus' scanners James could see the storms that were now spreading across the entire North Atlantic.

As the Arrow flew low, more portals opened and the ship's complement of hover tanks were sent out, along with a small number of remaining Zioronian troopers. Then as the Daedalus descended, still more portals opened and many of the Order troops who had been fighting boarders now headed for the ground battle.

Captured enemy airships were brought down to the island as well and they were piloted into the docking hold of the Daedalus where they could later be reverse engineered. Newton and Rainbow, with the help of the Deborah and Kerubim flew their airship into a large ship docking cradle. As they disembarked, some of the ship crew met them and arranged for a shuttle.

"You are needed on the ground." They were told.

The shuttle landed Newton and Rainbow in the staging area near the main entrance of the Rath. Kit and Mrorna were there to meet them. They went together to meet with Shet and many of the other battle leaders.

An area had been cleared just inside the main entrance of the Rath and Boris and his engineers had set up a holo-tank and a full control centre. Everyone was there. The mission team were again united and all the Battle Leaders had been assembled. A portal opened at one end of the control centre and Michael and a troop of Malakim stepped through.

"It looks like we are all here." Al quipped, "If the enemy wanted to utterly destroy us, here and now would be the time."

"Yes that's certainly a possibility, Alaquandi." Michael grinned at him, "But it is my hope that with all of us here we can end this destructive war."

Shet came forward and bowed low to Michael, who automatically raised him up.

"Shet," he bowed in reply, "I am Melki, but from the future and I honour you."

"It is an honour and a blessing to serve." Shet answered.

"It is time to end this." Michael said, "I am told that you have a plan."

Shet pointed to Captain Simon and also beckoned Newton and Rainbow over.

"Newton, Rainbow," he introduced them, "this is Zealot. He has been inside the heart of the Rath and knows its internal structures. Here we have a good reconstruction."

A plan appeared in the holo-tank showing the interior of the Rath. Other things were shown, including locations of military forces, the known structures of the deeper levels of the Rath and the tunnel that the Tecorah were still digging. The damaged power sphere could also be seen resting in the upper docking areas, where the Elementals and their Zoel companions were working on it.

"I wondered if it was possible to break into the centre of the Rath from above." Shet pointed, "But we were told that there was too much damage there and that the doors to the Ring below are sealed shut and impregnable. We have fought hard so far, but there is no mistake, the enemy have actually withdrawn most of their fighting strength into the heart of the Rath. Those we have been fighting so far were just a holding force. Enemy fleet ships have also fled to an unknown location. We control the island, but not the Rath itself. The enemy have control of the Ring and so can bring more troops in from elsewhere or if they wanted to they could just abandon the Rath. Even so, the entrance via the lower regions is swarming with Gorenge and Anakim. The only thing stopping them from opening portals of their own or teleporting more of their fleet in to attack us is the defensive shielding and wards we have built here. We could still be in for a big fight. But I am hoping that the enemy know all this too. They probably couldn't comprehend us being able to strike quickly and immediately."

Shet waved at Newton and Rainbow.

"You two saved us before from certain death." He said, "Can you do it again?"

"What do you want us to do?" Rainbow asked, while Newton just looked stricken.

Shet pointed at the holo-tank and at the empty area just above the Ring itself.

"Could you use one of the captured enemy airships to teleport into that space?"

"If the enemy haven't changed the recognition codes..." Newton hummed, "but they aren't that dumb."

"We might be able to get around the codes using the stasis field generators," Rainbow added, "If we were able to scramble the resonation frequencies we might be able to slip inside and pop!"

The two of them looked at each other and nodded.

"You will need a strike force to go in that ship." Kit stepped forward, "We will go, and we will capture that Ring and shut down the shields and wards."

"You won't be going alone," Shet said to Kit, "because I will give you the best we have to go with you. Also, we will need a very big distraction to keep the enemy busy."

I had brought my people to the meeting and looking around I could see quite a few of the original Russians that had fought beside me in Utnapishtim back in 1918. With them were the soldiers of their families, men and women who had fought in many conflicts over the last century. Niamah had seen me earlier and we now stood close together, along with Al and Kit, and Finvara, Al's father, standing behind us. Kit had Mrorna with him. I could see them holding hands and I smiled to myself. Surreya, Hilli and Grim, Fay and Tarmal had also stepped forward.

"I volunteer myself and the White Knights." I spoke up, and the Russians gave a loud "Huzzah!"

"It is only right as the first Order host that we fight in this strike, as we have always fought beside each other."

I could see Kit nodding and Grim looked at me and nodded as well. Shet, son of Awdame could see that I'd made a good request.

"So be it." He said, "And as our distraction..."

"I and my Cymbrogi will lead the attack into the lower areas of the Rath." Arthur called.

"We are with you!" called Finvara.

Other battle commanders across the room began calling, Michael, Virey, Weaver, and Burgess.

Across the room, Melki bowed towards his future self, as they were in telepathic contact, "And I will lead the attack through here." He pointed to the other entrance, which was still blocked, "Once the wards are down," he continued, "the

Tecorah and Humdrid will be able to break through and we will be in the heart of the Rath."

"When the Ring is captured," Grim added, "we will be able to reactivate the power sphere. The Elementals have repaired as much as they can and if we open the bay doors, they, the Deborah and the Kerubim can enter."

"And what of the Romany and Stone people?" Rom asked.

"Continue to hold the entrances so that none of the enemy can escape." Shet said.

Chapter Thirty-Seven

Hell

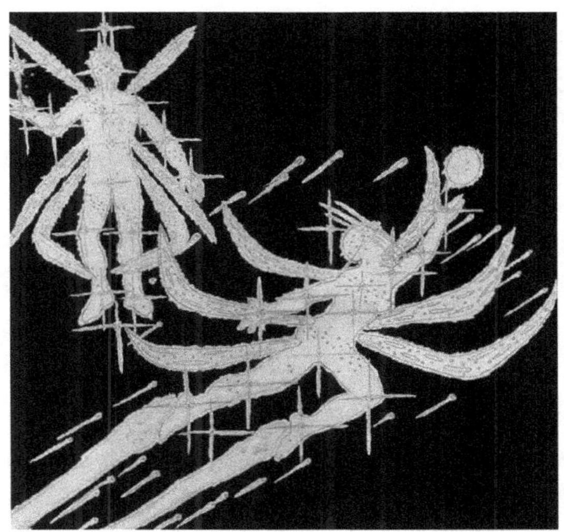

As always, we went into battle with a prayer. It was one thing we never neglected. Some would think that perhaps it was just a religious observance, a ritual habit, but for those of us who had fought the Nephalim for many years, it was as vital as air to breathe. We weren't just fighting against flesh and blood. The Elohim Logoi always reminded us that we also had invisible forces at work against us. While we fought, physically, there were many of the A'sidhe and other tribes of the Corridor deep in trance, projecting their traces into the spiritual battle. Our prayers and our spiritual focus enabled them to see more clearly and fight more effectively.

As Arthur gathered his forces at the lower entrance to the inner Rath, our attack force, to be led by Shet himself, took portals up to Daedalus. One of the enemy airships had been brought to the engineering deck and parked not far from the sphere that had been the prison that held Mrorna and her companions. Mrorna herself looked across at it grimly as we marched from the portal station towards the captured ship. The Daedalus bridge had been docked near the portal station and Captain John James had come over with his engineers to help his son Newton and Rainbow work on the ships engines and generators. While they worked, the rest of us were able to have something to eat and get ourselves ready. I took the time also to talk to Niamah and Kit and Al, and to just rest together for a bit.

Arthur chose to use heavy lancer constructs and to attack immediately. As usual, the Bear led the way himself through the entrance. Beyond was a warren of large tunnels. Small sensor constructs were released and went in front of the main force, looking for enemies and more importantly, looking for traps and mines. The enemy had set up barricades and the lancers fired heavy weapons, filling the tunnels with fire. It was hard to manoeuvre in the tunnels, but the lancers were able to fire through walls, create new tunnels and wear down the enemy shields. The process took time, and like the Spartans at Thermopile, the enemy placed themselves in the bottleneck and stood firm. Many of these were big Anakim and Gorenge, all heavily armoured.

Like all battles like this, it often just came down to who was stronger and who was better. Arthur and his lancers, followed close behind by heavily armed infantry, were able to confront the enemy positions and with sheer firepower break down the shield walls then fight up close. Personal shields gave some protection, but having a good aim and a heavy mace or sharp blade was the answer. Blood flowed.

I gathered us all together. There were about one hundred of us, on the deck outside the captured enemy ship. We were wearing the light white Order armour and heraldry of the White Brigade. Our ordinance was heavy blasters, shielded swords, and our flight sleds were attached to the sides of our boots. I would be battle leader, Grim, Surreya, Hilli, Niamah, Al, Kit, Mrorna, Fay and Tarmal would protect Rainbow and Newton as they worked on the Ring system. Vassilli Zabolotsky, Leonov Kurbatov and Boris Rujansky were each unit commanders of twenty troopers each, belonging to the Russian Whites. Grrr-tuk-moor was also there with thirty Boars Tusk Brigadiers', carrying heavy cannons and portable shields as well as explosives. We were ready to fight.

The American, Captain 'Zealot' Simon waited for us at an engineering station and one of the engineers had turned on a holographic screen. Under his helm, boots and gauntlets he was still wearing his US Air-Force uniform. All the members of the team that had gone back in time (except for Newton and Rainbow who wore engineering harness under their armour), were shield clad, that is, naked except for helm, boots, belt and gauntlets. Many of the Russians, those who had grown up in the Raths among the A'sidhe were shield clad too. I noticed that Niamah, Al, Hilli and Kit were all painted up with battle wode, while Surreya had the red war-paint of the Djinni. In battle, the body shields could be opaqued or camouflaged or left transparent. The Tuskers wore a bio-engineered skin under their armour.

"Battle Leader Ryan." Simon saluted me, "I have the intelligence you need for this mission."

"Thank-you, Captain Simon." I returned the salute, "What can we expect in the centre of the Rath?"

All the soldiers gathered around to look at the projection. The engineer tweaked the projector and the image grew in size. We could all clearly see the interior layout of the Rath as Captain Simon had seen it, before his escape. The detail was impressive.

"You must have an eidetic memory." Boris Rujansky said.

"Yes," Simon nodded, "I do. What you are seeing here are all the main load bearing structures and heavy equipment, barriers, tunnels, doors and open spaces. Also, there is the Ring."

"But there were other structures," Boris, always the engineer, "stuff that could be moved. Were there other ships in there?"

"They used the Ring to manufacture ships and refit them." Simon remembered the portals and what came out of them, "They even produced new soldiers. The new ships were bigger than these ones we captured. They needed the roof to be open for them to fit in under the Sphere that was above."

"But will the ship fit in there?" Boris insisted, "What if we teleport into an object?"

Rainbow had just arrived from her work and she stepped in, "We don't need to worry about that Boris. In fact, technically, our transport will not even arrive, but we certainly will."

Newton turned up then, wiping his oil stained hands with a cloth.

"Rainbow's right." He said, "We have found a way to teleport the ship, but we will also be doing so at a lower resonation."

Kit looked up at that, "That's how I entered that time sphere over there." He pointed.

"And rescued me and my people." Mrorna grinned at him.

"We can change the field resonation in our suits and even form full stasis fields if required." Rainbow said, "It means that we can, at the right frequencies, literally walk through walls."

"It's dangerous." Boris was frowning.

"Yes it is." Rainbow continued, "That's why we don't usually use it on the battlefield because falling through floors and being unable to interact with our environment around us is quite pointless, but..."

"We only need to be in that state for a very short time." Newton finished her sentence, "We are going to teleport in, using the captured ship, but at a lower frequency resonation. No matter what is on the other side, we will, for that moment of transition, be able to coexist phase shifted with other matter that doesn't match our frequency. All we need to do is disembark, res up to the normal frequency and our ship will teleport away. We will be inside, and do what we do best."

I grinned at that, "And what do we do best, Newton?" I asked.

"We kill Nephalim!" he laughed.

"Too right!" and we all laughed together.

How does one describe this battle in Hell? Not long before, we were confident and laughing, now we faced legions of the enemy. We had teleported successfully and simply stepped out of the ship bay, resing up and phasing into the interior of the Rath. Even before we did that, we could see them. The great plaza of the Atlantis Island Rath was crawling with enemy forces. The portals were all open and people were coming and going. They were preparing to evacuate, but they were still there.

As we appeared, there was a bang as our bodies displaced the air, and we dropped to the plaza floor, right in the middle of the Ring! Zealot's intelligence was perfect, and we formed our battle lines and opened fire. The element of utter surprise gave us what we needed. The enemy fell in their hundreds as they were unshielded and most were unprepared. While Newton and Rainbow attached their control devices to the central Trilithon of the Ring and the Altar Stone, Al pulled out the old key staff and replaced it with the one we brought with us. I ordered my Russians to move forward as the Pigrians gave heavy covering fire. Then the Pigrians put their shields down and we were walled in.

Most of the enemy had fled initially, but it wasn't long and I could see one of the Nephalim Baals leading them back down the streets of the Rath. It was Baal Molech. I could see his characteristic red armour. He had with him a combined force of Gorenge and Nephalim warriors. We looked at each other through the shield wall my Pigrians had erected, and Molech gave the order to his officers. They began firing at the shield.

Behind me, Rainbow and Newton had closed the portals, but kept the address. I could see Al concentrating as he interfaced with the Ring A.I. Normally, anyone, even a skilled key-master like Al would be instantly killed by the A.I. as a foreign intruder, but Newton and Rainbow had hacked the system and were working hard to control it. Then I looked up. Shrikes had flown into the plaza and they began to attack our shields from above. Not good. Our time was shorter than we hoped.

Down in the bowels of the Rath, our forces struggled as the enemy would withdraw behind the impenetrable protection of their ward curtains, and then come out to fight in unexpected places. Arthur and his generals were frustrated as the game of cat and mouse progressed – but who was the cat and who was the mouse? The enemy it seemed, controlled the circle that stood around the heart of the Rath. Arthur reluctantly called the troops back to a safe distance from the ward curtains so the enemy warlocks were unable to use their tricks. Finvara had seen a whole battle group vanish as the ward curtain in one gallery suddenly leapt forward and swallowed them. Fin withdrew with the survivors and when the curtain moved back along the gallery, their fellow warriors were found dead. It happened in two other places, but Arthur was determined that it not happen again, so they pulled back and set up shield walls of their own. If the enemy wanted to fight, then let them come out and do so!

Shet stood with me as we watched what was going on outside our shield wall. If that wall fell, the enemy would flood in. Would we be able to hold the Ring long enough to shut down the wards of the Rath?

Al stood within the virtual reality of the Ring A.I. To him it seemed as though he was in a maze.

"Turn the next right then right again." Rainbow's voice told him. Al followed her directions and as he turned the final corner, he discovered what looked like a portal stone, lodged in a dolman. Standing next to the stone was a Nephalim warlock, in his grey robes. The warlock tossed his robes aside and Al could see that under the robes he was armoured in mail and carried a spear. With a hiss, the warlock leapt forward to the fight. Al smiled to himself, pulled one of his custom made silver pistols from his belt and shot the warlock dead!!!

Arthur got the report immediately from Virey and his Zioronians, a section of the ward curtain had suddenly gone down and they could see through it!

"Go through!!!" Arthur ordered, "Get as many through as we can before they close it up! And bloody fight!!!"

Zioronian tanks, constructs and troopers went through the break in the curtain, with Virey leading the way. They met resistance instantly in a large flat arena. Valorians. Virey and his Zioronians screamed in rage at their ancient enemies, who had fought against them for millennia out among the stars! The black armoured Valorians responded in kind. They were not just mercenaries, but expert assassins, trained from birth on their hell-world of Cootac. It was a matter of honour for both sides, so there was no blaster fire, just edged weapons and no shields! This was how it was meant to be. Virey and the Valorian Master-of-Arms had nodded agreement. The Valorian was accompanied by two large Dar Mae Kae warriors. The Dar Mae Kae were an alien species enslaved for war. They were huge monsters, their bodies literally like stone, yet covered in some kind of organic infection. Their heads were covered in a hood concealing their faces, all except for their red glowing eyes. Rebreathers released gases they needed that stank like sulphur. Virey had fought them before and he was ready. Valorians and Zioronians alike, the same race, yet mortal enemies beat their armoured chests with their weapons and roared war-cries at each other! Then they ran at each other and the clash made a loud sound like thunder!

Data was streaming into my helm display of the battles around us. We had made our breach, but things could easily turn into a stalemate if there wasn't a way to push the battle onwards. I was looking over at Shet, and I could see his eyes through the visor of his helm. He was going into the battle trance state. He was beginning to shake with the energy building up in him. He wanted to fight badly. Perhaps I should just unleash him?

Sometimes the best defence was an offence. We gathered in our battle squads, all except for Kit and his team, who would remain to protect Newton, Rainbow and Al as they worked on the Ring systems. The rest of us formed up.

"We go straight for the leader." Shet's voice sounded far off as the trance fell upon him. Tactical data was flowing from his helm computer into ours. We knew what we had to do. The Pigrians began with a barrage of their heavy cannons, launching rockets as well as particle beams into the Rath around us. As they fired, we opened the shields and went out. The Pigrians followed, carrying their big weapons and firing as they went, opening the way ahead of us. Shet himself was restrained. I could see the trance making him shake as we moved into the streets between the buildings of the Rath. The enemy were firing their weapons back from behind their shield walls. They weren't moving forward to meet us, but waiting for us to come to them. Shet was grinning, and so was I. Yes, here we come! The last line of buildings between us and the enemy was nothing but rubble by the time we got there, destroyed by the heavy weapons fire. That was what we hoped for.

We could see the enemy line just ahead. The weapons fire between us was heavy and there was a lot of damaged building rubble. Our battle line drew up and we found cover. Shet's orders came through the helms. With our suit shields on maximum and activating the force tool functions of our gauntlets, we waited for the right second, then the whole line moved into the rubble and we began to toss the wrecked building material onto the enemy positions!! We had to work quickly, throwing the largest and heaviest chunks first. Whole walls and large stone blocks were sent hurtling forward. The enemy tried to fire their weapons but that only turned the falling material into broken shrapnel and slag. We kept throwing the rubble while the Pigrians fired into the buildings near the enemy positions, to create more confusion and block their escape. The point of all this was quickly made obvious as the enemy positions got literally covered with heavy material. Even with their shields the rubble was a heavy weight that was hard to move. Move it, they did try, but by then we were on top of them as well, setting shield charges and cutting our way in. The enemy had no time to form up or retaliate in any organised way. It meant that we could get right in close to them, and the Pigrians brought up the heavy weapons and were firing almost point blank at the enemy shields. The shields fell and we swarmed in. Shet himself was the point of the spear. He broke through the enemy line and went straight for Molech himself! Now it was our shielded weapons we were using, the neutron maces and Zioronian designed 'solar swords' that could cut through almost anything. Shet had acquired one of those weapons as well as the 'blessed' sword of Michael and he began to cut a swathe through all who tried to approach him. The trance gave him incredible strength and speed and the Gorenge and Anakim warriors were unable to stop him.

We were all fighting around him and I had battles of my own, so briefly I lost sight of Shet, but all of us could still hear him. Molech, being a Baal, had the ability to enter trance himself, but he was surprised by the ferocity of Shet's attack. Molech carried a huge sickle sword and he had a flame thrower attached to his other gauntlet. Shet ignored the flames and he managed to get really close, so close that their shields hissed and spat from the contact. Molech tried to pull free from the embrace but Shet wouldn't let him. Before Molech could bring his sword down, Shet had one blade pushing up between Molech's legs and the other pushing down on the nape of his neck. Molech's shields held, but Shet wasn't aiming at that. With a mighty heave, Shet lifted Molech off his feet and smashed him down on his head. I found out later that a squad of Pigrians fired their cannons right on his chest. The Baal's shields failed and he was reduced to burning ash. How appropriate for a fire god, whose worshippers would burn their children alive to him in sacrifice.

Without Molech, the enemy forces broke and fled deeper into the Rath. We didn't follow them but I had the main entrances to the plaza put under guard and shielded. We now had total control of the centre of the Rath.

I returned to the altar stone in the centre of the Ring. Al was still standing holding the Ring Key and interfaced with the A.I. Newton and Rainbow were still working.

"We are nearly done." Rainbow told me, "Al has one more barrier in the system to get through and then we will have the wards down and can open the doors above."

"That's very good." I nodded, "Keep me informed."

While Al had closed down a lot of the ward security walls, the main system had yet to be found. The virtual reality environment of the Ring A.I. was getting harder to navigate. Warlocks protecting the wards and other functions of the Ring were getting better at resisting. Al was suspecting that they might have been more than just manifestations of the Ring A.I. He wasn't sure what that meant. But if these warlocks were programmers, not programs, then they had access to the Ring system and that meant an altar stone and key. Al wasn't happy and he told Newton and Rainbow so.

"To be honest," Newton sighed, "I've been suspecting the same thing."

"There are strange things going on in the system." Rainbow added, "Or I should say systems."

"Systems?" Al wondered.

"It's only a hypothesis...." Newton said.

"I think that there is a second Rath connected to this gate." Rainbow said, "Possibly even another Ring complex. Someone is controlling this system remotely and that is why we are finding this so difficult."

Al turned a corner in the virtual maze within the Ring cyberspace and he gasped as he was confronted by an open portal at the centre.

"Do you see what I see?" he asked.

"You're right." Newton said to Rainbow, "There's a second system."

"So what do I do?" Al asked, "Do I go through?"

"No, no, NO!" Newton was emphatic, "Not a good idea at all."

"Why?" Al was tempted anyway.

"They have a firewall." Rainbow told him, "It would fry your brain. Log out and come back to us. There's a better way to deal with this, once for all."

Al closed his eyes and woke up standing next to the altar stone in the centre of the Ring. He twisted the rod of the Ring Key and pulled it out from the stone.

"Better get the team here," Newton said, "and Walter too."

Hilli and Surreya found me at the front and we morphed into Ren-form quickly and made the short flight back to the centre of the Ring. As we landed, Grim, along with Newton and Kit came to meet us.

"What's to report?" I asked, "Can we shut the wards down?"

"There's a problem." Newton told me.

"There always is." I nodded.

"Someone is controlling the Ring from another Rath." Rainbow told me, "Which means...."

"Which means we need to go there." I responded, "I know how it works, been using portals since 1918."

We gathered together. I looked over at my son Kit. He was holding Mrorna's hand. We quietly checked our armour and weapons. Niamah came over to me and we held each other close.

"We are going to do this." She whispered in my ear, "I love you."

"I love you too." I kissed her, "Whatever is on the other side, we will face it together."

I looked into the eyes of my family and friends. Unspoken, we knew what we had to do. I put my helm on the ground, and there in the centre of the Atlantis Island Rath we drew together into a circle of prayer. Grim, Tarmal and Fay, Surreya and Hilli, Kit and Mrorna, Rainbow and Newton, and Niamah and I, we quietly held each other.

Grim, always so priestly, prayed a simple prayer.

"There are no magic words," he began, "just a simple faith that we commit our lives to. We put our faith into action and fight this fight. We ask this, let us tear the darkness down and restore the light, in the Name."

"For Yeshua." We whispered.

Chapter Thirty-Eight

Last Stand

"We've found it!" Rainbow cried.

The portal opened before us and Newton yelled, "GO! GO! GO!"

We had our sleds on, but we stepped through the portal and found ourselves in the middle of a side corridor from the plaza of the other Rath. It looked quite different. My helm scanners told me that the temperature was freezing. Ice covered the surfaces of ancient passageways. Our scanners also told us that enemies were approaching fast! Using the sleds on our boots, we flew upwards then along the short corridor, flying out into the other plaza. We had to be quick. There were enemy troops everywhere! Atalanti and Medusa Nephalim, Valorians and their Aryan masters wearing black and death heads on their helms, the elite warriors of the Nephalim were here in huge numbers!!!

Suddenly we found ourselves in the middle of a firefight. Our personal suit shields were soon glowing with weapons heat and we knew we had to do something to get that fire off us or we wouldn't get home!

"Down into the centre of the Ring!!" Grim flew down into the middle of the fire. I knew what he was doing.

"Yes!" I followed, "They can't fire on us down there!"

The space in the middle of the Ring wasn't actually that big and the enemy were soon flooding in! Grim and Al got to the altar stone first, but there were already Neph wizards there and someone was locked into the stone with a staff. There was no not recognising who that was! It was Graud himself, grinning back at us like a maniac! How could he be here? He had obviously escaped from the destruction in the distant past.

"We have twelve seconds…" Newton's voice called over the coms, "signal is strong."

The shooting had stopped in the middle of the Ring, but we were facing huge numbers swarming in. We landed right on top of Graud and his wizards. With a cry I turned on Graud who was still smiling like a maniac! We both had swords and were quickly at it.

While we were fighting I was only vaguely conscious of the data streams scrolling across the top rim of my helm viewer. Newton and Clarrissa must have been very busy. Not only were they working to get the wards around the Atlantis Rath down, they were also working to hack into the A.I. of the mystery thirteenth Rath that we had just discovered. I didn't know then, but they were losing the battle.

Twelve seconds were up and our exit portal appeared in the middle of the Ring. It was a matter of flee or remain stuck where we were. Reluctantly I took one more swipe with my solar sword at Graud who easily evaded me. He was still laughing at me as Kit and Grim grabbed the back of my utility pack and dragged me back through the portal as it was closing. I thought I could still hear that bastard laughing at me even after the portal had shut!!! He was always the better fighter. He would have killed me in the end if we hadn't been forced to leave.

We were back in the centre of Atlantis Island Rath and our whole team were all there, panting with exhaustion from our fight. But we had done what we had hoped to do. Clarrissa and Newton were grinning at us. Renim were flying through the centre of the Rath and the big docking bay doors above us were finally open.

"The wards are down and our people are pouring in!" Newton cheered, "We have control of the Rath!"

Portals were opening all over and the troops were coming through. My helm viewer was telling me of the military success as enemy forces either died fighting or committed suicide rather than accept capture. It would take about twenty minutes for the job to get done.

"We lost the hack into the other Rath Ring." Rainbow told me, "When the escape portal closed, they put up a firewall. We will never get back in now."

"Any idea where they are?" I asked.

"Just somewhere very cold." Niamah came up beside me, "But that Rath could have been anywhere on Earth or anywhere in the Multiverse for that matter."

"We have no idea of the address at all." Newton added.

I nodded. "We have won a great battle." I said, smiling, "We will no doubt have a lot to investigate, but for now, it's time to celebrate."

EPILOGUE

The Atlantis Rath A.I. was named Anu. We were able to convince him to accept our occupation. There was a lot to clean up in the aftermath of the battle. Most of those who had been in the heaviest fighting, including my own team and myself, well, we were stood down to rest. Fresh troops were brought in to hold the Rath, clean up the mess and trace hunters were sent through the Ring portals to clear the air spiritually speaking of enemy traces that would no doubt try to hang around.

Boris Rujansky and his engineers insisted on doing most of the restoration work and we soon had the Rath operational. While the A'sidhe of the Seerlie Court sent in Danu to hold the newly occupied Atlantis Rath, most of the rest of us returned to Utnapishtim.

There was some time off due, but before then, Yeshua wanted to hold a council at Utnapishtim and settle the return of the Antediluvians to their own time. We gathered on a great open field in the Annwn, beside the waters of the Hubur River not far from the Djinni city of Irkalla. A throne had been set up for Yeshua and Surreya and her Djinni prepared a great feast for the host that gathered together.

The great Oberons and Morrigans of the Seerlie were there, as were the Commanders of the Fleet, and of course Shet and his people who had been such a great help to us all.

Yeshua had left his throne empty and chose instead to walk among the people, chatting and enjoying the party. He was quite fond of parties.

Niamah and I were hanging around with Kit and Mrorna as well as Captain John James and Grim. I saw other members of our team around the place. Al was accompanying Hilli about the field and it was obvious that they were now on very friendly terms. The same was true about Kit and Mrorna, who were always holding onto each other and kissing often. Niamah was very pleased with the match and she kept kissing me as well, something I was very glad for her to do!

Tarmal and Fay were there with their Zioronian crew and Newton and Rainbow who were helping them do some repairs on Arrow which were postponed for the party.

Yeshua came and found us and gathered a big group of us not far from the shore of the river.

Most of the Antediluvians were there and Yeshua had Shet and Melki beside him. Yeshua raised his arms and we all went quiet.

"Dear friends!" He called out to us, "We have won a very important victory. While war is never a good thing, this war is one we have had to fight and we have been able to break this link into the ancient past that Graud had hoped to exploit. The New Guard forces ruling over much of Eurasia and parts of Africa have been deprived of any support or supply from the past. We have broken their technological advantage and are now in a very good position to strike back and thanks to our occupation of the Atlantis Rath, we should be able to take back the Kilimanjaro Rath in Africa soon."

That brought a cheer from many.

"It is just the beginning." Yeshua continued, then he looked right at Shet, "It is the beginning for you too Shet. You have proven yourself true in battle, but also as a good and wise leader and your people love you. But this is not your time. You belong in another world of a long time ago from now. You and your people need to return. When you return to your world, plant a pillar on the first land you put your foot upon and there establish for yourself a capital city. You are destined to be a great ruler and will be the founder of a mighty Kingdom."

Yeshua turned towards the Hubur River where there were a number of large ships moored. The ships were Renim piloted and had large open decks. The behemoths and other antediluvian beasts were already aboard and the Elementals and Zoel were there as well. Rom and his people had gathered, and also Raph and the Kerubim, along with the Stone People warriors who had joined with them. Ramps onto the ships had been lowered to the shore and the people went up on board. Shet watched with Yeshua as they all were loaded on. Hilli and Surreya also came with a large number of Renim and Djinni who loaded goods, food, and other useful and valuable things onto the ships.

"We are giving you these ships and all the treasures and supplies we can load onto them for you to use as you build your city." Yeshua told Shet, "Use these well."

Finally, those of us who remained on shore were there with Shet who remained. Yeshua took him into his arms and blessed him. Then Shet waved to us and joined his people. Yeshua raised a hand and we could see a portal forming behind the ships, opening like a curtain. The boarding ramps were raised and the ships moved off through the portal, vanishing into the mist beyond. Then the portal closed behind them and they were gone.

Afterwards, Yeshua came to Niamah and I and sat with us on the grass.

"Any thoughts Walter?" he asked me.

"What about Graud?" I asked firstly, then, "And also, what about Nimrod and his Asherim?"

"Well," Yeshua shrugged, "Graud is out there somewhere doing what he has always done and no doubt we will meet him again soon. As for Nimrod, Ishtar and Lilith, they are now ruling over the New Guard. Somehow they escaped and they are now in Europe. They had hoped to keep their plans secret, but now we know. We will fight them openly."

"I look forward to resolving all of this." I said.

"There is much more yet to be revealed." Yeshua replied, "The battle between Darkness and Light, the Two Trees of Life and Death, it is only really just beginning."

APPENDIX

This story includes a number of different groups and there can be some confusion in identifying who is who. Hopefully by showing this "family tree" of all the different species and people groups, there can be some clarification. The Vansadagaadians refer to the present Eon as the Twelfth Great Cycle. Our Universe is the twelfth continuum since the creation of the Vansadagaadian Corridor – eleven universes before this one colonised by the Vansad and other Eldar races.

The Logoi

Are a multi-dimensional eternal and transcendent Being composed of many individual personas as a collective consciousness. The Logoi is an expression of the Source of all life and the Ground of All Being. Through Avatars, the Logoi actively engage in the creation of life throughout the Multiverse, through panspermia or by aiding successful civilisations to terraform and colonise worlds in new young universes.

Eldar Races aka **The Elohim Council** or **The Powerful Ones**

These are ancient sentient species whose civilisations have survived to migrate from the universe of their origin to other universes when their own universe ends. The Eldar are client races of the Logoi and aid the Logoi in the creation process of new worlds for colonisation and seeding. Some of the oldest Eldar races include the Elementals: Aesir (Air), Terrestrials (Earth), Tritons (Water), Astari (Fire) and Gaeans (Life).

Younger Eldar races include the Zoel: an alliance of species including the bee-like Deborah and their client symbionts the ant-like Tecorah, the bird-like Ziv, the Dinosaurian Torgar, Amphibian Tor-ahn and the aquatic Mer.

The Vansad

A very ancient Eldar race, the Vansad are the origin of all Humanoid species. The Vansad, with the Torgar, the Peeleens and the Rogan built the Vansadagaadian Corridor. Via the Corridor, the Vansad, their allies and client civilisations left their dying universe and entered a younger universe. The Corridor continues to exist as a pocket realm where most of the Vansad have the seat of their civilisation.

The Dark Eldar

An alliance of ancient Eldar species, including the Kraken, the Nagda and Zeebub.

Altatudes

A Vansad splinter culture that left the Corridor.

The Shile

A group of related species also called "Greys" known as an aggressive Eldar colonial culture and excellent geneticists. They breed client species known as Humanimals: e.g. B ardel, Chipperwaals, Pigrians and other "uplifted" species.

The Seelie Court

Another Vansad splinter culture, but loyal to the Elohim and the Corridor. The Seerlie are made up of twelve Royal A'sidhe Tribes:- e.g. Elves, Tuatha De Danann, Huldra, Djinni, Malakim (Angels), Solitary Faeries, Asgardians, Olympians, Immortals, Pict'Sidhe, the Egyptian Ennead/Pesedjet, Mu-Lemurian Faeries. All these live on Earth or the Sol System.

The Unseelie

A Vansad group which helped form the first Pandemonium, including Pandemons, Wraiths, Goblins and the DarMaeKae.

Twelfth Cycle Races of the Datum (Our current universe)

While Eldar species directly colonised the new universe, new sentient species were "seeded" and evolved independently. Torgar/Saurian seed races – The Gorenge were the original seed species of Earth and evolved into two species – the Terran Saurians and Changlings/Shape Shifters. Another Saurian species is the Kaloni Torgar who co-existed with a Shilean seed species called the Kaloni. The Draconians are a gigantic Saurian race that later joins the Second Pandemonium.

Shilean seed races

Using star-seed the Shile engineered new colonial species e.g. Humdrid, Telcan, Cheen and many species of Humanimals. Shile factions – Blue, Grey, White species. The Igigi are also a Shile group.

Bene Elohim/Vansadagaadian Seed Species

Humans – one of the most common splinter genus groups.

Nubirans – a dominating colonial species that has caste species including a ruling caste True Nubirans (The main Royal Family, descended from Anu may be Draconians using Human hosts as Avatars), Anunnaki Warrior Caste (includes various Saurian species as well as Homo Nubirans), Igigi Worker Caste (which also includes the Shile Grey Order working as geneticists).

Lahmu – a human seed group and original Inhabitants of Mars. After the destruction of the surface of Mars, the Lahmu divided into a the original Martians/Plazashans and those who colonised Earth and founded the colonies of Mu and Lemuria.

The Second Pandemonium – Founded by the Altatudes Falshon, Deimos and Phobos and includes members of the Dark Eldar and Unseelie, as well as Draconians. Other important members of the Pandemonium include the Valorians – a human group from Earth working as mercenaries, that broke away from the Aquani to colonise Cootac and Valor. They are known as Men In Black. DarMaeKae – a very alien species probably silicon based symbiont.

Nephilim/Anakim – infertile half-caste children of Anunnaki and Adamu. The Anakim are giants.

Original Terrans – the original human seed Homo species of Earth which are now extinct, although Indigenous Australians and some Bushman tribes are most closely related. Adapu – the infertile slave species created by Enki and Ninhursag after the Igigi revolt by genetically engineering original Terran genes combined with Enki's own genes. Adamu – Modern Homo Sapien Sapiens. The second slave species engineered by Enki and Ninhursag. Two were actually children of Enki by two different mothers, Adamu and Titi. The Elohim liberated the Adamu from slavery to Enlil.

Manhome – Adamu people led by Awdame and Haveh (Adam and Eve – formally known as Adamu and Titi) after the exile from Edin. Kayyinim – Children of Kayyin (Cain), who later built cities in the land of Nod and became known as Nodin. Assuririm – Children of Assur, son of Awdame and Haveh. Cushim – Children of Cush, son of Awdame And Haveh. Cherubim Daughters of Hebel – Children of Hebel (Abel) who live in the Cherubim Tree. Sethani – the Royal Tribe of Shet, son of Awdame and Haveh. Romany – Children of Rom, son of Awdame and Haveh. They are the trader tribe. Manloreans – a Nodin people descended from Lahmech. Jubalim – the bardic tribe. Jabalim – herders of cattle. Tubal-kayyim/Vulcanim – blacksmiths. Hecate – Witch Daughters of Naamah (later became the Ragdelon). Bursar – Vampire blood children of Kayyin. Aquani – a Sethani people who left Earth just Before the Deluge and established colonies Off-world, including Zioron and Zaltar.

Modern Groups

Melkizedek Order – the Vansad/Human order formed by Shem to battle the Enemy on Earth. Petra – replaced the Melkizadek and includes PETRAD, the Petra Research and Development group. Petra communities and Petra Security later develop into the Free States after the Time War. The Free States – includes the North American States, Free Britain, the Scandinavian states, Free Russian States, the Caucasus Free States, Israel, the Free States of Africa, the Free States of Australia Pacific.

The Mystery of Iniquity – the surviving Children of Enlil and Marduk, forming evil royal Anunnaki bloodlines. The House of Babylon – Founded by Marduk son of Enki, controlling much of Mesopotamia and Egypt before moving to Rome and then later to London. The European Pandemonium are loyal to the line of Marduk. The House of Canaan – Founded by Enlil, but defeated in war. This group, also known as the Atalanti moved to the Americas where they ruled from Atlantis Island and Mt. Shasta.

Medussa – An alliance of the Pandemonium, Atalanti and other Shedu groups. The New Guard – the Medussa occupying force of Europe after the Time War.

ABOUT THE AUTHOR

Christopher Glen Beck (Dip T, BA Visual Arts/History)

Christopher Beck is a teacher, artist, historian and social scientist, Biblical critical scholar and imagineer. Born in Brisbane, Queensland, Australia he currently lives in Poatina, Tasmania.

Chris has always been imaginative, a dreamer and a deep thinker. Science fiction and fantasy, Bible stories, ancient myths and legends and conspiracy theories have fascinated him since childhood. This story, his first novel, has its origins in a primary school playground imagination game of make believe. Aliens live among us and there is a secret war going on between them for our world. Big ideas for a kid in grade two!

Chris also loved the stories he heard in Sunday School, however always wondered what really happened. In particular, the Noah's Ark story picture books always had a funny looking banana boat with the animals heads sticking out – this image and scenario just didn't seem believable to him.

So, he imagined a very different world, where advanced technology coexists alongside magic. Hence, he created elves with blasters!